MW00605996

HOLD ON

LINDSAY MCKENNA

Blue Turtle Publishing

Praise for Lindsay McKenna

"A treasure of a book . . . highly recommended reading that everyone will enjoy and learn from."

—Chief Michael Jaco, US Navy SEAL, retired, on Breaking Point

"Readers will root for this complex heroine, scarred both inside and out, and hope she finds peace with her steadfast and loving hero. Rife with realistic conflict and spiced with danger, this is a worthy page-turner."

—BookPage.com on Taking Fire
March 2015 Top Pick in Romance

". . . is fast-paced romantic suspense that renders a beautiful love story, start to finish. McKenna's writing is flawless, and her story line fully absorbing. More, please."

—Annalisa Pesek, Library Journal on Taking Fire

"Ms. McKenna masterfully blends the two different paces to convey a beautiful saga about love, trust, patience and having faith in each other."

—Fresh Fiction on Never Surrender

"Genuine and moving, this romantic story set in the complex world of military ops grabs at the heart."

—RT Book Reviews on Risk Taker

"McKenna does a beautiful job of illustrating difficult topics through the development of well-formed, sympathetic characters."

—Publisher's Weekly (starred review) on Wolf Haven
One of the Best Books of 2014, Publisher's Weekly

"McKenna delivers a story that is raw and heartfelt. The relationship between Kell and Leah is both passionate and tender. Kell is the hero every woman wants, and McKenna employs skill and s empathy to craft a physically and emotionally abused character in Leah. Using tension and steady pacing, McKenna is adept at expressing growing, tender love in the midst of high stakes danger."

—RT Book Reviews on Taking Fire

"Her military background lends authenticity to this outstanding tale, and readers will fall in love with the upstanding hero and his fierce determination to save the woman he loves.

—Publishers Weekly (starred review) on Never Surrender
One of the Best Books of 2014, Publisher's Weekly

"Readers will find this addition to the Shadow Warriors series full of intensity and action-packed romance. There is great chemistry between the characters and tremendous realism, making Breaking Point a great read."

—RT Book Reviews

"This sequel to Risk Taker is an action-packed, compelling story, and the sizzling chemistry between Ethan and Sarah makes this a good read."

—RT Book Reviews on Degree of Risk

"McKenna elicits tears, laughter, fist-pumping triumph, and most all, a desire for the next tale in this powerful series."

—Publishers Weekly (starred review) on Running Fire

"McKenna's military experience shines through in this moving tale . . . McKenna (High Country Rebel) skillfully takes readers on an emotional journey into modern warfare and two people's hearts."

—Publisher's Weekly on Down Range

"Lindsay McKenna has proven that she knows what she's doing when it comes to these military action/romance books."

—Terry Lynn, Amazon on Zone of Fire.

"At no time do you want to put your book down and come back to it later! Last Chance is a well written, fast paced, short (remember that) story that will please any military romance reader!"

—LBDDiaries, Amazon on Last Chance.

Dear Reader,

Welcome to the Delos Series! *Hold On* is Book 5, a big book that is about Callie McKinley and Beau Gardner. Hold On is about Army Delta Force operator, Sergeant Beau Gardner and Callie McKinley. If you read *Forged in Fire*, then you met Callie because she was the younger sister to Dr. Dara McKinley.

Callie spends six months of the last five years at Hope Charity in Kabul, Afghanistan. She helps to take care of fifty young Afghan children. Her hobby is belly dancing and at the Thanksgiving USO show at Bagram Army Base, she and Callie bring the house down with their belly dancing routines. And that is where Beau Gardner, who is on Matt Culver's team, falls for her.

And when he goes to the charity to help out, but also to meet Callie, he hits a proverbial brick wall. Callie knows he's chasing her. She's tired of military men running her down out of lust just to get her in bed with them. Beau, however, sees much deeper into fiery, redhead, Callie, and he goes about proving it. Just as they connect, the next day they are going out to a 'safe' Afghan village to render medical aid. On the way there, Dara, Callie, Matt Culver and Beau, are ambushed.

Beau is willing to give his life to get Callie back to safety, but there is a daunting thirty-five miles between them and protection. Can he get her home? Will they be attacked? Beau is falling in love with the courageous civilian who doesn't quit and does everything he asks of her. Is there a future for them?

Let me hear from you about the Delos series. Happy reading!

Dedication

To my readers, worldwide, who loved Morgan's Mercenaries. Thank you for supporting this 45-book family saga-series! Now, you have a NEW one to read . . . Delos series! I hope you fall in love with the Culver family as you did with the Trayhern family. Happy reading!

CHAPTER 1

SERGEANT BEAU GARDNER wasn't Delta Force for nothing. Black ops sometimes required stealthy moves, and after seeing fiery redhead Callie McKinley belly dancing for the troops at Bagram, he set his sights on her. Of course, four thousand other salivating, panting males wanted her, too. Dara McKinley, a tall, gorgeous blonde, and Callie, her younger sister, had sent every man in the chow hall into erotic spasms as they watched the women's pulse-raising belly dances.

Of course, his team was with him, and their leader, Sergeant Matt Culver, had already set his sights on the blonde, so that was one sister off the table. Beau didn't care; he really wanted that green-eyed beauty who'd danced into his heart as she twisted, turned, and swayed to the music in her purple and silver costume.

Callie had taken the fast dance, whereas Dara had performed a slow, sensuous version. It was Callie's flashing green eyes, wicked smile, and gyrating hips that had sent the men leaping to their feet, wolf-whistling, clapping, and yelling their approval. These women certainly knew how to bring the house down, big-time.

Beau had been at Bagram for five deployments in a row with the same Delta Force team, and the two gals and their sensational belly dances were a welcome relief during an otherwise depressing Thanksgiving holiday, when all present were half a globe away from their families. As Beau watched Callie's full breasts, flared hips, and statuesque body swaying before him, he decided he had to meet her—one way or another.

Oh, he wasn't fooled. He knew there would be a hundred or so men crowding that hall to the room where the women would be changing into their regular clothes afterward. They'd be knocking on the door repeatedly, calling out their names, asking them out to dinner, lunch, or whatever they might want.

Beau grinned and enjoyed the rest of the sisters' act. He knew all the guys, including him, really appreciated that the women had given up their time to come here and entertain them. They didn't have to, and in Beau's heart of hearts, he tried to tamp down his own lust. But not having a woman for nine months was a monk's choice, not his.

If his ma, Amber Gardner, could have read his mind, she'd have boxed his ears proper and sent him to sit in the corner like a dunce. A wolfish smile tugged at his lips. Good thing she was in Black Mountain, West Virginia, and he was here in Afghanistan! Beau always liked a challenge.

Two days later, Beau had done enough sleuthing to find out all about Callie McKinley. She was a volunteer with an NGO named the Hope Charity. She worked at a Kabul orphanage five days a week and lived here on base on weekends. There was a section of B-huts for women, which was where she stayed when not working, and Beau was able to find out exactly which B-hut was hers.

He wasn't about to show up on the porch of her B-hut and introduce himself, because that would be too pushy. No, he needed a better mousetrap than that.

Given that it was Thanksgiving week, and blizzards were dumping snow on the mountains twenty-five miles north of Bagram, causing havoc with flights, the folks on the base were pretty much on vacation.

His captain had released Matt's entire team for the next seven days, but they couldn't go anywhere other than Afghanistan. However, Beau saw that as a golden opportunity. He also found out that Matt Culver was already playing security guard at the orphanage because he had his eye on Dr. Dara McKinley.

Beau decided to corner him in the locker room when Matt returned to base. Beau was catnapping in the locker room when Culver waltzed in later that night.

"Hey, bro," Beau mumbled, rousing himself.

"You still here?" Matt asked, surprised. He went to his locker and opened it up.

"Yeah, I wanted to talk to you about your extracurricular activities at the Hope Charity." He stood up, stretched like a lazy cougar, and walked over to the other wall of lockers, where Matt stood. "You're taking those two belly-dancing gals to that charity every day, right?"

Matt grinned and sat down on a bench, untying his combat boots. "Yeah. So what?"

Beau straddled the bench. "So, I'd like to meet Callie McKinley."

Matt gave his friend an amused look. "She'll turn you down, partner."

"Is she married?"

"No. Dara says she's single, and there's no one special in her life right now." He pulled off the boots, tossed them into his locker, and pulled out a set of Nikes. "You got that look in your eyes, Gardner. That never bodes well for me. And right now I'm connecting with Dara, and I don't want you messing things up for me."

Beau gave his friend a wry grin. "Naw, I wouldn't do that to you, Matt. I got my sights set on Callie. You can have Dara. She's a fine-lookin' woman, but not my type."

"Yeah," Matt huffed, shaking his head. "She's brainy as hell—and the biggest worrywart I've ever met." And then he flashed Beau a grin. "But that hasn't stopped me."

"I want to drop by tomorrow at the orphanage to casually offer my security services. Might be a good way to combine a good deed with getting on Callie's right side."

"You're truly a wily coyote, Gardner."

"Where I come from, back in Black Mountain, West Virginia, we call that being 'a wolf in sheep's clothing.' I just want to meet her and see if any sparks fly between us."

Chuckling indulgently, Matt pulled on the sneakers. "Oh, you'll get fireworks all right, Gardner. Callie isn't stupid, and she doesn't suffer fools any more than Dara does. She'll see straight through you and shoot you down quicker than you can say 'wolf!'"

"Well," he drawled, "I gotta try."

Shrugging, Matt stood and shut his locker. "Okay by me." He grinned, patting his friend's broad shoulder. "I can't wait for you to drop by so I can enjoy watching you get shut out of the belly-dancer sweepstakes."

CALLIE COLLIDED WITH a tall, wiry Army man in a big hurry as she turned a corner in the building where the orphanage was housed. Gasping, she began to fall, but he reached out to straighten her, his large hand wrapping firmly around her upper arm.

She was assailed by a wave of first impressions. First, his eyes, intense and gray, like those of a hawk. *A hunter*, she later recalled thinking.

His face was oval, with high cheekbones, shaggy black hair, and a longish beard. She was acutely aware of his monitoring just how much strength he needed to set her upright.

"Oh," she gasped, "I'm sorry," and she felt his hand fall away. Her skin tingled and it was pleasant, reminding her that six months without any sex made her yearn to be stateside once more.

"My fault, ma'am." He took off his green baseball cap. "I'm Sergeant Beau Gardner. You must be Callie McKinley?" He held his hand out toward her.

Callie didn't know if she was more shocked by his manners or by his knowing her name. This wasn't her first rodeo, and as she pushed her hands against her jeans she was sure this guy was black ops. She shook his hand.

"Oh," Matt Culver said, entering the room with Dara, her sister. "Callie? Did you meet Beau?"

Callie frowned. She gave a measured look to the tall, well-muscled soldier, who stood casually, his M4 rifle slung over his shoulder, the barrel pointed down. "No. Do you know him, Matt?"

"Just a little," he said, walking with Dara over to the coffee machine. "Beau is on my team."

"Yes, ma'am," Beau told her, drowning in her forest-green eyes. "I thought I might come over here and help Matt with security. Our team has the next week off, so it seemed like the right time to offer you some help." He saw her fine, thin red brows flash downward.

"Did you see us belly dance a couple of nights ago, Sergeant?"

Ouch. Beau kept his face relaxed, but he was definitely detecting that this redhead had already outed him. "Yes, ma'am, I did. You two ladies were the hit of the evening. But then, I'm sure you've already been told that."

Callie jammed her hands on her hips, looking up into his face. "And the reason you're really here, Sergeant?"

This woman was not only smart, but she had the prettiest bow-shaped lips he'd ever seen. Beau could almost taste them beneath his hungry mouth. But first, he had a hellion standing here, her eyes flashing. Beau was never good at lying, and if he wanted a woman, he went after her, fair and square. "I saw you dance, ma'am. I wanted to introduce myself to you, hoping that you might consider going out to have a pizza and beer with me later, after we return to Bagram."

Callie glared at him. "Not even," she said through gritted teeth. Huffing past him, she stalked over to the coffee machine and poured herself a cup. So why did she feel badly about catching him red-handed? Beau wasn't bad-looking and he was Delta Force, the cream of the Army's crop. And despite his patient, good-ol'-boy smile and that Southern drawl, he probably belonged to Mensa and had a sky-high IQ to boot.

At least he hadn't lied to her. That was new. *Refreshing.* Lies fell off men's lips faster than a bee could gather honey. They took it to an art form at Bagram.

"Look," she said coolly, holding the cup between her hands, "we just had a market down the street get bombed yesterday. We could really use more security right now." Her lips thinned. "But I've been around Kabul and Bagram for five years. I know your type. So while I'd love to have you and your rifle around, I really don't want your attention. Are we clear on that?"

When his lips turned up into an amused grin, Callie felt her heart lurch in her chest. What was *that* all about?! Flustered, she didn't even wait for him to respond, spinning around on her heel and hurrying down the hall. The children at the orphanage needed constant care and attention. And right now, they were receiving a midmorning snack in the kitchen.

Still, she couldn't get that lazy, boyish smile of his out of her head. Damn him! This wasn't the first time she'd been chased down by some soldier from the Army base. But it *was* the first time one of them showed up where she worked. That was different, and so, apparently, was he.

As Matt came and stood beside Beau, sipping his coffee, he murmured, "Told you so."

Beau shrugged. "First battle may be lost, but not the war," he said, and went over to help himself to the coffee.

Callie lost sight of both Matt and Beau. She knew Matt since he and her sister were serious about each other. He'd more than proven his intentions to support the orphanage and had been here when the Taliban had blown up some IEDs in the market a block away. Matt had swung into action, preventing the Taliban from shooting into the orphanage and possibly wounding the terrified children, or hitting one of them. Her sister, a pediatrician, had only been here for a week, and the orphanage had become Grand Central Terminal for little ones and pregnant mothers needing her medical help.

Now Callie was dead on her feet at the end of every day—and her feet hurt plenty. Noon came and went. They had fifty hungry children to feed, from a few months old to age fourteen. Every day, Callie and her four Afghan widows, plus the director, Maggie, had their hands full.

At one point, Callie saw Beau Gardner walking around, peering intently into some of the rooms. Their eyes met and Callie growled a low warning in her throat, whirling away. She wanted nothing to do with a man right now, and she hated being chased. This guy was determined to bother her, and she sensed he wasn't about to quit any time soon.

Midafternoon, one of her little charges, a young girl of ten, had wandered down the hall, holding her new shoes as she walked barefoot on the cold floor. There was no heating in the orphanage because it cost too much to keep it warm. Charities didn't usually have that kind of money, anyway.

Callie hurried down the hall after her as she disappeared into what was known as "the big room" out in front, but when she turned the corner, she came to an abrupt halt, totally unprepared for the sight that awaited her. There was Beau Gardner, his weapon on his back, leaning down and smiling as he spoke in Pashto to the little girl. She was shy, her eyes downcast, her finger in her mouth, but she was allowing Beau to gently coax first one shoe on to her bare foot, and then the other one.

Callie's heart swelled as she observed how gentle this man was, his large hands helping the child stand while urging her second shoe onto her foot.

The little girl smiled shyly as he lowered her foot and released her thin little arm. Callie couldn't catch what Beau said, but whatever it was, the child reached out and tentatively touched his beard. The look in her eyes made Callie feel a rush of heat into her lower body. Beau was a man, and a complete stranger to this child. And yet he had such charm, and that easygoing smile of his . . . She saw him kneel so he could give the child his full attention.

Beau slowly lifted his hand, gently grazing her long, black hair, moving a few uncombed strands across her shoulder. And when he smiled, Callie groaned inwardly. The man was a damned magician! If he could charm that little girl, who was very, very shy, and especially afraid of any man, then Beau was someone to be very wary of. And yet Callie found herself wanting him to smile at her like that. It was an intimate, warm smile. She could literally feel that sunlight energy around him, and she saw the little girl responding to it. So was she!

Uh-oh, Callie thought. This guy was trouble—big trouble! Turning, Callie quickly left, hoping he hadn't been aware of her presence. That was all she needed now, an attractive soldier who might tempt her to let her guard down. These guys were nothing but heartache on two feet. She'd learned her lesson years ago and sworn to never, ever get entangled with another military man as long as she lived.

But Beau Gardner interested her, damn it! Gritting her teeth, Callie headed to the kitchen to help feed the children. "Soldiers" started with an "s," she reminded herself. And "s" also stood for "stupid," if she thought for a blinding instant that Beau Gardner was going to be different from the rest of the male pack. She was sick and tired of men seeing her as a sex object and not a human being, especially after she and her sister had performed their belly dances before the entire facility.

Boy, had that been a miscalculation for someone who wanted to stay out of the spotlight!

BEAU AND MATT had just walked around outside the orphanage, and now they moved into the big room. During their conversation, Beau learned that yesterday, during the bombing of the market, two truckloads of Taliban had raced down the street outside the wrought-iron fence, spraying bullets everywhere until Matt had shot the driver of each truck. A day after the bombing he was allowing the children to have their midafternoon nap out in their normal slumber area. The four Afghan widows and Callie were getting all the children to lie down on their soft mats, covering each with a blanket because in late November, it was damned cold.

Beau watched Callie speak softly to each child, give him or her a smile, snuggle them into their blankets, and make sure that their small pillows were nestled beneath their heads. Callie was maternal, no question, and Beau tried to tear his gaze from her and keep moving down the hall, checking the back doors as well as the windows. He took his security duty as seriously as Matt did. When he'd finished his rounds, he found himself in the office again and set the M4 rifle aside to pour himself a cup of coffee.

He had his back to the door when he heard a sudden movement and twisted around to look over his shoulder.

"Oh," Callie said sharply, "you're here."

He grinned. "I guess I am. Come on in," he drawled. "I don't bite. Would you like a cup of coffee?"

She looked flustered, unsure, licking that full lower lip of hers, sending his imagination on a wild erotic spree. He forced himself to rein it in.

Callie hesitated, standing in the doorway, torn between her instinct to get to know him and her solid vow never to get involved with a military man, especially here.

Beau could tell she really wanted that cup of joe. "Come on," he coaxed. "I promise not to jump you."

A slight smile . . . maybe a grimace . . . and then she made a decision. "All right," she murmured, hurrying over. "But I don't have much time. We have to get the kids' dinner started in the kitchen."

Beau poured her a cup. "Here you go." He handed it to her, then moved to give her space, because she was obviously wary of him. Standing aside, he sipped his black brew, watching her add cream and sugar to hers. "You gals are busy here all the time," he noted.

Pushing some strands of hair off her cheek, she said, "It's always like this. And with those bombs going off down the block, the kids are scared to death."

"I can't blame 'em," Beau said. "It's no way for anyone to live."

Callie felt herself losing her edge and immediately drew herself up. Damn it, why did Beau Gardner have to be so appealing? She saw amusement in his gaze and was thankful that at least he wasn't staring at her like he wanted to strip her clothes off. Instead, he was leaning casually against the bookcase behind him, looking completely relaxed.

"Where do you live?" she asked, unable to hide her curiosity.

"I come from a no-name place called Black Mountain, West Virginia. Bet you never heard of it," he teased.

She shrugged. "No . . . I haven't. You seem to have a way with kids; that's why I asked."

"Oh, that little tyke who was carrying her shoes around earlier?"

"Yes. She just arrived here five days ago," Callie explained. She shook her head. "She lost her parents, and the village wouldn't take her in. No one had room for another hungry mouth to feed."

Hearing the sadness in her smoky voice, Beau said, "This is a pretty desperate country, and children and widows suffer the most."

"True," she agreed. "So where did you get your touch with kids? Do you have lots of brothers and sisters?"

This was important to her, and Beau was silently delighted to find a door that she'd opened up to him. "I've got two younger brothers, Coy and Jackson. Now they're in the Marine Corps. And growing up, since I was the oldest son, it was my job to herd them so they'd stay out of trouble." He offered a wry grin. "And believe me, three boys can get into an awful lot of trouble when they're young."

She smiled a little. "Boys are always hard to raise," she agreed. "That little girl . . ."

"Yes?"

"She's been so frightened since coming here. I found her a pair of shoes that would fit and keep putting them on her, but she keeps taking them off. The floors here are cold."

"Well," Beau said, "she's probably grown up barefoot all her life and isn't used to shoes just yet."

"That's what I thought, too," Callie said, frowning. She didn't want to look into his eyes, didn't want to feel her body signaling that it was coming back to life, hungry and wanting. As much as he tried to hide it, Callie knew he felt it, too.

"Well," she said, moving toward the door, "that was sweet of you to take the time to help her on with her shoes."

"She just needed a little TLC, was all," he said. "Kids and adults are like that, you know?" He pinned her with a knowing look.

Halting, she stared hard at him. "Sergeant? Do I look like a vagina and boobs on two legs?"

Shocked, Beau blinked once, recognizing the anger behind her harsh words. "Why . . . er . . . no, ma'am. I apologize if I insulted you. I meant—"

"Oh," Callie growled, "I know exactly what you meant, Sergeant. Look, I'm not interested!" She turned, disappearing out of the office.

Phew! She was redheaded for a reason, Beau thought, continuing to sip his coffee. And bold, too. A corner of his mouth hitched upward. He liked her spunk and her fire. He wondered what had happened that had made her so defensive.

"Well," Matt said, entering the room, "that went well."

Beau gave him a dark look. "You heard?"

"I've got ears like a wolf," Matt said, walking over to grab a cup of coffee. "I told you: she isn't going to be easy."

Shrugging, Beau said, "That's okay. Something tells me she's been real hurt by some military dude. She's gun-shy, is all."

"Oh," Matt said, grinning, "and you're going to fix that, right, Gardner?"

"Well, I have a way with animals and babies. Maybe I can turn on my backwoods charm and get her to trust me."

"Really? Does that mean you're coming here tomorrow?"

"Sure. Why not?"

Shaking his head, Matt walked toward the door. "You are a certified glutton for punishment, my friend."

"Yeah, well, I've survived worse than this," he called back.

Matt halted at the door. "You're fighting a losing battle with Callie."

Chuckling, Beau said, "Most likely, but I'd rather be here than anywhere else right now."

"You've got it bad, brother," Matt said, then disappeared around the corner.

"Yeah," Beau murmured. "I think I do." He had to admit it—he liked Callie's spirit. Hell, he liked redheaded women, and there wasn't anything to dislike about this spunky gal. Now he just had to keep that door open between them, and slowly open it more and more.

Beau was Delta Force and competitive by nature, but he also knew he couldn't push Callie into anything. No, this gal was going to lead him on a merry chase. But she wasn't going anywhere soon, and neither was he. Her time at this orphanage was ongoing until late March of next year. And he sure as hell was going to be around through March himself before going stateside once more.

All he had to do was spot Callie walking quickly from one room to another, watching that sweet sway of those killer hips of hers, and he was lost in the fog of lust. But it was more than that drawing him helplessly to this maternal, nurturing belly dancer. From what Beau had already glimpsed of her, he was even more determined than ever get her into his arms and into his bed.

CHAPTER 2

B Y THE THIRD day at the orphanage, Beau had been pleased to observe that Callie was less grumpy toward him. Between his rounds with Matt inside and outside the orphanage, he'd volunteered to help change diapers at the diaper station. He'd told Maggie, the owner of the orphanage, that he was good with babies and if she wanted, he'd feed them, bathe them, and diaper them.

Well! She'd jumped at his offer, and he found himself in what they called the "baby room" when he wasn't on his security walks. And by now, he was used to the rhythm of the busy, overcrowded orphanage.

Beau was dealing with a three-month-old baby girl as her nine-year-old sister, Aliya, stood nearby, looking on. Aliya watched as he placed the tyke on the soft white blanket spread across the table where diapers were changed. He was busy talking to Aliya in Pashto, drawing her out, making her feel comfortable in his presence as he unpinned the soft cotton diaper from the gurgling baby girl. He smiled down at the little one, her green eyes wide as he gently removed the dirty diaper, dropping it in a nearby bucket of water and bleach. He'd also volunteered to clean dirty diapers and put them in the aging washing machine at the back of the orphanage afterward.

Callie peeked in through the open door, her attention caught by the low, soft conversation between Beau and nine-year-old Aliya. It seemed impossible that a man of his height and size could move so delicately as he slipped a fresh diaper beneath the baby's bottom. She had to admit it: just watching him made her heart turn over with emotions she hadn't felt for a long time.

Beau was truly a sight, with his height and set of broad shoulders, his Kevlar vest over his long-sleeved blue tee. His jeans fit his body to perfection, and Callie could no longer ignore it. But it was Beau's low, crooning voice in that Southern drawl of his that mesmerized both her and the baby as he expertly pinned each side of the infant's diaper into place with safety pins. He made sure her little crocheted booties were snug on each of her waving feet, brushing her black hair aside from her round face with his spare fingers.

"Are you done?" she now asked, coming into the room. Callie leaned over, giving Aliya a warm hug.

"Just about," Beau murmured. He rearranged the baby's wool pullover. "Cute little thing, isn't she?" He slid one hand beneath the baby's tiny neck and the other beneath her buttocks, lifting her up and handing her over to Callie.

"She's adorable," Callie admitted, gently taking the baby. "I'm ready to feed her now."

Nodding, Beau said, "She's all yours. I've got these to rinse out." He grinned, leaning down and picking up the tall plastic bucket filled to the brim with wet diapers.

Callie laid the baby against her shoulder, patting her back gently. "You've done this a time or two, haven't you?"

"Told you before," Beau said, smiling broadly, "I have two younger brothers, and my ma put me to work as soon as I could handle a diaper, clean it, and replace it on them. It wasn't lost on her that I was good at it." He chuckled, moving past her and heading down the hall toward the laundry room.

Callie frowned, sliding her hand comfortingly along the baby's back. Ever since she'd snapped at him a few days ago, he'd acted as if she no longer existed. No more hungry looks. No more anything. Yet, Beau had made himself quite indispensable around here, just like Matt Culver. They were good men and brave soldiers, and they cared about this place and the kids. It wasn't a game to them, although Callie didn't fool herself. Matt was here because he was attracted to Dara. Her sister was definitely falling for the Delta Force sergeant, too—she could see it.

And now, Callie couldn't still her curiosity about Beau Gardner. Any guy who could happily change a diaper got her attention!

Beau had just finished placing the diapers in the washer when he felt someone enter the laundry room behind him. He turned, seeing Callie standing there, frowning at him, confusion in her expression.

"What?" he teased. "Got another diaper job for me?" he asked as he straightened, turning on the machine.

"Are you doing anything tonight after we get back to Bagram?" she surprised him by asking.

At a momentary loss, Beau said, "No. Why?" He watched her move nervously from one foot to another. He stood there, hands at his sides, holding her clear, green gaze.

"Would you like to join me for some beer and pizza tonight?"

Well, hell, you could have knocked him over with a feather! Beau remained serious, trying not to let the surprise show in his face. "Sure, I'd like that. Do you have a favorite place?" There were several pizza joints at Bagram along restaurant row. He opened his hands. "I promise I'll conduct myself as a gentleman.''

Callie's expression subtly changed, and he sensed that she wanted to trust him. And she could; Beau was as good as his word. He knew Callie wasn't a woman he could hog-tie and carry off to his bed with a few sweet words.

"Okay," she muttered. "Let's pick something out later. I need to get back to work."

And she was gone, just like that. Swimming in elated shock, Beau grinned and hoisted up the clean diaper pail he'd just filled with water and a bit of bleach. Maybe if he pretended to ignore Callie, she'd come to him. Well, tonight was going to make or break whatever hopes he had. And damned if he wasn't interested in her on more than just a lusty level.

He'd been with her three solid days here, putting in twelve hours a day, and he'd seen the work and care she put into this orphanage. He liked the love she extended to the children, who clearly adored her. There was nothing to dislike about Callie McKinley and more to like—much more.

"TELL ME ABOUT yourself," Callie said, sitting with Beau at a table in the rear of the busy, noisy pizzeria. It was raining outside and he'd picked her up in a Humvee earlier at her B-hut. How he'd gotten his hands on one, she didn't know, but she didn't ask. It was probably because he was black ops and could finagle a vehicle to drive her across the base to the restaurant.

Beau had changed out of the clothes he normally wore at the orphanage. Instead, she could smell the fresh soap on his skin, telling her he'd showered earlier. And his hair was washed and somewhat tamed around his neck and below his ears. He'd even trimmed his beard. Callie liked the black chinos he wore with a light gray sweater beneath his black leather jacket. He looked dangerous to her—and he was. She sensed it.

She tried not to think of it, but she realized that her body was yearning for his touch, his mouth on hers, his hands exploring her. The man was sensual as hell, and she wished she could ignore it, but she just couldn't.

"Well," he drawled, "my pa is a tanner up on Black Mountain near our cabin. A lot of hunters from all over the state use his services after they kill a deer. He's well known for the quality and softness of the hides he tans. My ma stays at home. She had the three of us boys, has a huge garden, cans in the late summer and fall, and puts up food for the coming winter. She's also a crochet queen.''

Beau watched Callie delicately eat the pizza, fascinated as he watched her lips move, forcing his body to behave itself. He was damn glad that she couldn't see his growing erection.

"Why did you join the Army?" she asked between bites of pizza.

"My pa was in the Marine Corps for four years. He wanted all of us boys to serve our country and told us to choose a service. I liked the Army, and my two younger brothers went into the Marine Corps."

"How did you get into Delta Force?"

Beau wiped his fingers on the paper napkin after finishing off his fourth wedge of pizza. "My pa taught us boys how to hunt, shoot, and track when we were real young. The neighbors up on top of the mountain, the Thorn family, used to join us in the fall when it was legal to hunt deer. Floyd Thorn always brought his oldest daughter, Baylee Ann Thorn, along with him. The three of us boys used to track with Baylee. She was better at it than we were." He smiled fondly, remembering those times. "But to answer your question, I guess I was good enough that Delta Force came hunting me down and invited me to join them. Before that, I'd been a ground-pounder, a combat soldier, was all."

Her mouth turned up as she took her second slice of pizza. "Delta Force is well known to take the cream of the Army crop. So there must have been something really special about you, Beau. You were more than just a soldier."

He warmed to her using his name. Callie was clearly having a battle within herself, trying to keep her distance, yet wanting to know about him. Beau gave her a shrug, sipping his cold beer, his gaze flitting across the darkened restaurant, filled mostly with groups of men at tables. He was one of the few who had a woman with him, because men far outnumbered women here on this base.

"I think it was because of my hunting and tracking skills."

"It sounds like it," she agreed.

"What about you?" he asked, holding her thoughtful green gaze. "Tell me where you're from. Where did you grow up?"

Callie smiled a little. "I was born in Butte, Montana. My dad is an orthopedic surgeon and my mom is a registered nurse. We live on my grandparents' ten-thousand-acre working cattle spread, the Eagle Feather Ranch, outside the city. My grandpa Graham McKinley runs the ranch. My grandma Maisy is an accountant for the ranch and works at home."

"So you're a bona fide cowgirl?" he teased, giving her a warm look. Beau saw a slight flush come to her cheeks.

"My grandpa put me up on my first horse when I was three years old," Callie recalled. "He told me years later that I yelled my head off because I was scared."

Beau couldn't take his eyes off her animated, heart-shaped face as she talked about the incident. He was happy to see that Callie was finally relaxing, at least in stages. He'd put this stage at a three out of ten.

"About the closest I got to a horse was riding the Thorns' mule," he now confided. "All of us boys would walk half a mile up to the crest of the mountain where they lived and beg Mr. Thorn for a mule ride. Then the three of us would pile onto the mule's back for a spin around the property. We felt pretty special, and I always enjoyed those rides."

"That was really nice of him to do that for you," Callie said. She picked up her mug of beer and took a sip.

"Hill people stick together," he pointed out. "There's a bunch of families who live up on Black Mountain, and we all support one another. I know a lot of folks call us 'hillbillies' and look down on us, but we're there for each other whenever we're needed."

Shaking her head, Callie muttered, "I hate it when people show their prejudices like that."

"In Dunmore, a pretty large town south of us," Beau went on, "my ma always ran into that kind of thing. She didn't wear the latest fashions, so people would shun her, ignore her, or pretend she wasn't standing in line to get waited on."

He saw flashes of anger and, yes, regret in Callie's eyes. Wow! His little redheaded spitfire could sure get pissed off in a hell of a hurry! Beau withheld a grin over that discovery.

"That's just plain wrong," Cassie sputtered. "I'm sure it hurt her feelings."

"The hill people living on Black Mountain didn't often go down to the lowlanders' towns," he said. "We were pretty self-sufficient. We raised our own meat, we hunted, we had big gardens, and we helped one another. Mr. Thorn, for example, would take his mule and ride him over to other parts of the mountain and plow up the ground for other folks so they could put in their gardens every spring. My pa would help him when he could. He and Floyd would go hunting and kill enough deer for everyone. After they skinned and quartered them, they'd take the meat to the elderly folks on the mountain who couldn't hunt any longer."

"I like that about your folks," Callie confided as she finished her pizza slice. She pushed the last wedge toward Beau. "Finish this off, Beau? I'm stuffed!"

"You sure?" he asked. "You could take it back with you for a midnight snack."

"I'm very sure. And I'm glad to see that you know how to share."

He chuckled and picked up the last wedge. "What? You have some guy in your past who'd steal pizza out of your hands so he could gobble it down himself?"

His heart somersaulted as she smiled—really smiled at him—for the first time. Beau thought he'd died and gone to heaven in that moment. Callie was always beautiful, but when she smiled, her green eyes shone with a radiance that went straight into his heart and lit him up inside. He decided he liked making her smile.

"I've had that experience, yes. Not often, but when it happened, I never saw him again. That kind of attitude tells me a lot. Specifically, I realized that he was selfish and put himself first instead of thinking about others' needs. I don't keep people like that in my life. Ever."

He munched thoughtfully on the cheesy, salty pizza. "Kinda thought that. You strike me as a gal who doesn't suffer fools—at all."

"No, I don't." Callie scowled and wrapped her slender hands around the cold mug of beer in front of her. "And I haven't made up my mind about you yet, Beau, but I am drawn to you. I just can't figure out why . . ."

His brows rose. "Maybe because I'm a good-lookin' brute?" he teased, watching her cheeks flood with color. He knew he wasn't hard to look at, but he also wasn't one of those handsome hunks on the covers of the romance novels that his ma loved to read, either. Beau considered himself ordinary-looking, and that was fine with him.

Sitting back, Callie absorbed the warmth dancing in his eyes. "To tell you the truth. I wasn't looking for a man. I don't need a relationship getting started here at Bagram. Besides, you guys are interested in only one thing, and I'm not interested in anyone who's just focused on having a good time."

"Sounds like you've had one too many bad experiences around here," he said, suddenly becoming serious.

"Yes, one too many," Callie muttered. "Which has me confused about you. You didn't lie to me about why you showed up at the orphanage."

He munched and then swallowed. "My parents never put up with liars. We boys learned to tell the truth when we were real young. We were taught that your word was your bond, and you never went back on it. And I suspect that, you being a ranch gal from the West, your parents and grandparents are a lot like my parents in that department."

"Hah! You'd better believe it," Callie laughed, then got serious again. "I just can't figure you out."

"You mean, I'm like a Chinese puzzle box?" he coaxed with a chuckle.

"You're black ops. You've been trained to assume a cover, to be something you aren't. You're all chameleons. That's what has me concerned."

"Look, Callie," he said, dropping his casual demeanor and looking directly into her eyes. "What you see is what you get with me. I'm not trying to hide anything from you. Am I attracted to you? Yes. Do I think you're an incredible dancer? Yes."

"You're either the most honest guy I've met here at Bagram, or you're the best liar I've ever run into," she laughed.

Finishing off his pizza, Beau wiped his mouth with the paper napkin.

"You're not a target, Callie. I never knew much about NGOs or the work you gals put in, but being with you this past week has given me a whole new appreciation for your commitment to those kids' welfare." He continued holding her gaze; he'd never been more honest than he was right now. "There's just something special about you, other than being a highly talented belly dancer. It would be an honor to get to know you better."

How could she turn down this man? He seemed to have all the right words and answers for her. Callie sat there, the vibration of his low, Southern voice feathering through her, making her want things she knew she shouldn't want. There was a simplicity to Beau Gardner, a down-to-earth quality. He was a man close to the land and to nature, and that called to her. She was the same way, having come from a hardworking ranch family.

"I just don't want to get into a relationship," she warned him. "I've been suckered in before, and I swore I wasn't ever going to be used again."

He pushed the aluminum pizza pan aside, resting his arms on the table, and then shocked her with his next words. "I'm not the kind of man who plays games, Callie. I've been up-front with you from the moment we met. I really am drawn to you for many reasons." He opened his hands. "And I'd be telling you the world's biggest windy if I said I didn't think you're the sexiest woman I've seen in a long, long time. And sure, I think about what it would be like holding you in my arms, in my bed."

Wow, this guy called it like it was! Callie sat there, stunned, hearing the grittiness in his tone, seeing the sincerity in his eyes. She wrapped her arms around her chest protectively, staring back at him. "Beau, are you always like this with a woman you want?"

He shrugged. "Well, to tell you the truth, I'm always honest with a woman who interests me. I don't play games, Callie. If there's a connection, that's great. If there isn't, then there's nothing I can do to change that, is there? I happen to think there's something special between us."

Blunt and honest. How refreshing was that? Callie felt the clench of hunger ramping up within her. "I've got to tell you, I'm not open to one-night stands."

"I'm not either," Beau agreed quietly.

There was no doubt in her mind that he was telling the truth. And that was even more alarming as she found herself fantasizing what it would be like to . . .

"Then what do you want?" she asked, needing to hear the words.

"I'm not sure, because you're different. You call to me, to . . . well, to my heart." He gave her a sheepish look. "Normally, my heart isn't in the mix. Oh, there's certainly physical appreciation for a woman who interests me, but for whatever reason you grabbed my heart from the moment I saw you dance.

That hasn't changed. It's just gotten stronger. The more I get to know you, the more I like what I see. What do I want from you? I'd like you to trust me enough to see what draws us to one another. I don't know where it's going, gal, but I'd sure like to find out. Wouldn't you?"

Okay, the ball was in her court. Callie gave him a speculative look. "You're either the smoothest operator I've ever run into, or you really are who you say you are. I know that you black ops guys are good at getting what you go after. You can turn into what we want you to be, so you know how to approach us women. Black ops guys are known to read a human being better than ninety-nine percent of the rest of us on God's green earth."

"I don't disagree with your analysis of us, Callie. When we're undercover, we do use those skills. But I'm not using them on you right now. And I hear you loud and clear that you don't trust me," he acknowledged, folding his hands.

Feeling guilty, Callie knew she'd hurt him. "Look, Beau, I'm sorry to be so defensive, but I've been used in the past, more than once, and I never want to go through that again. That's all," she added, feeling unsure of how he would respond to her fragility. Most men would just get up and walk away, she knew, or ignore her words and scheme to get her into bed anyway.

Nodding, he said, "I got that, gal. I saw the pain and the nervousness in your eyes when we met. All I can be is honest about who I am and what I need when we're together. Just like you are with me now," he said with a brief smile.

"Well," she mumbled, leaning on the table with her elbows, "I'll give you this: I don't think any other guy would try to impress me by changing a baby's diaper or cleaning out a diaper bucket."

Chuckling, Beau met her rueful smile. "Well, to tell you the truth, I love kids and babies and grew up helping my ma earn pin money by babysitting the tykes on Black Mountain. Believe me, I had my hands in more baby poo as a kid than you could ever imagine."

Callie's heart began to slowly open as he made his shy admission. Could there really be one man on this testosterone-laden base who would be honest with her? She'd been lied to, manipulated, and disappointed so many times before that her heart couldn't stand any more.

But there was something so honest, so clean and refreshing about Beau Gardner that she felt all her walls, all her defensiveness, begin to melt away. Between his country-boy drawl and his sincere gray eyes, he made her feel special.

Later, Beau walked Callie up to the porch of her B-hut. The weather was rainy and chilly, and she hunkered down in her hooded black wool coat. He kept his hand cupped beneath her elbow as he walked her down the sidewalk. Once they were protected by the overhang of the roof, Callie pulled her hood off and began to dig in her purse for the key. A part of her wanted to turn, push up on her toes, and kiss this man, but another part resisted.

She was waiting to see what he was going to do, and she found herself wary again. She just wasn't sure what her reaction would be if Beau tried to kiss her.

"Found it," she muttered, pulling the keys out.

"Good enough. I'll see you tomorrow morning at the van, okay? You go ahead and get inside, and then I'll leave."

"You don't have to do that," Callie protested.

"Oh, yes, I do." Beau continued to swivel around, looking into the darkness and light rain. "Too many women in the past have been attacked as they were entering or leaving their B-huts." His shadowed eyes met hers briefly. "Believe me, you're not going to be one of them."

Her hand shook as she placed the key in the lock. "Thanks," she said a little breathlessly. "It's nice to have a personal guard dog." She slipped inside. "Good night, Beau. Thanks for the pizza and beer." She saw him smile, lift his baseball cap to her, and then settle it back on his head.

"My pleasure, ma'am. Sleep well. I'll see you in the morning. Good night."

Callie pushed the door closed, her heart pounding with the need for more of Beau. He was being the essential gentleman, which was exactly what she'd wanted. So why did she feel so damned disappointed that he hadn't gripped her arm, hauled her against him, and kissed her senseless? Because she knew he could have, but he hadn't.

There were four rooms with doors within her plywood B-hut. She knocked on Dara's door quietly, not wanting to wake up the other two women, who were already asleep. Dara didn't answer. Grinning, Callie would have bet anything that Matt Culver had lured her over to the Eagle's Nest. It was well known on the base that the black ops groups had their hideaways where they could take a woman, make love to her, and do it without having to worry about the MPs breaking in to ruin their night.

Turning, she moved into her small, cramped quarters across the hall from her sister's room. Callie wanted only happiness for her big sister and was proud of Dara for becoming an MD. But Dara didn't understand the allure of a black ops soldier the way Callie did.

Although he had a stellar reputation, Matt Culver was still a guy, and Callie was afraid he going to use her sister and then walk away. Maybe she'd have a talk with Dara tomorrow morning at chow to warn her off Matt. But would her sister believe her?

Not that Matt Culver seemed like the playboy type. The look in his eyes when she'd catch him looking at her sister was more than lust. It went far deeper.

Muttering to herself, Callie shook her head and shut her door, locking it. She had enough problems of her own with Beau Gardner suddenly popping up in her life. He seemed so damned sincere, and so far, he was scoring very low on her BS meter. In fact, he was off the meter entirely.

Well, she'd wanted honesty, right? And he was giving it to her. Shedding her clothes, she decided to take a hot shower in the morning when it was light. Callie never liked to walk over to the shower area after dark. There were too many male predators on this base, and in her five years here, women had been mugged and raped. That was not a place she wanted to go.

Instead, she had a large aluminum bowl, a gallon jug of water sitting beside her dresser, a washcloth, and some soap in a Ziploc bag. She would give herself a spit bath and then go to bed.

WHEN CALLIE'S HEAD hit the pillow and she snuggled down into her bed, she immediately began to think about Beau. She loved his low, soft drawl, that boyish twitch of his lips, the warm amusement in his piercing gray eyes—eyes that missed nothing.

She was sure many people had been fooled by Beau's good-ol'-boy de- meanor. He exuded patience, care, and a sense of protectiveness that appealed strongly to Callie. The man was the whole package for a woman seeking someone steady and reliable in her life. Callie had often dreamed of finding a man who liked babies, and Beau had such a way with the little Afghan girls. That morning, when he'd arrived, they had surrounded him, shy but wanting to be in the sunlight of his aura, his care, and his open, giving warmth. Often, she'd see Beau kneel down, tie a shoelace, help a little girl with a coverall strap that was hanging off her small, thin shoulder. He'd tighten it up just a bit to keep it from falling off again.

Afghan girls were taught to fear boys and men. It was all part of a tribal culture aimed at suppressing women. Unfortunately, it started early, when little girls had barely begun to walk.

But Beau was a highly unusual man, and these children, who had lost their parents and grandparents, basked in the warmth of his quiet, gentle presence. Callie had tried to escape being affected by him, but it was too late now—her heart was already getting involved, no matter what she did to try to ignore it. So what on earth was she going to do now?

CHAPTER 3

CALLIE HEARD DARA enter the B-hut at 0600 the next morning. She could barely hear her sister whispering to Matt Culver out on the porch as she held the door open. Her heart sinking, Callie realized that they'd been together all night over at the Eagle's Nest. Happiness for Dara warred with her concern that Matt was like every other man on this base: wanting sex and nothing else from a woman.

Her sister was still pretty innocent about military men, who went for months without sex and were horny as hell. On the other hand, Dara wasn't the type to tumble lightning-fast for a guy, as she seemed to be falling for Matt Culver.

Callie couldn't blame her sister: Matt was an incredibly good-looking man, confident, brave, and demonstrating the best manners. And that didn't even touch his sky-high intelligence. Then again, Delta Force men were dangerous that way—a lethal combination of brains and brawn.

Sighing, she heard the door close and Callie opened hers, peeking out. Dara appeared wrapped in euphoria, her eyes soft, all the tension she usually carried now gone. There was no question that they had made love last night, and probably this morning, too, judging from the drowsy, satisfied look in her sister's eyes.

"Want to go take a shower?" Callie asked her.

"That's a very good idea," Dara agreed. "Just give me ten minutes and I'll go over with you."

"Great," Callie said. "Is it still raining outside?"

"No, just high humidity, a lot of sharp, cutting wind, and darn cold," Dara reported, opening her door across the hall.

"Knock on my door when you're ready, okay?" she asked Dara.

"Yes, will do . . ." *For sure*, Callie thought, *Dara is in la-la land.* Callie easily recognized that look. It came with super orgasms and lots of them. Matt Culver must have been one hell of a lover, along with his other talents. But then, the Delta boys were always in high demand. The women here weren't stupid; they hooked up with the strongest, the sexiest, the brightest warriors available. It was a case of natural selection at work. Right?

Callie groaned and pushed on her clogs, wrapped herself up in her yellow terry-cloth bathrobe, and put her bath and hair towels into her bag. She tossed in shampoo, soap, and conditioner, and she was ready to go. She expected that she and her sister would catch up over morning chow.

"YOU LOOK LIKE you've just arrived from another universe," Callie teased as she and Dara found some seats midway through the hundreds of tables and benches. The chow hall at 0630 was relatively quiet compared to what it would be like in an hour. This building held a lot of hungry men and women for three square meals a day.

Dara sat opposite her, dressed in a pair of black wool slacks, a red turtleneck sweater, and a black wool blazer. "Is it that obvious?" she asked coyly, scooping scrambled eggs onto her fork.

Chuckling, Callie said, "How many orgasms? Must have been a lot, judging by the way you looked when you came in." She saw Dara give her a horrified look. "Oh, come on, Dara, this is between us girls. Orgasms do exist, you know. And after all, you're a medical doctor," she said, grinning wolfishly.

"You are so crass sometimes," Dara muttered, trying not to smile.

"How many? Come on, tell all to your little sister . . ."

"Lots. That's all you get to know. And now I'm going to change the subject."

"I'd sure like to be in your shoes," Callie sighed. "Or out of them!" She ate her oats and saw her sister's cheeks turn red. Dara was conservative, elegant, beautiful, and introverted. Unlike Callie, who was the exact opposite. Callie knew she was attractive, but she'd never kidded herself that she was the beautiful sister. Dara was the one with that soft, natural blond hair that fell like a cloak around her shoulders.

"What about that other Delta guy? Beau Gardner? He seems to really like you," Dara pointed out. "Sometimes, I see him watching you, and the look on his face belongs to a man who yearns for his woman."

"Yeah, to get into my pants," her sister mumbled.

"Oh, that's mean, Callie. He's as nice as Matt is."

"Yes, and look what happened to you once Matt came along!"

Dara grinned and shook her head. "Okay, so this isn't my norm with a man. I know it takes me months to warm up to a potential prospect."

"Yeah, this one took . . . what? All of six days? Wow, you're setting a new personal best for yourself, Dara."

"Jealousy will get you nowhere," her sister laughed. "Come on! He's a wonderful person. I really enjoy being with him."

Callie sobered. "But, Dara, you're going to be gone in another four days, back home in Alexandria to finish your residency. Matt Culver is staying here until March, and what then? God only knows where the Army will send his team next. He's a shadow warrior—not the best type of guy to hook up with."

"Matt's enlistment is up next March, Callie, and then he's getting out."

Brows raised, Callie said, "Really?"

"Yes, and did you know his family lives in Alexandria? He's coming home to Virginia to help his mother run Delos, her global charity."

"Oh," Callie murmured thoughtfully. "So that makes a difference. After all, he'll be in your area."

"It does make a difference," Dara agreed. She sighed. "Callie, I'm falling for this guy. He's the real deal. I realize I don't have your experience with men, but I have enough to know Matt is someone I'm very serious about."

"And is he serious about you?"

"I believe so."

Callie stirred her oats. "I just don't want to see you get hurt, Dara."

Reaching out, Dara squeezed her hand. "I know that, Callie."

"Yes, well, I can tell you from too many experiences that falling for a military guy isn't the best choice."

Dara munched on her toast. "So what's with you and Beau, then? Sometimes I've come out of my examination room and found him watching you from a distance. Not stalkerlike, but he'll be diapering the babies or helping the little ones, and he'll lift his head and watch you pass by."

"Really?"

"Yes."

Shrugging, but secretly pleased, Callie said, "I'm too busy to check out who's looking at me."

"Well, I swear, he looks like a puppy dog who's falling in love."

"Great!" Callie choked. "Just what I need."

Laughing, Dara smiled over at her. "Callie, you're young, you're beautiful, and you have a killer body most women would die for. I see the looks you get here in the chow hall every morning."

"But I don't want to be a damned sex object, Dara. You know that."

"Well, you and I agree on that one. I want a man who treats me like an equal too. One who respects me . . ."

"Like Matt Culver does?"

"Yes." Dara's voice went soft. "He's wonderful, Callie. I tried to ignore him when he met us outside those exit doors after our belly-dancing routine.

But he has a way about him." She sighed. "He's so sensual. And charming. And funny. He even makes me laugh, and you know how few men can do that!"

"Well, it sounds pretty good, and I'm happy for you, sis," Callie agreed. "Enjoy your last four days here, and don't forget, we're driving out to that Shinwari village. It's all set up. You'll be doing your medical rounds for women, children, and babies in the village, and I'll be handing out shoes and winter clothing to the children."

"Are Matt and Beau going with us, I hope?"

"Yes. You worry too much, Dara. I don't think Matt would let you go out there without him."

"I know," she admitted ruefully. "I never feel safe here, Callie. I mean, I want to volunteer my time with you and the Hope Charity. But I'm never relaxed. Well, I take that back. Last night, I was *very* relaxed."

Callie snickered, shaking her head. "Well, if nothing else, keep going to the Eagle's Nest every night with him and you'll be loosey-goosey by the time we drive that twenty-five miles to the village."

Dara's eyes became huge. "Callie! How did you know about the Eagle's Nest?"

"Gimme a break, Dara. I've been on Bagram six months out of every year for the last five years. You get to know the base and how it operates."

"So, have you been to the Nest?"

"No," Callie said pertly, "but I've heard about it from other women who have been there. They say it's like an apartment."

"It is. And it's soundproof."

"Good thing," Callie said drily, giving her sister a wicked grin.

And then they both laughed, their hands over their mouths, looking more like teenagers than women who could, at any given moment, be putting their lives on the line.

BEAU WAS SWAMPED by the children the minute he and Matt arrived inside the orphanage. They had made their cursory inspection outdoors, and seeing the children warmed Beau's heart as he and Matt moved into the mudroom. They kept their M4s against their chests so a child couldn't accidentally bump into a barrel and get hurt on the cold metal of the weapon. The boys gravitated to Matt, and the girls flowed around Beau. In part, it was because they both spoke their language, which created trust. The children's openness and their happy chatter made the men smile.

Beau greeted Maggie and watched Callie disappear into the kitchen, where breakfast was being prepared for the children. He called the girls to accompany him to the big room, and they followed him like little ducklings. They all knew he brought wrapped candy, and their small hands reached for it when he patted the stuffed pockets of his cargo pants.

Matt had taken the boys to one corner of the big room, and Beau took the girls to another. In Afghan society, if an American soldier gave a little girl a piece of candy or food, the boys would come and attack her, beating her up until she gave up her prize to them. The boys were vicious when it came to intimidating a girl. They let her know from the time she took her first steps that she was valued far below any goat or donkey in the village.

As Beau sat down on a chair, he pulled his weapon to his back, getting it out of the way as the girls crowded excitedly around him, their eyes shining with eager anticipation, their small hands opened toward him, begging him for some candy. He smiled, spoke softly in Pashto to them, and pulled out a bunch of wrapped candies. As he held his large hand down toward them, he saw how different the girls were from the boys.

The boys would have charged forward, fighting and hitting each other, grabbing for as much candy as they could get. Instead, the girls waited, their eyes large with excitement. Beau told them he would start with one girl and allow each to take one piece in turn.

The girls were patient as Beau handed out all the candy to them. Then he called them over, asking them to sit down around his feet and eat their prizes. Across the room, he saw Matt had his hands full with the shoving, pushing boys. All it took was a deep growl from him in Pashto to stop the tussles, and they backed off, thinking they were going to get cuffed or struck with a belt or a switch.

Instead, Matt told them to sit down and be still. And they did.

Beau smiled and watched his charges slurping up the hard candy, licking their small fingers and smiling as they enjoyed their treats. He would remain with the girls until they finished their candy, because if he didn't, the boys would try to come and take it away from them. And more than a few were looking longingly his way.

Beau gave them a dark, unspoken look of warning that they were not welcome. The boys remained sitting, squirming, but no longer fighting among themselves. Matt handed out one piece of candy to each of them. Beau chuckled to himself, glad he'd gotten the girls. They were far easier to work with than those wild little boys.

He happened to lift his head and was surprised to catch Callie staring at him. He wasn't sure what the look on her face meant, but he smiled over at her and she promptly turned and left the room.

Beau wanted to tell her how pretty she looked this morning in her purple turtleneck sweater and dark gray cotton trousers. She wore her red hair in a long ponytail down her back, and he itched to slide his fingers through that molten crimson mass.

His dreams had been torrid last night, and he'd awakened this morning with a painful hard-on. Even worse, he'd also awakened with an ache in his heart—for Callie. This was clearly going to be about more than sex.

Unconsciously, he rubbed the area of his chest where his Kevlar vest rested. Callie was a complicated person, and Beau understood her distrust of men in general. Of course, getting hit on all the time was nerve-wracking, not to mention infuriating, to a woman. He remembered his father telling the boys one time how he'd met their mother. Amber had been beautiful, fawned over and chased by every boy on Black Mountain, when she was in her early twenties. Beau remembered how his father, who was a patient man, had gotten her to choose him over all her other suitors. He had treated her with respect, never tried to sneak a kiss from her, and took her on long walks instead, talking to her about what was important to her. What were her dreams? Her goals? What made her happy? What made her laugh?

His father was a wise man, Beau decided, and he swore he would apply that same philosophy to Callie.

"Here."

Looking up, he saw Callie was holding out a washcloth. "You've got a bunch of little girls with sticky fingers, Gardner. Clean them up so they can come and get breakfast, okay?" She smiled one of the sweetest smiles he'd ever seen.

He grinned crookedly and thanked her. One by one, Beau dutifully cleaned every pair of little hands thrust up into his face. It took about ten minutes, but the girls' mouths and hands were wiped clean of candy. He shooed them down the hall to the kitchen, and they ran like little wild horses, their hair flying behind them, giggling and laughing.

It lifted his spirits as well. Children were innocent. They needed protection and support. Sadness moved through Beau, because all of these children had been ignored by their villages and left to starve to death. They had no place to go. If he could have, Beau would have adopted the whole brood of them, but that wasn't reality. And it broke his heart, because their lives in this harsh corner of the world were never going to have happy endings.

Matt was busy schooling the wayward boys, and it was clear that they were listening to him. Beau smiled to himself, watching his sergeant speak to the boys in Pashto like a native. He was a good leader, not one who used bullying tactics to get them to do what he wanted.

Beau had seen real changes in the boys since he'd been at the orphanage, and it was all thanks to Matt. He had stopped the boys from hitting or attacking the girls, which was a huge triumph. As the last boy left and walked, instead of raced, down the hall, Beau sauntered over to Matt. The boys and girls were now integrated at the tables. These boys were going to learn to respect the girls. It was a good lesson for both genders as far as he was concerned.

Matt pointed with his bearded chin toward the front door. It was time for another stroll around the grounds of the orphanage.

CALLIE GROANED, SITTING down in Maggie's empty office and pushing off one of her shoes. It was three p.m., and all the children were down for their naps. Her feet were aching, and she longed to sit down and rub some of the soreness out of them.

"Here," Beau said, placing his M4 aside and sitting down on the stool in front of her chair. "Let me do that for you."

Callie hadn't even heard him enter the office. "Don't tell me you give foot rubs, too!" she said incredulously. Grinning gratefully, she set her shoe aside.

"Yes, ma'am, I do. My ma has weak feet. I think they call it 'fallen arches.' I used to watch my pa take each foot separately and gently massage them. She got so relaxed that sometimes she'd fall asleep on the couch while he massaged away. She always felt better after he worked on them." Beau held up his long, spare hands. "I got lucky, Callie. I got his hands." He reached for her right foot.

"I would *love* a massage," Callie sighed. "I need shoes with better arch support, that's for sure." She leaned back, and the moment Beau's hands enclosed her foot, she felt the magic his mother must have felt when Beau's father began working on her feet. His hands felt wonderful!

"You know, you work too hard around here, Callie," he drawled. "Now, just close your eyes and go far away in your mind. I'll take care of these poor, sufferin' feet of yours." And he did, running his hand up and down her arch, her skin warm and velvety beneath his seeking fingers as he pushed and cajoled those tight muscles to loosen them up.

"Ohh . . . ," she whispered. "That feels so good, Beau . . . thank you . . ."

His mouth curved faintly as he began to knead her flesh, taking each toe, gently moving it, getting it to relax. The soft sounds emanating from Callie's throat pleased him.

He wanted to do something for her. God knew, she flew around this place, helping the four widows and then assisting Maggie with tons of paperwork in her office. Callie was constantly on her feet, and he'd never seen her take a break.

"Must be that belly dancing, 'cause your ankles and calves are truly fine," he murmured, sliding his fingers from below her knee downward.

Callie sighed, utterly relaxed. "Everyone works hard around here. And hey, you can do this any time you want." Barely opening her eyes, she studied his bent head as he focused solely on her leg, ankle, and foot.

"Well, you and I are going to be in this neck of the woods until next March, so let me know when you need another boost." As a matter of fact, Beau was making some long-range plans for them both.

He would, of course, have to go on missions with his team, but they'd also get a few days' rest at Bagram. Then he could call her up and ask her out, or do something special to gain more of her trust. He'd been looking for an opportunity to talk to her today, and by sheer luck, he'd found her here.

"Mmm, you've got a deal," Callie murmured. His hands were strong but gentle. *He truly does have magic hands*, she thought as her cranky feet began to glow with improved circulation. When he was done with one foot, he leaned down, retrieved her shoe, and eased it back on, placing it beside him on the wide stool.

"Are we ready for the other foot?" he teased, already picking it up and coaxing the shoe off her foot.

"Ohh, for sure . . . thank you . . ." Callie felt absolutely adored. Worshipped, as a matter of fact. Her mind rejected that image, but she couldn't help but feel spoiled rotten by Beau Gardner. His hands soothed her sore feet, and as he kneaded her ankle and then her calf, she could do nothing but sigh with pleasure.

The way he monitored his strength against her flesh told her he'd be a sensitive lover. Clearly, he wasn't the kind of guy to show off his strength to women, and this was a refreshing change for Callie.

She began to doze off, and it wasn't until Beau placed her shoe back on her foot that she roused herself.

"Feel better now?" Beau asked, gently tapping her ankle.

"Like night and day," she admitted, her voice husky as she sat up, rubbing her eyes. "I must have dozed off. I never do that!"

"Only for about ten minutes," Beau said. He eased off the stool, walked over to retrieve his rifle, and snapped it back into his chest harness. "The kids will be down for another fifteen minutes. Would you like a cup of coffee? I'm having one," he said, gesturing at the freshly made pot sitting on the back shelf in the office.

"That sounds good," she said, still trying to wake up. "My feet feel wonderful. I guess I owe you," she offered, feeling suddenly shy.

"Uh-oh," Beau teased her mercilessly, pouring her a cup and then adding the sugar and cream she liked. Stirring it, he turned and walked across the office, handing her the mug.

"What?" Callie demanded, thanking him for the coffee. Her eyes moved upward, meeting his. There was such merriment in their gray depths that she felt embraced by an invisible energy coming directly from him to her.

"Well," he drawled, returning to the coffeepot, "you said that you owe me. Now, what am I to think about that?" He sauntered to another chair that sat near hers.

Callie rolled her eyes. "What's your favorite flavor of ice cream?"

"I'm kind of ordinary. I like chocolate."

"Not Rocky Road? Chocolate almond fudge?"

Shaking his head, he enjoyed seeing Callie relaxed and not tense or on guard. "No. But I do like nuts and whipped cream on it when I can get it. Does that count?" His lower body went on red alert as she rewarded him with that luscious smile of hers. It lit up her whole face, her green eyes radiant.

"Well," Callie continued, "I happen to be friends with a gal who's in my B-hut. Carrie works over at the ice cream parlor on restaurant row. She knows I have a weakness for ice cream and usually stores my favorites. I go over once a week, usually on a Saturday afternoon, and get a cup of Rocky Road slathered in hot fudge."

"I see," he said. "It's nice getting to know a little more about you. What else do you like to do if you have a chance?"

She sat back, holding the mug in her lap. "When I get home, I get thirty days' vacation, and I head straight for my grandparents' ranch. I pull on my jeans, my cowboy boots, my cowboy hat, and a long-sleeved white blouse, and go out and get my favorite mare and go riding."

"What does it do for you?"

Callie was struck by the depth of his question. "Peace. Quiet. A chance to heal myself from all I see over here, every day." She gestured around the room. "I love my family very much, and just getting to be home with all of them heals me, too."

"This work could suck anyone dry," he agreed quietly.

"My parents taught us to make a difference, Beau. Be something positive. Dara was inspired to go to medical school and become a doctor. I wanted to work in a more grassroots capacity, I guess. I wanted to effect changes, one person at a time. I signed up with Hope Charity out of Los Gatos, California. I have an apartment there, and when I get done with my thirty days at my parents' ranch, I go home to that city. I work as an office assistant for Hope until it's time for me to do my six months overseas here, at Kabul."

Nodding, Beau added, "Saving one child at a time by giving each a hug?"

Callie gave him a long, studied look, and felt her heart begin to truly open to this man. He wasn't like the others, she realized from their unexpected conversation. Never did he talk about himself, what he had accomplished or done in his life. If he talked, he talked in terms of his team. Or his family. It was never about him as an individual.

"You know," she began, searching for the right words, "you and I are probably more alike than I ever realized."

Beau's mouth twitched. "I think we're both people who believe in being a role model, being present, effecting change. I wouldn't always say that in my line of work that's true. Sometimes, we take down the bad guys. Sometimes, I have to kill someone."

"But you're killing to protect the innocent, those unable to defend themselves. You protect the villages, the people who live in them. You know how bad off they are. They barely enough food to feed themselves, much less anyone else. And on top of that, you take out the bad guys. You also protect our soldiers from IEDs, ambushes, and attacks. Most of all, you find high-value targets, men who are entering Afghanistan to kill or enslave the villagers."

At that moment, there was something so alive, so pulsating, so magical between them, that all Callie could do was absorb the sensation. This was the first time they'd both unveiled their feelings.

Her vulnerability, and his own, took her breath away. She saw from his eyes that he not only felt it, too, but understood that something special was taking root between them.

Callie had no name for what had just leaped to life and now burned brightly, encompassing them. It almost made her momentarily breathless, just knowing that she could plumb the depths of Beau as a human being. Not just as a man, but as a person who was open and unafraid to stand before her. How rare a gift that was!

She saw the tumult in his eyes, his feelings emanating like a warm summer rain, enfolding her and holding her safe and protected. Ever since she'd started dating, Callie had had this deep, secret dream of the perfect man for her. But that quickly got knocked out of her as she made one mistake after another with men who disappointed her or used her. Beau was unexpected. She knew black ops guys who were type A tigers. Yet Beau appeared on the surface to be a laid-back type B, easygoing and not competitive. It appealed strongly to her. She liked a man who could be strong when needed but also put away that masculine hardness and connect with his more gentle side. To her shock, Beau was demonstrating it daily. She saw him when he was going on security rounds outside the orphanage. He was all type A male, from his hard, alert expression to the decidedly protective energy around him and the tension he carried from being on guard.

Right now, he'd put that part of himself aside. Except for her father and grandfather, Callie had never seen any other men with these two distinct facets to themselves. That was why she had wished mightily to meet a man like them. But she never had.

Not until just now . . . And maybe dreams did come true. Callie just wasn't sure, but her heart certainly was. She knew men could be gentle and nurturing, because she'd seen it in her own life. And after so many bad choices and mistakes with men, Callie had decided she was an idealist and that Beau might be the man of her dreams after all. Time would tell.

CHAPTER 4

C ALLIE WAS EAGER to have dinner with Beau tonight. After he'd massaged her feet, he'd gotten up to attend to his security rounds. Later, near quitting time, she found him diapering three babies in a row. The four Afghan widows took great delight in seeing a man diapering a baby. They stood around the table tittering, hiding their smiles behind their hands. These women were deeply curious about Matt and Beau—especially Beau, because he not only diapered the babies but fed them and rocked them when he wasn't on security rounds.

Callie knew Pashto well, although she wasn't formally schooled in it like Matt and Beau were, and enjoyed watching the widows giggling and whispering. She realized that Beau was the real deal: he was unfailingly gentle around women, granting them instant respect. He listened without interrupting them as so many men often did. Even more surprising, he asked what they thought about specific topics.

Callie was sure that these women were eyeballing Beau as perfect husband material, but they'd never admit it. Still, it was that boyish smile he shared with them as they watched him diaper their babies that stole her heart. The guy was so damned different from any other man she'd met.

And his tenderness called strongly to her. She had begun to feel a bit jealous of Dara when she saw Matt drop in on her between patients. He would touch her with such affection that Dara's eyes would grow soft. Yes, Callie could see there was genuine love growing strongly between them, and she was beginning to like Matt a lot. Maybe her sister *had* gotten lucky and would be spared going through the fools Callie had met in her search for the right guy.

Callie moved on, wanting to watch Beau but knowing that sooner or later, one of the widows would probably spot her. She returned to the kitchen, preparing the area for tomorrow morning's breakfast of hot cereal and milk for their charges.

"Hey," Beau called later as he halted at the entrance to the kitchen. "Matt's ready to roll. Do you need a hand getting things prepped for tomorrow morning?"

How like Beau to volunteer, she thought. In a few short days, he'd grasped the routine of the orphanage. Turning, she said, "No, but thanks anyway. Give me five minutes and I'll be ready. Is Dara finished with her last patient?"

Beau nodded, leaning casually against the jamb to gaze appreciatively at Callie. Her hair was mussed, and she hadn't had time to stop and comb some of those loose tendrils near her cheeks. His fingers itched to slide them back over her delicate ears, but he told himself, *Not yet*. He could see how relaxed Callie was around him now. That was progress.

"I don't suppose you might consider going out for pizza and beer tonight with me? I'm buying," he offered casually.

"Do you live on that stuff?"

He chuckled. "You got me. Guilty." He saw a slight smile tug at those soft lips of hers. Beau was ready to give his right arm to taste her; he sensed that Callie would be a hot, hungry lover. She would never be passive or make the man do all the work. No, he'd bet a year's pay that she'd be one helluva lover, taking as much as she gave. She was the kind of woman who pulled out all the stops, a wild woman in disguise. He'd seen that natural, earthy woman in her belly dancing earlier.

"How about you choose a place to eat and I'll buy," he offered.

"Well," she said archly, finished wiping down the counter and folding the cloth, hanging it over the spigot, "I do owe you for giving me the most wonderful foot massage I've ever had. Do you like hamburgers and french fries?"

"That combo sounds like music to my ears," he said, meeting her radiant green gaze. For a split second, Beau saw something else in her eyes, something that shocked him: barely disguised lust. For a moment, he thought he was making it up. But no, it had definitely been there.

"Let's go to Duffy's, then. First, though, I'd love to go back to Bagram to grab a quick hot shower. Could you meet me at 1900?"

Beau almost said, *You've got a date*, but bit it back. "Sounds good. I'll drop by your B-hut."

CALLIE DIDN'T WANT to look too closely at why she wanted to shower, wash her hair, and use her jasmine-scented soap on her skin. She had brought two special outfits to Bagram. One was a nice evening black wool pantsuit. The other was a long black wool skirt. She could use the pantsuit blazer with it.

Dara had already taken off with Matt, who was taking her to the fanciest restaurant on base: a Middle Eastern one reputed to have the best food in Afghanistan. Dara had been so excited—and she looked beautiful in a pale gray pantsuit and emerald-green turtleneck, with her golden hair down around her shoulders.

Callie knew that Matt loved her blond hair free, not caught up in a ponytail, which was how Dara wore it during office hours.

Now Callie wanted to look beautiful tonight, too. She had already accepted the fact that Beau was growing on her, and so far there was nothing to dislike about him. Callie sternly warned herself it hadn't been that long, though, and she wanted to take this one slow.

But damned if her hormones hadn't kicked in when he looked like a lazy cougar sunning himself on a mountain ledge in the kitchen earlier. The guy was sensual in a quiet, powerful way, always reminding her that a hunter and predator lived just beneath his placid exterior.

Callie had no doubt that he was far from laid-back when out on a mission. Beau's gray eyes gave him away, and sometimes, if he sensed something amiss, she saw him come online as a warrior, that energy gathering around him like a lethal storm. Right now, he was allowing her to see what she termed his "downside," when he wasn't being threatened or having to chase after a high-value target.

Looking in her closet now, she decided on a deep pink cowl-neck sweater to offset her black wool pantsuit. Fluffing her hair, she walked over to the mirror for a critical appraisal. Highlights of copper and gold blazed through her long, lightly curled hair as it cloaked her shoulders. She added a pair of small gold earrings to emphasize strands of her hair.

Long ago, she'd been given a one-ounce bottle of jasmine perfume for her birthday by her parents. It had to have cost them an arm and a leg, Callie now realized, and it was straight from Paris. She'd always loved that fragrance since she had first breathed it at the age of four, when her mother had allowed her a dab on the inside of her tiny wrist. Callie sniffed all day, not wanting to wash away the wonderful fragrance from her arm that night. Her mother had smiled and told her that when she was eighteen, they would buy her a bottle. It made her warm with memories.

Dabbing on just a tiny bit on the insides of her wrists, Callie tried to tell herself that she was doing this for herself, not Beau. In fact, she couldn't get images of that lazy smile out of her head, or his careful, constant attention to those Afghan children. He was truly a babysitter of the best kind.

When she thought of him diapering babies, she immediately focused on his large, beautiful hands. She wondered what it would feel like to have him touch her as a lover. Callie didn't fool herself for one moment. No matter how much Beau had backed off from her, she knew he wanted her badly.

Could he be wearing her down, little by little? Probably. He wasn't black ops for nothing. Still, he had promised her he would be a gentleman, and to her, that meant he could look but not touch, unless she signaled otherwise.

The light scent of jasmine enveloped her for a moment and she inhaled it, taking it deep into her lungs. Tonight, she would put on a bit of makeup. Her long red lashes emphasized her green eyes, but she added a touch of moss-colored shadow above them. Her cheeks were naturally ruddy, and whether she liked it or not, she blushed often and deeply.

Callie had hoped she'd grow out of such a teenage response, but she never had. To her relief, her mother was the same way. Dara was more like their surgeon father in other ways. Choosing a soft pink lipstick that went with the color of her sweater, Callie stood back, critically assessing herself.

What would Beau think? He'd always seen her, with the exception of the night of the belly dancing, without any makeup. Her hair had never been down; it was always in a ponytail, like Dara's. This was definitely a different Callie he'd be squiring around tonight!

BEAU KNOCKED AT the front door of the B-hut right at 1900. As Callie locked the door to her room and turned, she could see him through the small window. He was dressed in his chinos and a cream-colored sweater with his black leather jacket over his powerful upper body. His hair looked recently washed, and she smiled to herself, placing her black leather bag over her right shoulder and opening the door.

Beau whistled. "You clean up mighty purty, Ms. McKinley."

Callie felt the heat rush into her cheeks. "Thanks, Beau. So do you."

"I managed to grab a shower, too," he said, opening his hand toward her. Would she take it?

Wanting to touch this man, Callie slid her smaller hand into his. She felt the calluses on his fingers, the dry warmth of his skin against hers. "Thanks for the compliment. It's kind of nice to clean up, put on some nice clothes, and feel pretty every once in a while."

Beau was drinking her in as if he were seeing her for the first time, and he was obviously impressed by the changes in her appearance. Callie couldn't help but preen a bit. On her part, she observed a man who could no longer disguise his desire for her.

Beau felt the soft warmth of her hand in his and felt those small calluses she'd collected working hard around the orphanage. His nostrils flared, catching her female scent along with the subtle fragrance of jasmine. He closed the B-hut door and it automatically locked. It was dark and windy. When Callie drew her wool hood over that mass of beautiful red hair, he grimaced. His fingers practically itched to thread through those strong, shining strands. "Ready?" he asked.

Curving her fingers around his, she said, "Ready."

"I feel like I'm the pumpkin in some fairy tale," he teased, cutting his stride for her sake. "You're the beautiful princess, and I'm the country bumpkin."

"You're hardly a bumpkin—maybe more like a wolf in sheep's clothing?" Callie liked the way they seemed to casually sway against one another as he led her to the Humvee parked along the curb. She could hear the jets taking off and some helicopters at the other terminal coming in to land.

The air was always filled with the smell of kerosene used by the choppers. And sometimes, when the wind would change direction, she'd get to inhale the dry desert scents instead. Tonight, the sky was dark and forbidding; it would probably rain soon.

Beau chortled as he opened the door for her to step inside. "You're a woman with intelligence, no question. I'm probably closer to that wolf you're talking about than a bumpkin."

At least he was being honest with her. She settled into the seat of their cold vehicle, and once Beau climbed in and shut the door, she was aware of a shift between them. This was their first real "date." They had both gotten dressed up in this part of the world, and they both knew they were curious to discover what the possibilities were for a relationship.

She looked at him and reflected on his rugged profile. She could certainly see the warrior within him. She just had to make sure her heart didn't betray her by falling all over itself whenever he looked at her.

Her pulse ratcheted up when he gazed down at her thoughtfully, almost as if he were looking through her. Could he actually reach into her heart to see how she felt about him?

Beau drove onto the two-lane street. "Are you hungry?" he asked.

"Starving, to tell you the truth."

"Good, so am I." *Hungry for you*, he thought, but Beau kept the words trapped in his mouth. "You look beautiful tonight."

"Thanks," Callie whispered, a catch in her voice, clasping her hands over her black leather purse in her lap.

"I notice you're wearing different shoes. How are your feet feeling now?"

"These are my 'good' shoes," she said, "and they have a nice arch in them. My feet are still smiling from the massage you gave me today."

"Good," Beau murmured. He drove down another street, stopped, and made a left. Restaurant row was always the busiest place on this base, and tonight was no exception. He'd phoned ahead and gotten a reservation and a very private booth for them.

"They've got sweet potato fries here, and they're a personal favorite of mine. My ma makes the best sweet potato pie you've ever eaten. She puts thick marshmallow cream on it and sprinkles pecans through it."

"That sounds delicious. My mother taught us how to cook and bake. Dara was actually a lot better at it than I was, though."

"So," he said as he parked in the lot, turning off the engine, "what are you especially good at?"

"I make a pretty mean apple pie. And I'm really good with piecrusts. The secret is not to knead it too much. Otherwise, it gets tough and won't melt in your mouth."

"Remind me to invite myself over to your house for dessert some time." He grinned, climbing out of the vehicle.

Before Callie could open the door, he'd come around and opened it for her. The night was blustery, the wind cutting, but there was no rain. Just heavy humidity in the air. She appreciated Beau's sheltering her with his body as they walked up to the busy restaurant. Once inside, Beau found the hostess, who guided them to the rear of the establishment.

They were given the last booth, which was very intimate compared to the others. She looked over at him as she slid into the booth. "Okay, how did you score this booth?" she asked, grinning.

Beau handed her the menu and said, "I got lucky when I called over for a reservation." His eyes sparkled. "What? You think I paid someone off to get this booth because it's private?"

She had to smile as she looked over the menu. "The thought crossed my mind." She shook her head wonderingly. "You're always planning, aren't you? I guess that's the mark of a good military man."

"Hoping is more like it," Beau admitted, losing his smile. "I think we have something good between us, Callie. I'm hoping you'll want to keep exploring like I do."

She saw that need deep in his shadowed eyes, heard the sincerity in his low voice as he folded his hands on the table. "I wasn't looking for a relationship, Beau."

"Neither was I."

"How can this go anywhere?" she demanded. "You're black ops. I know how you guys appear and disappear. And women never know where their men are, what's happening, or if they'll ever return alive."

"Sure, it can be hard on a woman," he agreed. "But don't you think it's tough on the guy involved, too? He's out on an op, doesn't have a clue as to what's happening to the woman he loves, if she's doing okay or not, or a thousand other things that life can throw at her while he's away."

"You've got a point, Beau, but I don't want to live that way. I tried before, and my heart just can't take another broken relationship again. It hurts too much."

He felt the anguish beneath her words. "Did you lose someone who was in black ops, Callie? I feel a lot of pain around you. I see it in your eyes, and I hear it in your voice."

The waitress came and Callie held back on her response, ordering a hamburger and french fries. Beau ordered the same thing, only with sweet potato fries instead. She wanted to distance herself from him, because every time she was near him, she felt her resolve crumbling. Sure, Beau was a great guy—honest, kind to children, respectful to women.

But he was black ops.

The waitress left their drinks and took their menus, leaving them alone.

Callie took a deep breath and then began, "In my first tour at Bagram, I fell in love with a Special Forces sergeant. I was pretty green, young and starry-eyed. Chet was black ops. He and his team were always going out with the Delta boys and disappearing for weeks, sometimes months at a time. He'd show up at my B-hut at all hours of the night, often after coming back to Bagram. I couldn't handle it, Beau. The danger he was in, my imagination taking off and thinking the worst . . . And I knew he loved what he did. Finally, at the end of my six months here with the orphanage, we split up, and I went home with a broken heart. I honestly don't think he ever loved me. I was someone to have sex with. I didn't realize it at the time, but six months later, I'd figured it out."

"I'm sorry, Callie. The guy should have come clean with you from the git-go. At least that way you'd have had a choice to make instead of being hood-winked."

Shrugging, she sipped her coffee. "He's like most of the guys here, which I soon discovered the hard way."

"Have you met anyone who really cared for you?"

His question made her wince. "'Care' as in a real relationship where it wasn't only about sex?"

Nodding, Beau drank a sip of his beer. "Yes."

"No, I haven't."

He sat back, spreading out his long legs beneath the table, bracketing her legs but not touching them. "What would it take to convince you that I do care about you? And that it's more than just wanting to have sex with you?" Beau searched her face, her expression still dark and thoughtful. She'd been hurt often, and that was tough for an idealist like her. Unfortunately, the men she attracted were hard-core realists who wanted her body, not her heart.

In his case, he wanted everything from her, and was willing to give her back exactly what he got.

She looked at him, clearly concerned. "I don't really know. I'm scared, Beau. Scared of myself, even more than I'm scared of you, at this point."

He felt a bit of hope begin to grow. "Really? How so?"

"Look, I have to be honest with you," Callie began, her cheeks flushing a deep pink. "I like you, Beau. I'm sure you can feel that. I'm even beginning to trust again, which is no small tribute to you. But then I remember the guys who disappointed me, and my own stupidity in letting it happen again and again. And then I get scared and pull away from you."

Nodding his head, Beau asked softly, "Callie, I need to know if you feel we have something special between us." He slowly moved the cold, beaded beer between his spare hands, studying her.

Without hesitating, she said, "Yes, I do," her mouth tugging toward a smile. "You're different from other men, and you're interested in what I think. That's new for me. You ask me serious, deep questions, and no guy has ever done that before."

"Because I want to know all of you, Callie. Sure, your dance dazzled me, but I was more taken by the fire in your eyes and the passion you were expressing in that dance. I don't know how else to explain what I sensed and saw about you. You're all heart, and that makes you different from the women I've known before. In a lot of ways, you remind me of my mother, because she's a very passionate woman, and an idealist, like you." He smiled ruefully. "Not that I see you as my mother. You share her passion for life and that touches my heart deeply."

She sat there, aware that she was losing not only the battle but the war. Realizing this brought mixed emotions. "I don't know what's happening with us, Beau," she muttered, "I really don't."

"Me either, gal."

Her heart pulsed when he whispered that endearment in a roughened tone.

"What I'd like to do," Beau proposed, "is just keep doing what we're doing, and let the good experiences build up. I'll make every effort to be with you at the orphanage in Kabul when I'm back on base. And I'd like to take you out, maybe for an ice-cream cone at your ice-cream parlor that hides the Rocky Road."

She let a grin escape as he went on. He certainly had her pegged already, including her weakness for Rocky Road! He was the most perceptive man she'd ever met, that was for sure. And he certainly paid close attention to her desires.

"And don't forget, we have some nice dinners ahead, and those future foot rubs you've already signed up for, yes?"

Callie sat there, feeling guilty as hell. This man was trying to navigate around all her bad experiences, and his sincerity was obvious as his gaze gently held hers.

She felt a tingle of excitement. This was real. It was really real!

"And you'll keep on cleaning out the diaper pail and diapering the babies?" She watched that chiseled mouth of his draw into a boyish grin.

"Sure 'nuff."

"I think," she said falteringly, opening her hands, "that feels like a good plan, Beau. Let's give it a try and see how things go."

"I got it," he promised her. "And for now, let's enjoy our night together, okay? I have a lot of questions for you."

All her guilt and worry fled beneath his coaxing smile and those gleaming gray eyes of his as he sat up. "What kinds of questions?"

"About your childhood. What kind of cute little girl were you in the first grade? What was your favorite thing to do in school? How many little boys' hearts did you break?"

Her lips formed a faint smile. "I was a freckle-faced little girl with pigtails in the first grade. And I had a heck of a temper. One little boy pulled one of my braids, and I turned around and smacked him in the face with my fist. That earned me a trip to the principal's office."

Chuckling, Beau said, "Somehow, I already figured out you were a hellion from the time you were born."

"Well, my mom could sure attest to that. I was the second born, and she thought she had it timed to get to the hospital to birth me. My dad, who's a surgeon, ended up delivering me in the backseat of our car."

"It's that red hair," he promised her, his heart swelling as she smiled.

"That's what Dad said."

"Does your mother have red hair?"

"Yes." Callie opened her purse and drew out her iPhone, going to her family pictures, turning it around, and handing it to him. "There's all kinds of family photos there. Help yourself."

Callie watched his expression carefully as Beau held the iPhone and slowly scrolled through the photos. He turned it around, holding a photo up to her.

"This is you in the first grade?"

"Yep, that's me. Two front teeth missing." She laughed.

"You were a very, very cute little girl," he murmured.

"I wasn't the classically adorable type like my sister, Dara," Callie protested. "There were plenty of other girls who were prettier than I was."

"Impossible," Beau growled. "You look incredibly beautiful to me."

Heat streaked up from her neck and settled right into her cheeks. Callie wanted to slide down under the table.

"And I like your blushes," Beau added, recognizing her embarrassment.

"I was a tomboy," she admitted. "Dara was the feminine one. All I wanted to do was ride my horse with my grandpa on roundups, gallop in the pastures and be with him and his wranglers. Dara always liked dressing up, using cosmetics, and playing with her hair and nails." She touched her red strands. "I just wanted to get it out of my way so I could see where I was riding."

"You're not a tomboy now," Beau said, handing her back the phone. "You're all grown up now and one hundred percent woman. I can barely see those freckles of yours."

Groaning, Callie said, "I hated those freckles. I can remember how many times I cried, wishing they'd go away. The boys at school called me 'Spot.' I was so embarrassed by it."

"If I'd been there, I'd have taken on those boys and told them never to call you that again, or they'd answer to me."

Callie believed him. "Have you always been this protective of people you care about, Beau?"

"Yeah, pretty much. I sometimes think that's the reason I went into Delta Force—to protect the innocent, those who couldn't defend themselves. My pa drilled into us boys from an early age on that we were protectors. We were stronger than women, more athletic, bigger, and that made us responsible to protect and provide for those we loved and cared for."

"You certainly do," Callie agreed, sliding her phone into her purse. She remembered that the only photos he had of his family were taped on the inside of his locker door. Beau wasn't allowed to carry anything personal on him.

The waitress returned with their meals and they dug in, eating in companionable silence. Callie enjoyed watching Beau eat. He ate quickly, as if starved. She was surprised when, about halfway through his meal, he put some sweet potato fries on her plate.

"For you," he said.

She met and held his gaze, feeling every nerve in her body yearning for him. Her thighs clenched, and she knew what that meant. How she wanted to kiss Beau, to feel his strong mouth slant across hers, take her, breathe his life into her, infuse her and inflame her with his touch. She knew he would willingly do that and more. So where did sexual need end and a true relationship begin? Callie had never found that place, that was for sure. And Beau was so unique compared to the other men she'd dated that Callie had no yardstick to measure him by. If only she weren't such a coward. If only she had the equivalent of a set of balls so she could walk into his arms and kiss him until they melted together. If only . . .

CHAPTER 5

"SEEMS LIKE YOU and Beau are getting along nicely," Dara said as she and Callie ate breakfast at the chow hall the next morning.

Callie pushed the oatmeal around with her spoon, frowning. "You're right."

"Don't look so happy about it." Dara smiled over at her. "Why so glum?"

"Because I really like the guy, and I'm fighting it."

"Why would you do that?"

Callie gave her older sister an impatient look. "For obvious reasons. You know my track record of relationships with military guys. None of them have ever worked out."

"Maybe he's different, Callie. I know the little girls at the orphanage idolize him, and kids and dogs aren't wrong about people."

Callie concentrated on her hot oatmeal, listening despite herself. "I don't know. I'm confused, Dara. And scared."

"Afraid to get hurt again, right?"

She stared over at Dara, whose blond hair was back in a ponytail. "Bingo. I don't think my heart can take another breakup, to tell you the truth. I don't want to like him because he's Army. He's in a black ops job that leaves a woman hanging and wondering if he's going to survive the next mission or not." She pulled the spoon from her mouth and waved it warningly at Dara. "And Matt is in the same line of work. You're leaving in a few days. You won't see him for how long?"

"He's got leave coming up for Christmas, and we're planning on seeing a lot of each other then. He's invited me to his family's dinner, and I'm going."

"Okay," she said grumpily, "Matt has to come back here after that, though. He's got a few more months until his enlistment is up. You're going to worry the hell out of yourself about where he's at, Dara. I know you. Worrying is the number one thing you do best."

Smiling a little, Dara nodded, cutting into her breakfast steak. "That's true,

I worry a lot. I got Grandma's gene on that one," she said wryly.

"Thank God I didn't get it," Callie said with feeling. "I see what it does to you. And when Matt has to deploy back here, you'll go crazy with concern for him."

"I know . . . but it's only a few months," Dara said. "And in my residency I'm so busy eight to sixteen hours a day, I don't have time to worry. It's when I get home that it really hits me. He's promised to stay in touch via email and Skype when he can."

"I'm sure he will. These Delta Force boys are out on ops more than they're back at their HQ here at Bagram. You're not educated on the military like I am, Dara. And don't forget, I fell for Chet five years ago. He was Delta Force. I know the type."

"I remember that debacle," Dara said sadly, giving her a commiserating look. "I remember how much it tore you up to break up with him."

"I had to, for a lot of reasons."

"But isn't Beau different from Chet?"

Snorting, Callie said, "Light years different. I can't even compare the two personalities. The only place there's agreement is that they're both Delta Force."

"Then why not give yourself a chance with him, Callie? You're young, beautiful, and single. I know you have dreams of settling down, eventually working stateside for the Hope Charity and raising a family someday."

"Because Beau is Army. His enlistment is up in June of next year. I asked him if he was going to reenlist and he said yes, that he wanted to put his twenty in."

"Oh," Dara said, frowning. "Well . . . that's not good for you."

"No, and if I married the guy—not saying I would . . . but if I did? He'd be off on some top secret mission to some armpit nation, and I'd know nothing. I'd be left behind to take care of the house, myself, and any children we had."

"I can't argue with your experience," she said. "But I really think Beau is nice. And he seems to get along well with you. Does he make you happy?"

"Yes," she muttered. "I really like being with him. And I'm having one hell of a time keeping my hands off him."

"So are you saying that if he wasn't in the Army, you'd pursue him? Or"— she grinned—"let him pursue you?"

"Yes. But that's not reality. And I'm not sure I can try again, Dara. I can't. My heart can't take another blow like that."

"You have had your fair share of broken relationships over the last five years," Dara agreed quietly, buttering her toast. She brightened. "Well, who knows? Maybe fate will intervene in a positive way. Maybe you'll see a door open that wasn't open before regarding the two of you."

Callie shook her head. "You know, you're a bigger idealist and dreamer than I ever was, Dara. You always have been. I'm a realist in comparison to you." She smiled at her sister. "I don't see how that could have happened."

Shrugging, Dara said, "Well, Mom always said to dream big, and the cosmos will take care of the doors flying open in front of us to make it happen."

"As much as I love Mom, I've found in the last five years that my dreams do not intersect with reality. I'm trying to be more pragmatic now. I can't afford idealism in my personal life anymore."

"I always hold out hope for the hopeless, Callie."

"Well," she said, "you're a doctor. You have to be in that mode."

Waving her knife in Callie's direction, Dara said, "Maybe you should have a little faith, sis. You know, sometimes life turns around and twists us in unexpected ways, making the impossible look possible. Even for you."

"Dreamer and worrywart. Dara, I can't live like you do," she said, and managed an apologetic but loving smile for her sister. "A heart can only take so many hurts, so many disappointments, and then you have to protect yourself from ever getting hurt again."

"Matt isn't like that."

"Well, that's good to hear. And I'm truly happy for the both of you. He seems like a really responsible, steady guy, and I've seen how he looks at you. He's fallen for you hook, line, and sinker, sis. But you have for him, too."

"Well," Dara murmured, "I'm getting there. I haven't known him that long, but I do like what I see, and I like how he conducts himself with me, with the children at the orphanage. He's a good person with morals and values that agree with my idea of integrity."

"Yeah, Beau's the same," Callie muttered, shaking her head. "The guy is a stand-up dude. He's got the same morals and values as Matt. And it sure calls to me, but I'm just so damned afraid to open up my heart one more time."

"You're holding out for a relationship like Grandma and Grandpa have," Dara agreed. "They're so devoted to one another, still so in love with one another." She brightened. "We were so lucky to grow up on their ranch, especially since Dad was always at the hospital. Even today, they live different lives from our grandparents, but they clearly love each other."

"I know, I know. I guess." She finished her oatmeal and pushed the bowl aside. "My idealism starts to show, because I do dream of a relationship with a man like Grandpa or Dad. They're devoted to their wives. We saw it every day as kids growing up. I mean, for example, Grandpa would come in from working somewhere on the ranch, and he'd have a handful of wildflowers for Grandma in his hand. Or, he knew she loved See's Candies, and he'd make a special trip into Butte to buy her a box for no reason. And he'd make her hot chocolate at night with lots of whipped cream, because he knew she loved to have a cup of it before bedtime. That's the kind of marriage I want, Dara. The other day, Beau massaged my aching feet at the orphanage and brought me a cup of coffee. It reminded me so much of something Grandpa or Dad would do. That's the kind of man I want. I want him to love me so much that he's looking for small but special ways to show me he loves me."

"Well," Dara said, brightening as she slathered strawberry jam on the toast, "Grandma is the same with Grandpa. She makes him special meals all the time. Things he loves, like roast beef and potatoes, or tuna and noodles. She's just as devoted to him, Callie. Each has their way of letting the other know on a daily basis that they love one another, that they're happy with one another."

"I know," Callie whispered, shaking her head. "And I've always dreamed of that kind of marriage. To a man who worships me and who I can worship."

Dara gave her a wicked look. "Beau massaging your poor, tired feet? What would you call that, hmm? How many men have you known who cared enough about you to ease the cramping and pain I know you get in those feet at the end of some days at the orphanage?"

Callie nodded. "I guess I didn't see you pass by the door."

She chortled. "Couldn't help it. I was walking by Maggie's office and saw you two together. I thought it was sweet of him to do it, Callie. Now, maybe Beau was originally taken with your belly dancing, but he's clearly a cut above the sex-hungry studs salivating to get you into bed. This guy really cares about you. He's paying attention to you in ways I've never seen a guy do before."

"I know," Callie sighed, confused.

Dara munched on her toast. "I just hope something happens that will give you two a common doorway you can both walk through together. I'd love to see you in an ongoing relationship with one another."

BEAU NOTICED HOW remote Callie was in the van on the ride to Kabul that morning as he sat in the backseat with her and Dara, always alert to his environment.

Matt rode up front with their driver, Mohammed. There wasn't much talk on this part of the ride, because no roads in Afghanistan were safe. Beau and Matt had their work cut out for them as they watched other pickups, white ones, buzz by them. Any one of them could have held Taliban with weapons. And of course, bomb makers would dig holes at the edges of the highways, burying IEDs in the hope that a driver would run over one of them the next day.

Beau saw sadness in Callie's green eyes this morning. What was she feeling? Had something happened to her last night or earlier this morning that he didn't know about? Beau would make it a point to ask her once they got past feeding the children breakfast.

He waited and caught Callie walking into Maggie's office after the children's breakfast was finished. He knew she had about fifteen minutes before helping teach the children to read. He sauntered in and gave her a hello smile as he picked up a mug.

"You're looking sad about something," he said, pouring himself a cup of coffee.

"Just life," Callie offered, shrugging as she backed off to give him room.

"Did you hear bad news I should know about? Your family? Your grandparents?"

She shook her head. "No, everyone is fine back home."

"Maybe you're missing them," he reflected. "After all, it is the holidays."

Callie wanted so badly to walk up to Beau, wrap her arms around his waist, and rest her head on his chest. She knew without a doubt that he'd embrace and hold her. "Well, there is that. I love Christmas, Beau."

"Tell me about it," he said, leaning up against the bookcase and watching some of that sadness dissolve. "What kind of Christmas does your family celebrate?"

"Oh, a wonderful one. My grandparents are very old-fashioned. They have a sleigh that their two horses haul around the ranch in the snow. And we always get tons of snow." She sighed and smiled a little. "We have this family tradition where Mom stays at the ranch making apple cider with wonderful spices, warming it up for us. Dad is a killer doughnut maker. He makes them by hand and fries them up in a fryer. While they're doing that, my grandparents take me and Dara on a sleigh ride under quilts that my grandma made eons ago. We bundle up and take off down a long, sloping hill and into the woods. It's so wonderful and beautiful. You get to see the snow on the evergreens, the sun sparkling on the snow being pushed off the limbs by the breeze. By the time we get back to the ranch, Mom and Dad have hot apple cider and warm doughnuts on the table waiting for all of us. We tell them of our adventures, and we all sit around the huge oak table and have so much fun and laughter together."

"Sounds like the kind of old-time Christmas postcard my ma collects," he said. "And I can tell you're pining away for your family."

"I don't normally stay here in the winter," she said. "But Maggie's volunteer fell sick, and I took her place. Usually, I'm in Kabul and Bagram from March through September of every year, but I always love being home for the holidays. It's a chance to be with my family." She looked over, seeing that Beau understood. "What about you? How does your family celebrate Christmas on Black Mountain?"

"Oh," he said, his mouth curving, "it's not as fancy as your sleigh ride over hill and dale, but another family on the mountain, Dot and Henry Barker, invites everyone over for an old-fashioned hayride. We get a lot of snow, too, and if the weather cooperates, they hitch up their team of Clydesdales to their hay wagon. They invite everyone down to the bottom of the mountain where they live. Each family brings food for a huge banquet. Henry's a blacksmith, and his wife, Dot, is best friends with my ma. Jason, their son, ran with us growing up. We were tighter than fleas on a dog." He smiled a little in memory. "He's now in the Army, and he's been in Afghanistan. Sometimes, I get to see him. Anyway, the Barker family puts on this shindig about two or three days just before Christmas for everyone. The families living on Black Mountain always look for ways to celebrate life and do things together. Going for that hayride with the Barker family is the highlight of our Christmas celebrations on the mountain."

"That sounds wonderful, too," Callie said softly, feeling encircled by his invisible warmth. Her heart yearned to be closer to him. "I like sharing things like this with you," she admitted. "I love your stories about Black Mountain and the people who live there."

"And," he said, easing away from the shelf, "that's why I think you love working for a charity. It's just a big, noisy, crazy family, too." He grinned, setting his emptied cup aside.

Callie didn't want Beau to leave. She wanted to keep delving into him as a person. "I love talking with you. You always remind me of home and what I'm missing."

He smiled a little, settling a cap on his head. "Well, at least you know that next year you'll be home for Christmas and can be with your family." As he walked over to her, he lifted his finger, moving a few strands of her red hair behind her ear. Instantly, she felt that tingling pleasure where his finger barely brushed her ear. "Family is everything," he added. Taking a few steps away from her, he said, "I'd really like to take you to the fanciest restaurant we have on base tonight. Are you game?"

Callie felt herself drowning in his calm gray gaze. Again, she loved that feeling of protection wrapping around her when he looked at her. "Don't tell me you dance, too!" she teased.

"Well, now," Beau said, "I might try a slow dance or two with you after dinner, but I'm not exactly Mr. Silverheels out there on the dance floor. I was raised on square dancing, which is like a foreign dance to most folks nowadays," he chuckled.

"Yes, I'd like to dance." She saw hope burning in his eyes once more, saw yearning, too, for her. "Okay, a slow dance or two; let's see how we do."

"I'm game if you are," he said, giving her a lopsided smile. He pointed down at his combat boots. "I truly have two left feet, so we'll have to be careful. I don't want to step on your poor toes."

It would be a way to be close to him, and Callie felt her lower body clench, grow achy with need. How desperately she wanted that kind of intimacy with Beau.

"Well," she said dryly, "let's take it a step at a time," and she walked out of the office, hearing him laugh at her intended pun. His laughter vibrated throughout her. Beau pushed every feminine button she owned, and Callie looked forward to tonight and more moments like this. And she knew she'd be tempted by Beau's masculinity, his longing for her. It would be hard not to take another step toward him. And maybe she should . . .

CALLIE'S NERVES WERE screaming as she looked at herself in the mirror. She knew that Chelsea's, the most expensive restaurant in Bagram, would cost Beau a lot of money for dinner.

She smoothed her hand down the long black wool skirt she wore tonight with an apricot silk blouse under a black blazer. The outfit brought out the highlights of her freshly washed hair. There wasn't much she could do with it because it had a slight curl, but it looked nice tonight, a shining mantle hanging loosely around her shoulders.

When Callie turned eighteen, her grandmother had given her a family heirloom of earrings, small white pearls set in gold. Her great-grandmother had passed them on, and now she was wearing them. And the choker of white pearls gleaming around her throat was warm and special to Callie. Touching them, she felt beautiful and swore she could feel the love of her family as she wore them tonight.

Her hands were trembling because she was excited, scared, and torn. Earlier today, she'd seen that Beau had wanted to kiss her after he'd surprised her by placing strands of her red hair behind her ear. It wasn't anything aggressive, but it was there, as if being gently offered to her for her consideration. The man knew how to fluster a woman, no question. And she was flustered. Her body was hot, hungry, and she ached below, something that was happening more often with Beau. All he had to do was look at her, and she felt herself growing damp.

She pulled on her black wool hooded coat, picked up her black leather purse and leather gloves, and left her small room. Dara had departed with Matt earlier, and Callie wondered if they were over at the Eagle's Nest again.

She admitted it: she was envious of her sister. She'd have loved to be spending time there with Beau. Swallowing, Callie walked down the hall to the door, seeing Beau waiting for her outside.

Tonight, the sky was clear, the stars glittering in the sky as she opened the door. When she stepped out on the porch, she smiled up at Beau. Tonight he was wearing a suit! It was a dark blue sport coat with a white cotton shirt beneath it, and a conservative blue tie, along with what she thought might be dark blue slacks. "Wow, you clean up well," she teased, smiling.

"So do you," Beau murmured, appreciation in his tone. "I should have made a reservation at Chelsea's before this," he added. Beau reached around her and closed the door, making sure it was locked. "Ready for a nice dinner?" he asked, reaching his hand out to her.

Callie took it, relishing the warmth and strength of his fingers curving around hers. "I am. This is a really nice break for both of us. Kind of reminds me of being back home."

"It does for me, too," he agreed.

She had come to want his hand in hers. This time, as he descended the stairs, he brought his hand against the small of her back, guiding her down the sidewalk. Callie found herself moving closer to Beau, almost beneath his arm. If he noticed it, and she was sure he didn't miss a thing, he didn't take advantage of their closeness. As good as his word, he stayed in control of his emotions.

Her heart stirred again with need of him, and she felt caught up in the powerful heat they generated whenever they were together. If only she had the courage to do something about it. If only . . .

CHAPTER 6

"HAVE YOU BEEN to Chelsea's before?" Beau asked Callie as he opened the door to the restaurant.

"No, but I've heard about it."

"I'm in the same boat as you," he admitted ruefully.

"I'm just a ranching girl. I'm used to the local café in town, not something fancy like this," she said, looking around. The place was warm and intimate. There was soft music playing, and she saw a big dance floor at one end of the restaurant. A number of couples were already on it, dressed in their civilian clothes. Although there were a lot of civilian contractors on the base, Callie knew that military men and women never went anywhere in uniform unless they had to.

A maître d' came up to them dressed in a black and white tuxedo, looking formal and somewhat officious. Callie watched Beau handle the situation with quiet authority. It was as if the slick-haired maître d' knew power when he met it; he gave Beau a crisp nod, walking them to a cream-colored, leather wraparound booth.

Callie noted all the fancily dressed women and the men in suits and ties. She was proud of Beau, thinking he looked every bit as good as the others. And she'd bet a lot of them were officers.

But Beau carried something else: an obvious huge dose of confidence, which made him stand out. Once they sat close to one another in the U-shaped booth, another waiter dropped by to get their drink orders.

"Would you like a bottle of wine?" Beau asked her. "I know you like white."

"I know most guys prefer beer."

"That's true. But none of my team is around to see me sipping a glass of wine," he said with a teasing grin. "They'd rib the daylights out of me. But I'm always willing to stretch myself, and I'll try whatever wine you'd like to order."

"Figured as much," she laughed. "I like white wine, but I'm not too keen on reds." He passed the wine list over to her.

"Would you like to pick one?" Beau saw her cheeks grow a little pink. They were both out of their element in this place, and he didn't want to embarrass her. "Or would you rather I do it?" He'd had training in such details. When undercover, a Delta Force operator had to have knowledge of such things.

"No, I think I can do this," Callie assured him, giving him a wry look. "Do you like dry, semisweet, or sweet wines?"

"Whatever you want is fine by me," he said agreeably.

"Are you always this easy to get along with?" she teased, watching his grin widen.

"With you, yes. My enemies would tell you differently," he added blandly.

Callie held back a laugh. "I'll bet," she said. Choosing a wine, she gave the waiter their order and he left. "Wow," she said, "this is really a posh place, isn't it?"

"Sure is. Beats anything we have at Black Mountain."

"I like that you don't put on airs."

"Well," Beau said, "I'd sure get caught in a hurry if I tried." He absorbed the deep green of her eyes, seeing that she was enjoying herself. He loved seeing her smiling as she was right now. He was finding it harder to fight his attraction to her and was grateful that the white linen tablecloth draped over his lap hid his physical reaction to her.

"I like the music." Callie enjoyed the soft, melodic sounds. Everything about this restaurant was truly first-class. "I've had girlfriends tell me about this place and how much they liked it. Now I can see why."

"It's quiet. That's what I appreciate." Beau opened her white linen napkin and handed it to her. He then opened his own. "My parents have never been to a place like this."

"I know Mom and Dad have, but I don't know about my grandparents. They love their ranch, they love their life, and are fulfilled in ways I don't think many people ever are."

"That's the way my folks are," Beau said. "They rarely leave Black Mountain. We got our family and extended family living there. All we have to do is walk half a mile in any direction, and we'll be at some relative's cabin."

"I'd love to go there someday," she said wistfully. "It sounds perfect."

"Well, if you're coming my way for a visit, I'll let you show me your family's ranch in return. The place sounds pretty magical to me."

Warmth settled in her heart. "I'd like that." And she would. Just being around Beau melted all her resolve and the shields she hid behind. He made everything seem possible.

She changed the subject. "You seemed really confident when you came in here."

"In our training, especially undercover work, we have to be familiar with every kind of scenario." He smiled a little. "Back home we have a knife, fork, and spoon." He gestured to the place setting before him. "Here? You get a gazillion different pieces of flatware. In training, we were taught which one to pick up and use first. We have to know wines and food as well."

"Then," Callie confided, "you can help me out, because I've never seen this much silverware in my life!"

He reached out, placing his hand briefly over hers. "I have your back, gal."

Just the way he said "gal" with that roughened drawl made Callie swear he was a magician, using his touch, his gray gaze, his boyish smile, to weave a spell inside her, one of hunger combined with need. "Thanks. I hate embarrassing myself in public."

"I know. Me, too."

She asked, "What else do you know about me? And don't pretend to be dumb, because you Delta guys are the smartest of the lot. I know you study me, Beau. Sometimes I can actually feel it."

He placed his hand over the back of the booth, his arm inches from her shoulders. "Does it bother you?"

"No. But I can feel when you're doing it."

"I can't help myself, Callie. You're one beautiful woman. Sometimes at the orphanage I'll see you do something, and I'll watch the play of light against your hair or skin. I think how pretty you are, whether I'm seeing your profile or a full-face view. And of course, I'm captured by your hair, but I think you already know that."

"You're just like Matt Culver," she teased. "He loves Dara's blond hair down, too."

He reached up and placed one finger lightly on her hair and moved a strand away from her eyes. "Can you blame us?"

It was such a gossamer touch, but it was driving her crazy because she desperately wanted Beau to touch her more. "No," she said, a little breathless, "I can't. I know that guys like women with long hair."

A waitress from the bar came over and delivered their bottle of wine and two glasses, and then poured a little in one for Beau to taste.

"Here, you're our official wine taster," he said, sliding it over to Callie. "Tell her what you think of it."

Delighted that he was making her an equal partner in this enterprise, Callie tasted it and nodded to the woman that it was fine. The waitress poured the wine and left. A busboy came by, delivering a basket of freshly baked artisan bread and some warm zucchini muffins.

Beau handed her the basket. "You first."

"I know what you want," she said, giving him an amused look.

"Oh? Which do you think I want?"

"The muffins. I'll let you have them."

"You're pretty good," Beau congratulated her after she took some dark bread and pulled over the butter dish. "Guess I'm pretty transparent."

"More than you know," Callie said, meeting his smile.

AFTER DINNER, BEAU asked Callie, "Are you ready to dance?" They had both ordered steak with a baked potato, sour cream, and butter. Callie had turned down dessert, but Beau had asked for the hot apple pie. It had been delicious, but he declared that it couldn't touch the one his ma made. The vanilla ice cream, however, was outstanding.

Callie wiped her lips with the napkin. "I'm stuffed, Beau. I'll probably go out there and waddle around."

He chuckled. "Now, come on," he said, and slipped out of the booth, extending his hand toward her. "Just try one dance. If you don't like it we can skip a second one."

"I'm going to be rusty," she laughed, preparing him for the worst.

"Okay, then. We'll be rusty together," he promised, his hand on her back, leading her to the other end of the restaurant.

Beau made it so easy to slip into his arms, and the music was soft and romantic. There were at least fifteen other couples on the wide dance floor. Callie felt comfortable but was glad there were other dancers around them so she wouldn't stand out like the klutz she was. She might be graceful and confident as a belly dancer but ballroom dancing was pretty much foreign to her. The moment Beau's hand wrapped gently around hers and he slid his arm around her waist, drawing her near but not too near, Callie knew he'd danced a time or two before.

"For someone like me who has no problem whatsoever doing a belly-dancing demo, I'm a set of nerves out here," she muttered.

He smiled down at her, the intimacy springing strongly between them. "That's because you're in charge of your belly dance, and you know what you're doing. Out here, I'm the great unknown," he said modestly.

She relaxed a little more because Beau obviously knew what he was doing. "I suppose they taught you guys how to ballroom dance, too?" His eyes gleamed, and she smiled because he wasn't going to tell her. "So they taught you high-class manners, ballroom dancing, wines, and what else?"

"Oh, sweet woman, we can't go there. I'm top secret. Remember?"

The endearment feathered across her and she accepted his teases. Moving a bit closer to him, Callie inhaled his male scent, the fresh soap he'd used earlier, the desert fragrance that was a part of the Afghan landscape.

He was the only one with a beard and longish hair in the establishment. Callie noticed more than a few men, probably officers, giving him a sharp glance, as if noting he was black ops of some kind. They might not have known if he was a SEAL or Delta Force, but they knew he was different from the rest of them. That made her proud of Beau. He didn't seem to care one whit if anyone stared at him or not. His gaze was solely on her.

"I like the way you smell," he rasped, leaning over, his voice low and intimate.

"I was thinking the same thing about you," she admitted.

"Hmm, mental telepathy. That's a good sign," Beau noted, moving her easily and with confidence in a slow circle. Amazingly, she had no trouble following him.

"I don't know," Callie admitted, her senses woven into him, her hand in his, feeling his body supporting her yet not demanding as he guided her around the dance floor. She could feel the throb of his strength and masculinity and instinctively absorbed it, wanting more.

"Those pearls make your skin radiant. Did you know that?"

"No . . ."

"My ma loves pearls. My pa bought her some for their tenth wedding anniversary, and she cried and cried over them. They were the real kind, not the freshwater ones, but from the ocean. And when she wore them for the first time when they went to church, she looked radiant, too." Beau looked down, gazing into her upturned face. "Like you. Pearls bring out your perfect complexion."

Beau saw the warmth in her green eyes, saw those wonderfully shaped pink lips of hers part beneath his compliment. How he wanted to lean down and brush his mouth against hers, but he reminded himself to let Callie take the next step, if there was one. She swayed knowingly with the rhythm of the music, the beat just a natural part of her dancer's instinct. His hand had settled low on her back, and he could feel the movement of her hips beneath his palm. They brought to mind the way she had done those hip snaps and rolls the night she had belly danced for the troops. He knew he was having trouble keeping his erection down and was glad he'd buttoned his suit jacket to hide it.

"My great-grandfather gave these pearls to my great-grandmother, and they've been passed on down through our family. Dara got a beautiful Tiffany brooch of sapphires and diamonds, and I got the set of pearls."

"Well," he drawled, "you got the best deal of all, Callie. The pearls do nothing but show the world how lovely you are."

There was such sincerity in Beau's praise that she couldn't resist it and whispered, "Thanks." And then, Callie moved closer, her breasts brushing lightly against his chest, her nipples instantly peaking. Her lower body urged her to get even closer, and she let herself follow its urging, placing her head against his shoulder. She closed her eyes, feeling Beau's arms tighten, bringing her against him gently. It was just enough, and Callie sighed, swaying with the music, surrendering to Beau's lead. She felt a rush of sizzling fire and her urgent hunger arcing through her. Unable to suppress it, she caught her breath.

"Okay?" he asked, his lips near her ear.

Callie nodded, not trusting her voice. Ever since she'd met Beau, she'd wanted this. Just this. Feeling him hold her close, absorbing his maleness, the controlled power of his body beneath his clothes, that sense of protection he bestowed upon her.

She felt as if he were her own personal guardian, shielding her from everything bad in the world around them. Never had she felt that, from anyone. It just felt so natural to fall in step with Beau, to follow his lead, to hear the steady beat of his heart, as if he never got stressed out.

Unconsciously, she rubbed her cheek against the soft fiber of his jacket, longing to open it, loosen his tie, unbutton that starched white shirt, and place her hands across the amazing breadth of his naked chest. Her hand tightened in his, and he slowly drew their clasped hands against his chest in an intimate gesture. Like lovers.

Only, they weren't. She sighed, her hips just naturally moving slowly against his own, wildly aware of his thick erection against her belly, of his wanting her. It felt as if all her inner wetness was preparing for him to enter her. There was dampness between her thighs, and her panties were already soaked. All this, and he'd never even tried to kiss her! Yes, she was in real trouble now!

It had been a year since she'd made love to a man, but she knew that time was drawing to a close as she felt his narrow hips rolling against hers. A deep moan threatened to escape her as they moved closer to each other, their need and growing desire overriding all their caution.

She felt his lips press against her temple, his moist breath sighing against her flesh. Straining upward, her breasts firming, her nipples crying out to be touched and ravished, Callie lifted her head. And as she did so, she closed her eyes, seeking and finding Beau's mouth. The brush of his lips against hers was featherlight, as if it was a gentle introduction. A low sound caught in her throat as she stretched, wanting more of him. The second time he kissed her, he slanted his mouth over hers, inviting her to respond, waiting, not pushing or forcing himself on her. Her breath quickening, Callie's hand slid upward and curved around his strong neck, pulling him down, bringing his mouth firmly against her own.

When she heard his low growl, she felt herself melting into molten clay to be kneaded, formed, and shaped by his hands, his slowly moving body, and the hungry heat of his mouth that he'd restrained as he celebrated their first contact.

Callie lost all sense of place and time as their mouths moved in sinuous concert with their bodies along with the music. It was as if Beau were making love to her out on the dance floor, connected from their mouths to their hips, his arm possessive, like a male animal claiming his mate. The power of that sensation rocked her world as her senses exploded with the taste of him, the masterful way his mouth took hers. Yes, he was very adept at loving a woman slowly, deliciously, and confidently.

Reluctantly, Beau eased his mouth from her soft, wet lips. *Damn!* he thought. *One of us has to be aware and restrained out here.* Hell, it was the last thing he wanted to do right now, but the music was ending and they couldn't stand out in the middle of the dance floor fused together.

He smiled down into her half-closed eyes, seeing the arousal doing a slow, deep burn. Yeah, he felt the same way, his body hardened to the point of making him want to bend over in pain.

"Come on," he rasped thickly, releasing her but keeping his arm solidly around her waist. He could see that she was disoriented, and as they slowly walked off the floor, he took her aside. She was still floating from that unexpected kiss she'd initiated.

Bringing her over toward the wall, in the shadows, his hands settled lightly on her upper arms.

"Callie, I need to know what you want to do." He wanted so damn badly to love this woman the whole night through, to claim her and show her how much he could pleasure her, make her cry out and scream with needing him. Beau wanted to give her everything she deserved and more, because all of him was engaged with this.

Callie's lips had been hot silk against his, just as sensuous as her belly dancing. He looked deep into her eyes, which were still dark with longing.

"I want . . ." She tried to think, her slender red brows moving down for a moment. "You . . ." The word was almost torn from her lips. "And . . . I'm so afraid, Beau . . . so afraid . . ."

"Don't be," he rasped against her ear, kissing her hair. "It will be all right. Wait here, and I'll get your purse and pick up your coat." He'd already paid the bill, so that was out of the way. She gave a jerky nod, as if still swimming in that invisible cloud of pleasure. He recognized the look and smiled a little, brushing his knuckles against her cheek. "I'll be right back, sweet woman."

Callie nodded. Beau's one kiss had loosened her and made her desire trump any fears she'd been holding on to. Her needy body was insistent now;

she'd gone too long without sex, without release, and his kiss had undone her, sprung open the latch and released her need, making her a prisoner of lust and hunger that could only be quelled by letting Beau love her.

When he walked over, helping her on with her coat and handing her the strap of her purse, she felt as if she were walking in a dream, only half present in this reality. But she couldn't fight the need any longer. She just couldn't.

He placed his arm around her shoulder as he pushed the door open, guiding her down the walk.

"Where are we going?" she asked, her voice sounding faraway, as if they were standing in a tunnel.

"The Eagle's Nest, Callie. You know about it, don't you?"

She licked her lips, relying on Beau to guide her, her arm wrapped around his waist as they slowly walked to the parking lot. "Yes . . . but . . . isn't it occupied?"

"Not to my knowledge," he said, his voice low but amused.

"But . . . Matt and Dara . . ."

"We have two Eagle's Nests," he told her, opening the door to the Humvee. "They're at opposite ends of the warehouse."

She stood there. "Oh," was all she could manage to say. If nothing else, Delta boys were prepared for all possibilities. They must have believed in the old SEAL saying, "One is none, and two is one." It meant that you should have two of everything, just in case.

"You still want to go over there?" Beau demanded, tipping her chin up, her eyes meeting his. "This is up to you, Callie. I'm fine with anything you want."

Her panties were soaked. Callie could feel her juices between her thighs. Whatever battles her mind had waged about him, her body had won the war. "Yes, I want this. I want you, Beau." She lifted her face to him, feeling the heat, the animal hunger radiating off him, enveloping her, mesmerizing her, and taking her to a place where only pleasure awaited them.

"You have me, sweet woman. Climb in, okay? It's a short ride over there."

Leaning her head back, closing her eyes, she wanted to remain cocooned in the special heat and masculinity of his body, his arms, and his mouth. Her lips tingled and she could taste Beau on them, along with the apple pie and coffee. Now she was hungry to taste him all over.

She didn't try to think. Her body refused all questions, humming along like a Formula 1 racer wanting to tear down a track.

She wanted Beau's hands all over her just as her hands wanted to explore that tall, powerful body of his.

"Talk to me, Callie," Beau urged her quietly as he drove down the road.

"About what?"

He smiled indulgently. "Are you protected? Do I need a condom? I'm clean, by the way . . ."

She groaned. "Oh, that . . ."

"Yeah, it's a necessary part of our lives. Tell me what you need."

She could feel her body gnawing and hungry. "I'm on birth control pills. I'm clean. And I hate condoms."

He chuckled darkly. "Good to hear, and I agree about condoms. Not my first choice, either."

"Good," she whispered, sinking back, her whole lower body turning molten. Beau's kiss had been searching, giving, and taking. He had tasted her gently, then, confirming his instincts, relished the promise in her lips. She could feel the low reverberation in his chest as he'd taken her mouth, cherished it, then given it back to her. He had deepened the kiss until she swore she could imagine him licking her everywhere. Just . . . everywhere . . .

The promise in that one kiss was stamped throughout her yearning, ravenous body. More than anything, Callie knew Beau could fulfill her. And never, in her entire life, had she wanted to make love to a man more than him.

Where had her caution gone, or her concern that Beau would be like Chet—here today, gone tomorrow? It wasn't fair to compare the two, and Callie knew it. Yet, Beau wasn't going to give up his career, either. He had already made that choice, and she wasn't a part or a consideration of it. So what drove her into this seething storm of arousal that had suddenly overtaken her and wiped out her common sense? Her fear of the future?

There was no disputing that Beau wanted her. She saw the glint of the hunter that he was in his eyes. She felt his animal hunger, a primal warrior quality that had unveiled itself as she'd kissed him. Callie knew she had no one to blame for this decision except herself. She had claimed him with her offered kiss, and he had responded. That was the promise he'd made to her. She had to initiate. She was in control. So far.

Right now, Callie felt like a plane spinning out of control, hormones raging, lust in charge; she had gone too long without orgasms, without the pleasurable touch of a man in her life. Instinctively, Callie knew that Beau would treat her as an equal partner tonight. He wouldn't be like a rutting stag in heat.

Just the way his mouth had lightly fitted against hers on that first grazing touch, Callie knew he was going to be an exquisite lover. And was that the reason she'd decided to do this? To share his bed? To be in his arms, an active, giving, loving partner?

No, she had to face the facts: not only did she know he would love her thoroughly, love her first, strive to give her all the pleasure possible, but she also knew his heart, his emotions, would be involved, too.

Closing her eyes, she took a deep, ragged breath, surrendering to her arousal and her need for this man—in every possible way. Tonight, she was going to give Beau Gardner her heart, her body, her soul. Callie had no idea where this would lead either of them. And at the moment, she didn't care.

CHAPTER 7

CALLIE HAD NEVER been inside the Eagle's Nest and was surprised to find it resembled a studio apartment. There was a cozy living room with a couch and chairs and a kitchen with a stove, microwave, and refrigerator. The bedroom was at the other end, with a purple velvet spread across a king bed flanked by small tables.

What she liked the most was the bathroom. It had a tub—something she missed desperately—and a huge, two-person-size glass-enclosed shower. The green and white tile floor shined beneath her feet. The carpet in the living room was beige, the walls white, a few pictures hung here and there. The place had no windows, which she missed, but that was understandable, since they were deep inside a huge warehouse on the base.

Beau locked the door and turned, moving toward her. "Well?" he asked. "Does this meet your expectations?"

She nodded. "It's even nicer than I heard from other women who had visited this place," she admitted, pulling off her wool coat.

Beau hung it in a nearby closet. "These two apartments were built by the first Delta Force team entering Bagram in 2001 onward." He moved around, settling his hands on her shoulders, searching her eyes. "We bring women we care about here when we want quiet time together. Sometimes, it's a place to talk and share and learn about one another. Sometimes it's about love. Sometimes sex. But not always."

"That's what I heard from my friends," Callie said, nodding.

"The guy you fell in love with? Did he ever bring you here?"

"No. I never knew about this place until a year after that." She looked around, feeling the warmth of the quiet room. "It's got a nice, peaceful feeling."

"The best thing about it is, it's private." Beau moved his hands gently up and down her upper arms. "Sometimes, when there's a big football or basketball game going on in the States, a bunch of us guys who are off duty will come over here. We'll have beer, eat nachos, and watch the game."

"Typically male," Callie murmured.

He grinned. "Guilty." Beau smoothed back some strands of her hair from her shoulders. "We're here, Callie. Together. Tell me what you want."

And with that one question, she knew she had to give him her honest answer. "You, Beau. I want you."

"Well, you have me. You had me the first moment I saw you."

"But I don't know where we're going, Beau. A part of me is scared to death and another part wants to leap off that cliff with you and just be a risk taker." She felt delicious sensations throughout her body clench as he swept her hair aside and kissed the sensitive nape of her neck.

"Relationships are always about risking one's heart," he murmured, leaning over, his lips trailing more slow, soft kisses down her neck. "You have to know something, Callie," he added, easing away. He cupped her face, fixing his gray eyes on her glistening green ones. "I'm taking as much of a risk as you are. My heart is completely involved in this. It's not just about having sex with you. It's me wanting to love you the very best way I know how." He searched her eyes. "I'm not going to get up afterward and walk out on you or never see you again. What I want with you is long-term. I want to share that journey with you, if you'll let me."

She trembled. "Yes . . . that's what I want . . . what I need, Beau."

His mouth pulled slowly into that smile she loved so much. "Then come to bed with me," he said, his voice thick with emotion as he slid his hand into hers, leading her.

Beau made it seem so easy, and it felt natural to be with him. He had turned on a light in the kitchen and darkened the rest of the place. She pulled off her blazer and put it down on a bench at the end of the bed. Then she watched him shrug out of his suit coat and place it beside her blazer. She sat down and pushed off her shoes and he joined her, doing the same. They both felt the unspoken urgency to be together in every possible way.

She stood, stepping out of her long black skirt and slip, and as she pulled the apricot sweater over her head, she saw his face change, his hungry gaze taking in her lacy white bra and panties. Callie owned only one set of what she considered "girly" lingerie, and tonight she had worn them. Now, standing before him, her whole body responded to the primal look of a man wanting his woman.

And she wanted him just as much.

Oddly, Callie did not feel embarrassed as she watched him disrobe, but if she'd thought she was needy before, she became shaky with lust as he stood before her. How she wanted to touch him, kiss him, feeling his powerful, tight body against her own. Without a word, she walked to the edge of the bed, shimmying out of her lacy panties. And before she could unhook her bra from the back, Beau was there, the silent ghost that he was, now with mere inches between them, the heat rolling off his body, his powerful erection barely grazing her belly.

"I want to do this," he rasped, sliding his hands around her back, unhooking her bra. As he pulled the straps down her arms and let the bra drop near her panties, her breasts fell free. She saw his eyes narrow and leaned into him as his hands cupped her breasts, the weight of them in his callused palms, sending sheets of fire radiating within her.

She whimpered as she leaned into his strong hands, desperately wanting him to touch her nipples. As if reading her mind, he brushed their peaks with his thumbs, and her knees crumpled, a low moan of relief issuing from her.

"You're so sensitive," he growled, taking her to the bed, lying her down, and coming alongside her. She was curvy in all the right places, her breasts full and taut. Beau watched the play of light and dark against her soft, feminine body, from her breasts to her hips to her firm, curved thighs. His heart was pounding in his chest, his erection pressing into her, and he heard her gasp as he moved his thumb across her deep-pink nipple, which begged to be further explored by him.

And he was ready to do just that. Nothing existed for him but the sound of her whimpers, her hips restless and pleading against his. As he leaned over, capturing that delicious peak with his lips and drawing it into his mouth, she cried out, her fingers digging into his shoulders, now moaning his name. He smiled as he licked and sucked on her nipple, feeling her begin to dissolve in his arms, against his hard erection. She was alive, hungry, and most of all, as bold as he'd expected her to be. That red hair was a warning for every man who might prefer a passive lover, because Callie McKinley was quite the opposite.

As he left her nipple, her hand moved and curved around his erection, sending a bolt of fire through him, the jagged pleasure ripping up his spine, making him growl with appreciation. He saw that faint smile on her lips, saw the huntress in her eyes, and he slid his mouth against hers, celebrating their coming together, absorbing her lush curves, the strength of her hips and belly against him. Beau took her mouth with a hunger that matched her own. He knew what she wanted, and he was more than willing to give it to her.

Callie gasped as his fingers trailed down across her belly. He captured one of her legs beneath his own, opening her thighs. The moment his fingers trailed across her mound, she trembled. His fingers moved through her slick, heated folds, and she cried out his name as he explored her with a leisure that built an immediate, throbbing ache at her entrance.

Her hands gripped his broad shoulders as she lifted her hips against his hand, wanting more of his touch, wanting him to stop the gnawing ache that was driving her insane.

Beau's nostrils flared as he dragged in her sex scent, his fingers coated with the fluids from her body. Her red curls were saturated, the insides of her thighs gleaming wet, and she was so ready that all he could do was deepen that kiss, his tongue moving provocatively against her own, creating a rhythm that made her whimper against his mouth. Then her fingers began to dig frantically into his shoulder as he sought the swollen, silky knot at her entrance, and she cried out when he found and stroked it.

Ordinarily, a woman took time to build and prepare for entry, but Callie was already there, telling Beau how much she wanted him.

"I need you," she gasped as he left her mouth. "Beau, don't tease me. I need you inside me. Now. Now!"

"You've got me, sweet woman," he growled, rising, moving his knees between her damp thighs. The scent of her, a combination of musk and wildflowers, filled his nostrils. She didn't wait but urgently moved against his erection, coating it with her heated moistness, moving up and down against him, sending him into a hurtling ache of fire ready to explode from within. Beau barely maintained control as he moved to her entrance, his hands sliding around her hips, cupping her cheeks, drawing her up against him, feeling her response build until he knew she could wait no longer. Her lashes shuttered closed and her head fell back against the pillow, her back arching upward, wanting him.

As he slowly eased into her, he felt how tight she was. Beau knew that it had been a long time since she'd made love with a man, and he leaned over her, his fingers moving through that flaming red hair of hers, capturing her gently, holding her in place. Moving his mouth across her lips, tasting her uneven breath, he rasped, "I'm taking us slow, Callie. I don't want to hurt you. It's been a while for you, hasn't it?"

He saw her barely nod, her eyes dazed and deep green, saturated with arousal, lost in the heat boiling between them. Yes, it would probably kill him if he kept his rock-hard erection in tight check; he had never wanted a woman more. But he wanted to build her pleasure, feel her orgasm swell around him. Her body was like heated satin against his, a sheen of perspiration building as their breaths grew shallow, urgent. He tried to hold on to some small part of his mind, to give her, from his heart and soul, the love he felt for her.

He slowly eased into her, feeling her small body give beneath him. The last thing he wanted was to hurt her, so he thrust into her gently, then pulled out, then eased into her again, hearing her moan, hearing those sweet sounds build in her throat.

But he had miscalculated her ability to be patient. In fact, with her athletic strength built from hours of belly dancing, she insisted on pulling him deeper and deeper into her, despite his wish to spare her any possible discomfort.

Callie knew what she wanted and went after her climax with a vengeance as Beau gritted his teeth, trying to hold back until he felt her begin to build rapidly toward it. Callie came first, and he allowed her to set the rhythm for them. Every stroke sent him deeper, her channel tightening around him, the fluids hot and juicy as he groaned with pleasure, knowing his release would soon join hers.

Now he felt contractions begin, heard her gasp, felt her fingers dig into his shoulders, demanding what was hers. Beau would have surrendered to her wild needs, her hunger that truly matched his own, but he was damned worried about taking her as hard as he ached to do. And when her strong, slender legs wrapped around his hips, he knew he was lost, because she thrust her hips boldly, seating him as deeply into her as she could.

And then, he felt her body spasm, a violent contraction around his, squeezing the hell out of him, making him hiss through clenched teeth as an avalanche of boiling heat scalded through him. Callie screamed, clinging to him, her body arched against his, his name spilling from her lips, her eyes tightly shut as she felt the explosion throughout her lower body, sweeping him away with her.

The violence of her orgasm engulfed him along with her, erasing what was left of his resolve, igniting a fire that burned every cell in his body. Now, freed of his restraints, he thrust repeatedly into her, milking her orgasm, cries of satisfaction pouring from her as he finally gave her what she wanted.

He held her in place, his fingers locked into the thick strands on either side of her head, her body quivering, gripping him almost to the point of torment as he took her, caressed her, and felt her scorching orgasm continue to undulate throughout her, bringing her to tears.

Beau couldn't hold back any longer; the sweet tightness of her body, the hot moisture surrounding him, was his undoing. He pressed his sweaty brow against hers, his fingers gripping her hair, groaning as the fire contracted through him, racing down his spine, slamming into his tightened balls, and jettisoning deep into her hungry, needy body. His whole body shook with the power of his release.

Callie continued moving against him, her hips twisting, sucking him in, draining him until he collapsed against her, panting, the sweat sliding between them.

Beau breathed heavily against her hair, the strands tickling his nose and face, the sweet smell of her filling his lungs, filling him. He groaned her name, releasing her silky strands and enclosing her shoulders with a sweep of his arms. He held her tightly against him, locked within her welcoming body,

feeling her hands move restlessly against his back, stroking him in the aftermath, loving him.

He had no idea how long he lay against her, his angular, muscled body
against her own soft curves. He wasn't ready to leave her—overwhelming
emotions poured through him. There was something so powerful, so nurturing
about their union that all he wanted to do was absorb what it had awakened in
him and share it with Callie.

Beau knew it had been good for her, too. In fact, he'd barely been able to
hold off long enough to let her come first. Now, weak beyond belief, he lifted
himself off her, hearing her mew like a hungry little cat that wanted to keep
him close. He reluctantly slid free of her and then brought her against him as
he lay on his side.

He used his leg to draw her lower body close to him, holding her fully
against him. Her tousled hair spilled across his arm like a red cloak, and gazing
down at her, Beau felt his heart open completely. Her russet lashes were like
soft fans against her pink cheeks, her lips slightly swollen from the power of
their kisses. Her breasts brushed against his hairy chest, creating tiny fires of
pleasure for him. She was still breathing hard, the sheen of perspiration making
her shadowy body gleam in the soft light.

He took a mental picture of her in his arms, the beauty of her body glow-
ing in the aftermath of their lovemaking. He never wanted to forget this
moment. She was radiating satisfaction and pleasure, all because he had loved
her so well, so completely. Now he leaned down to kiss the corners of her
luscious mouth, which were drawn upward in a happy smile, letting Beau see
how much he'd pleasured her.

Then he kissed each of her eyelids, the intimacy between them strong and
unbroken. He wanted to bind her to him, his mouth moving to her satiny
cheek, then back to her mouth again. His hand ranged from her sleek shoulder
to cup her breast, hold the rounded weight of it in his palm, as he heard a
sound of pleasure vibrating in her throat.

He just couldn't get enough of her. There were so many ways he wanted to
please her so he could hear again and again those small, soft sounds emanate
from her, telling him he was satisfying Callie.

In his world, a woman's body was an altar to be worshipped at, tended to
and cherished. He gently captured one rosy peak, pulling it into his mouth,
suckling her. She cried out softly, then pressed herself wantonly against him,
letting him know she loved everything he was doing. He slid his hand downward, cupping her buttocks, allowing his fingers to move to that sweet curve
between them. His fingers were saturated with her juices, and he knew she was
ready for him once more. The naturalness, the trust with him, was unbroken,
and it humbled Beau as nothing else ever would. Callie had given him her

heart, her sweet, beautiful body, and that damn near brought him to tears. She had overcome her fear of what might happen, thrown her lot in with his, and taken a chance.

He didn't want fear stopping her or making her hesitate where he was concerned. He was here today, and God knew he wanted to be with her tomorrow, too, and the tomorrow after that.

Beau had only two more nights to convince Callie of his intentions, because he knew he was being sent on another mission. He was almost desperate to give her enough physical pleasure to capture her heart once and for all. But could he do it? Could he convince Callie that he was worth risking abandonment and disappointment, which she'd been programmed to expect from a man? He knew they could climb this challenging mountain, because he believed what they had was stronger than anything he'd ever experienced with a woman. And yes, he was falling in love with Callie, a woman as natural as nature herself.

Callie was no game player. Beau felt his heart swell so powerfully with love that it nearly overwhelmed him. His primary purpose now was to keep her safe, make her happy, hear her sparkling laughter, absorb the husky quality of her voice after they had made love, explore with her how she saw the world.

As he felt her move her hips in anticipation of his entering her again, he smelled her sweet, seductive fragrance. He instantly became hard again, so quickly that it surprised even him.

A raw cry tore from her as he lifted her leg across his hip, giving him full access to her. And as he eased two fingers into her entrance, feeling that sweet knot swollen once more, he took her mouth, took those melodic sounds emanating from her, drinking them deep into himself, wanting to consume her on every level.

He slowly entered her, twisting his fingers, widening her, feeling her contractions respond to his strokes as she shuddered against him. And as he moved deeper, her breathing became faster, lighter.

Lifting his mouth from hers, he recaptured her hard nipple, suckling her, and she screamed, bucking hard against him, clinging to him as she was swept away by another orgasm. He found her center again and stroked her there, feeling her entire body clench around his fingers. Her sobs sounded like music to him as he continued his rhythmic movement, and she came again and again with a violence that staggered him. She was now his, completely, in every possible way.

CALLIE DIDN'T KNOW what time she awoke in Beau's arms, her body resting against his, the simmering heat once more beginning to build within her lower body. There were no windows to reveal whether it was night or morning. Beau slept deeply, his breathing slow and shallow against her, his arm possessively around her waist, holding her to him.

Closing her eyes, her head on his shoulder, her arm curved across his narrow waist, she realized she'd lost count of how many orgasms he had coaxed from her. Right now her body shimmered like the radiant heat waves one found moving across the hot desert floor.

She had to admit it: never had she felt as fulfilled as she did right now. This man knew how to love her, but even more important for Callie was the intimacy they'd shared afterward. Beau was fully present, fully involved with her, and whenever he placed his mouth against some part of her body, she felt his heart and soul engaged with hers. And when he smiled knowingly into her eyes, she felt her heart explode with such happiness, she could barely breathe.

Not only was he worshipping her physically, which she had never before experienced, but Beau kissed her as if they were long-lost lovers finally reunited.

When Beau touched her, he seemed to be holding her soul gently within his loving hands. Best of all, Beau caressed her with a tenderness she'd never experienced from a man, and it left her sighing with fulfillment. Now all she wanted was to be close to him, to love him, to hear him groan or growl as he slid deep within her.

Callie finally understood what bliss was. It was far more than physical gratification. It was when two people were so attuned to each other, their hearts opened fully, transcending the physical world into a whole new sphere of experience.

Looking up at Beau's sleeping features, she smiled softly, wanting to lift her fingers and graze his cheek. His face was free of tension for the first time since she'd known him. That deliciously shaped mouth of his was slightly parted, his breathing deep and slow.

She also thought of how humble he was, and yet how superior he was to other men she'd known. He might have called himself a country bumpkin, but truly he was a warrior of the first order. His mind was sharp and deeply intuitive, with a mature insight into life, and into her. He was complex, layered. There was so much to learn about him . . . and she couldn't wait to see Beau continue to reveal himself. The thought excited her as nothing else ever had. He reminded her of a treasure chest that had been placed before her, and she had been offered the privilege of opening it. This was the greatest gift she'd ever received from a man.

How had she gotten so lucky? She'd been ready to classify him with the rest of the men who'd pursued her for sexual conquest. Now she saw that Beau, by showing her unconditional love, was in a class by himself.

CHAPTER 8

CALLIE STRETCHED LANGUIDLY as sleep lifted from her. She sighed, feeling Beau's lips against her brow, placing small kisses there. She slowly lifted her lashes, struck by his tender gaze as he watched her begin to wake.

"You are so damn beautiful when you start to pull out of sleep," he told her, caressing her cheek. "I want to wake up like this every morning with you."

She purred and leaned into him, her breasts against his chest, feeling his erection pressing into her belly. "Mmm, that feels so good," she whispered. Then, "What time is it, Beau?"

He lifted his head, glancing at the clock on the dresser opposite the bed. "It's 0300. We still have some time left."

She gloried in the warm, hard strength of his arm curved beneath her neck, holding her protectively. "I think," she said, her voice husky, "I dreamed you up, and none of this is real. I'm simply in a wonderful dream." She saw his mouth turn up, his eyes crinkle with his smile.

"Well, then, sweet woman, we're both dreaming the same dream." He slid a few strands of hair away from her ear, nibbling on the other one.

A cascade of heat skittered down through her as he licked her ear, and Callie sighed. She felt boneless, sinuous, sexy, and desired.

"Mmm, let's keep dreaming together then," she laughed, meeting his warm gray eyes. How delicious that she could trail her fingertips across his cheek, run them across his full lower lip, and watch his eyes become heavy with arousal. "I like touching you," she whispered. "All over. I wish . . . I wish we had more time together." She knew that at 0600, she had to be back at her B-hut to prepare for her day at the orphanage.

"Well," he offered, catching her fingers in his, "there's tomorrow night. Shall we continue what we've started here?"

Her entire body flooded with anticipation. "Yes, definitely."

"Good." He grinned, then, with a grimace, added, "Because the day after that, I'm being sent out on an op."

Instantly, Callie's feelings of well-being were replaced by fear.

Beau saw her eyes widened as he assured her, "Don't worry, it's just routine stuff." He leaned over, and his kiss told Callie what she needed to know: that he didn't want to leave her any more than she wanted him to go.

Her mouth responded, her lips parting beneath his, a rush of her sweet breath into him, and he tasted her and inhaled her feminine scent. God, he was desperate to claim her, to let her know that he wanted her for a thousand reasons. But if her response to his kisses was any indicator, Callie was more than willing to give them a chance.

As he broke the kiss, their breaths becoming heated and quickening, he said, "More than anything, Callie, I want you in my life. I know I'll be gone sometimes, but I'll always be coming back here to Bagram, to you, to your arms. And to our bed."

Her fears were temporarily pushed aside by the depth of his commitment to her. "I don't know how this is going to go," she admitted. "Of course I want you, Beau, but I know your commitment to the Army has priority over us."

Although it hurt to hear those words, he couldn't argue with her. He twisted a strand of her hair around his finger and then released it. "When I met you, Callie, I never dreamed you'd give me a chance to prove myself to you, that I wasn't just chasing you down to get you into bed. You stole my heart from the beginning, and the more I've gotten to know you, the more I want every last damn second I can squeeze out to be spent with you. I'll give you everything I can. I know the Army owns me for now, but when I come off an op, I'm heading your direction, and if I have my way, we'll spend as much time together as possible."

Nodding, she closed her eyes, burying her face against his neck, her arm slipping across his shoulders, holding him tight against her. She almost said, *I'm falling in love with you,* but bit back the words. "I want this to work too, Beau," she whispered unsteadily. "I hope it can."

"Let's have some faith in us and our future," he urged her quietly, stroking her unruly, mussed hair, moving his hand down her spine. "I don't have any answers for us yet, Callie. But I'm going to try to think outside the box and see if I can come up with a better plan." He kissed her temple. "I want you in my life. You have to hold on to that. I don't want to let you go. We still have some time together here at Bagram, so let's make the most of it. Okay?"

"Yes," she managed to say, feeling her heart starting to break. "When I'm with you, I feel hope, Beau. I feel as if we can do this."

His mouth softened with relief. "Then let me hold our hope in my heart, Callie, for both of us. Hold on, will you?"

"I'll hold on," she whispered, leaning up, grazing his mouth with her lips.

★

DARA GAVE CALLIE a curious look as they sat down in the chow hall later that morning. "You look different. Happier, maybe?" she asked, salting her eggs.

"Beau and I were at the other Eagle's Nest last night," Callie admitted, and saw her sister's eyes widen with surprise as she stirred sugar and milk into her oatmeal.

"Really! Well, Matt and I were in the other apartment." Dara smiled, remembering their night together.

"I kinda figured you were." Callie's mouth quirked. "I didn't hear a thing. Did you?"

Dara grinned a bit self-consciously. "No."

"Good."

"Wow!" Dara suddenly admitted, "I'm shocked—about both of us! What on earth is happening, sis?"

"Don't ask me," Callie grumped. "I've already been around the block with one Delta guy. And now I'm a glutton for punishment, and I'm doing it again." She frowned. "Actually, that isn't fair to Beau. He's nothing like Chet. In fact, he's just the opposite."

"I think he's a good guy," Dara agreed, "just like Matt. They're made from the same genetic pool, I swear."

"Well, they are good friends and teammates," Callie offered. For whatever reason, her oats tasted delicious this morning. And she was starving. It had to be because she and Beau had made love three times last night. Her body still glowed with the memory of his hands, worshipping her.

"Yes, Matt loves him like the brother he never had."

"Well, at least you know Matt's coming home to you," Callie said enviously.

"Give yourselves some time, Callie. It's very possible that Beau's career will change course."

"I don't know," Callie admitted. "This is so different for me, Dara."

"How is it different?"

Blowing out a puff of air between her lips, Callie said, "I've had enough relationships, unlike you, to know when a man is really into me. With Beau last night . . . Dara, I've never been so well loved in my whole life. He was caring and tender with me, like a dream come true. I honestly didn't believe men like him really existed."

"That's wonderful," Dara murmured, giving her a warm, sisterly look. "I know you've had some pretty rocky relationships in the past."

"Like you haven't?" Callie demanded archly, lifting a brow.

Dara had the good grace to blush. "Well, putting it that way, yes, my two affairs ended up being certified disasters. Until Matt."

"See? Even your voice softens when you say his name," Callie observed, smiling.

"And yours doesn't?" Dara laughed, amused. "Sorry, but it's happening to you, too. Every time you mention Beau, your voice goes an octave lower."

"He affects me so deeply, Dara." Callie was now serious. "My heart pounds every time I think of him, or remember his smile, or his sexy drawl— now, that's a real turn-on for me."

"Hmm, sounds serious. As a doctor, I'd say you're infected, but that doesn't sound very romantic, does it?"

An unwilling grin tugged at Callie's lips. "No, he's not a virus, Dara." And at that, both women giggled, their bond even stronger now that they were both in love.

BEAU SURPRISED CALLIE that evening when he picked her up at her B-hut. He drove her directly to the Eagle's Nest and announced, "Tonight, sweet woman, I'm cooking for you."

Surprised, she said, "Really? I didn't know you cooked!"

"I learned when I was a kid—my ma taught all three of us boys the basics, and I started creating my own recipes." He chuckled. "So today I went over to the base exchange and bought us some groceries so we'd have more time with each other—and to get us off the restaurant merry-go-round."

"I like the way you think, Beau," Callie said approvingly.

"I haven't poisoned anyone yet, so I think you'll be safe." He flashed her a grin.

"This is so nice," she whispered. "Thanks for doing this."

"What? Did you think I was going to tie you to the bed and not let you go?"

His teasing drawl brought out her own grin. "I really didn't know what to expect tonight, Beau. I just knew I wanted to be with you."

"Same here," he admitted, darting a look in her direction as he drove into the warehouse parking lot. "I want every moment I can spare to be spent with you."

They worked in the kitchen side by side. Beau even had an apron for Callie and tied it around her waist, because she didn't want to get her brown wool slacks dirty. He had thoughtfully brought veggies for a healthy salad and assigned the job of preparing it to her. She also cut up some cheddar cheese in small squares to sprinkle on top of it. To her surprise, the kitchen was well stocked with spices, plus lots of other items in the refrigerator, not just junk food.

"We have a couple of guys on our team who could be considered amateur chefs," Beau told her as he salted and peppered their T-bone steaks, now sizzling in the frying pan. "They're the ones who really amped up our spice cabinet."

"I think it's kind of nice that you guys have this place," Callie said. "It gives you a chance to slow down and relax."

Beau turned the steaks and thought about how to answer her. "It isn't always about bringing a woman over here," he told her seriously. "One guy is going with this Air Force air traffic controller, and they love to play chess. They meet over here whenever he's not on duty, and they really go at it with one another. They're good friends and both are married to other partners." Beau grinned. "I'm a checkers kind of guy. Chess isn't for me."

"Checkers? You know," Callie said, "I grew up with them, too. My grandparents always played a game on Sunday evenings after dinner. They taught Dara and me how to play, so when we were older, the four of us were able to play together. We'd have checker's tournaments. It was always a lot of fun." She smiled fondly. "I often think that sometimes they let us win so we wouldn't lose all the time."

"Well," Beau murmured, "because they love you, they wanted you to grow up with positive experiences under your belt."

"Did you and your family play any games together?"

"Yeah, my mother was stuck on Old Maid."

"What's that?"

He gave her a wink. "Old Maid was a card game out of the 1840s, I think. My grandma played it with her, and my ma still has the cards she originally owned. So when we boys were old enough, she taught us how to play it. It's like a standard card deck, except one of the cards is an Old Maid. And whoever ends up with it *is* the Old Maid. It was nothing fancy, but we three boys got a lot of mileage out it," he chuckled.

"My grandmother told us that people used to play a lot of card games back in the Depression era," Callie recalled.

"Yeah, no one could afford to go out to a restaurant, go to a movie, or do much of anything else," Beau agreed, turning the steaks again. "Card games were big because they brought families together, so they were more than just fun times for competitive types."

Within minutes, everything was ready. Callie took their salads to the table, and Beau brought the dinner plates with the steaks on them. He'd bought some French bread, too, and Callie had slathered it with butter, wrapped it in foil, and heated it in the oven. She placed the warm, buttery bread in a basket and set it on the table between them. Beau pulled out her chair so she could sit down. She loved that about him. He was always the gentleman.

"Tomorrow, by the way," Beau began as they dug into dinner, "Matt and I will be going with you two and Mohammed to that Shinwari village."

"That would be terrific!" she said gratefully. "It's a service the Hope Charity offers that village four times a year. We're just lucky Dara is here now so she can offer medical support to the villagers."

Nodding, Beau said, "Matt and I know the northern area pretty well, and it's considered fairly safe."

"Nothing is ever safe out here," Callie muttered, chewing the delicious steak. "I mean, it's a pro-American village, and this will be my fifth trip out to it, but I'm always a little concerned."

"Well, it's winter, and usually the Taliban slinks back to their own villages or across the Af-Pak border to sit out the winter. We should be safe going to and from the village."

"That's what I told Dara, but you know how she worries. She's already jumpy about it. I told her it would be an easy day for all of us, and it gets us out in fresh air and sunshine, if we're lucky."

"Actually, it's supposed to be overcast with a possibility of rain here at Bagram. That village sits at seven thousand feet, so they'll probably get snow if the mountains decree it," Beau pointed out.

"Mountain weather is always fickle," she agreed. "Well, we'll be dressing warmly," she promised.

He sobered and held her gaze. "When we get back, Matt and I are expected at HQ to prepare for the op I mentioned this morning."

Beau could see her struggling to keep her expression positive. His heart swelled with love, and he knew he would do whatever it took to protect her from life's disappointments.

"You know that as soon as we land back here at Bagram, I'll be on the cell phone to you. Okay?"

Dara might have been the chief worrywart in the McKinley family, but Beau sensed that Callie wasn't too far behind. She cared so deeply for others that he knew she was naturally going to worry about him.

Callie forced a slight smile and said, "Of course, Beau. I understand. I can't wait to see you when you're back."

"I know . . . and I'm sorry. I hate to see you worry," he said, reaching across the table, his hand over hers for a moment.

"You can't help it, Beau. It's okay."

That stuck like a lump of coal in his soul. Now he was beginning to understand why Matt was looking forward to separating from the Army. It helped that he already had a job waiting for him Delos, the network of charities his family ran. But since meeting Dara, Matt had been positively ecstatic that he was leaving the military.

If Beau hadn't been emotionally involved with Callie, he might not have appreciated Matt's reaction. But now he did, even more than he wanted to admit.

Squeezing her hand, he said, "We'll make this work, Callie. I promise."

His promise came from a place deep within him, and Callie could feel it. She knew Beau came from a family, a tradition, where a man's word was his bond, not to be broken unless death interceded first. She suddenly felt close to tears. "And I promise to wait for you . . ."

Beau swallowed hard, holding her luminous gaze. It was more than he could ever have hoped for from Callie at this young stage of their budding relationship with one another. "We're going to make this work," he rasped, sliding his fingers across her cheek. "I always want you in my life from now on, Callie. Somehow, I'll figure out a way to make that happen."

BEAU MOVED HIS fingers, lingering along Callie's back, listening to her shallow breaths, feeling the dampness on his neck and upper chest. Callie's hand moved weakly through the sprinkle of dark hair on his chest.

Their first session of post-dinner lovemaking had left them exhausted; they had eagerly moved together with a sense of hunger and urgency. Now, at 0200, he'd awakened, driven to love her again, but this time as tenderly as he could. And this time, Callie came undone within his arms. He had felt her tears on his shoulder afterward and wasn't sure what they meant.

Was she devastated that they were having to part so soon after having met one another? Or was she torn apart by the prospect that he might be in danger?

Beau didn't know, and so he leaned down, kissing her closed lids, tasting the salt of her tears. "What are these tears all about?" he asked thickly, smoothing her silky hair away from her face so he could see her in the shadows.

Callie barely opened her eyes. With trembling fingers, her voice low and apologetic, she whispered, "I-I don't know. I rarely cry. I'm crying because you're going to be gone, in danger again, Beau. I'll worry . . . I'm sorry . . ."

"Hush, gal, I want you to share everything with me. You know Delta teams are the best. I have you to come back to, Callie. I have every reason to survive, and I will." He gave her a tender look. "Tears don't upset me, either. My ma taught me a long time ago that they were cleansing." He smiled deeply into her wounded eyes. Cupping her cheek, he leaned over, breathing in her scent, that musky wildflower mix that made him ache to take her all over again.

"Don't ever be afraid to cry around me. I know a lot of guys are uncomfortable with a woman's tears, but the way I see it, you're just clearing out some dark memories or emotions."

She sniffed a bit. "Do you ever cry, Beau?"

He lifted his head and his mouth twitched. "Now, can you keep my secret?"

"You know I can."

"My pa cried sometimes, and he did it in front of us boys. And that's where we learned it was okay to let go, to give in to our feelings. We were taught it was nature's way of healing us from the inside out." He slid his fingers through her hair. "Yes, I cry. Now, do I do it in front of my team? No way." His mouth turned upward. "But there've been plenty of times in the Army where I've sought a quiet, out-of-the-way place and let my tears fall."

"Do you feel better afterward?"

"Always. How about you?"

"Always."

"See? We can be crybabies together. Just another thing we share," he teased gently, seeing her sad smile and trembling lower lip.

"I think I'd like your parents," Callie said. "My mom and dad aren't so much that way, but my grandparents are."

"It could be a generational thing, you know? Or it could be because I was bred in the hills and we do things differently from the lowlanders." Beau smoothed her hair from her face. "Hey, I have something to tell you that should cheer you up."

"What?"

"I called my ma on my sat phone while we were over at the orphanage earlier today. I asked her to send me a deck of Old Maid playing cards, and I told her I'd finally found a willing partner."

Callie couldn't help but laugh. "And I suppose you're going to teach me how to play when those cards get here?"

Beau cradled her in his arms, and she realized she had never felt as safe as she did right now. Beau, while a big tease sometimes, was a consummate warrior, and it was especially evident right now because he was bristling with protectiveness toward her.

"Sure. I thought that once I get off that op, we can come over here to the Nest and make dinner and then afterward, I'll teach you how to play Old Maid."

It was impossible for her not to laugh, and he laughed with her. After this last bout of lovemaking, Callie had admitted to herself that yes, she was falling in love with Beau, and she now knew she had no intention of stopping it.

Her unexpected tears were really about her feelings, but she wasn't going to tell him that. She didn't want to make Beau feel bad about choosing to remain in a career he loved.

And she realized that she was willing to be in his life as long as they lived, for however long that meant. Right now, Callie accepted her fate, because Beau gave her so much in return.

"Come here," he growled, lifting her into his arms and easing off the bed. "I'm going to get you a bath started. I know how much you love them." He set her upright on the bed and then gathered the purple velvet spread around her shoulders, tucking it in so she wouldn't become chilled. "Stay here for a moment. I want to get the water going in that tub for you."

Callie loved to watch him walk around naked, his shoulders so proud and thrown back, his long legs powerful, his strong calves muscled. And he had the cutest rear she'd ever seen. There was nothing, absolutely nothing, about Beau that wasn't beautiful to her.

When he came back about five minutes later, she could see that he was a man with a plan. "Okay," she murmured, "what's going on here, Beau?"

"Nothing, sweet woman." He brought out a white silk bathrobe from the bathroom and helped her into it. Then he leaned down and swept her into his arms and carried her over to the couch. He sat her down, bringing one of the big pillows at one end for her to prop herself up against. "I've decided you deserve a world-class foot massage first before I fill that tub with water for you."

"Oh, Beau, you're kidding me," she said gratefully. She adored his foot rubs.

He sat down near her feet and uncovered one of them, placing it against his thigh. "Now, why would I kid you about that, gal?" He slid his long fingers around her delicate arch and began to gently move and pull at those muscles, getting them to loosen up.

"Ohh," she whispered, leaning back, closing her eyes. "You've utterly spoiled me, Beau. That feels sooooo good . . ."

"Better than your orgasms?"

She laughed and opened one eye. "No way. You bring out the best in me, you really do. I've never had so many orgasms in my life!"

He seemed pleased about that. His hand slid up her ankle, and he forced himself to focus on relaxing her calf muscles, a place she seemed to hold stress.

"Well, you bring out the best in me, too," he confided. "I don't normally come three times a night. I knew you were the right woman for me."

"How could you know that, Beau?"

He slid his thumb along the muscles of her calf, hearing her sigh. "I felt it the night I saw you belly dance."

"Really?" Callie scrunched up her face in disbelief.

Beau laughed and went on, "Hey, maybe every other man in that chow hall that night had a hard-on, but I was seeing something else in you. Something deeper. Of course I wanted you in my bed, but not just because you were a sexy dancer."

Her snort shifted into a sigh as he continued kneading her foot.

Beau finished her other foot and then rose. "I'm going to start your bathwater."

When he returned, she could see that he was becoming erect. "Looks like doing foot massage does something else for you," she teased.

He glanced down and smiled. He leaned over, pulling the silky robe from around her. "That's your fault," he rasped, sliding his arms beneath her naked body and lifting her up against him. "It's time I spoiled you a little more," he announced as he kissed her forehead, carrying her into the bathroom. He nudged the door shut and then eased her to her feet. "Bath time."

"Are you going to wash me, too?" She met his gaze, her whole lower body feeling how much he wanted to be inside her.

"No, I'd like to, but you know what?" He pointed to the shower. "One of these days, I'm going to give you the sexiest washing you've ever had under the shower." His look was feral as he took her hand, helping her step into the huge garden tub, now filled almost to the top with warm water.

Callie gave him a big grin as she took the proffered washcloth and soap. "I'm really going to look forward to that."

"You should, gal. Now, while you're getting your bath, I'll take a shower all by myself and miss you like crazy."

She chortled. "Fortunately, it won't be for long."

He shook his head. "Just lounge and enjoy the water."

Sighing, she sank into the heated tub, closed her eyes, and murmured, "Beau, you're unbelievable."

CHAPTER 9

C ALLIE TRIED TO appear calm and unworried as she entered the white van. Mohammed, smiling, told them all "Good morning!" as they climbed in. He had been hired by the Hope Charity and was their driver. When he wasn't doing errands for Maggie and the charity, he would pitch in and help at the orphanage. Only twenty-one, the black-haired, green-eyed Afghan was always upbeat and smiling. Callie loved his optimistic attitude, and it rubbed off on everyone. He was the kind of person, in her opinion, that just made a day go better, even a bad one. She smiled over at Mohammed, speaking to him in her Pashto. Today was Dara's last day at Bagram, and they were driving out to a nearby Afghan village—a safe one, Callie had assured Dara.

Callie made this trip once a month, and when she did, she brought either a physician, a dentist, or an optical team with her. This time, she was bringing Dara to help set up a medical clinic for the village's women and children. Once that was ready, Callie would distribute winter clothing and shoes to the children.

At the van, Callie saw Beau climb into the seat behind the driver. Matt helped them into the van and then rode shotgun, sitting in the front passenger seat with Mohammed, his M4 beside him. Callie felt a definite sense of tension running through the two Delta Force operators and wondered if her sister had picked it up, too. Judging by Dara's worried look, her fingers moving restlessly in her lap, she probably had. It was never secure going out beyond the wire, the safety of Bagram.

Callie saw both men check their weapons, extra-alert and more intense than usual. Both men were clearly in warrior mode.

Earlier, Dara had been anxious and had confided in Callie that she was glad the two Delta Force operators were going with them today. She felt jittery about leaving what little safety there was at Bagram. The village they were heading toward was thirty-five miles north, near the slopes of the mountains, in a small, water-rich valley.

Callie had tried to ease her sister's fears, and having Beau and Matt along seemed to have settled most of her sister's civilian nerves. Now Callie forced her own anxiety down, keeping on her game face, pretending all was business as usual. Being able to sit next to Beau helped quell Callie's anxiety, and he appeared his usual, unflappable, easygoing self. Once, their eyes met and Beau traded a slight smile with her. Her body continued to glow from their lovemaking earlier that morning, and her sister had that same fulfilled look. Callie was grateful that they had both started the day being loved by these men.

The morning sun was slanting across the flat desert landscape as Mohammed chatted away in Pashto with Matt. They left the safety of Bagram and headed north on a two-lane black asphalt highway.

Dara tried to relax, her hands knotted in her lap. Matt had urged her to wear hiking boots today because villages were muddy this time of year and there was no place on this trip for a nice pair of leather shoes. Not only that, but both he and Beau had their huge sixty-five-pound rucksacks with them, stuffed with whatever they felt they might need.

Callie knew both men were prepared for anything, and because it was winter, Beau had urged her to "dress down and dress warm." The village sat at the foot of the mountains, surrounded by snow and in freezing temperatures that were normal for November. Callie was wearing her hiking boots, heavy jeans, and a white silk camisole instead of a bra. She didn't like bras, and any time she could get away with not wearing one, she did. She'd chosen a bright red mock turtleneck sweater, a toasty combination of merino sheep's wool woven with silk. The sweater kept her warm but not hot.

Her black hooded nylon down coat fell around her hips, keeping her warm, and instead of wearing her unlined leather gloves, Callie had opted for "serious" fleece-lined gloves. She wore a black and red knit cap and a knitted scarf wrapped around her neck. There was no way she was going to freeze outside in this weather.

Between her and Beau sat Beau's huge rucksack. Knowing him, he had covered every possible need for any emergency. He had insisted she put a small knapsack together for herself, which she normally didn't do, but she grudgingly carried some protein bars and several quarts of water, knowing the village did not have a well. Few of them did; the villagers relied on a nearby stream or river for water.

The village they were visiting today sat near a small river, which could have been foul, polluted, and not drinkable. No one had ever reported on its purity. The mountains hovering over this valley made their own weather, and snow could fall in the blink of an eye this time of year.

There was little conversation except for Mohammed merrily chatting away with Matt in the front seat. Both Matt and Beau wore radio headsets, earpieces, and mics close to their lips so they could be in constant touch with one another. That further upset Dara, because she thought they were wearing such gear because they expected to get attacked, but Callie assured her sister this was a normal part of their uniform when they were out on a mission. Dara seemed willing to accept Callie's explanation.

Callie found herself less tense because she was sitting next to Beau. She was well aware that cars and trucks were often attacked on this lonely road. It was usually frequented by military convoys only, and they drove special trucks with trained drivers looking for IEDs planted beside the highway.

Beau had his rifle in a chest sling, the barrel pointed upward toward the ceiling of the van. Matt's M4 was also up, and Callie saw his finger near the trigger. She realized that these men were on full alert and was both reassured and anxious, knowing they might have sensed potential trouble but weren't sharing it with her and Dara. But if they truly felt there was trouble nearby, Callie knew they'd have told Mohammed to turn around and go back to Bagram. They would not put them in danger if they thought it was close.

Because Dara had never gone outside the confines of the base to visit a hamlet, Callie understood why she was worried. She had assured her sister they would be safe and that the people of the village would be very grateful that a real American doctor was coming to treat them.

Dara had regularly visited here once a year while Callie was in Kabul but had always worked only out of the Hope Charity in the major city. This was her first drive out to a nearby village. She had balked when Callie first asked her to come assist the villagers, but her sister cajoled her, telling her sweet stories about the babies who needed her help, and pointed out that villagers had no way to get medical services.

That had persuaded Dara, but the recent market blasts in Kabul had set Dara on edge as never before. She was simply not cut out for this kind of violence. Of course, no one was! However, the people of Afghanistan had been forced to endure war and violence for decades.

The desert began to shift and change from flatlands to bumpy hills covered with brush. They were slowly climbing, gaining elevation, and now Callie could see the snow-capped mountains in the distance. They were tall, rugged, and powerful looking, with dark, gathering clouds over the peaks, promising snow later today or tomorrow.

Soon enough, halfway through the narrow valley, Callie spotted the familiar thin ribbon of a dark green river off to their left. She saw trees, too, but the leaves had fallen, leaving bare branches in their stead. Towering evergreens stood in thick profusion alongside the naked trees.

Mohammed slowed the van and turned off on a heavily rutted, muddy road. It had rained up here, from what Callie could tell; she saw wheel ruts from carts drawn by donkeys or horses. The van bumped along slowly, and Dara gripped the arm of the seat.

As they approached a stand of pine trees, it appeared that the van would have to be steered between them. Beau and Matt suddenly became far more alert, alarming Callie when they suddenly took the safeties off their M4s. Did they see something? Callie knew Beau had gone over to HQ before leaving Bagram, getting the latest reports on the area. If any attacks had occurred in the last few days, he'd know. The good news was, there had been no reports of enemy activity. So what were both men studying so intently up ahead and to the right of their slow-moving van?

Beau moved his weapon, and Callie tried to scoot toward Dara so he had room to maneuver in case he had to use it. She still tried to appear relaxed beside her sister, but in truth, her heart was hammering away.

Trees and brush surrounded the van as it negotiated the deep, muddy cart ruts, barely moving through them at a sliding, slipping crawl. The wheels spun, the van moving sideways as Mohammed fought to keep it on the road. Dara gripped the armrest tighter, her gaze moving quickly from one side of the road to the other.

Matt and Beau were on full alert, braced as they continued to peruse a particularly enclosed area. Callie could see nothing. It was as if this stretch of the road to the village was walled in by sixty-foot pine trees and brush. Anxiety shot through her, and she worked to keep her expression calm, recognizing the signs of Dara's barely suppressed panic.

When Matt spoke quietly to Beau in his mic, Callie couldn't hear their exchange, but her instincts were on high alert. There was now a real sense of danger hanging over them and she gulped. Matt and Beau positioned their rifles on their shoulders, and Callie barely breathed, knowing something was terribly wrong up ahead.

And then the windshield shattered, exploding glass fragments everywhere, like sharp, glittering shards of ice.

"Get *down*!" Matt roared, aiming his M4 out the shattered windshield.

Dara lurched for the floor and Callie did, too. The deep-throated firing of the M4s hurt her ears as the van lurched from side to side.

Mohammed screamed, and then their vehicle skidded sideways as a *thunk, thunk, thunk* of bullets was fired into the careening vehicle.

Callie covered her sister with her body, holding on tightly to Dara. She felt the van suddenly lift off on one side. *Oh, my God*, she thought, *we're crashing!*

She clung to her sister, now balled up into a fetal position on the floor. They had been ambushed! She heard Beau's voice above the roar, and Matt answered, the sounds around her cartwheeling together. Now she was panicking, too!

The van fell on its side, sliding off the road and slamming into the tree line, where it came to an abrupt stop.

Callie gasped, flung halfway across the seat. She grunted, flailing, as she tried to get up. Matt leaped out of the passenger side door. Once out, he tried to jerk open the van's sliding door to free them. Her ears hurt as the roar of Matt's M4 and the returning *chut-chut-chut*-ting of enemy AK-47 rifle fire converged. She couldn't see the enemy but she saw the winking of gunfire coming at them from deep within the pine grove.

Callie's ears hurt, and she twisted around, knowing she was a target as bullets tore into the van. Beau gripped her, shoving her hard between the front seats, trying to get her out of bullet range and behind the dashboard.

Matt was outside the van, firing slowly and carefully into the grove. Where was Mohammed? Callie pushed up on her booted feet, twisting her head toward the driver, and saw to her horror that he was slumped over, dead, with half his head missing.

Callie cried out and, panicked, tried to scramble out of the van. Dara was screaming in the back, having been thrown off the floor and into the wall of the van during the crash. Never had Callie felt so naked, so vulnerable, as she did right now.

The firing stopped momentarily.

"Get out!" Matt yelled as Callie struggled toward him. He kicked at the passenger side door wide open. Beau cursed, trying to jerk it open the sliding door open from inside. It was jammed shut!

"Exfil!" Beau yelled to Callie, meaning she needed to exfiltrate the van as swiftly as possible. Matt hauled Callie out the passenger-side door. He ordered her to stay down behind him. Dara was next as Beau pushed her roughly forward between the two front seats. Matt caught and dragged Dara out, pushing her down behind him, next to Callie. He lifted his M4 at the wall of trees, ready to fire.

Beau leaped out, right behind Dara, his eyes narrowed as he warily searched the wall of green facing them.

"Take her," Matt snapped, guiding Callie to her feet. "Get into the hills! We need to separate. We can't go together. We have to split up the Taliban force. Once you get hidden, call for help from Bravo and wait until the quick reaction force arrives."

"Roger that," Beau said, gripping Callie's arm. She'd fallen into the muddy road on her hands and knees, and he moved her swiftly to the rear of the van once he'd pulled her to her feet. He halted behind the van and jerked open the hatchback, telling her to crouch so she wouldn't become a target. He hauled out both rucks and brought one over to Matt, dropping it beside him.

Quickly, Beau returned to the rear of the van, shrugged into his ruck, and grabbed Callie's hand, pulling her to her feet. Settling her muddy fingers around his web belt, he growled, "Come on, stay low and stay close to me, Callie. Don't let go of my belt."

Callie clung to that belt because her life depended on it. In seconds, Beau was crashing through the wall of evergreens opposite the attack.

Bullets started flying again, and Callie's world consisted of ear-splitting sounds, branches snapping off near her head, and bullets whizzing just past her ear as she ran. At one point, she swore she felt the heat from one bullet pass her cheek; it was that close.

Beau was crouched, on full alert. She didn't know how he could move so quickly with such a heavy pack on his back, but he did. The earth was spongy and muddy; Callie felt the sucking of the clay on her boots as she slipped and slid along the path.

They continued toward what she thought must be a river, and to her relief, she found that the deeper they moved into the grove of evergreens, the less fire they had to dodge. Finally, the firing ceased.

That was when she heard the sounds of the mud sucking at their boots and a gathering wind beginning to blow. Beau continued to trot through the woods, moving among the trees. Callie was breathless as she tried to keep up with him and tried not to worry too much about Dara. She knew Matt would protect her, just as Beau would try to keep her safe.

Callie had thought that the market bombing this past week had been terrifying, but this was far worse. Now she was the target, in hostile territory, with only one man, Beau, to keep them both alive.

Her lungs were burning and her breathing ragged and loud. Finally, Beau paused for a moment, looking around for a huge old tree. He slowed down slightly and gripped her hand. Using the width of the evergreen as protection from gunfire, Beau led her behind it, his M4 up and ready to fire again.

"Sit down," he urged her. "We need to rest a minute."

Nodding, Callie collapsed into the wet pine needles, grateful to sit for just a moment to catch her breath. Beau crouched down near her, pulling off his water tube from across his shoulder.

"Drink," he coaxed, handing it to her.

Callie gave a jerky nod, seeing how nearly colorless Beau's eyes were now. This was the warrior in him, she realized, sucking down the cold water from the CamelBak he carried on his ruck. It tasted so good! She hadn't realized how thirsty she'd become, and now, sated, she pushed the tube back into the loop on his shoulder.

He turned, his gaze stripping her naked as he looked for any injury she might have sustained. "We were ambushed," he told her in a low, raspy voice. "A large, unknown Taliban force hit us, and Matt and I split up to avoid leading them into the village. You and I are heading for the river, and we'll remain in the hills for as long as we can. Matt and Dara are heading for the higher mountains. I'm calling in help from Bagram, but right now we need to get as far away from this van as we can." Beau continued to look around the area. Everything was quiet. "Are you injured at all, Callie?"

"N-no, just scared as hell. I-I wasn't expecting this."

He snorted quietly. "We weren't either. We checked all resources back at Bagram. The area was supposed to be nonlethal. The Taliban has obviously decided to become active now, even though winter is setting in. This is a new strategy for them." Beau kept the rest of his thoughts to himself. The Taliban was constantly changing its tactics. In the past, when the first snows fell on the mountains, they would slink back to their villages or across the border and take a break. Now they were apparently still roving through the area. This was bad news for them: no village was "safe" anymore. He felt bad for the sisters. Callie had mud splattered on her cheek, and her eyes were filled with fear and anxiety.

He handed her the M4. "Hold this while I get my sat phone out of my ruck. I need to call Bagram. If we're lucky, we'll meet a Night Stalker helicopter and two Apache gunships a couple of miles away from here, get picked up and flown back to Bagram."

He stood, shucking off his ruck. Callie held the huge, heavy rifle between her hands. She was no stranger to rifles and pistols, having grown up with them at the family ranch. But this rifle, the M4, was lethal-looking.

She watched as Beau shrugged out of his pack and laid it on the wet forest floor, then quickly opened it up.

Her eyes widened. There were several bullet holes through one side of it and she heard Beau curse beneath his breath as he tore open the ruck, his hands immediately going to the shredded area.

"What?" she asked hoarsely. "What's wrong?" She saw the disappointment for a second in Beau's expression and then, just as quickly, his game face was back in place.

He picked up his sat phone, and she could see it had been shattered by a bullet. "Damn! I can't call Bagram," he muttered. Dropping the destroyed phone into the torn pocket, his mouth thinned.

"W-what does that mean, Beau?" He looked grim, and it scared the hell out of Callie.

He turned to her, his voice low. "It means we can't make contact with our HQ at Bagram. We're on our own." He touched the radio headset he wore. "This radio I'm wearing only has a mile radius on it, Callie. That means we have to get within a mile of Bagram in order to put in a call for help."

The way his mouth flattened, the way he looked at her, the concern burning in his eyes, she felt more afraid than she had in her entire life.

"Doesn't Matt carry a sat phone on him, too, Beau?"

"Yes, he does, but that doesn't guarantee us anything." He reached over, rubbing her arm with his gloved hand. "They're going into the mountains to escape the Taliban, Callie, and in the mountains it's twenty times harder to get a signal out for help. Matt was depending on me to make that call." He tightened his jaw, clearly distressed. He didn't like to let anyone who depended on him down, and now four lives were at stake. "I can't do a damned thing about it."

"B-but," she stammered, keeping her voice low, "couldn't Matt make a call at some point?"

Shrugging, he muttered, "I don't know. Nothing is for sure right now, Callie," and he looked deep into her frightened eyes. His hand grew more firm around her upper arm. "Listen to me. We're going to have to make our way back to Bagram without any help at all. That's a thirty-five-mile hike one way in forest, hills, and finally, some flat desert."

"Oh, God," she whispered. "But what about the Taliban?"

His eyes narrowed as he slowly scanned the area, listening for any unusual sounds. His gaze came back to hers. "They're going to be chasing us, that I know. Unfortunately, we don't know how many are in the group." He shook his head. "I don't even know if we were able to divide up their group by splitting up and going opposite directions. I'm hoping we have." He patted her shoulder. "You're going to have to be brave, Callie. We're in for a brutal run for Bagram, and I'm not going to sugarcoat it for you. That doesn't serve us at all."

"Okay," she said, her voice shaking. "Just tell me what I need to do, Beau."

He smiled tightly, briefly grazing her bright red cheek. "Hang on to my belt. If I suddenly crouch and stop, you do the same. Try not to step on any branches that might snap and make noise. I've no doubt that the Taliban has trackers out and they're following our muddy footprints." He pointed to the mud beneath the brown, pine-needled floor. "It's going to be easy for them to follow us, so I'm going to head for the river with its rocks and gravel along the banks. That should slow them down and, hopefully, throw them off the track."

He turned, frowning, his gaze penetrating the gloom of the forest surrounding them. "Whatever you do, don't speak, and try not to cry out. If you need something, jerk on my web belt. I'll try to slow down enough so you can keep up, but this is going to be tough, so just do your best." He gave her concerned look, and she knew he was worried about her.

Knowing how much he cared helped her tamp down her anxieties. "I'll do it," she promised, grim. "I'm so scared, Beau, for us and for Dara and Matt, too."

His eyes flickered with emotion and then he tucked it away. Emotions could get a person killed. "Your sister is in the best of hands with Matt. He'll take good care of her, Callie, so don't worry about her. Just put all your energy, your heart and soul, into keeping up with me. We've got to make it to that river to throw them off our trail or they will capture us."

He didn't want to say anything other than that, because Beau did not want to have to tell her he'd give his life for her without a moment's hesitation. If they were captured by the Taliban, he knew he'd die fighting for both of them.

Beau purposely didn't go to the worst-case scenario. If they caught Callie, they'd rape her, videotape it, keep her a prisoner, and eventually, either behead her or sell her as a sex slave across the Af-Pak border. She had no idea how brutal the Taliban were and what they would do to her. Every cell in his body screamed, "Protect her!" He'd get her back to the safety of the Army base or die trying.

"Ready?" he asked her, quickly closing up his ruck, standing, and shrugging it back on his shoulders.

Nodding, Callie got to her feet, rubbing her gloves down the sides of her jeans. She was muddy and wished she had some water to clean off her gloves and the knees of her jeans. But that wasn't going to happen. Looking up between the tall trees, she saw more and more gray and turbulent clouds drifting over the valley where they stood. "Couldn't we go to the village for help, Beau?"

Shaking his head, he belted up, took the M4 from her, and clipped it on his chest harness. "No. The Taliban would expect that. And if that village gave us safety, the Taliban could attack and kill a lot of the women, children, and men to try and find us. We can't risk it, gal."

His lips brushed her temple, and she closed her eyes, feeling that powerful sense of protection that Beau always gave her. His kiss was unexpected but couldn't have come at a better time—she realized how badly she needed his touch, his assurance.

"Okay," she said, easing away. "I understand. I don't want anyone else killed." She felt tears behind her eyes and forced them away. "My God, did you see poor Mohammed? He was shot in the head."

"Yeah," Beau uttered. "he was a good man. He didn't deserve what he got."

"They'd do the same to us, wouldn't they?"

He saw the stark terror in Callie's eyes. "Not if I have anything to say about it. Matt and I and the rest of our team do this kind of thing all the time. We're used to working among the enemy. We're good at what we do, Callie. Just keep your faith." He picked up her hand, settling it on his web belt near his left elbow. "Okay?"

Beau didn't want her going to pieces and was depending on her rugged roots as a rancher's daughter, raised in the wilds of Montana and accustomed to a harsh environment. Beau was betting that Callie's backbone was made of titanium—and now it was going to be tested.

"Okay," she said, her voice more steady. Her hope rose a little as he reached back with his gloved hand, squeezing her hand around his belt. Appreciating his thoughtfulness, Callie felt her throat closing with terror of the unknown. She pushed it back. Beau needed her courage, not her fear.

However, she worried about Dara. She trusted Matt's abilities, but her older sister wasn't in great physical shape. Nor was she the type to work out, like Callie was. She would be a huge liability to Matt now that they were making a run for it. Callie was glad that she'd put in her three or four days a week at the gym in Bagram. *If ever a workout would pay off, it's now,* she told herself.

She not only did belly-dancing exercises, she also ran three miles most days on a treadmill. Would it be enough? She didn't know, but she wasn't about to put Beau and herself in jeopardy if she could help it.

Beau looked one last time behind them and then silently moved out at a strong pace. Callie watched what he was doing, so she could emulate his movements. He was careful not to step on any branches that might crack or snap, alerting their enemy to the direction of their whereabouts. Thirty-five miles! It seemed daunting to Callie as she tried to keep up with Beau's long-legged stride. They had soon covered a good distance across the floor of the woods that surrounded them. Everything was silent, but that scared her, especially because there were no birds calling. All she could hear was the wind sifting and singing through the evergreens above them.

They could have died in that van if not for Matt and Beau's quick thinking. Was Dara injured? She hadn't appeared to be. She was white with terror, but Callie hadn't seen any blood on her. But things had happened so swiftly as the two operators had grabbed them out of the van, heading in different directions, that she couldn't really tell. Her heart was pounding, her mouth open as she tried not to make any noise as she breathed. Beau was in a crouch, his M4 ready, and she had no doubt that the Taliban was following them. And the mud on the ground was making them easy targets to follow.

Oh, God . . ., she prayed. *Please help us!*

CHAPTER 10

THEY REACHED THE river in two hours, and by the time they did, Callie was sobbing for breath. Beau had slowed down a number of times so she could rest briefly, and she felt guilty as hell. She was sure that she was slowing them down so much that the enemy would easily catch up with them.

Beau had done his best to find places that hid them—at least, better than if they were just strolling through the open forest. There were hills scattered throughout the region, and often he would find a rockier area for them to cross, rather than continuing along the forest's floor. This left far fewer tracks for their hunters to follow.

Now, her lungs burning, she pressed her hand against her chest as Beau led them to the area where the woods thinned out. Ahead of them lay the dark green waters of the river. It wasn't a wide river, maybe two hundred feet across, with blackish gravel on the shoreline.

Beau suddenly surprised Callie by taking her hand off his belt, bringing her beneath his arm, and holding her close. Callie groaned and sagged weakly against him, grateful for the sense of safety he provided.

"Hold on," he murmured against her ear, kissing her temple. "I'll get you out of this or die trying."

His voice was low and husky, and Callie clung to him, now absolutely terrified. Never had death seemed so close. Would they survive? They could be killed, or even worse, taken prisoner and tortured.

Callie had heard too many gory stories, seen too much evidence on the Internet of what al-Qaeda and the Taliban could do before trotting out their tortured prisoners for the rest of the world to view.

She pressed her face against Beau's shoulder, inhaling his scent. There was so much she wanted to say to him, but this wasn't the time. Besides, he wanted their talk kept to a minimum.

Still, she was heartened by the tender way he cradled her against him, silently infusing her with the strength and confidence that would get them out of this situation.

Sliding her arm around his waist, holding him, she swallowed back her tears and her terror. Sure, she wanted out of this, but that wasn't an option.

"How are you doing?" Beau asked, his voice low, lips against her mussed hair.

"Are you serious?" Callie heard herself saying, and managed a half grin.

"I know," Beau admitted. "I feel the same way. But look—our team has been up and down this river often," he told her. "It goes for about fifteen miles, winding in and out of a lot of hills before we have to strike out away from it. The rocks will hide our tracks and slow the Taliban down. You can't find tracks in gravel unless they're really obvious."

He looked up as the first raindrops struck his face and turned, easing his arm from Callie and drawing her hood up and over her hair. "It's going to rain, and probably snow later," he told her. "Is that jacket of yours rainproof?"

"Yes."

Nodding, he pulled up the hood on his cammo jacket, the bill of his baseball cap protecting his eyes from the rain, which was now gaining strength. "There's a small cave about half a mile south of here. It's never been used, as far as I know, by Taliban or by the goat herders, mostly because it's pretty small. It's not big enough for a band of goats to huddle inside it. Locals will know about it, but the Taliban usually isn't local."

"Are we going to hole up there?"

Beau checked his watch. It was now noon. "Rest a bit," he said, turning, holding her gaze. He saw a red scratch mark on her jaw. "That hurt?" he asked, lightly touching it.

"No. Why?"

"You were hit by some brush there."

"Oh." Callie's mouth twisted. "I don't even feel it, Beau."

"It's the adrenaline," he assured her. "When you're scared, adrenaline dumps into your bloodstream. You can have a broken bone and never feel the pain from it—or a bullet hole through you."

A cold chill worked down through her. "I don't feel the scratch, so I guess the adrenaline is working."

He watched the rain veil coming off the mountains somewhere behind them, stretching out across the narrow valley where this river twisted and turned. "This is gonna be a constant kind of rain for a while," he murmured, holding her gaze. "That's good news for us. The mud that's on our boots will wash off as we skirt the edge of the forest and walk in the gravel. It will make it nearly impossible to track us."

He didn't want to tell Callie just how damned skilled the Taliban were at following their enemies. A good tracker could literally study the gravel and be able to tell where a person had put down the heel of his boot.

Beau didn't want to make her any more anxious than she already was. Yes, he knew it would slow their enemy down, but it wouldn't stop them from trying to locate them. Their only recourse was to stay on the move. Unfortunately, he could see fatigue tightening Callie's flushed features.

"How are you holding up, gal?" He saw Callie's green eyes grow soft for a moment as he grazed her cheek, wanting in some way to help ease her anxiety and fear.

"I'm getting tired. I don't know how far we've gone, but I'm starting to stumble." She looked dismayed, and he knew she felt guilty about holding them back.

"We've probably made about seven miles so far. But we're heading west, not south. Bagram lies to the south. I had to take us here to the river, or we'd have been sitting ducks if we'd headed straight south from where the van was ambushed."

"So we still have thirty-five miles to go?"

"'Fraid so," he said, apology in his voice. "My first priority is getting you to as safe a place as possible. Then we can lay out a plan for moving south."

Her legs felt tired, and she could feel the beginnings of cramps in her calves, but Callie wouldn't complain. Beau had enough on his mind to keep them from falling into enemy hands or worse. She managed a sour smile. "I'd give anything to be in that tub at the Eagle's Nest right now." She watched amusement gleam in his light gray eyes for just a moment.

"I'll get you back there. Maybe not as soon as you'd like, but it'll happen. Just hang on, Callie." He patted her damp, muddy knee. "Come on, I need you to hydrate. If you don't keep drinking water, you're gonna cramp up, and that'll be painful."

Callie drank until she couldn't drink anymore, and Beau drank like a camel. He then pulled two protein bars from a pocket, handing her one after he peeled it open for her.

"Two things we have to do: eat and keep hydrated. We're burning up thousands of calories right now, and we've got a long way to go. Eat it all, okay?"

She did. The rain was thickening until it was a constant gray veil all around them. Sounds became muted, the drops plopping regularly on her jacket's hood and shoulders.

"Is this rain helpful for us?" she asked, hoping for good news of any kind.

"Yes, very. If it keeps up like this, and I hope it does, it can potentially wipe out some of our tracks on the floor of the woods."

"Beau, are you scared, too?" she asked him, savoring the sweet, tasty grains of the protein bar.

"Nah. This is routine for us." He gave her a wry smile, wanting to reassure her and dull her fear. "We're trained up for this, and you aren't. We know the dance out here in the badlands, Callie."

For the next two hours, drenched by rain falling softly around them, they made their way along the riverbank, always hidden by the line of trees. Callie never saw any enemy but heard gunfire from time to time, and that was all she needed to know they were out there, still hunting them.

Beau was a consummate hunter himself, reminding her of her grandpa Graham, who had taught her and Dara how to find and follow deer tracks. She didn't like to see any dead animals, so her grandpa had never allowed the girls to follow him deep into the Montana mountains where he actually went hunting.

Now she was getting a firsthand look at what Delta Force operators did, and if she'd thought their work was dangerous before, she had a whole new perspective on it now. Beau and Matt went out into godforsaken places like this, hunting down HVTs—high-value targets—and keeping the people of this country safe while they routinely laid their own lives on the line to do it.

Yes, Dara had every reason to worry about Matt. Callie was sure that if they were still alive, Dara also had a deeper appreciation for what he did than before. What motivated them to do this kind of thing? Patriotism? It was beyond Callie to understand how one could live in constant danger like this.

NEAR 1500, BEAU could feel Callie really beginning to lag. She was stumbling a lot and fighting to keep up with him, and he could feel her nearing a point of exhaustion. After finding a small cave nestled in one of the larger hills near the river, Beau led Callie through a wall of thick, tall brush that swatted at their faces and bodies. He gripped her hand and brought her close to him, using his own body as a shield to protect her as they popped out the other side, revealing the dark entrance.

Unsure whether or not the cave was occupied, Beau signaled her to move to one side of it and stand quietly while he went in to see if anything or anyone was in there. M4 raised, he crouched and disappeared into the gloom.

After five minutes, he gave her the all clear. Beau led her inside the cave, and guided her to its rear and then down a tunnel. Grayish light spilled into the other end of it, lighting their way. The area was oval, with rocks jutting out here and there, the limestone walls a combination of interwoven shades of white, light gray, and cream. There was another exit, a slender opening that looked like a ragged slit a giant hand had carved into the limestone with a huge blade.

"We can talk here in low voices," Beau reassured Callie, halting her in the small oval cavern. He released her hand and began to unbuckle his ruck, pushing it off his shoulders. "Make yourself at home." He smiled a little, hoping to lighten her mood with some positive news.

Callie slowly pulled the wet hood off her hair. Looking down at her muddy gloves, she pulled them off and sighed. She wished she had a comb as she tried to regather her hair into a ponytail, but the band holding her strands together had broken a while ago.

"Here," Beau urged, taking a dry blanket out of his ruck and placing it alongside the smoothest wall of the cave. "Set your gloves on some of the rocks and let them air-dry."

"And my coat, too?"

"That too," Beau agreed. He pulled out an empty plastic gallon jar from his pack and walked over to the slit, setting it down so the water could run off one rock and drip into it. He added purification tablets to it, just in case. In Afghanistan, bacteria could quickly infect and/or kill you if you drank untreated water.

The air in the cave was warmer than the outside, humid air. Glad to be rid of his vest holding pockets of ammo magazines, Beau put everything on one end of the blanket, where he could grab it in a hurry, if necessary.

"Have you been in here before?" Callie asked in a quiet tone. She was so happy to get out of her coat and hung it on a nearby jagged outcropping.

"Many times. Our team has camped in here during the daylight hours and then we go active at night." He stripped down to his dry T-shirt and cammos, taking off his baseball cap, running his fingers through his long, thick hair.

Giving Callie a critical look, he saw her fingers were white. Moving to her, he took her hands into his, feeling how cold and wet they were.

"They're pretty numb," she admitted, standing so close to him that she could feel the heat rolling off him. Even though the temperature was falling and it was chilly outside, they had been hiking at a fast, steady pace.

"Let's get you warmed up then," he growled, releasing her hands. Turning, Beau pulled out a sleeping bag from his ruck. He laid it out and opened it up. "Come here."

She came over, feeling how stiff her knees felt, how tight her calves were, screaming at her to sit down and rest.

As if reading her mind, Beau said, "Come on, sit down with me. I want to get you warmed up."

"Best invitation I've had all day." Callie grinned weakly, coming to sit on the soft sleeping bag.

Beau's arm went around her shoulders, drawing her against his tall, lean body. "You've earned this," he breathed against her hair, kissing her temple, wrapping her up beside him. She melted like warm honey against him, and he could feel her exhaustion. Callie, he was learning, was pretty good at hiding her feelings from him. However, Beau needed her to be honest about how she was doing so he could pace himself against her condition.

She wrapped her arm around his middle, snuggling beneath his arm, her face pressed against his chest, her knees drawn up against his lower body.

"Better?" he asked, inhaling her scent, closing his eyes for just a moment, loving her more than he could tell her right now. Beau could feel a slight tremor through her.

"Better," Callie whispered. "I needed this . . . thank you . . ."

He looked at her, concerned. "I want you to rest, Callie. Close your eyes. If you can nap, that would be great. We're safe in here." That was a lie.

"We aren't leaving here soon, then?"

Hearing the hope in her voice, he said, "We're staying here until dark. Then it will be time to move again. You've got about two hours to nap. I'll hold you safe, gal."

His words put out the fires of her anxiety, and Callie sighed, surrendering to Beau in every possible way. Her voice slurred as she whispered, "I'm worried about Dara . . ."

"She's in good hands with Matt. They'll be okay," he reassured her, sliding his hand down across her unruly red hair, the ends damp and rain-sodden. "Save your energy for yourself, Callie. Go to sleep . . ."

An hour later, Beau sat there on guard. One of them had to remain awake and alert. His mind whirling with thoughts, questions, he couldn't help wondering how Matt was doing. Dara wasn't nearly as fit as Callie, and he knew Matt would have his hands full trying to escape with her in tow.

Fortunately, his team had been trained to deal with unexpected conditions as they were, not as they would be if ideal.

He had let Callie think they were safe, and he held her, sharing his body heat with her, hoping it would dry her, warm her, and help her recoup. Night was a natural protection against the Taliban, who still didn't have night-vision goggles. Therefore, at night the enemy always camped somewhere, made tea, ate dinner, and then slept throughout the night.

Taliban were usually active only during daylight hours. Beau never took that as gospel, though, because some warlord from Pakistan might spend the money to buy his soldiers night-vision goggles. That would allow them to roam the night like the Delta and SEAL teams did.

His heart turned to Callie, and he looked at her tenderly. Her hair tickled his cheek, and he ached to take her out of this hellhole they'd just stepped into. Thirty-five miles, plus the seven miles they'd already walked to the river, was a lot for any person to undertake. It wasn't unusual for his team to cover ten to fifteen miles a night, depending on the territory and geological conditions. His body was so toned physically that without Callie in tow, he could have been halfway to Bagram by now—and a hell of a lot farther from the Taliban he knew were tracking them.

Callie. Damn, he was proud of her. She had been brave, hadn't complained once, and had kept her tears to herself. All she'd shown him was fierce determination in those green eyes of hers. She had heart, but he'd always known that about her. Callie was a fighter. She wouldn't sit down and cry or be a victim saying she couldn't do something. No, she'd stepped up to the plate, done what was asked of her, and kept up at the best speed she could. Damn, he loved this woman.

Beau moved that word around inside his head, allowing it to finally penetrate his heart. They hadn't known each other that long, but from the first there had been something beautiful growing between them. He'd known they'd be good in bed together, and he hadn't been disappointed.

The biggest hurdle was getting Callie to allow herself to maybe love him someday. Beau knew without question that he was falling in love with her. But their relationship was young and this unexpected ambush could shatter the dream he held for them, even if he was able to get her to the safety of Bagram.

She felt so damn small, soft, and curvy beneath his arm now, huddled up against him, her arm wound around his waist. He could feel the slight rise and fall of her breasts against his chest, exuding her special womanly fragrance.

He wanted to dream, damn it, but right now, sitting in this cave, knowing the enemy ranged this area routinely, he didn't dare unleash his imagination. He'd wanted to dream of a future for them, but now, this. Neither of them would have a future if he couldn't get Callie safely out of this hot mess.

His mind turned to Matt and his sat phone. If Matt could get high enough up a mountain peak, if the weather conditions cooperated, he might be able to shoot a call off a passing satellite, beaming it down to their HQ at Bagram. *Maybe.* Matt was probably wondering what had happened to them, as well. If he tried to raise sat phone contact with Beau, he'd fail and figure something had happened to the sat phone, or that it had low batteries. He wouldn't think the worst because equipment failed routinely out here in this unforgiving land.

But the worst could happen. And Matt had expected Beau to make that call to Bagram, to get two QRFs, Quick Reaction Force, out here to pick them up. But that wasn't going to happen. Ordinarily, Beau would not have felt as bad as he did right now because it was common for Delta Force operators to be pitched out into enemy territory without any means of contact. Radios went on the blink all the time. Some got shot up.

Communications in Afghanistan sucked at best, due to the interference from the mountains, and this was one of those inconvenient times. He did know one good thing: Matt had filed a mission plan with their HQ on going into this village: he'd advised that if they didn't arrive back at Bagram by 1700, the captain should put out an alert to find them. It was near three p.m., so two hours had to pass before their CO would hit the alarm button, knowing they were missing.

His mouth twisted as he watched the rainfall outside the cave slit. Drones didn't do well in this kind of weather, so none would be launched. He was aware that, being up in the mountains, Matt and Dara had probably run into one helluva snowstorm. While Beau and Callie were getting rain now, which was a mixed blessing, that could change, too.

His mind grappled with the realization that no action would be taken to find any of them until there was a big improvement in this messy weather. *Damn it.*

The only good thing was that the Taliban didn't like getting wet or cold, either. There were plenty of caves in the hills next to this river, where the enemy was probably hunkered down. He imagined them making tea, and then staying warm and dry until tomorrow morning.

Beau knew that if he and Callie left here at nightfall continuing to head south toward Bagram, they'd put a lot of distance between themselves and their enemy. But if the Taliban were on horseback . . . well, he didn't want to even go there.

Riding a horse and tracking the enemy was a lot faster than going on foot, and most Taliban rode horses. None of the possibilities for rescue looked good to Beau. He knew the military would try to find them—but right now, the inclement weather would prevent a drone from being launched into the cloudy sky. Sure, Apache helicopters operated in all kinds of weather and could fan out to try to find them. But where would they start to look? Their overturned white van, so well hidden in that copse of evergreens, would be invisible to the pilots manning those combat helicopters. And the van would not give off any heat signature either.

He hoped their captain would tell the Apache pilots to start at the Shinwari village they were supposed to visit. They might be able to send out a Black Hawk with a Delta team on board, to talk to the chieftain of that village. He could ask if they had ever arrived.

Beau knew the operators would then backtrack to the only road leading into that village. But they had been six miles away from the village when they were attacked. And with their lousy luck, the weather was probably going to turn to snow as the night deepened, with temperatures plummeting. Beau figured the rest of his team would be rabid to get out and locate them, no matter what it took, no matter the inclement weather. Delta operators worked, no matter the season or conditions.

But even if they found the van and Mohammed's body, they would have to conclude that the four of them had been captured by Taliban. Or else, they were on the run with radios on the fritz. Beau knew the operators would be looking for and following tracks to try to determine what had happened.

He wasn't sure what he himself would do in such a scenario. Their team would hope desperately that the four of them had escaped. The operators wouldn't know they'd split up until they started looking around for tracks, and Beau knew they would. Delta operators were good at putting puzzle pieces together, and sooner or later, their team would start to get the picture and realize they'd split up so they could make it back to Bagram.

And then? Well, that could be several days in the offing. Weather, especially snow, would cover up their tracks. On the route Matt had planned to take, snow would have wiped out any trail he left almost immediately as he moved up in altitude toward that pass at nine thousand feet.

Damn, this didn't look good. Beau had to focus on the knowledge that Delta soldiers didn't give up on teammates and wouldn't leave any man behind. They would expend every effort and scour this area mercilessly, trying to locate all of them.

Callie stirred, and he held her a little more tightly as she whimpered. It was a small sound, but it tore at him. And then she nuzzled into his chest, sighed, and fell back into a deeper level of sleep, her arm loosening across his waist, once more sagging against him. He leaned down, pressing a light kiss to her uncombed hair.

He worried about what her parents and grandparents would feel like once an Army officer drove out to their ranch to tell them that their two daughters were MIA. The devastation to their close family would be equivalent to a bomb going off in their home.

The fog of war, as Beau knew too well, was capricious at best. Was he glad that sat phone had taken the bullet meant for him? Yes. But it also put both their lives in jeopardy. Worse, Matt and Dara were in equal trouble unless Matt could get his sat phone to work in those damn mountains, which was pretty unlikely.

And that left both of them only one option: to go it alone and forget about being saved by anyone else. And know, for damn sure, the Taliban was hot on their trail and it was just a matter of time until they would locate and close in on them.

At that point, Beau knew it would come down to a battle, and that he had to protect Callie. She had to survive this—even if he didn't make it. He was responsible for her and would fulfill his promise to keep her as safe as he could. But would it be enough?

CHAPTER 11

C ALLIE MOANED SOFTLY, feeling Beau's lips against her hairline. She was so tired she wanted to remain in that deep, healing sleep, but she knew she had to wake up. Slowly, she inhaled the scent of his warm, strong body. Even now, it made her heart pulse, awakening the passion he had stirred within her before all this had happened.

She loved this man. She knew it and she admitted it. Life was too short to delude herself about her feelings now. She slid her hand up his chest, feeling his dry, warm T-shirt and the powerful curve of the muscles beneath it. For just a moment she languished in that in-between state, not really awake, not really asleep. Her senses were coming back now, and she relished the way his skin tightened as she smoothed her palm across his chest in a caress. She heard him chuckle.

"Hey," he murmured, kissing the top of her ear. "You need to start waking up, gal. It's time to get going . . ."

Making a muffled sound of displeasure against his chest, Callie tried to snuggle even more closely against him. She heard Beau give another slight laugh and he threaded his fingers through her hair, massaging her scalp, and that made her grateful for his tenderness under the circumstances.

"Now that I have your attention . . ." He smiled against her temple.

"Don't . . . stop . . . ," she said, her voice muffled against him. His fingers were making her scalp tingle and radiate with such delight that Callie sighed and sank into his care.

"You're such a pussycat," he growled, amusement in his low tone.

"Mmm, I am . . . You make me that way . . ." Her voice sounded far away, and Beau felt wonderful in every way to her. As she awakened more, Callie became aware of how stiff her legs felt as she started to untuck them from against him. Grimacing, she opened her eyes.

"Ah," he drawled, "the princess has decided to join the real world."

Snorting softly, Callie slowly eased into a sitting position next to Beau. Her thick, long hair fell around her, and she raised her fingers, pushing the bulk of it away from her face. Looking around, she saw it was now dusk outside the slit. "What time is it?"

"Seventeen hundred." Beau could barely see her face in the grayness. He cupped her cheek where the scratch lay against her jaw. "How are you feeling? And"—he pinned her with an intense look—"don't sugarcoat this for me, okay? I need to know what shape you're in physically, Callie."

"My legs," she muttered, straightening them out in front of her. "They're really stiff."

"Yeah, that comes from all the walking and trotting we did. Any cramps?"

Shaking her head, she rubbed her face, trying to fight the need to simply lie down on that sleeping bag and rest some more. "Just . . . tired. Really tired, but we've been running hard," she managed to say, her voice still drowsy.

"Yeah," he murmured, getting to his knees. He reached into his ruck and pulled out two MREs. "Hungry?"

Her stomach growled.

Callie grinned belatedly. "I guess I am. What are those?"

"MREs, 'meals ready to eat.' I always keep a bunch of them in my ruck. I'm going to fix us dinner and then we're gonna have to leave this nice, dry place."

Rising, her lower legs screaming in protest, Callie began to slowly do stretching exercises to ease the pain. "I need to go to the bathroom."

Beau pointed toward the slit. "Go over there. I promise, I won't watch."

"Like you haven't seen me bare-butt naked before?" she teased a little, the sleep beginning to dissolve.

"I think you have the nicest ass I've ever seen," he told her, preparing the MREs with quick efficiency. "But if I watch you, I'm likely going to say to hell with our food and carry you back here and make love to you."

Callie absorbed that growl of his. Even now, Beau was so damned sexy. But she knew he was teasing her. They were in a dangerous situation, and there was no way he'd compromise them like that. Keeping her tone light, like his, she said, "It's nice to know you appreciate my body."

"My appreciation stretches far beyond that sweet body of yours, but I can't show you right now, gal."

His thick, husky tone left no doubt in Callie's mind that he wanted her. It sent a heated riffle through her, landing squarely between her legs. "Not a good idea to go there right now, even though I'd like to," she admitted, standing and watching him work on the MREs.

"You're right. It's not the time to think about the good things life can bring us. We need to eat, hydrate, and then leave."

Nodding, she yawned, placing her hand against her lips. "Okay . . ."

Smiling absently, Beau watched her walk stiffly toward the slit. Outside, the rain continued to fall. The temperature was lowering, just as he knew it would. True to his word, he turned his back toward the slit, giving Callie a modicum of privacy.

For the next fifteen minutes, they ate in silence. Beau watched her carefully for clues as to how Callie was really doing. She was a rough rancher's daughter, and he knew she would never whine or complain. Aside from scratches from some of the brush they'd had to push through, she looked reasonably fit considering the ordeal she'd been through.

"That was good," Callie murmured, folding up the package and handing it back to him. "I'm so glad you're carrying these."

"It's what we eat when we're out on an op," he said, placing it back into his ruck. They never left anything behind. If the Taliban spotted their trash, it would tell them a lot. They would remember this cave as one to spot check in the future for enemies contained within it.

"Did you get some sleep?" Callie searched his darkly shadowed face.

"Someone has to remain on guard, darlin'."

Her heart widened with appreciation, and love for this man poured through her. He lifted his eyes to hers for a moment, and she felt that invisible embrace he always gave her. Gratefully absorbing it, she said, "You have to be exhausted, Beau."

"Nah," he murmured, finishing off his meal and tucking the used packet back into his ruck. "I'm used to this kind of gig."

Shaking her head, Callie whispered, "This is a hell of a way to find out what you Delta Force operators really do."

Nodding, Beau got to his knees, rummaging through his pack. "Well, for now you're one of us." He handed her a set of NVGs and pulled out his own pair. "We're going to wear these. It will help us see through the night. Ever worn a pair before?"

She took them. "No."

For the next few minutes, Beau instructed her on how to work them. "We'll be able to navigate through the night because we can see everything, including anyone in the area, human, animal, or bird. But I don't think we'll see any Taliban, because they hunker down and sleep during the night hours. They don't usually have NVGs like we do."

"That's good," she said, relief in her voice. And then she gave him a worried look. "Beau, does my family know what's happened to us?"

He decided to tell her the truth, hard as it would be for her to hear it. "Yes, I'm sure an Army officer has already visited them."

"Oh, God," she managed to say, her hand against her throat. "What would they tell them?"

"That you and Dara are MIA, Callie. 'Missing in action.'"

"Oh, no," she said softly. "They must be so worried!"

He reached over, gripping her hand. "It's going to be hard on them, because they aren't going to know what happened to either of you."

"B-but, will the officer tell them anything else? That we're being looked for out here?"

He nodded. "Yes, the officer will inform them that they're mounting a search for you, for sure. They'll most likely say that you two were heading out to an Afghan village to render humanitarian aid but didn't show up there, so you're officially missing."

She pulled her hand out of his, pressing it against her lips, tears glittering in her eyes. "This is going to tear them up."

"It will," Beau agreed quietly, packing his ruck and Velcroing it shut. "It's the hardest thing we have to do, and we hate having to do it."

"And what about your parents, Beau, and Matt's? Will they be told you're both MIA, too?"

"Yes, of course," he admitted heavily. His parents had never had an Army officer go to their cabin to inform them that one of their sons was MIA. He looked up to see the devastation in her shadowy green eyes, the way her soft lips twisted with grief.

"Callie," he said, and reached over, gripping her hand where it rested on her thigh. "Don't go there. You have to remove all your feelings from this situation. You can't operate out there in the night worrying about how this is going to affect everyone, you just can't."

Giving a jerky nod, Callie whispered, "I know . . ."

"Good." He gave her hand a comforting squeeze before he released it. "The best way to help your family is to focus on what we're doing right now. The more attention and alertness we put into our hike, the faster we'll get back to Bagram."

"I-I understand. And once we get to safety, will everyone's families be notified?"

One corner of his mouth lifted. "Count on that, Callie. And they'll do it just as fast as humanly possible so the families don't suffer unnecessarily." He saw a little relief enter her worried expression.

There wasn't a chance in hell that Beau was going to tell her that their safety was far from assured. Let Callie keep her hopes up for both of them.

IT HAD TAKEN Callie a good hour to get used to the flat, two-dimensional display of the NVGs she wore. Beau had a more advanced set that gave him three-dimensional capability, and he was doing his best to lead her so she wouldn't stumble or fall. The rain was constant, with more gusts coming their way as they threaded in and out of hilly areas along the river.

Beau had set a good pace, but not as fast as before, and for that, Callie was grateful. Rain ran down her face, but there wasn't anything she could do about it. Sometimes it blurred her NVGs. Her fingers were permanently cramped into a clawlike position around his web belt. The gravel was often thick, making her feel as if her sore legs were slogging through peanut butter. She could see everything in grainy green, which buoyed her. They never spoke.

Beau had warned her that they could only use hand signals, and that if she needed something, she should yank on his belt to alert him. Her gloves were still soggy and her fingers had become numb hours ago. Callie could see white wisps of her breath in the frigid air. She fought back tears of frustration and gamely trudged on, trying not to think about Dara and Matt or their families. She was sure everyone was distraught over the news that they all were MIA.

Callie realized that going through this ordeal was changing her feelings about going off to Afghan villages. Now she swore that if she was lucky enough to survive this situation with Beau, she was *never* going to another village outside the wire. It just wasn't worth it. She knew her family worried constantly about her working in Kabul six months of the year. Maybe she needed to take a step back and really look at her decision, and choose a different lifestyle for the future. She didn't belittle the good she'd done in the five years she'd spent off and on in Afghanistan. But at what price to herself and her family? Death by the enemy, if caught? She wanted to live. She was seeing everything she'd done thus far in this country through another lens right now. There were choices, for sure. And right now she had to focus on surviving so she could look at them when her life wasn't on the line.

Callie felt terrible that she'd tried to convince Dara that this would be a safe trip. How wrong she'd been! And what if Dara died? She shook off the thought. *Don't go there!* she told herself.

Distracted, she stumbled over a stone and reached out as she fell to her knees on the sharp gravel. "Damn!" she muttered, excruciating pain coursing through her.

Instantly, Beau halted and turned, dismayed at the sight of Callie on the ground, her knees bleeding freely through her jeans, her face white.

Callie sobbed, biting back most of the sound as she rolled over and tried to sit up.

"Don't move," Beau rasped, crouching beside her, his hand gripping her shoulder. "Tell me where you're hurt."

Groaning, she clutched her left leg. "Oh, God, Beau, it hurts . . . the pain, it's so much!"

"Where?"

His voice was low, quiet, and calm, and it moved her away from impending hysteria as she breathed raggedly, her fingers gripping her lower leg. "M-my calf . . . it's on fire!"

"Okay, let me look," he said soothingly, moving to her knee, leaning over her, running his hand knowingly down her left calf. The moment he encountered a huge knot of muscle, Callie cried out, the agony intensifying.

"Hold on . . . ," Beau said, and slipped his hands beneath her back and knees, lifting her up in his arms. It wasn't going to be the most pleasant ride for her because she was crushed against his rifle, not his body. Whimpers of agony jammed in her throat as she threw her arms around his neck. "I'm taking us deeper into the woods. There's a nearby cave, and we can rest there. You've got a bad leg cramp, Callie, but we can fix it. Just hang on . . ."

She collapsed against him, biting down hard on her lower lip as she felt the sudden, unexpected knifelike pain ripping through her leg.

"I-I'm sorry," she sobbed, pressing her face against his wet neck.

"Hush, it's all right. You're going to be okay, Callie. Just a few more minutes and we'll be there . . ."

The cramp in her leg seemed to multiply like angry, writhing snakes twisting her muscles, and all she could do was whimper, her lips tightly shut because she knew she had to be silent.

Oh, God! Had her cries alerted any nearby Taliban? Panic surged through Callie as Beau carried her into a narrow cave, the opening partially visible, the rest covered over with thick brush.

He moved quickly behind what he termed "a wing of rock" near the entrance. It was a wall of limestone, about five feet long. Behind it was a small room, which gave them a place to hide from possible prying eyes. He knelt on the dry dirt, placing her gently down and positioning her back against the smooth stone surface. Leaning close, he said, "Don't move and don't make a sound. I have to clear this cave first. I'll be back as soon as I can . . ."

He was gone like a shadow. Callie kept the NVGs on, watching him pull up his M4, unsafe it, and disappear. She tried to lean down and touch her cramped calf, but as soon as she touched it, more pain erupted around it. Teeth clenched, she leaned back, breathing raggedly, trying not to cry out in agony. She had never experienced anything like this before. It felt like knives repeatedly being thrust and twisted into her balled-up calf muscles.

For a while, she lost track of time, gripping her upper left thigh as if holding it with both hands would stop the pain from drifting up her leg. It didn't do any good. When Beau reappeared, she had no idea of how much time had passed. She watched as he placed his rifle against the wall, got rid of his ruck, and quickly opened it up.

Callie could hear herself breathing raggedly, the sound carrying around them. Guilt ate at her. She wasn't being quiet at all. She was putting them at risk because she couldn't gut out the pain. What must Beau think of her now?

"Here," he said quietly, "take your glove off and open your palm."

Stymied by this request, she did as he asked, and with her NVGs, she saw he had, of all things, a small saltshaker. What the hell? He shook the salt grains into her opened palm.

"Okay, pop the salt in your mouth. Now," he ordered.

What good was this going to do? She did as he asked and popped more salt into her mouth. By the time he'd put the saltshaker back into a plastic bag and dropped it into his ruck, the pain in her leg had started to reduce. Shocked, she stared at him.

"The pain is leaving," she managed to say. "What did you do?"

"Good! I'll tell you in a minute. I want you to lean back and relax. I'm going to get the rest of that charley horse worked out of your calf. And listen: try not to scream, okay?"

Beau quickly pulled up her damp pant leg up to just below her knee and gently wrapped his hands around that fist-sized knot in her calf. This kind of leg cramp was the worst you could get, and he knew just how painful they were. He felt her flinch as he brought his hands lightly around the knot.

"Is the pain still going down?" he asked her.

"Y-yes."

"By how much? Give me a percentage."

Her mind was swimming with the shock of the pain and she could barely think. "At least half," she gasped.

Beau said, "Good," and explained, "You're dehydrated, and this is what leg muscles do when they don't get enough water. That salt is replacing what was lost from your sweating, Callie. I'm going to give you more salt in another minute to continue to help reduce the knot, and then I'm gonna have to massage the rest of it out of your calf by hand. And it's going to hurt like hell and you're going to have to *not* scream. Okay?"

Callie gave a jerky nod. "I can't imagine it hurting any more than it does now." She saw Beau's mouth thin. His hands radiated heat. The skin was so sensitive that his callused hands around it made it hurt even more. But she didn't pull her leg away. "W-will it go away?"

"In time," he said soothingly. He gave her more salt and waited a few minutes. "What's the pain level now, Callie?"

"Umm, maybe forty percent compared to a hundred percent before I put the salt in my mouth."

He nodded. "That's good. Okay, hang on and jam your fist into your mouth."

He made a movement, and a scream tore up through her chest. Callie bit down on the fist she'd placed against her mouth. Her back arched, her nostrils flared, and a sob erupted from her as his fingers, long and kneading, began to work on the last of that angry, twisted knot.

For a moment, Callie thought she'd black out from the pain as it rolled up through her in wave after wave. And then, after the initial reaction, Beau's knowing fingers began to loosen those tight, gnarled muscles and got them to start relaxing.

Feeling the pain exploding within her, then going away minutes later made her breathe in ragged sobs, her hand still against her mouth. She opened her eyes to slits, watching as Beau leaned over her leg, his mouth set, his whole attention on the damned cramp.

Finally, the pain began to dissolve each time he nudged and forced another muscle to let go, to untwist and lengthen. She dropped her hand into her lap, breathing harshly, her head tipped against the rocky surface, eyes closed, shaking internally from that gutting agony.

"There," he murmured, beginning to smooth her muscles, stroking them, kneading them until they behaved once more. "You did good, Callie. Just try to relax now."

"Easy for you to say," she grunted.

Beau smiled, understanding how she felt. "You're going to be okay now, gal. I'll give you more table salt in a minute, and then you'll drink a couple of pints of water. We'll hole up here until you're stable again."

Closing her eyes, her breathing began to steady. It was not as explosive and harsh sounding as it had been, and she tried to ease her fingers out of a fist resting on her thighs.

"God, that was horrible, Beau," she gasped.

"Yeah, I know. I've had a couple of those myself. Everyone on my team gets them from time to time. They're no fun." He continued to smooth her calf, his hands firm, trying to get the muscles to remain relaxed.

Shaking her head, Callie muttered, "You guys really do go through hell."

"Sometimes," he agreed in a drawl. "But it's not always like what you're experiencing. We do a lot of good out there in the badlands, and when we nail an HVT, it's like Christmas to us. Makes everything we have to endure out here to find the sonofabitch worth it, believe me."

"I just never realized," she began lamely. "You guys suffer so much . . . so much . . ."

"Now, don't you wander down into that box canyon," he counseled, amusement in his tone. He gave her calf one more gentle stroke and then pulled her trouser leg down over it. "There, good as new."

She snorted, watching as he moved to his ruck. Callie held out her hand toward him and he shook some salt grains into it again. "What is this? The latest secret for dealing with charley horses?" she asked wryly, tipping her head back, allowing the salt to slide into her mouth and dissolve. She was starved for the taste of it, figuring it was a symptom telling her she was deficient in the mineral.

"Oh, just a little country medicine my ma gave me," he offered. Pulling out a quart bottle of water, he opened it and then handed it to her. "Sip, don't glug. We're gonna rest here for at least thirty minutes. You'll need to get water into your system, so go slow but sure."

Right now, Callie would do anything he asked of her. "Can I take off my NVGs?"

"Sure, go ahead."

"Beau, how are you doing?" she asked, concerned about him.

"Fine."

Callie's mouth twisted. "Would you tell me the truth?"

He chuckled again, that rumble through his chest. "I have never lied to you, gal. I'm not starting now, okay?" He moved his head in her direction after he pushed up his NVGs.

She couldn't see his eyes, but she could feel that invisible embrace again, and she hungrily soaked it up. "Okay," she whispered. "You just seem . . . well . . . indestructible—at least, in comparison to me."

"I am. I've had many years at this work. My body is primed for it. Yours isn't."

"I guess I'm slowing us down."

"I was getting ready to call for a rest anyway."

"Are you *sure* about that?"

"Yep. Now, keep sippin' the water, because you have to hydrate, or that charley horse will come back with a vengeance. I don't think you want another session with that, do you?"

"God, no!" she agreed.

"We're going to have to stop about every thirty minutes and hydrate you from now on. Even in cold, wet, rainy weather like this we lose a lot of water to sweating because of the pace we're keeping."

She dutifully continued to sip the water. "Tell me about the table salt, Beau."

He sat crouched in front of her, his long arms resting over his knees. "Baylee Ann Thorn's mother is a homeopath. She's our hill doctor up on Black Mountain. One time when I was home on leave shortly after joining Delta Force, I was telling her about the cramps I kept getting in my calves on long marches. She said to always carry a shaker of table salt because of the loss of salt in our sweat. If we took some salt grains, it would not only ease the cramp, it would get our electrolytes stabilized until we could get proper hydration. I found that to be true. Our whole team, including Matt, carries a saltshaker. They found out it works like magic."

"It sure did on me," Callie whispered gratefully. "It took that pain level down to nearly bearable until you started massaging that knot out of my calf."

"Yeah," he said softly and apologetically, "but this experience teaches you to hydrate, and we're just gonna have to be more watchful and stop to get you to drink more often."

"I'm a liability," she groused, unhappy.

Beau reached out, gripping her glove. "Hey, understand this, Callie. You're never a liability in my world."

She knew Beau was trying to stop her from feeling guilty and appreciated his low, warm response. Beau enclosed her hand, giving it a squeeze of reassurance. His courage was unflagging. "Ever since meeting you," she said, "I wanted to know what the rest of you was like."

He snorted softly. "Be careful what you ask for. Right?"

A faint smile tugged at one corner of her mouth. "I'm not sorry this happened, Beau. I always thought you were an incredible man. I felt your warrior side was pretty much hidden from me."

"Oh? That I came off like some type B office pogue?" he jested.

She smiled. "I loved the gentle side of you I saw at the orphanage. I knew you couldn't be Delta Force if you weren't a badass warrior."

Beau stroked her hand. "Well, now you've seen me, warts and all, gal. I hope this doesn't mean we're going to separate once we get back to Bagram."

Callie heard the teasing in his voice, his hand so warm and dry compared to hers. "If anything," she whispered, suddenly emotional, "you're such a hero in my eyes and heart. I just hope you don't think less of me and walk away from me if we make it back to Bagram." His hand tightened around hers.

"Not a chance of that happening, gal, so don't ever go that direction. You're just as courageous as I am. You're not a quitter. You're the fighter I always thought you would be if you were in a desperate situation. I was proved right." He released her hand and even in the darkness, he found her thick hair, stroking it gently. "If anything, I can't see my life without you in it after we make it back to Bagram. Okay?"

CHAPTER 12

B Y THE TIME dawn was rising on the horizon, Callie was exhausted. She had no idea how far they'd traveled. The rain had, thankfully, stopped a few hours ago, but her fingers were still wet and numb. Beau went around a hill; she was always amazed that he remembered where caves were located. He led her into one that required them to crawl in on their hands and knees, making her bite back a groan.

Once inside, the bare light revealed what she was beginning to call a "comfy cave." She heard water running, and with her NVGs on she could see water dripping from above into a small pool. She waited by the entrance as Beau cleared the place. There wasn't much to clear because it was oval shaped with rocky walls and fine silt for a floor. It smelled musty and humid from the outside air.

Beau came over, allowing his rifle to lie against his chest harness. He gripped her soggy, gloved hand and gave a gentle tug for her to follow him. Every step was agony, her knees feeling as if they would crack and fall off. She knew he was doing his best to keep them safe, and her heart swelled with love for him. He was at greater risk because she couldn't keep up a killing pace for hours on end like he could. She was painfully aware that she was no match for his ability to endure hardship.

She followed him to the rear of the cave, where it was darker. Callie had faithfully hydrated every half hour, and so far, there were no more of those horrible leg cramp events.

Beau brought her closer to him and whispered, "There's a tunnel here. It twists and winds, but at the end of it, there's another cave that has an exit point in case we need to leave in a hurry. Just follow me. Watch your step, because there are lots of rocks jutting out of the floor, and they can trip you up."

She nodded, saying nothing and trying to catch her breath. In another minute, Callie found herself in a second cave, which had another entrance-exit point covered with thick brush. Here, the cave floor was smooth, without silt or sand in it.

Even better, she saw another small pool of water. The cave wasn't high, perhaps seven feet tall, and was rounded, in comparison to the other one, which was more oval-shaped.

Beau shrugged out of his ruck near the pool, opened it, and laid out some items. He turned and pushed up his NVGs. "We can talk quietly in here," he told her. "You won't need your goggles anymore." He pointed to his ruck. "There's a washcloth, a bar of soap, and a dry towel I've laid out for you. There's also that water so you can clean up a bit."

Nodding, Callie pulled the goggles down around her neck. She rubbed her face and grinned weakly. "That sounds wonderful. Thanks . . ."

"I need to go back into the other cave and sweep it clean of our footprints," he told her. "I'll be back in a few minutes."

Nodding, Callie watched him move like the silent ghost he was. Beau had to be as tired as she was. Getting used to the rhythm of black ops, she knew he was preparing to rest during the daylight hours, when they would hide and sleep. They walked at night because they could roam unseen by nearby enemy troops. How far were they from Bagram?

Her stomach growled and she realized she was starving! Getting out of her raincoat, she hung it on a rocky outcropping and pulled off her gloves, all soaked and muddy. She placed each of them on a rock near her wet jacket. The idea of getting fed was very appealing to her.

She never heard Beau reenter the cave until he knelt down next to her at the pool. The light was increasing, and she saw the gleam of sweat across his face, seeing more clearly the toll their run was taking on him. "Is everything okay?"

"Yes," he murmured, washing his hands in the water. "It feels nice to get clean," he said, giving her a warm look. "How are you doing? I need a report from you."

She tried for a light smile. "Till today, I've never had my knees feel like they were going to crack and shatter on me."

"That comes from the rough country we're traversing. It's hard on all the body's joints, but especially our knees," he said. "How about that left calf?"

"It's still tender," she admitted, soaping the cloth, eager to wash her face and neck. "But it's not cramping, thank God."

He smiled a little. "Yeah, makes you a little gun-shy once a charley horse bites you."

For the next five minutes, they didn't speak. Once Callie cleaned off her face, neck, and hands, she handed the soap and washcloth to Beau. It felt wonderful to have a dry towel to pat off her face and neck.

Callie swore she would never take for granted the small, everyday pleasures in her life. Beau was on his knees, resting on the heels of his boots, and she could see the fatigue in his bloodshot eyes.

"If I wasn't with you, where would you be by now?" she surprised him by asking.

Beau smiled a little and hung the damp towel over a rock. He knew where that question was going. "We're making good time, Callie. In fact, by my estimate, we covered about ten miles. We've already turned on the south leg of our journey and we're roughly twenty-five miles from Bagram. Add on that seven miles we had to walk to the river first, and you've covered seventeen miles."

He saw her eyes widen with a pleased sense of shock. As weary as he was, his lower body stirred because she was so damned beautiful to him. "So see?" he teased. "We're doing fine."

"That's such good news," she whispered, then felt her eyes filling with tears. "I didn't realize how far we'd come."

"We're making progress, gal." Beau sensed her guilt over being slow and saw it clearly in her eyes. He'd gone through all the scenarios Callie was probably beating herself up over. She'd been out to this particular village four times a year, and she'd talked her big sister, who hadn't wanted to go outside the wire, into going with her to the village. Now she was guilt-ridden for placing Dara in this kind of danger. And even Beau didn't know what was happening with Matt and Dara. He wished he did, because then he could try to alleviate the terror he saw banked deep in Callie's eyes. He knew the doctor had no training or knowledge of this kind of situation, but she was with Matt and couldn't have been in better hands.

Callie, at least, was in decent shape, thanks to her belly dancing and gym routine. She was more physically fit than most other civilians, including her older sister. Beau was glad he had Callie with him, because she was a stubborn fighter who didn't give up. He was grateful for her strong Montana ranch upbringing, and he hoped Dara would dig deep and find that same strength. Otherwise, she and Matt were in a shitload of trouble up in those unforgiving mountains.

"Hungry?" he asked, rooting around in his rucksack.

"I'm starving," Callie admitted.

"Hmm, I like a woman with a good appetite." His eyes sparkled. "And who enjoys her food," he added, hauling out two more MREs. "Let's go over there and I'll spread out the sleeping bag and blanket for us."

"Let me help, okay?" Callie offered, needing to contribute something to their comfort level.

Beau nodded. "Okay," he said, pointing to the blanket rolled up in his ruck. "Why don't you take that over there and get our bed laid out?" He instantly saw gratitude in her eyes. Her hair was thick, mussed, and needed desperately to be combed. He might be able to find that small comb he carried in his ruck. Callie would be more than appreciative, but first things first. Food was their priority now.

Later, after they'd eaten and were leaning up against a part of the wall that was less rocky, Beau picked through his ruck. He found what he was looking for and presented Callie with a gift that made her gasp.

"A comb!" she whispered as she reached for it. "What else do you have in there?"

"Just some necessities," Beau chuckled, watching her quickly pull out the small black plastic comb, looking as if she'd been handed pure gold.

"How about a hot bath?" she suggested with a twinkle in her eyes.

"Yeah, I wish. I bet you're having fantasies about one right now."

"That's all I can think about!" she said, grinning. "A hot bath and getting the ache out of my knees and ankles."

He watched her begin to comb the damp strands of hair. "You have beautiful hair," he told her. It wasn't the first time he'd said so, but she grew warm with pleasure.

"Thanks," she said, sending him a grateful look. "I'll be so glad to get back to Bagram, where I can wash my hair, get this awful sweat off me, and the grit all over my skin . . ."

"The grit is the worst," he agreed, pushing the ruck aside. Callie had opened up the sleeping bag and put it on the floor. There was a dry wool blanket to put over them, and with the temperature in the cave in the high sixties, it would probably do the job.

"And you guys go through this all the time?"

"Well, on long-range missions, yes. A lot of the time we're dropped by helo into a particular place, far enough away so we aren't heard by locals. Then we steal into an area to perform our mission, after which we're picked up."

"And this is all because you have radio contact?"

He grinned. "Yeah. We always carry two sat phones on us. If one gets banged up and inoperable, we always have a backup. It's not a good thing out in the badlands to have a nonworking sat phone on us."

"I'd never have known what you really do out here if this hadn't happened to us."

"Well," he murmured wryly, "it's not something I think you'll want to repeat."

"Isn't that the truth!" Callie grumped. She gave her hair a pleased look, the strands shining in the low light, free of snags and knots. "Just getting my hair combed makes me feel better. Thank you."

"Looks pretty." Beau knew how much it meant to Callie to at least get cleaned up a little. Different things made women feel better. For him? He'd have given anything to have the hottest shower he could stand and just wash the damned grit chafing his skin raw. He couldn't have cared less about his hair.

"It feels so nice to get slightly cleaned up," Callie admitted. "Are we staying here for the day?"

"Yes, we are. It's stopped raining and it's probably going to start clearing up. We can't afford to be out in the daylight because the Taliban would spot us sooner or later. We need to hole up here, and we'll take off at dusk."

"It will be so nice just to rest," she murmured, continuing to comb her hair.

"I know. I'm ready to stretch out," he agreed.

"Are you staying awake?"

"I've got to," he said. "You know I've got to stay awake for both of us."

Frowning, Callie said, "That doesn't sound fair. What if we took turns? I could stay awake for two hours and then wake you up in two hours. That way, we'd both get sleep, Beau."

"Sounds good," he agreed readily. "You take the first two hours of sleep, okay?"

She gave him a sharp look. "No, Beau, you need to get some sleep first."

He tried not to smile. Callie wasn't dumb. "What? You don't trust me, gal? Think I wouldn't wake you in two hours?"

"No, I don't trust you on that, Beau. You're looking really tired. You haven't slept in forty-eight hours."

"I'll catnap," he assured her, smoothing out the sleeping bag. "Come on, you need to lie down. You can use my closed ruck as a pillow and I'll cover you up with the wool blanket. You'll be toasty, dry, and warm."

She gave him a wary look. "What kind of 'catnap'?"

He chuckled. "I can see I can't fool you."

"You look exhausted, Beau. I'm worried about you."

He reached out, caressing her cheek. "Sweet woman', I do this all the time. I'm used to it, and so is my team."

"Yes, but you usually *have* a team. Each man can take a watch and the rest can sleep. Instead, you've got to babysit me, Beau."

"Okay," he said more firmly, "lie down on your side here." He pointed to one side of the sleeping bag. "What I'll do is lie with you." He saw her eyes grow teary for a moment. Callie obviously needed some special care. Their escape from the Taliban was emotionally stretching her in ways she'd never experienced, and Beau sensed the toll it was taking on her.

"You'd actually sleep with me?"

"I'll catnap," he said, correcting her. "But I'll hold you, okay?" That was easy—nothing would ever feel so damned right to him for all the right reasons.

"I'd like that."

"Lie on your side and I'll join you," Beau offered, bringing the blanket up over her. Then Beau spooned beside her, using his arm as a pillow for his head. He wrapped his other one around her waist, bringing her against him.

Callie groaned. "Oh, Beau, this feels so good."

Beau couldn't have agreed more. "It does, and there's more of this to come once we get back to base." He wanted to keep Callie's hopes up. For now, he was enjoying the pure, raw pleasure of feeling her small body tucked alongside his longer one. Beau could give her warmth, a sense of security, and he knew that just lying beside him, she'd quickly drop off into sleep.

As for him, he lay there, his eyes open, listening to every last sound. Taliban were known to have frequented this cave precisely because it had pools of water in it. But while they drank from it, he wouldn't. The water was full of bacteria and God knew what else. It was okay for washing, however, and once Callie was sleeping deeply, he'd get up and refill their gallon jar with the water and put the purification tablets in it.

For a moment, he closed his eyes, his hearing keyed to every noise. He felt the soft rise and fall of Callie's breasts against his arm, but this was no place to make love, much as he wanted to. Dawn was coming, and he knew the Taliban would soon be awake and back on their trail. Worse, if they had horses, Callie and Beau would have much less time to elude their pursuers.

His mind ranged over Matt's situation with Dara. So much could go wrong up in the mountains. At least down here, it was warmer and not snowing. Up there, it was—another challenge for Dara to deal with. He worried about her. A lot.

Callie fell asleep almost instantly and Beau hated easing away from her. He knew that if he didn't, he'd fall asleep, and he couldn't let that happen. Instead, he rose quietly to his feet and picked up his rifle to check out the other cave.

He didn't want any surprises. There was a greater likelihood of Taliban moving around with the skies clearing. The sun would quickly dry up the area, the ground hardening once more. He hoped their run along the riverbed had slowed the enemy down. As far as he could figure, he and Callie had done everything right, or at least as well as they could have done under the circumstances.

With clear skies, Bagram would send at least one drone up to begin hunting for them. Beau knew that the black ops community would realize he and Matt would hole up during daylight hours and move only at night.

Still, he hoped there was already a drone in the sky searching for them. If nothing else, it could find their pursuers, and if it was a Predator drone, it could take them out. Predators carried Hellfire missiles and could easily remove a cluster of Taliban if it spotted them. And Beau was sure the Taliban was around, even though they hadn't seen traces of them.

It was a special gift for Beau to watch Callie restore herself with a deep, uninterrupted sleep—one he'd been able to give her. It was nearly dusk now, the sun lancing through the thick brush covering the cave's entrance, spraying shots of gold light on the rear of the cave wall. He stood near the tunnel, the M4 in his chest harness, simply watching the play of light against her clean, soft features. He would never tire of watching this woman wake up, aching to have her in his arms, her naked body against his, in the warmth of their bed. The dreams he had for them were so damned many, but wanting to share them with her was impossible right now.

He forced himself to leave her, moving silently down the tunnel. This was a popular cave, and he knew he was taking a risk by even stopping here, but Callie was physically and mentally exhausted. If she didn't get the rest she needed, they couldn't make that last push of twenty-five miles. It would take them to within a mile of Bagram, where he could finally use his personal radio.

This time frame would hold the most danger of all. There would be fewer hills, although he was going to move to a small mountain and use it as cover. The last four miles were wide-open desert, with only a few desert trees here and there.

This part of their journey would be the most hazardous of all, but because it was night, they had a chance to get back home without being seen. Still, as Beau well knew, nothing was guaranteed, and if the Taliban were roving around the area out of season, it threw more danger into the mix.

CALLIE HUNGRILY ATE everything in the MRE. Beau sat beside her, his long legs crossed. It was getting dark outside and she knew it was soon going to be time to move. He'd cautioned her not to talk because the Taliban was active from dawn through dusk. She hoped they were bedding down for the night somewhere other than in this cave. Earlier, he'd whispered to her that tonight they would walk at a fast, steady pace to reach Bagram. Then, within a mile of the base, he could contact his HQ by short-distance radio. Never had Callie wanted anything more than to be safe on that Army base.

By the time it was dark, they were on the move, leaving the cave behind. Overhead, the stars glittered in the ebony sky above them. The chilly wind blew around them, sometimes with unexpected harshness. They left the hills behind, heading toward Beau's next objective. It was about six thousand feet tall, with rocky slopes and covered with many groves of stubby trees.

Callie knew Beau wanted to thread through the groves to hide from any local Taliban. Her gloves had finally dried out, as had her parka, and it was nice not to have numb fingers as she held on to Beau's belt. She tried to walk as quietly as Beau did, and they continued on until near midnight on the slope.

At that moment, Beau suddenly halted and moved into a slow crouch, his M4 up, and pointed ahead of them. Instantly, Callie's heart took off at a wild gallop. He'd taught her to not move quickly; slow was definitely preferred, bringing less attention to them.

Callie's ears picked up sounds. *Pashto. Oh, God!* Gulping, she slowly crouched down behind Beau. Taliban? She was pretty sure of it. There were no villages in this area. There was low laughter and more talk. What was Beau going to do?

He slowly stood up and she followed suit, terrified. He turned and she followed, a huge tree between them and the Taliban encampment. Never had she wanted to be more careful about where she placed her boots. She kept her focus on the ground and hung on to Beau's belt so tightly her fingers ached.

Her heart was pounding in her ears so loudly she couldn't hear anything else. Beau led them downward for more than ten minutes before he stopped. Then, crouching, he brought his arm around Callie to draw her up against him. He could feel her tension and sensed her anxiety.

His lips near her ear, he said, "Taliban. Don't know how many. We're going to keep working our way down this slope."

"A-are there more?"

"I don't know. Just watch your step."

She nodded and slowly rose with Beau.

Beau looked around, his hearing never sharper. The gusts of cold wind certainly didn't help, but lucky for them, the wind was blowing in a direction that took their scent away from the Taliban. The group was bedding down for the night. He'd heard no horses moving around or snorting. This could be another band of enemy that was not tracking them.

He and Callie could have gotten unlucky and walked into their camp, and it had been a close call—too close! He could feel the terror coming from Callie because the reality of their situation had become far more immediate. Before, she'd asked how he could know that the enemy was searching for them since they were never visible.

He had smiled and told her that by the time she saw them, they would have been surrounded and captured. These people melted like ghosts in and out of the surrounding areas. Callie had looked at him skeptically, and he knew she didn't believe him.

Well, now she did.

Beau knew they had five miles to go to reach Bagram. He angled their approach steeply down the slope, hoping that Callie would watch her feet, since the rocks were sometimes loose. There were large, clear areas of hard dirt and not much brush now, and he tried to stay away from them because the more cover they had, the safer they'd be.

Suddenly, he froze, picking up noise, movement. Callie crashed into him. He absorbed the impact, remaining motionless. There, coming from below and to the left of them on horseback. Beau saw two Taliban soldiers. Their horses were tired, their heads hanging, their shaggy coats gleaming with sweat from being ridden hard for hours, or perhaps days.

Gripping Callie's gloved hand, Beau moved her to a nearby huge pine tree. Without a word, he guided her so that she crouched down behind it, fully hidden from their view. The riders were coming closer, and he had no way to hide her in a cave because there were none in this area. The Taliban were also wearing NVGs. *Sonofabitch!*

He turned, lips close to her ear. "Whatever you do, stay here. I have to take them out. Don't move an inch. I'll come back for you when it's over."

Callie wanted to cry out, but knew they had no choice. She nodded, and an instant later Beau had melted into the dark. Thanks to her NVGs, she could see him lean down and run, hiding among the trees and brush. She stayed crouched on her hands and knees behind the trunk of the tree and listened as horses clip-clopped closer and closer toward her.

Terror shot through her as she knelt, paralyzed by the fear, her head down against the wide trunk, trying to make herself smaller. How desperately she wanted to melt into the earth! Beau could be killed! She could die! Suddenly, Callie wanted to live so badly she could taste it in her dry mouth. Her heart was leaping out of her chest, she was so damn scared. She had no weapon and no way to protect herself—nothing! A sinking feeling of dread overtook her as the horsemen drew ever closer.

Meanwhile, Beau was calculating what to do next. He had no silencer on his M4, so he knew when he fired that the sound would boom throughout the area, alerting the other Taliban camp farther up the slope. He had no idea how many of the enemy were in it, because he couldn't peer through the brush to make a head count.

His mind snapped back to Callie. She was helpless, and the only thing she had going for her was a tree trunk to hide behind. He worried that the horses would smell her scent, and if she moved, their acute hearing would hear even the slightest noise. The Taliban were very attuned to their horses and would quickly pick up on their reaction.

Damn! He skirted the group, hoping that they would ride by the area, Callie remaining undetected. So much could go wrong, and worst of all, he was dealing with an unknown number of enemy. Were there more men behind these two riders? He didn't know that, either. This was when a drone would have helped him out, giving him an overview of the situation. That way, he could make better life-and-death decisions.

But right now, Beau had no drone info. All he had was his experience and one rifle against an unknown enemy force on horseback approaching the area.

Beau made a wide circle, trying to get in between the riders and the enemy camp. No one suspected he was out here—and that was his only advantage: the element of surprise.

Suddenly, he heard a shriek from Callie. Instantly, he turned, running down the slope as more raw screams filled the air. And then he heard the sounds of the men who had captured her. His heart thundered as he hurtled down the slope, slamming a bullet into the chamber, unsafing his weapon, and running as hard as he could. *No, not Callie!* They must have discovered her! *God . . . no!*

Everything started to slow down and Beau felt the icy sense of death close to him. He leaped over a small log, landing inside the barren slope. Two riders had dismounted, and at least four other men stood around her.

Callie was on the ground, struggling, as one man held down each arm, while others had splayed her on her back. Another man was on top of her, his legs bracketing her hips, tearing at her red sweater. She was fighting for her life, screaming out in terror, trying to get loose, but she didn't have a chance.

Another man had yanked her jeans, pulling them down below her knees, grinning.

Rage barreled through Beau, and he skidded to one knee, placed his rifle against a tree to steady it, and fired. The man sitting on Callie was hit with a bullet to the head. Beau's second shot took out the man who was holding her jeans. And then, as they toppled off her, Beau began to take out the four men holding her down. He saw the whole world change through the scope of his M4 as it bucked savagely against his shoulder.

The four Taliban left reacted, releasing Callie and going for their own weapons.

"Stay down!" Beau roared at Callie, who was trying to get up. He knew she'd be killed in the crossfire. Cursing, he finished off all four of the soldiers, who collapsed around Callie, now on her belly, hands over her head, trying to protect herself.

On his right, he heard new Taliban running down the slope toward Callie, and he knew they'd kill her. Moving swiftly from the safety of the tree, he ran past her, yelling, "*Down! Don't move!*" and then headed up the hill to meet the men racing toward her.

Beau saw the first Taliban, a soldier with an AK-47, appear on the rocky slope above him. Calmly, Beau crouched, taking him out. Bullets began flying all around him. He knew that the muzzle flash of his M4 would draw fire from the others, and the dirt shot up in geysers all around him. Some bullets ricocheted off nearby rocks, sending sparks flying into the air.

Beau released a spent magazine, slapping another in with the palm of his hand. Sighting, he took out two more soldiers. The men's screams continued, blending with the roar of returned AK-47 gunfire. The smell of spent ammo burned Beau's flared nostrils, but he remained stationary, watching behind his sight as each soldier appeared around the trees.

Suddenly, he heard movement to his right and heard the bark of an AK-47. The bullets whined in all around him and his left leg kicked out beneath him. He was falling, slamming into the earth. Grunting, Beau felt his left lower leg go numb. He'd been hit! *Sonofabitch!*

Callie's life was at stake, and he shoved to his feet, saw the shooter, and aimed at his head. Two more soldiers popped up, like Whack-a-Moles. They fired simultaneously at Beau.

A bullet slammed into his Kevlar vest, spinning him around. Beau grunted again, hitting the hard earth, rolling, taking his M4 with him. Two more Taliban were running toward him, wildly firing in his direction. He sat up and fired back, now barely able to breathe, the pain radiating throughout the center of his chest.

And then he heard the sweet thumping sound of several helicopters approaching them, and the sky suddenly lit up from a distance. A Hellfire missile exploded five hundred feet above where he lay. With a sigh of relief, Beau knew an Apache combat helo was on the scene!

The whole night erupted with rocks, dirt, and a booming sound that tore at his ears. The concussion wave rolled down the slope, tossing him up into the air. Beau landed somewhere below, momentarily stunned and disoriented. More important than anything, he had to get back to Callie and protect her.

Help was here, and he didn't know how they'd known. Maybe a drone had spotted them and the QRF had been triggered from Bagram. Forcing himself to his feet as pain raced up his left calf, he limped drunkenly down the hill— toward Callie.

Let her be alive. Let her be alive.

Beau had no idea if there were other Taliban around, and as he ran, he watched for any movement in the area. His breath tore from him as he hurtled down the slope toward that barren area where they'd captured Callie.

Oh, God, please let her be alive!

CHAPTER 13

BEAU SKIDDED DOWN the slope and saw Callie hugging the ground. As he ran toward her, his radio crackled to life, and the nearest Apache pilot told him that the area had been cleared of Taliban and the medevac would be landing at Beau's present location in ten minutes.

Beau told him he had Callie McKinley with him and quickly signed off. He knelt down beside her on one knee, pushing his M4 to his back. Callie was still lying on her stomach on the ground, her hands over her head, trying to protect it.

When he placed a hand on her shoulder, she screamed in terror.

"It's me," he shouted, raising his voice above the din of the helos now circling the slope like airborne wolves hunting their prey. The Apaches ruthlessly combed the entire area, continuing to look for enemy heat before allowing the medevac to land.

As she raised her face to him, Beau saw the terror etched on Callie's face, and the front of her sweater was torn down to her breasts, which were covered with a damp, wrinkled white camisole; her hair was disheveled and encrusted with dirt, leaves, and twigs. She gripped the front of her sweater, her mouth contorted in a sob, tears trailing down her dusty cheeks. She held her other arm close to her body. Had she been wounded?

"Help is coming," Beau shouted over the *thump-thump-thump* of the helos. He reached out again, his hands gently cupping her shoulder. "Where are you hurt, Callie?"

Shaking, she tried to form words but couldn't get them out.

Beau quickly looked her over. "Can you stand up for me?"

Tentatively, she nodded.

He leaned down, pulling up her jeans. Her white cotton panties had been nearly torn off her, and he betrayed none of his rage as he gently lifted her up, his hands around her waist. He felt Callie's fingers dig into his shoulders as she stood, wobbling. His leg was on fire, and he tried to anchor himself in case she fell or fainted. He couldn't think about the blood flowing down his leg or the injuries he'd sustained. Not yet.

"Callie? Where are you wounded?"

"M-my right arm . . . I think it's broken . . ."

Damn it! Beau brought Callie tenderly into his embrace, holding her. She was shaking violently now, her knees collapsing against him. Biting back a groan of pain, he took her full weight. Callie had become a frightened child, wide-eyed and terror stricken. And injured.

While he felt pangs of guilt for having left her alone, Beau knew that if he'd stayed behind they would have been overrun by the fourteen men he'd killed, wounded, or who had run off to avoid the fight. And he couldn't have defended the two of them if all of them had attacked at once. No, both he and Callie would have been dead, or the Taliban would have captured and raped Callie.

God, he hoped she hadn't been raped! He didn't know for sure, but she couldn't stop shaking. He continued to hold her tightly in his arms. She was so damn fragile and pale.

His radio crackled to life again, and he had to deal with the copilot radioing him from the incoming medevac. They wanted green chemical lights thrown out to show where to land. Beau eased Callie down, her back resting against a nearby tree. He told her he'd be right back and quickly pulled the lights out of his pocket. Half-running, half-limping into the huge empty space before them, he tossed them out after making sure the copter blades wouldn't shear off a tree limb or hit something that could snap off a blade.

Finished, he hurried back to Callie. He found her with her legs pulled up against her body, her arms wrapped around them, and her head buried against her knees. As he knelt in front of her, he gently placed his hands on her shoulders. Her head snapped up, her eyes glazed with memories that would never leave her.

There was so much noise surrounding them at this point that they couldn't hear anything else. Beau leaned down beside her ear.

"The medevac's landing, so stay where you are. The air from the blades is going to beat against us. I'll help you stand up as soon as the crew chief gives me the signal to board." He squeezed her shoulders. "We're going home, Callie. You're safe now . . . safe . . ."

THE WORLD HAD changed in an instant. Callie couldn't stop crying, because her broken right arm ached and throbbed. She knew it had been broken when one Taliban soldier had caught her, deliberately grabbing her right arm and violently twisting it. She'd been thrown off her feet and landed on her back in the dirt. And then they'd been all over her.

Now the buffeting by the medevac landing and remaining near takeoff speed was like invisible boxing gloves punching continuously at her body. She had no way to see; the night was black and moonless. If not for Beau and another crewman who'd helped get her on board, she couldn't have made it alone. Her emotions went from pure relief to abject terror over having been assaulted by six enemy men, all intent on first raping her and then possibly killing her.

There was no light inside the shaking, shuddering helicopter as they entered it, and Beau guided her to a litter attached to the bulkhead. She let him gently sit her down on it and place a helmet on her head.

Then Beau told her, "Callie, the medic wants you to lie down on the litter. I'll be near you. Go ahead, lie down. You might even like it."

Within seconds, the Black Hawk was spooling up and gravity was pushing her down into the litter. She began to become aware of the voices of other men. Some of it was jargon she couldn't understand, but the comfort and anchoring of Beau's large hand against her shoulder helped steady her.

Then she felt someone else's hands on her. A man's hand. With a cry, she surged up, striking out with her feet, violently pushing whoever it was away from her.

"Callie, that's the medic," Beau rasped. "He's got to examine you to make sure you have no more injuries."

"N-no!" she cried. "No man is touching me! Leave me alone!" she sobbed, nearly hysterical. She felt like a trapped wild animal, the adrenaline surging fully through her, her senses amplified. She needed to escape, but where? Only Beau's reassuring hand on her upper arm comforted her. "D-don't let them touch me, Beau . . . please . . . don't . . . ," she whimpered.

Beau instantly took over, explaining to the medic what had happened. Then he put his arm around Callie and asked, "Listen, are you hurt anywhere else besides your arm? Can you tell us that?"

Shaking her head, she said, "N-no. I just want out of here, Beau. I want to go home!" Her voice broke and she burst into tears again, burying her head in his chest.

She noticed that he smelled of raw sweat, dirt, and his own scent. His chest was heaving with effort, but his arms were stabilizing around her shoulders, and it made her feel secure in her broken world.

"Okay, no problem," he said, squeezing her gently. "It'll be a short ride to Bagram, and as soon as we land, there's going to be a gurney waiting for you. The staff will take you inside to ER, where they can help you, Callie."

"B-but, where will you be?"

"Right there with you, don't you worry, gal."

She sniffed, her nose running, the tears streaming unchecked down her cheeks. All Callie wanted to do was hide away from this violent world—a world that Beau was somehow able to deal with. She could not. The moment she closed her eyes, she saw those men on their approaching horses. They were wearing NVGs too, and she thought they would be able to see her hiding behind that pine tree.

Callie had jerked upward and started to run, but they quickly tackled her and she fell on her face, nearly knocked out.

She opened her eyes, blackness meeting her gaze. All she could see now was the faint green of the goggles everyone was wearing, including the two pilots up in the cockpit. Only Beau's steadying presence, his calm, low voice, thick with emotion, sustained her and stopped her from spiraling into total hysteria.

She heard men talking, heard Beau say something about a gunshot wound. But her mind was shattered by the violent attack she'd undergone, and the aftermath—Beau's hard, cutting voice earlier telling her to lie down and not move. Bullets spitting up all round her. One had grazed her hand, burning it. It ached even now as she clutched the torn red sweater to her body, shamed and humiliated by how easily those men had nearly stripped her clothes from her body.

Beau had told her to stay where she was and not move, but when she'd seen those two riders, she'd panicked. And of course, they'd immediately spotted the sudden, unexpected movement and then, her. She'd done everything wrong! *Wrong!* Why couldn't she stay where Beau had told her to, and why had she allowed fear to overwhelm her?

Miserably, Callie sank against Beau, her trembling beginning to abate. She felt the downward push of gravity, the pitch in the engines changing. Beau moved a little, helping her sit up.

"We've landed at Bagram," he told her huskily. "I'm taking off your helmet, Callie. It will get noisy until we can get you into the ER. I'll be at your side. I'm not leaving you, gal . . ."

His voice sounded terse, but in her state she wasn't sure what she heard except that they had finally landed at Bagram. They were home! They were safe! She helped him get the helmet off her head, and no one tried to touch her.

The door slid open, and there was a minimal amount of light on the tarmac where the helo had landed. Beau stood up, gripping her around the waist, helping her stand. Her knees were shaky and she clung to him, unsure whether the orderlies would see her to the gurney waiting just outside the door of the helo. She held her broken arm protectively against her body.

Everything was a blur. The noise of the jet engines combined with the Black Hawk's rotating blades, and Beau yelled something to the orderlies standing nearby. She saw them back off. Callie gripped the remains of her sweater to her body, not wanting anyone to see her like this, and Beau helped her climb up on it. And then the gurney was moving, and Beau was at her side. His strong, warm hand was once more on her shoulder, comforting her. The lights were bright as they wheeled her into the ER, and automatically, Callie lifted her left hand, the glare too much for her to take.

Finally, all was quiet. Her ears were ringing and the voices around her seemed muted. She had a hard time understanding people talking. The gurney was halted at a cubicle surrounded with light green curtains.

She heard Beau on his shoulder radio talking to someone. As she slid off the gurney and he helped her sit up on a table in the center of the cubicle, she saw him grin. As tired as he was, his mouth was able to curve upward.

"What?" she asked.

"Dara and Matt are safe," he told her, gripping her dusty hand. "Our CO just called me. They were rescued earlier and were flown into Bagram. They're on their way over here right now to see you!" His grin went broader.

Tears filled her eyes, and she whispered, "Oh, thank God . . ."

A male doctor in a white coat entered the cubicle. Callie saw his last name was Brennan. He had short black hair and blue eyes and was in his midforties. Instantly, the doctor's gaze shot to Beau, who was still talking in a low tone on his radio.

And then Dara entered the cubicle, her expression one of relief as she spotted Callie. She stepped around the doctor.

"Hi, Dr. Brennan. I'm Dr. Dara McKinley, her sister," Dara told him. "I'm registered here with the hospital and have a right to practice here."

Callie uttered a small cry and threw her good arm around Dara. They hugged each other, and then Matt entered the cubicle.

"Okay, Dr. McKinley, so long as you're authorized to practice, I'm fine with it." Brennan stared hard at the two Delta soldiers and told them sternly, "Family only."

Dara snapped, "He is family, doctor. He's my fiancé and he saved my life."

Brennan scowled but realized he was outnumbered, and given the circumstances he decided to back off. He stepped forward, gently lifting Callie's right arm to carefully examine the break.

Meanwhile, Matt went over to greet Beau, and the two men heartily embraced one another, relief that they'd both survived in their faces. And then Callie realized Beau looked pale beneath his tan. What was wrong with him?

Before she could ask him, he turned to her. "Callie, I'll be back in about half an hour at the most." He touched her cheek. "Dara will stay with you until

I can return. I'll be back, I promise."

Giving a nod, and before she could ask anything, the Delta Force operators left the cubicle. Beau was limping, her gaze on his muddy pants, and she knew something was wrong. But what? She wanted to ask, but Dara was talking to the doctor about her broken arm. Dara was here, however. She was cleaned up, wearing civilian clothes, looking weary, but all right. Her sister remained right beside her, like a guard dog.

"Thank goodness you're okay!" she told Dara, tears springing to her eyes. "They told us you were rescued earlier."

Dara smoothed Callie's red hair away from her face. The strands were matted with dust and debris.

"Are you really all right, Dara?"

She shared a tired smile with her. "It was rough, but we're okay. Callie, what happened to you and Beau?" She couldn't keep the strain out of her voice. Callie appeared to have been rolled in the dust. She was positively filthy, with fine gray dust all over her body, coating her face and neck.

Callie closed her eyes. "I-I can't talk about it right now, Dara. My arm . . . it hurts . . ."

Leaning forward, Dara gently slid her arm around Callie's shoulder. "It's all right," she whispered. "Everything's going to be all right, Callie. You're here. You're safe . . . I was so worried about you . . . about Beau . . . Thank God you're alive . . ."

Matt reentered her cubicle, and Callie saw he had his operator's expression in place.

Tears trickled down through Callie's dusty cheeks. She sniffed and tried to wipe them away, her hand trembling badly. "Why was Beau limping? Did you know that he saved my life?"

Matt moved around them. "He took a gunshot wound to his left calf, but he'll be okay. I just took him down to another cubicle here, and there's a doc who's going to fix him up. I'll go find out his full status, Callie." He noted her pain-filled eyes. "I'll be right back."

Callie sniffed again and Dara pulled a tissue from her pants pocket, slipping it into her sister's hand. "What happened?" she demanded quietly, holding her sister's stare. Dara recognized the signs of deep shock.

"Later," she muttered, wiping her eyes. "I'm so desperately in need of a shower, Dara." She choked, squeezing her eyes shut. "Just a shower . . ."

"I'm having her taken to X-ray," Brennan said to Dara. He looked Callie up and down. "Do you need rape counseling, Ms. McKinley?"

Dara gasped, her gaze flying from Dr. Brennan to her sister. *Rape?*

"N-no. Just get me something for the pain in my arm, okay?" Callie asked the doctor.

Brennan gave a brisk nod and said, "I'll get an orderly to take you to X-ray. In the meantime, please lie down."

Callie grimaced as the doctor left. "He's got the bedside manner of an alligator," she rasped, wiping her eyes with the damp tissue.

Dara came closer, her arm around Callie's slumped shoulders. "Rape? Were you raped, Callie?" She tried to hold it together. She didn't want to hear Callie say yes, but her sweater was torn, dirty, bloodied, with brain matter splattered across it, and she was disheveled.

Even now, Dara could see bruising around her sister's slender throat. What had happened?

"I was almost raped," Callie croaked, then laid her head on her sister's shoulder. "It was awful, Dara. We were on the run. The Taliban was closing in on us. Beau had me hide behind a huge pine tree and told me to stay put. He had to sneak around a group of Taliban. He was going to come up behind the riders and take them out. There must have been six more soldiers behind them." Tears dribbled down her cheeks and she licked her lips, tasting the salt, the grit of dirt on them.

Dara held her breath, absorbing her sister's words. "So what happened?"

"They found me because I ran when I should have stayed put," she muttered, lifting her head, trying to move her shoulders to get rid of the tension. "They galloped over and captured me. I started screaming and fighting them. Beau heard me and came running back." She closed her eyes. "They'd taken me down, yanked my sweater apart, tearing it, pawing at me. And they were holding me by my wrists and ankles, Dara. They'd pulled my jeans around my knees when Beau attacked them." She pressed her hand to her eyes, a sob escaping her. "It was—horrible . . ."

Dara held her gently in her arms, and Callie gripped her with her good arm, clinging to her, as if to release her would be to lose her forever. "I'm so sorry, Callie. How awful. But thank God, at least you weren't raped. That's the good news." Dara felt a huge sob work up and out of Callie. She held her sister, stroked her dusty, mussed hair, wishing she could get her to a shower and help her clean up.

Callie smelled of sweat and fear, and Dara forced herself not to cry with her. Right now, Dara had to be the strong one so she could care for her sister and give her a sense of safety.

An orderly came in to take Callie to X-ray, but Dara gave him a hard look and a firm shake of her head, warning him silently to come back later. The young man hesitated, saw the situation, lifted his hand, and gave her an apologetic look, quietly exiting.

Soothing her little sister, Dara kept whispering, "You're safe now, Callie. You're safe. It's going to be all right. You're in shock right now, and I'm sure you feel like you're flying apart inside."

She knew because she had felt the same way when running with Matt up that mountain to escape their enemy. This was so much worse than she could have imagined. Brave, vital Callie had been reduced to a huddled mouse, her eyes wild with terror, dark with anguish. Dara had never seen her like this before. Callie was in constant pain from her arm, traumatized by the near rape and the threat of a horrific death.

"I need to know how Beau is!" Callie demanded, lifting her head, no long-er trying to stop the tears from running down her dirty face. "My God, Dara, he took all of them on! One man against all of those sick, murdering bastards. He exposed himself to them to save me." She pressed her hand to her face, bowing her head, a wracking sob tearing out of her.

Matt reentered quietly, his gaze cutting to Dara, and she saw beneath the mask on his face, the tightness of his mouth, his eyes alive with emotions. "Can you get me the head nurse?" she asked Matt. "Now, please?"

"Yeah," he said, studying Callie for a moment. Turning, he left the cubicle.

In moments, the head nurse, an Army major about fifty years old, entered into the cubicle.

Dara said, "I'm Dr. McKinley. This is my sister, Callie. She's been through hell. I need you to authorize that women only be with her, no men. And I need to get her cleaned up. Is it possible to place a stabilizing splint around her arm for now? It appears to be a closed break. I'll escort her to X-ray after she gets cleaned up."

The nurse nodded. "Yes. I'll get a woman doctor to take over here. Stay put."

Matt reentered and stood at the end of the examination table, saying noth-ing, silently appraising Callie's condition. Her sobs stopped and she lifted her head, her eyes swimming with tears.

"Beau?" she croaked.

"He's okay," Matt said soothingly. "The bullet in his calf went clean through, and they're patching him up right now, Callie. He took a bullet to his Kevlar vest and there's a big bruise, but that's all. He's going to be fine. They'll release him in probably half an hour."

Pressing her hand to her chest across the torn sweater, she whispered, "Oh, thank God . . ."

Dara motioned to the table. "Matt? Can you get me a gown over there for Callie? I want to get her out of these filthy clothes right now."

Matt walked over and handed her a gown. "Call me when I can come back in," he said, giving her a light squeeze to her arm.

"Yes," Dara said. "Stand guard out there, okay? The head nurse is getting her a removable splint. Let her in, but don't let anyone else in until I'm done dressing Callie. And if that Dr. Brennan comes back, tell him we've got this covered. We no longer need his services."

"You got it," Matt murmured, trying to curb a grin. Dara was pissed off. The blaze of anger in her eyes was something to behold. His woman could command legions with that voice and look, no question. She had one hell of a temper when she wanted to demonstrate it. Matt made a note to keep that in mind.

The head nurse quickly returned with the removable splint. "Will you wash the area, Dr. McKinley? And then I'll place this support around her broken arm," she said.

In minutes, Callie had a waterproof, removable splint on her arm, and Dara could already see the relief from the pain in her eyes. She thanked the nurse, who then left. "Let's get you out of these clothes," she murmured. "You'll feel better in a clean gown."

Dara suddenly felt the threat of tears and pushed them back. Right now, Callie needed her to be strong, guiding, and supportive. As she helped Callie into the gown, Dara saw bruising all over her body, front and back. And so many scratches and gouges. She didn't know the details, but Dara strongly suspected the men had held her down on rough, rocky ground when they were about to rape her.

Terror, combined with rage, roared through Dara, but she swallowed hard and kept her calm face on. In a matter of minutes, Callie had a blanket over her shoulders.

Grabbing another cloth left by the head nurse, Dara fashioned a sling for her right arm, and as soon as she tied it around her neck, Callie sighed.

"That feels so much better," she whispered with relief, leaning back against the gurney, closing her eyes. "Thanks, sis. I don't know what I'd do if you weren't here . . ."

"I'll be with you every step of the way," Dara promised her, her voice breaking. She watched as Callie was placed in a wheelchair by a woman orderly. Dara insisted on pushing her out of the ER. She knew the women's showers and locker room were located in the basement from her own experience hours earlier, and she took her sister down there to help her get cleaned up.

Callie stood for a long time beneath the warm shower stream after Dara helped her wash her dirty hair and put conditioner into it. She also had her turn so she could soap up the places on her body where Callie couldn't reach because of her broken arm. Never had Callie been so grateful for Dara's help.

"Did you call Mom and Dad to say I was found?" she asked, the water running over her shoulders and back.

Dara nodded. "Yes, everyone's been notified. I called them. They're overjoyed. Mom asked you to call her when you felt up to it."

"Can you call her back and tell her I'm okay? Right now, I'm a ball of up-and-down emotions. All I want to do is cry. Don't mention the near rape. I don't want them to know. It will just upset Mom and Grandma horribly."

"Don't worry," Dara promised her, gently washing her upper arm and then carefully washing her wrist below the splint, making sure she was clean. "As soon as I can get you assigned a private bed in this hospital, I'll call everyone and let them know. Okay?"

"F-fine, thanks. How are you doing, Dara?" She stared into Dara's eyes. Callie could see exhaustion and terror still rooted deep in them.

"Listen, we'll talk more about our adventures tomorrow, okay? Matt got me out of that awful ambush and we're both okay. Better off than you are, presently." She managed a little teasing grin. "But you'll bounce back, Callie. I know you, and this isn't going to hold you down."

But Callie didn't feel sure about anything. "I worry about Beau. He never told me he was wounded."

Snorting, Dara finished crouching down to wash each of Callie's feet. "Why am I not surprised? These guys are Delta Force, Callie. They don't complain about a little gunshot wound. They just want to focus and get the mission completed. And he sure did that with you, didn't he, sis?"

CHAPTER 14

Dara thanked Dr. Ann Bartel, Callie's newly assigned physician, for being there for her sister. She had been responsible for getting Callie placed on the orthopedic ward floor, away from all the noise and hectic activity. When Ann suggested an antianxiety medication for Callie, her sister refused it. She wasn't a pill taker and hated medications in general. The only medication she would take was an antibiotic, but it had to be truly necessary for her to agree even then.

Dara saw her sister's energy ebbing away. She understood—she was dealing with her own exhaustion and stress from escaping the Taliban, who had pursued them in the mountains. Dara promised her she'd call their parents and grandparents before she left with Matt to get some sleep in the Eagle's Nest.

After they left, the small room became quiet. It was still dark outside, and Callie had no idea what time it was. She missed Beau, and she was worried about his wounds. She desperately needed his calming presence, because she was beginning to come apart, little by little. When she closed her eyes, she saw flashes of the whole violent scene where she had been caught and captured, the men laughing at her as they splayed her on the ground, ripping at her sweater and jeans. Callie had never felt so helpless or enraged, unable to fight back except to scream for help.

There was a soft knock on the door, and Beau stood there, grinning. "How's my special gal doing?"

"Beau!" she whispered, sitting up in bed. "Are you okay?" Callie saw he'd taken a shower and had changed into a clean Army uniform. He was wearing a dark green olive T-shirt, his desert camouflage jacket open over it. His hair and beard were damp, his gray eyes clear. He stepped into the room and quietly closed the door behind him.

Beau gave her a tired smile and limped over to her bed, reaching out and gripping her left hand. Her right arm was in a sling. "I'm fine. How are you doing?" he asked, searching her exhausted features.

"I'm whipped, but also hyper," she admitted. "What happened to you? Why didn't you tell me you were shot, Beau?"

He released her hand and caressed her hair, which now, washed and combed, fell like a bronze waterfall around her shoulders. "Not much time to tell you," he teased. "We were a little busy out there, weren't we?"

There were tears in her eyes, and he could see Callie trying to fight them back, but the effects of all the violence she'd experienced were deluging her. "Busy . . . I guess that's an understatement. Did you have your leg looked after?"

"It's okay," he drawled. "They cleaned it out, slapped a bandage on it, pumped me full of antibiotics via a nasty shot in the ass, and said I'd be fine. I took a hit to my Kevlar, so I have a big, pretty-looking bruise on my chest, and it's nothing to write home about." He looked deep in her eyes. "Now, you need to tell me how *you're* doing."

She closed her eyes, loving his hand as it caressed her hair. The need for his touch was overwhelming. "Dr. Bartel wanted me to take an antianxiety pill," she rattled. "I told her no. I-I just needed you, Beau." She lifted her lashes, clinging to his warm gray gaze, filled with love. Even now, with terror still coursing through her, Callie could see Beau's unspoken love for her. His hand was gentle as he moved it across her gowned shoulder, his fingers sliding down her left arm and capturing her fingers.

"You'll always have me," he promised, his voice gritty with emotion The words meant a helluva lot more to Beau than she realized, but he wasn't ready to speak to her about it yet. Right now, Callie was in deep shock and needed his reassurance. He wanted to be there for her as much as possible under the circumstances. "Look, I have to get over to my HQ at 0900 this morning." He looked at the watch on his wrist. "It's 0400 now. How about I sit in that chair near your bed? You need to sleep, Callie. I can stay until 0800. You've run for nearly three days. Rest is what will help put you back together again."

His calming words soothed her, and she gripped his hand. "You're right." She searched his exhausted face. "Have you been able to call your parents to tell them you're okay?"

"No, not yet. You were my first priority, Callie. The Army has already called them and told them that I was no longer MIA and that I'm fine. After I see my captain at 0900 this morning, I'll call them from HQ and chat with them. Did Dara get to your family yet?"

"Yes, she called them for me." Taking a sharp breath, she whispered, "I-I just feel so shaken up, Beau . . . scattered . . . in pieces. I've never felt like this before . . ."

"You could have died out there, Callie. That's the bottom line. And you didn't, but you have to take care of yourself right now. I'm sure your family knows you'll call when you feel up to it. Don't be hard on yourself."

Nodding, she released his hand. "I'm so tired, Beau. And I'm wired, like I can't come down off that cliff of anxiety that just keeps ripping me up. It won't go away . . ." How she wished she could crawl into his arms and be held. But it was impossible, and she was grateful he'd stay with her in the room while she slept. "Will you come back after seeing your captain?"

"Yes, for sure. With my leg in this condition, I don't know what they'll do with me. My CO will probably give me some downtime."

"At least you can't go out on ops," she said, and noticed his eyes lighten with humor for a moment.

"That's for sure. Right now I've got an eight-week sick-time chit from the doc saying I'm not going anywhere. I'm not sure what the captain will decide to do with me underfoot." He leaned over, kissed her forehead and her cheek, and murmured, "Now, come on, lie down and I'll tuck you in. I want you to sleep, sweet woman'. Sleep heals."

Callie agreed and lay down on her left side, getting her broken arm in the sling comfortable against her gowned body. Beau tucked her in and she closed her eyes, needing his calm presence. He'd actually been shot and could still act as if it wasn't the end of the world. She'd been violently attacked and was having trouble dealing with the memories that kept surfacing when she least expected them, spiraling her back into terror like a broken record that played over and over again.

Beau left her side and turned off the overhead light, plunging the room into darkness. She heard him moving to the chair and sitting down. "Will you be able to sleep, Beau?" she asked, closing her eyes, the exhaustion flooding through her bruised, aching body.

"Oh, real easy, gal," he promised. "You just sleep like an angel, Callie. I'll be here if you need me." Rubbing his face, he tipped his head back against the comfortable lounge chair and was instantly asleep.

CALLIE FELT DRUGGED as she slowly awoke, hearing the door open and then quietly close. Instantly, her mind went on red alert, and adrenaline surged through her. She jerked up into a sitting position, then gasped with pain as the sudden movement jarred her broken arm.

"Whoa, Callie, it's me, Beau."

Her heart was pounding like a drum and she realized that light was peeking around the venetian blinds covering the only window. "Oh, Beau. Thank God! You scared me for a minute . . ."

Limping over, Beau could see the terror in her eyes, which were no longer drowsy but wide-open with alarm. "Sorry, gal, I didn't mean to wake you up like this." He reached over and carefully moved her toward him. Callie was breathing erratically, in that flight-or-flight mode he knew all too well. The wounding to her psyche, her emotions, was pervasive, and Beau felt helpless to combat it for her. He understood it was all internalized within her. Without the proper training and mind-set, anyone would react like this.

"I just left my captain," he told her, brushing her hair away from her face as she rested against his shoulder. "He's not sure what to do with me. I'm on sick call and so he's putting me on mission planning at the HQ for now."

"Does that mean you'll be leaving me?"

He heard the panic in her tone. "He's giving me until tomorrow to be with you. Then," he said apologetically, "I'm back on day duty Monday through Friday. I'll get weekends off."

"I-I wish we weren't here, Beau. I wish we were over at the Eagle's Nest, just us two."

"I can make that happen, Callie. But first, we need to get your doctor to sign you out of here."

Nodding, she sat up. "I don't want to be here. If I could just be alone with you so you could hold me, I'd feel so much better."

Because he'd forsaken her during the firefight, Beau felt a pang of guilt. "Sure, I'll go look up Dr. Bartel, and you can tell her what you want."

"Thank you, Beau. I'd really appreciate that."

"Have you eaten yet?"

"No. I'm not hungry."

Frowning, Beau muttered, "Gal, you're going to have to eat something. I know you're going through a lot, but the best thing you can do is eat and get your strength back. I'll go find Doc Bartel, and on the way back, I'll swing by the cafeteria and grab you a tray of breakfast vittles, okay?"

She nodded, hating that she felt so wimpy and needy. This wasn't like her at all. Callie had always been the strong one in their family. Now she could feel herself falling apart. Her world as she knew it had shattered into a million pieces out there on that Afghan slope. "Yes, I'd love that. Thank you, Beau."

Beau's gut churned. What was going to happen to Callie? Would they send her home? Did Maggie and the Hope Charity have anything to do with her decision making or not? He had so many questions and no damned answers as he went through the cafeteria line, getting a breakfast he hoped she'd want to eat.

Callie was so damned pale, and he knew she was on mild pain meds for her broken arm. His mouth tightened into a thin line, and he couldn't forget that he'd left Callie unprotected when she needed him the most. How many times had he replayed his tactical decision-making process? Could he have done it any differently? Beau didn't see it, but maybe discussing it with Matt Culver would help. Or it might not. Beau had five years in as a Delta Force operator, all of them here in Afghanistan. He knew the land, the players, and the tactics. He simply didn't see another option besides trying to hide Callie and get to those riders before they got to her.

But she'd not listened to him and had moved, making herself an immediate target of those riders. He hadn't expected that. She'd gotten so scared that she'd run. It was a normal reaction for a person without military training, and Beau couldn't fault her. Callie was already feeling guilty for talking Dara into going along with them to that village. He wasn't about to pile more on her shoulders for her decision to run, rather than stay hidden.

AS HE LIMPED toward the hospital elevators with a breakfast tray in hand, Beau wondered what this backlash might do to their budding relationship. Would Callie be so broken that it would dissolve as a result?

He lived in a special hell where that question was concerned. So far, she hadn't said the words, but she could. And then what? He was falling in love with her. Right or wrong, he wanted a life with Callie, but this debacle had thrown everything up into the air. And Beau had no idea where it was going to land. The military owned his ass. He couldn't walk away and remain with Callie, even though he understood her need to have someone she trusted at her side. She was falling apart before his very eyes.

He had no training for a civilian trauma like this and didn't know where to go to ask hard questions about what Callie's changed demeanor meant. She wasn't the same person as before, but then, how could she be? He'd been shot twice now, and Beau recalled how the first experience had changed his attitude toward his future. He had taken a bullet in his right shoulder. Fortunately, it was a flesh wound, but it stopped him in his tracks.

Life became more precious. He didn't want to waste it as he had before. Things had become more serious for him. That first time he'd been shot, the experience had matured him and made him more sober about his future.

Before being wounded, he'd thought he was bulletproof. But then, he'd found out from talking to other operators who had been wounded while in Delta Force that the same thing had happened to them. Major life changes occurred.

As he took the elevator up to the ward floor, Beau knew he needed to talk to someone about this. Callie's trauma was something he needed to understand better; he had to find someone who was an expert on rape or near-rape experiences. Right now, he felt ignorant and knew he could inadvertently do more harm to Callie as a result.

More than anything, he wanted to be there for Callie because he loved her. Taking a deep breath, he walked down the hall to her private room and lightly knocked, letting Callie know he was there.

She opened the door. Surprised, he saw her in a pair of her jeans, a soft apricot sweater, socks, and a pair of leather shoes. "Come in," she said, standing aside.

"You're dressed," he said, bringing the tray to the rolling table.

"Maggie just dropped by to see me while you were gone. She'd stopped by my B-hut and Dara happened to be there, and she gave Maggie some of my clothes to bring over to me. I actually feel halfway human again."

Closing the door, Beau nodded. "Maggie was here?" She was Callie's boss.

"Yes." Callie sat on the bed, her legs hanging over the mattress.

Beau wheeled the tray table over to her, taking the lid off the plate that held scrambled eggs and buttered toast. "What did she say?"

Callie grimaced and picked up the fork with her left hand. She was right-handed, so it was an effort to use it. "I told her I was going home, Beau. My parents called me right after you left the room. They want me to come home to the ranch. So do my grandparents."

He nodded, helping her by adding the strawberry jam to her toast. "How do you feel about that?" He saw Callie's eyes grow teary for a moment and then the tears were gone.

"I want to go home." Her voice quavered and she shook her head. "I told Maggie I need home. I can't stay here anymore, Beau."

Relief raced through him, but he kept his reaction to himself, weighing the fragility in her expression and hearing the pain in her voice. "How did she take it?"

"She understood."

"Will you work for the Hope Charity stateside then?" Because right now, Beau felt strongly that Callie needed the safety, the constancy, of her family and the ranch she grew up on to help her work through this experience.

"No, I quit." She shrugged her left shoulder. "I've never done something like that before, Beau. Right now, I just need home. Family. Time to figure out what I'm doing. I thought I knew . . ."

"I agree," he said quietly. "Was Maggie upset with your decision?" Beau hoped not.

"No, she was fine. She said she understood completely."

"Did she leave the door open for you to go back to work for the charity again if you want?"

"She did," Callie said.

Beau smiled a little and took her fork, putting a load of scrambled eggs on it. "Open that pretty mouth of yours. You need protein."

It was such an intimate pleasure to feed Callie. She had been pushing that fork around in the steaming scrambled eggs but not eating them, and Beau knew she needed to eat or else. There was that warm connection shimmering between them once more. He could feel it. And he could see the relief in Callie's eyes as he spoon-fed her the breakfast. When she'd finished the eggs, he pulled off chunks of toast, handing them to her.

Yes, this one event was life-changing, and it scared him, because he wondered if, somewhere down the road, Callie would walk away from him, too.

"Could we go to the Eagle's Nest, Beau, after breakfast? Dr. Bartel has released me and I want to spend whatever time is left here with you."

"Sure," he murmured. "We can do that. I'm not due back at HQ until 0900 tomorrow morning."

She wiped her hand on the paper napkin he offered her after eating both pieces of toast. "Thanks," she whispered.

"When do you think you'll be going home to Montana?"

"I'm not sure yet. I got a call from Dara, who's looking into it for both of us. She has to get back to work at her residency in Alexandria, Virginia."

"But you'd fly home to Montana. Right?"

"Yes."

"Gonna be cold and snowing there, gal," he teased, removing the tray. He'd poured her a mug of coffee, and she gratefully lifted it with her left hand.

"I know, but that's okay. I'll be home." Because right now, home was *safe*.

"And that's the right place for you right now," Beau agreed. He heard the tenor of her voice and understood that the Montana ranch and love and people who would support Callie while she worked through her trauma.

Beau wished more than anything that he could be there. He ached to be with her, but he saw no possible way for it to happen.

By 1100, Callie had been released from the hospital and Beau had driven her over to the warehouse where Eagle's Nest One and Two were located. Once he had walked her to the second-story apartment, she asked him if Dara and Matt were in the other unit. They were. She asked if Beau would go get Dara because she needed to talk to her.

Dara came to see her about fifteen minutes later, alone. "Beau and Matt are having coffee down at the cafeteria," she told Callie, shutting the door. "You look better this morning," she said, coming over and sitting with her on the leather couch.

"Thanks," Callie admitted, "but inside I feel shattered, Dara. I can't explain it. I wanted to talk to you because you know me so well."

Dara came and sat next to her on the couch, tucking one leg beneath her, facing Callie. Placing her hand on her sister's shoulder, Dara said softly, "Hey, you've been through hell. And I'm sure you're feeling like you're going crazy inside."

Callie moved her hand across her stomach. It would sometimes roll with nausea before settling down once more. "There are times when I feel like vomiting, Dara. It hits me out of nowhere. I'm not thinking about it or anything else, it just hits me like a bolt out of the blue."

"It's called a vagus nerve response, and it's your emotional reaction to the trauma working its way out of you," Dara said. "Everyone handles trauma differently. Some people get nausea. Others vomit. Some faint. All of it's a normal reaction to terror and feeling like you're going to die, Callie."

With a grimace, Callie grumped, "Great. Just what I wanted to hear. How long does it last, Dara?"

"Usually a week or two at the most. It just goes away on its own."

"How are *you* doing this morning, Dara?" Callie asked, noticing that her sister looked at peace. There was an aura of stability and happiness around her, and the shadows beneath her sister's eyes were gone. Her mouth was soft and relaxed.

"Much better. Getting a good night's sleep in Matt's arms really helped."

"Good. Because I'm feeling horribly guilty about telling you that it was safe for us to go out to that village, Dara." Callie gripped her sister's hand. "I'm so sorry I pushed you into going with us." Her voice broke, her hand tightening around Dara's fingers.

"Oh, Callie," Dara whispered, gently squeezing her sister's hand," I don't blame you. How on earth could you have known it was going to happen? You'd been going out to that village four times a year for years, and it was always safe." She looked at Callie and firmly told her, "Do not blame yourself, okay? I don't blame you at all. It was my call to go or not, and I made it."

"Really? You're not angry with me about all this?" Callie whispered, wiping her eyes. She was so grateful seeing Dara's face shining with love for her.

"Silly goose!" Dara said, ruffling her red hair. "I would never blame you for this!"

"W-what do Mom and Dad think? Are they blaming me?"

Dara shook her head. "No, not at all. I was able to explain the course of events to them during the phone call. How could they blame you, Callie? If anything, they're so relieved we're both alive and safe, nothing else matters."

"And Grandpa? Grandma?"

"They're overjoyed we're alive and safe. You're such a worrywart! You're going to win the title from me! Everyone wants you home so they can show you how much they love you."

"I'm sure they want to see you too," Callie put in shyly.

"Of course, but I have to get back to work first. I'm fine, really."

"But what about Christmas? It'll be here soon . . ."

"I know. And before all this happened, Matt was getting thirty days' leave to go home and see his family in Alexandra, Virginia. He asked me over a week ago if I wanted to see him on leave, and I told him, 'Of course!' He invited me to be with him at their family Christmas dinner, and I said, 'Yes, absolutely.'"

"Oh," Callie whispered, disappointed. "Then you won't be home with us?"

Frowning, Dara said, "I'm going to talk to Matt about spending two weeks of his leave with his family and then maybe flying home for a week to be with all of you. We had already planned a short vacation in Hawaii for the last week. I really want everyone in our family to meet him anyway. It's a perfect time to do it."

"That sounds good," Callie agreed, some of her sadness lifting. "I'd love to have you at home, even if it's after Christmas and only for a week."

"Me, too, but I get two weeks of vacation starting January first and not before that. It would be the ideal time for Matt and me to fly to Montana and be with all of you for that week." She patted Callie's hand. "But let's see. I have to talk to Matt first. He's got a huge Turkish-Greek-American family flying in. The whole family is going to be there at his parents' home until mid-January. I don't know what other plans are in the offing, so I'll check with him about this the first chance I get."

"But if Matt couldn't come with you, would you come home anyway?"

"Of course I would, Callie. I miss everyone, too." Dara smiled gently. "What about you and Beau? I know there's something serious going on between you two."

Pain pierced Callie's heart. "I'm falling in love with him, Dara. Please don't tell him that, though, because I've never said anything to him about it."

Dara's smile grew, and she confided, "That's so wonderful! Matt said Beau is serious about you. He's never seen him this serious about a woman before."

"Yes, but he's stuck here at Bagram. I'm going home. It's Christmas, and I wish so much that he could come home and be with me in Montana."

"Have you told him that?"

Lifting her head, Callie looked around the quiet apartment. "I thought if I could get Beau here to the Nest, I'd ask him, but I don't know if there's anything he can do about it. Seems his captain is keeping him here at Bagram for eight weeks while he heals up from that bullet wound."

"Then," Dara urged her, holding her worried gaze, "you need to ask Beau if there are any other ways they might allow him to come to Montana to be with you."

"My God, we've been through so much in a short amount of time, Dara. I've come unglued. I'm not thinking clearly. Not like I used to . . ."

Nodding, Dara said, "Yes, I understand and it's because of the shock you're in right now. But couldn't you tell Beau something so he knows how important he is to you? You've never been one to be afraid to ask for what you want, Callie." She smiled a little. "Don't be shy about this, okay?"

Giving a jerky nod, Callie whispered, "Okay . . . I'll think about it . . ."

CHAPTER 15

B EAU SAT DOWN with Matt Culver in a quiet corner of the chow hall. While Dara visited Callie, they decided to get breakfast and coffee. He laid out the whole story of his run to get Callie back to safety to his team leader from beginning to end.

Matt rubbed his beard and leaned back in the chair after he finished. "You did the right thing, Beau," he said. "But I don't know if Callie could ever appreciate the decisions you had to make, and why you had to make them the way you did. I'm sure she was scared out of her mind. I saw it often in Dara. They're civilians. They live in a fairly safe society where bullets aren't flying every day. They aren't used to being hunted."

With a grimace, Beau nodded.

"She moved and she made a target of herself," Matt added. "That's what tipped your whole plan into chaos. If she'd stayed unmoving, those two riders would probably not have seen her at all. But horses are good at detecting the least movement, and she made a bad choice."

"Yeah," he muttered, "I know it, but I'd be damned if I'd bring that up to her. She's already feeling a ton of guilt about talking Dara into coming with her to that village."

"Better left unsaid," Matt agreed, frowning. He shook his head. "She still trusts you, though, and that's important."

"But that could change."

Shrugging, he said, "Yes, I suppose it could. How is she feeling right now?"

"I'm no shrink, but to me, she's fragile and barely holding it together."

"That's not unusual," Matt said. "At least she wasn't raped. She had the shit beaten out of her and got a broken arm, but the worst didn't happen."

"I have no experience with a woman who's had the tar beaten out of her, Matt. You read in the newspapers about domestic abuse and assault, but to actually see it is a whole different story. I mean, we see how the women and children of an Afghan village react to abuse, which is exactly how Callie is reacting now."

"Trauma is trauma," Matt said, somber. "Dara had her share of it, but she was never assaulted by the Taliban like Callie was. There's a huge difference between being chased and never catching sight of the enemy, and having the enemy capture and almost kill you."

"It's a very big difference," Beau muttered. "I don't know what to do for her or say to her, Matt. She doesn't want to be touched by any man, other than me."

"Because you've proved she can trust you. Hell, Beau, I'm no shrink, but your heart's in the mix and so is hers, whether either of you realizes it or not."

"I'm afraid I'll do or say the wrong thing. I mean, what the hell is the right thing to say to her? That everything will be fine? I don't know that, and you know we don't go around promising things we can't deliver."

Matt shook his head. "I know. I don't have any words of wisdom to impart to you, bro. I wish to hell I did. I've got my hands full with Dara and her post-traumatic reactions. It's dicey for both of us, but in different ways. I think you have a rougher path to follow than we do."

Beau felt the weight of the challenges settling around his shoulders. "At this point, I'd rather be facing Taliban hordes than dealing with this situation with Callie."

Matt eyed him. "Do you love her, Beau?"

The words were spoken so quietly that it caught Beau off guard. Matt's expression was open, and he wasn't wearing his game face. Beau said, "Yes, I'm falling in love with her. It started from the moment I saw her belly dancing in that show in the chow hall. Nothing's changed in my attitude toward her since that time."

"Then," Matt counseled, "the best thing you can do is keep doing it."

"We've not even admitted it to one another, much less talked about it. She's never said those words to me, either. I'm pretty sure she does love me, because of things she's said, but until I hear it . . . I'm not taking anything for granted."

"Hey, pardner. I saw her studying you at the orphanage when you didn't realize she was watching you. What I saw in her eyes was a woman very interested in what her man was doing."

"I hope so. Sometimes, I see her giving me a look that I swear is love, but she's never said it out loud to me." Beau had known Matt Culver for five years, and he trusted his judgment of things.

"When you love someone, a touch, a kind word, a look, can give them everything they need from you. It's not a good time to broach the topic with her, I agree. Let her tell you what you can do to help her. Ask Callie a lot of questions, Beau. That will keep you from making those damned assumptions about what she's feeling. You will know exactly what she needs and how she responds."

"That sounds good," Beau murmured, giving his friend a grateful look. "You should have been a shrink." He grinned a little.

Matt snorted. "Being a team leader is tough enough. And trust me, I'm on eggshells with Dara right now, too. One moment, she's strong and solid, the next, she's starting to emotionally go to pieces on me. She'll burst out crying. Or she gets a nightmare and wakes both of us up. I never know when it's going to happen and neither does she. We just try and take it a minute at a time." He slid Beau a sympathetic glance. "And you're going to have to do the same in your situation. Callie can't help what her emotions are doing to her right now. She's had her whole worldview shattered, just like Dara."

WHEN DARA RETURNED to Nest One, Matt and Beau had arrived and brought to-go boxes of breakfast with them. Beau left the apartment to let them have breakfast with one another and walked up to the second floor of the warehouse, where Callie was staying at Nest Two. He opened the door and found her puttering around in the kitchen, making them coffee. His gut tightened and he closed the door, locking it.

"Did you have a good talk with your sister?" he asked, coming into the kitchen and leaning against the counter. Callie's cheeks had a little pink in them and hope sprang up in Beau. As she looked up at him, he saw her green eyes weren't as murky. Was that hope he saw in her eyes, or was it a slight lessening of stress?

"I did. It helped a lot." She turned on the coffeemaker. "Want coffee?"

"Sure," he murmured, "thanks." Beau saw her left hand tremble slightly. The apricot sweater brought out her pale skin and highlighted her red hair, now loose and free around her shoulders. She was beautiful even now. He ached to hold her, but her right arm was in a sling.

"Want me to get the cups down?" he asked, assuming she was feeling awkward about having to use her left hand.

"Yes, please."

"How about if we have coffee in the living room?"

"That sounds nice," she said.

"Go sit down. I'll bring it over in short order."

Callie nodded and walked to the couch, sitting down on one corner of it, pushing off her shoes, and tucking her legs beneath her. "Did you get to talk with Matt?"

"Yes, I did." He placed the mugs next to the coffeemaker.

"Were you two comparing notes on us and your experiences?"

"We were talking mostly about the ambush and what happened afterward." He did not want to divulge the details. She still seemed too fragile to cope with anything that would further upset her. "Mostly tactics and strategy," he added. "What did you and Dara talk about?"

"We made our plans to get out of Afghanistan," she said. "Dara has made arrangements for us. She'll go to Alexandria to finish her residency at the hospital."

"And you?"

"I'm going home. Dara has all the flights set up. We'll take Kuwait Airways out of Bagram to their country and then get a U.S. airline flight to Seattle, Washington. From there, she and I will take different flights to get us home."

He brought over the cups of coffee, carefully placing one in her left hand, and she thanked him. Beau saw her struggling with her emotions, trying to act normal when she was nowhere near it. He hurt for her and sat near Callie but left some room between them. "At least you'll get to spend Christmas with your family."

"I'm so looking forward to it, Beau."

"From the stories you told me already, it sounds like it's exactly what you need to heal up from this experience." He saw her eyes cloud with pain, her lips thin for a moment.

"Did you know that Dara will be spending Christmas with Matt and his family in Virginia?"

Brows rising, Beau said, "Looks as if things are serious between them."

"Very. I guess this experience made Dara realize she truly loves Matt, and vice versa."

Beau felt tension move through him, hearing the confusion in Callie's voice. Matt had known Dara for just a little longer than Beau had known Callie, and their relationship was moving full speed ahead. He saw Callie wrestling with that knowledge and clamped his mouth shut.

"She's two years older than you," he noted, sipping his coffee. "Years do make a difference between how people see the world, Callie."

"I guess . . . it just seems too soon. I don't know." She shook her head. "Who am I to judge anyone? I'm feeling so screwed up inside I don't know where I am from one minute to the next. I have nonstop anxiety, and I feel like I'm whipsawing back and forth every few minutes emotionally. It's crazy stuff."

"It's the trauma, gal. In time, these sharp ups and downs will start smoothing out."

She gave him a distressed look. "Will they, Beau?"

Her expression nearly unstrung him. He set his cup down on the coffee table in front of the couch. Unsure of where they stood with one another, Beau wasn't going to risk rejection by moving too quickly. "Would you like to come and sit beside me? I can hold you for a while if you want."

Callie closed her eyes, taking in a ragged breath. "That would be nice, Beau."

He eased up and moved around her. She scooted down so that he could sit with his back against the corner of the couch. That way, she could lean into his right side while keeping her broken arm comfortable in the sling.

As she slid up to him, he bit back a groan of pleasure as she fitted against his body, turning toward him, her cheek resting on his shoulder, brow against his jaw. And just as before, her arm slid across his hard, flat belly. This time, she made allowances for her sling, and it took a few moments to get herself in a comfortable position.

Then, and only then, did Beau ease his arm around her shoulders, being careful not to put pressure on her upper right arm. "How are the bones in your arm feeling?" he asked, still tasting the silky strands of her hair.

"As long as I take the ibuprofen, the pain is dialed down to a gnawing ache."

"You do know that pain actually slows down the healing process?" Beau knew that Callie didn't like taking drugs. He couldn't blame her. He didn't either.

Callie nuzzled into his shoulder, inhaling his clean scent. She could feel Beau's skin tighten in response to her hand resting languidly across his belly. "I know, but Dr. Bartel wanted to give me a narcotic painkiller. I once took a Percocet, and it knocked me out for three hours solid. So I don't do opium- or opioid-based drugs. I don't want to be knocked out, Beau."

"I understand, gal," he said, moving his fingers lightly against her upper arm. "You comfy now?"

"Yes," she uttered, closing her eyes. "You're my very best medicine, Beau. I hope you know that."

His heart swelled with hope when he heard her soft, wispy words. "I hope I'll always be that for you, Callie." Beau wanted to say so much more, but he felt her body begin to sag against his and knew how tired she was. He also knew pain could take a person down until they were exhausted. And she was definitely at that level.

"Just take a nap," he urged her in a drawl. "I'll sit here and be your big, warm teddy bear blanket."

Callie managed a partial laugh. "Teddy bear? Beau, I saw you out there in action. If anything, you were like a lethal snow leopard."

"You can make me whatever you want," he said, kissing her hair and loving that small purr of pleasure in the back of her throat. Wanting to shake himself, Beau hoped that whatever they'd had before this grueling experience was still intact. But given all she'd gone through, how could it be? Unsure of their tentative relationship with one another, Beau knew he had to approach Callie slowly and with a world of patience. She was in shock. She couldn't sort much out right now. And she sure as hell couldn't sort out their feelings for each other presently. Patience was the key.

CALLIE AWOKE SLOWLY. She was warm and it felt good, compared to the icy cold she'd felt for nearly three days. Her brain was groggy and she felt the ache of her right arm in the cast. As she slowly stretched, she realized she was in a real bed, not a hospital bed. The clock on the nightstand read three p.m.

Surprised, Callie remained on her left side, her knees drawn up toward her body, the blanket toasty over her. Never again would she take for granted a warm, dry blanket or a downy, soft pillow beneath her head. She slowly opened her eyes, taking in the quiet apartment. The only light on was in the kitchen. Focusing, she saw Beau sitting at the table with a lot of papers spread around him, plus a computer. He was hunkered over the Toughbook laptop, a scowl on his face, eyes narrowed on the screen. She didn't know what he was working on, and then remembered that tomorrow morning he was due at HQ to work on missions for his Delta Force brothers.

She ached to be in his arms and recalled falling asleep in them. Beau must have carried her to bed. He had a rugged-looking face, made even more masculine by that beard and shaggy hair. Absently, she wondered what he would look like without a beard, and his hair cut and trimmed in civilian fashion.

Her gaze settled on his sensual mouth, and she felt vague stirrings in her lower body. At least the attack hadn't completely killed off her libido. Callie had been worried about that, and wondered if she'd ever let a man touch her intimately again. Would every man bring back that black-bearded Taliban soldier who had dismounted from his horse and chased her down, then grabbed her to satisfy his lust for a woman?

She'd done so much wrong. *So much.* Her heart ached with all the stupid, unthinking mistakes she'd made. At least Dara wasn't angry at her, and for that, Callie was relieved. But what of Beau? He'd told her clearly not to move from hiding behind the trunk of that pine tree. Looking back on it now as she lay warm and comfortable, Callie realized she had been safe there. Those riders would not have seen her, so why had she bolted? Why had she panicked and run? By doing so, she'd exposed her hiding place and put Beau into jeopardy, too. Would he have been wounded if she'd just listened to him and stayed where she was? A small voice told her no. That made her feel even worse.

Right now, Callie didn't like herself very much. Beau had to be horribly disappointed in her. He was probably angry because she'd gotten him wounded twice. And yet, her heart cried out for him, for his mouth on hers, his arms around her. If not for him, she knew now that she'd have been captured, raped, and probably kept a prisoner or sold as a sex slave. She could have been dead instead of being in his dry, warm bed.

She wanted to cry, because thanks to her anxiety, lack of trust, and panic, she'd gotten him injured. That was the last thing she'd ever want; she loved Beau—those feelings had been growing within her since their first meeting. There was no one else like this West Virginia soldier. He had morals, values, and integrity. He had never tried to take advantage of her and had always treated her with respect, as an equal. And he doted on her . . . a real first in her relationships.

Pushing her face into the pillow, Callie choked back a sob of remorse. She was a hot mess, that's all there was to it. She couldn't ever recall another time in her life when she'd wept so often. It just wasn't like her. How badly she wanted Beau at her side—wanted him to hold her again and kiss her senseless. Make her forget her life-and-death mistakes.

But it was all a dream, because tomorrow morning, she and Dara would be on a flight out of Afghanistan, heading home, while Matt and Beau remained behind. At least Dara had something wonderful to look forward to—Matt would be with her for thirty days. Callie wasn't the jealous type, but the hurt in her heart was real as she realized she'd allowed Beau to slip through her hands. She'd been a big disappointment since the ambush, clingy and needy. She'd certainly revealed that she wasn't as brave as he'd needed her to be, and as a result, Beau had been forced to risk his own life to save hers.

Callie uneasily drifted back to sleep, tears silently streaming down her cheeks.

BEAU HEARD CALLIE stir and looked up from the table where he was working on a mission plan. She slowly sat up, the blue blanket he'd tucked around her falling to her waist. She pushed her fingers through her thick red hair, her eyes puffy and drowsy-looking. He sat up, envisioning her waking up in his bed beside him. It seemed like a dream that could never come true again, but Callie inspired him to dream, to want. No woman had triggered his heart like she did. He slowly rose, pushing the chair back and walking over to her.

"Hey," he drawled. "You look like a princess waking up from a long, long sleep." He smiled at her as he sat down at the end of the bed. He longed to kiss those lips of hers, remembering that kiss with her days earlier. Beau wanted to take her into his arms, but her sling prevented it.

Her mouth tightened a little as she sat up and crossed her legs beneath the blanket, her left hand resting protectively against the sling.

"What time is it?" she asked huskily.

"Dinnertime. Five p.m. to you civilians and 1700 to us military types. Is your arm bothering you, Callie? Are you in pain?"

She nodded. "I need to get up and take more ibuprofen," she muttered.

"Let me get it for you," he said, rising from the bed. She had put some in her purse when she came over to the Eagle's Nest. Beau opened it and found the prescription bottle. He brought back a glass of water and one of the white tablets.

"Here you go," he said, and dropped the tablets into her palm. She looked half-awake, and Beau understood—shock made people sleep a lot. Sleep was the antidote to working shock out of their systems. He sat down on the edge of the mattress, handing her the glass of water.

Callie softly thanked him, took the tablets, and handed him the half-empty glass of water. "What were you doing over there?"

Beau set the glass on the nightstand. "Matt was over at HQ and brought the laptop and our mission intel to me. I'm working on that right now. Are you hungry? Anything sound good to you for dinner tonight?"

Making a face, she muttered, "I'm not hungry yet. I'm still waking up."

"Maybe a cup of fresh, hot coffee? I just made some for myself."

"That would be nice," she said, giving him a grateful look.

He eased off the bed. "Okay, come join me in the kitchen and we'll look through what's in the fridge, and I'll put something together for us."

Callie nodded, immediately missing him as Beau casually sauntered across the room to the kitchen. He was being so solicitous to her, and she'd done nothing to deserve it. He seemed immune to what had happened to them last night. How could that be? Was he really that different from other men? Was it military training that made that difference? Even though he had a bullet hole through his calf and a bruise on his chest where another bullet had struck his Kevlar vest, could he really feel like nothing had happened to him, to them?

Shaking her head, she threw off the cover and scooted over to the edge of the bed. Bathroom first. Cold water on face afterward. She felt drugged, unable to wake up and be alert. What was wrong with her?

Beau gathered up all the reports and put them in files, setting the laptop on the coffee table. He felt a lot of confusion from Callie, saw the yearning in her eyes for him. But at the same time, he saw that she was dealing with the assault and the images of men dying around her, on top of her. Her focus was probably not going to be on him. Or them. If there was a "them."

If only he could be with her in Montana. He could be the one person who could listen to her without interrupting her. Her feelings were deep and dark, and that worried him. People who went through this kind of horror, as he well knew from his time in Afghanistan, often didn't emerge from its grip. Would Callie be one of those casualties? How many women had seen a man's head come apart because of a bullet while he sat on her?

Was there a possibility that they could still have a relationship? Beau wanted that more than he wanted to breathe. He feared that when Callie went home to people who loved her, they wouldn't be able to help her as much as he would because only he knew the depth of her wounding. He had been there. A part of it.

The wounds of war never depended on what people had done—only on who was left to remember them. And the memories for him, and for Callie, were as bitter as any he'd ever known.

CHAPTER 16

B EAU STOOD NEAR Callie at the fixed-wing terminal the next morning. The sky was overcast, and it was definitely going to rain. He had already taken her luggage to the Kuwait Airways luggage cart a few minutes earlier. A hundred other civilian contractors, mostly men, were in the Operations area, waiting to board too. He saw Matt with his arm around Dara's shoulders, off to one side. Trying not to envy their intimacy, Beau focused on absorbing every second of Callie's final minutes with him.

He wanted so badly to tell her he loved her. Last night, after making her dinner, she had been so exhausted, she'd almost passed out, and he'd slept on the couch, a blanket tossed over him. She had not asked him to join her in bed, and that had cleaved his heart wide open. Beau reminded himself that she was most likely remembering his abandoning her. That or feeling guilty as hell about endangering both their lives.

He knew that Callie had been tired, and he could tell she was emotionally up-and-down, so it wasn't the right time to discuss anything important, even though she was leaving the next morning. Beau might not ever see her again.

Sadness gripped his heart as he took her in, loving every inch of her. She had turned away, watching the airline's boarding ramp being pushed up to the middle door of the awaiting airplane. Now Callie looked desolate, grief-stricken. Her sad green eyes were almost lifeless, and her beautiful mouth was set tight. Beau was sure her broken arm was acting up, too. He knew there were all kinds of pain Callie was wrestling with, from physical to psychological to emotional.

She had closed up on him last night after dinner, and he wasn't sure why, but he felt as if Callie had left him. Sure, she was still in the same room with him, but it felt as if the light she always carried so brightly within her had been snuffed out.

He didn't want to believe that. She had been such a sunbeam in everyone's lives before the ambush and assault. Now she was a shell of her former self.

This morning, he'd helped her with her hair. She'd wanted it plaited into one long red braid after she'd gotten her shower. It was a special pleasure for Beau to sit on the bed, brushing her thick, silky red hair. They'd even laughed a little, and Beau ached to lean over and kiss the soft nape of her neck, and then make love to her. But Callie was treating him as a dear friend, not a lover, so right now, he'd settle for that.

He wondered if, after she boarded that plane for home, she'd forget him. To remember him would be to recall the experience that had robbed her of so much. He let himself sink into despair, seeing a future without the auburn-haired pixie who had stolen his heart.

Callie had worn her black wool pantsuit with a bright green tee beneath the blazer. He'd tied off her braid with a green ribbon of the same color. With her small gold earrings and a little makeup to hide her pallor, she looked almost the way she had that first night. Right now, that night seemed like a dream to Beau.

The doors of Ops opened up and a female flight attendant called them to come and board the flight. Out of the corner of his eye, Beau saw Dara lean up and give Matt a passionate kiss good-bye. He wanted to kiss Callie, and she turned to him, reaching out, her left hand meeting his. She slipped a piece of paper into his hand.

"This is my email address," she said. "Just in case you feel like letting me know how you're doing."

Beau's heart leaped as he opened up the paper, memorizing her email address. "Yes, I will," he said, his throat tightening with a multitude of emotions he couldn't show her. The soft strands of hair around her face only made her that much more beautiful to Beau. God, he wanted to kiss her! There was such confusion and darkness and yearning in Callie's eyes as she looked earnestly up at him. Was there a pleading quality deep behind her request?

She looked like a beautiful bird among the mostly dully dressed male population, walking out between the doors toward the airliner.

To hell with it. Beau wasn't going to let Callie go without kissing her. He reached out, sliding his arm around her waist, drawing her close to him. If she didn't want that kiss, she'd let him know right now. Hope lit up her sad green eyes, and her hand came to rest against his chest.

"I'm here for you, Callie," he growled, leaning down, capturing her lips, wanting to tell her through his kiss just how damned much he loved her. To his relief, Beau got no resistance from her; instead, as he slanted his mouth against hers, he heard a whimper catch in her throat and felt her fingers dig into his shirt. She was warm, wet, her lips hungry and eager against his. Callie couldn't press herself against him because of the sling she wore, so he held her lightly, his hand floating against the small of her back, aching to love her.

Beau didn't want that kiss to end, but he heard other people leaving Ops for the plane and knew he had to release her, let her go. Easing his mouth from hers, he stared intently into her half-closed eyes. Now he saw a faint sheen of gold in them. She'd had gold flecks in her eyes before the ambush, he suddenly recalled, and heartened, he smiled a little unsurely and released her, touching her cheek briefly with his fingers.

"I'll be in touch, Callie. I promise. I'm here for you if you need me. Never be afraid to email me about anything, okay?" Beau knew she would need to talk to someone who understood the anguish she was experiencing. Whether it was him or someone else remained to be seen.

She smiled brokenly as she stepped away from him, picking up her purse. "I will be in touch, Beau. Thank you," she said, her voice choked. Her eyes suddenly moistened, and she blinked the tears away. Reaching out, she grazed his bearded jaw. "Thank you for saving my life . . . I'm so, so sorry I disappointed you . . ."

What the hell? He opened his mouth to protest, but Callie was already gone, walking quickly toward the opened Ops doors. Where did she get the idea he was disappointed with her? Confusion made him stand there paralyzed for a moment, not sure what to do. Run after her? Stop her? Ask what she meant by that crazy statement?

Eventually, Beau let it go. He wasn't sure what Callie was thinking, but it was erroneous as hell. He'd never told her he was disappointed in her. He never would.

She was in emotional shock, traumatized, and maybe not thinking clearly. Still, Beau rubbed his chest where his heart lay, because her words had hurt him deeply.

He joined Matt at the windows, watching the Kuwaiti airliner slowly trundle out to the ten-thousand-foot runway. A light, misting rain was beginning, the clouds low and gray. Beau felt as if his heart had been torn out of his chest. He wanted to be on that plane with Callie, not watching her leave him behind.

Matt turned to him. "How are you doing, bro?"

"I've had better days," Beau muttered, afraid to trust himself to say more.

"Yeah. Me, too," Matt agreed grimly.

Beau met his group leader's gaze. "At least you're going home in two weeks and you'll be with Dara."

"And I am so looking forward to it," Matt said, his voice thick with feelings. Glancing over at Beau, he said, "I'm sorry our captain decided to keep you here at the base."

Shrugging, Beau said, "I guess I'm stuck creating missions." He watched the jet anchor at the end of the runway. So many emotions tore through him and he swallowed hard, sitting on them. After the jet took off, he watched it until it disappeared into the gray clouds. Then Matt clapped him on the shoulder.

"Come on, we've both got work waiting for us at HQ."

THREE DAYS LATER, Beau received an email from Callie. He was nervous but excited to read it as he opened up his personal email inbox on the HQ's computer. The last three days had been pure hell for him. Matt was already bringing the team together for another mission in two days, and he was stuck back at Bagram. His leg was slowly healing, so he was hobbling around the office like a three-legged horse.

Beau's disposition wasn't as even-keeled and charitable as it had been, and he frequently lost his temper. That just wasn't like him. If not for Matt pulling him aside and listening to him, he felt as if half of him had left the station the morning Callie had walked out of his life.

Now there was an email from her. Eagerly, he read:

Hi, Beau. I'm home. It was a grueling flight, and I didn't realize just how sensitive I was to everything. Dara traded seats with me on the flight because guys would walk up and down that narrow aisle and brush against me sometimes. I couldn't handle it. It was a stupid reaction, but I couldn't deal with it. Thank God Dara was there. I felt safer, more secure, in that middle seat. There was a woman civilian contractor in the window seat, so that was good. It's only men who scare me, and I understand why, but I still feel threatened.

The Seattle airport was large and noisy. Going through customs, people were crowding around me, everyone in a hurry, wanting to get home. I felt as if I were crawling out of my skin. I wanted to scream. I wanted quiet. I couldn't handle all the chatting, the noise, the pushing, and the bustling about. By the time we got out of there, I was an emotional wreck. Dara took me to a women's bathroom and I stayed in there to get away from it all for a while. That break helped me get my act together.

I felt so stupid, so weak, Beau. It's as if my skin has been turned inside out, and I'm so raw and emotionally volatile. I was never so glad to get off a flight as I was in Butte, Montana. Seeing my whole family waiting for me was like coming to you, walking into your arms. I had a feeling of safety, and of being loved.

My parents are worried about me. I can't talk about what happened yet. I know they want to understand, but not yet. My grandparents, thank goodness, aren't pressing me about it, and it's easier being around them. Grandpa Graham is a lot like you: he asks me lots of questions. And he's okay if I don't completely answer them. He's so wise and I feel so safe around him.

How are you? How's your leg doing? Is it on the mend? What's the weather like there? I just talked to Dara yesterday evening and she's so excited that Matt will be home in less than two weeks. She deserves to be happy. Is there going to be a USO show for you guys at Bagram?

Have you heard from your family? How are they doing? I'm sure they're sad you can't be home for Christmas.

The weather here is picture-postcard beautiful. I took ten photos with Grandpa's Canon digital camera and he helped me convert them into small JPEGs for you. I took photos of the ranch that I'd like to share with you. Please let me know how you are? Be truthful about it. Don't tell me you're 'okay.'"

Beau, I miss you terribly. I'm sure you don't miss me because I was such a pain in the ass, but I have to once again thank you for saving my life, giving me my life back, and I'll always be grateful to you, Beau.

Big hugs,
Callie

It felt as if someone were carving up his heart with a dull steak knife. Beau printed a copy of it and then saw the ten photos Callie had sent along. He scanned them rapidly, hoping there was one of her among them. There was! His heart hammered as he looked at the photo of her with her grandparents, standing together against a pipe-rail fence. On either side of them were horses with friendly looks on their alert, shaggy faces.

But Beau's gaze stayed focused on Callie. She was in a red knit cap, her hair loose and free around her white parka. Grandma Maisy was on her right and Grandpa Graham on her left. Between them, how pale and strained Callie looked.

Beau's mouth tightened. He missed no details, not in his line of business, because missing a detail could get you killed. The darkness in Callie's green eyes scared him. She was trying to smile but couldn't quite carry it off. Her arm was still in a sling.

Now he had no doubt—he needed to be with Callie. Would she ask him to come visit her? Would she hint in that direction or give him a clue as to whether he was welcome or not? Or had she gotten as close as she could to asking for him to walk back into her life by saying she missed him desperately? Women talked in code, that was for damned sure. He was a man of action, and it was painful to do nothing.

Beau turned away to answer the emails from his own family. He decided to hold off on answering Callie's email for a bit. He was never spontaneous about important decisions, and he wanted to read it more carefully.

GRAHAM MCKINLEY WATCHED his granddaughter cleaning out one of the oak box stalls in the horse barn. He stayed out of her line of vision. It was a wintery midafternoon, and he'd been in the house earlier when he'd heard a muted scream from behind Callie's bedroom door down the hall. And then, minutes later, she'd hurried down the hall in her winter gear, racing out the porch door and following the shoveled snow trail that lead to the horse barns.

His wife, Maisy, was in the office at the other end of their huge, three-story home. She wouldn't have heard Callie's scream. From the day she'd come home, Graham had known that his granddaughter was still suffering from her experience in Afghanistan. She'd been home five days now, and every day, she had worsened, it seemed. No matter what the family did, it didn't help her. What would?

It hurt Graham to hear his granddaughter crying when she thought no one else was around, hiding out in the stables to get the privacy she needed. She couldn't use her right hand yet, but Callie was creative. Holding the pitchfork beneath her left arm, she could lean down in the stall, slide it along the concrete floor, and scoop up a bunch of straw and horse poop. She would then walk it out to where she had a large wheelbarrow nearby. The gray horse that had been in there, Ghost, her favorite thoroughbred mixed quarter horse, was standing quietly in cross ties, watching her.

Something had to be done to help Callie. Graham eased from his position in the shadows and quietly walked down the aisle in her direction. Ghost nickered a hello and Callie looked up. She wiped her nose with the back of her sleeve, straightening after dumping the load of manure and straw into the wheelbarrow.

"Grandpa! What are you doing out here?"

He smiled a little, picking up another pitchfork hanging on a wall hook. "Might ask you the same thing, Callie. Want some help cleaning Ghost's stall?"

"Well . . ." Her voice faltered, and she gave him an embarrassed look. "Sure . . . I guess . . ."

"Come on," he said gruffly, sliding his arm around her shoulders and giving her a gentle squeeze. "Let me help you." Her eyes were dark with the pain she carried within her. Callie had never asked for help; she and Dara had grown up independent and self-confident. This was a side of Callie he'd never seen.

"O-okay . . ."

For the next fifteen minutes, they silently worked together. Callie was still crying and sniffing. Graham knew his granddaughter well: she was a stubborn little thing, and until she was ready to reveal what she was carrying inside, no one could pull it out of her.

Her nose was red and her eyes were red-rimmed. They worked quietly together, and pretty soon, the stall was cleared. Graham brought over a fresh bale of wheat straw and threw it into the stall. Then he pulled out his Buck knife and cut the twine around the ninety-pound bale. Callie helped him spread it all around, a nice mattress for Ghost, who would appreciate the fresh, clean-smelling straw. The barn had fifteen box stalls, and every one of them needed to be cleaned every other day.

It was a constant job, and one that Graham's wranglers normally did. But his men and women were on holiday, and he was short-staffed.

"This was awful nice of you to help out here," Graham told her, taking both pitchforks and hanging them back on the barn wall. "I'll get Ghost and bring him in here."

"I'll go get him a flake of hay," Callie said, turning toward the stacked alfalfa.

Afterward, Graham asked her, "What else were you going to do out here?"

Shrugging, Callie whispered, "I don't know, Grandpa . . ."

"Want to sit with me over there?" He gestured with his gloved hand toward two metal chairs sitting near the open door of the tack room.

Callie nodded, trying to stop crying. Just her grandfather tucking her beneath his arm and pulling her against his tall, strong body made her feel better. As they sat down, she said, "Grandpa? You were in the Marine Corps. You've never told anyone about it, or what you did when you were in."

He smiled a little, resting one boot over his knee. "Well, mostly because what I did was top secret, baby girl."

Her eyes widened, and she stared at her sixty-five-year-old grandfather. "Really?"

"Yep. Why?"

She melted beneath his warm blue gaze, feeling his love for her. Wiping her face with her fingers, she said, "The man who saved my life—Beau Gardner . . ."

"Yes?"

"H-he reminds me so much of you in some ways. He's Army black ops and top secret, just like you. He's very kind and gentle. He never raised his voice, always had a smile for me. Even in the worst of it, when we were running to get away from the Taliban, he seemed so calm, so sure of himself."

"He's Delta Force, right? I recall Dara calling and mentioning that Beau was one of the men on Matt Culver's team."

Nodding, Callie whispered, "It's so hard to talk about this, Grandpa. N-no one understands . . . but Beau did. Just being around him calmed me down immediately. He just has a way with me, like you do."

"He sounds like a very special person, Callie."

"H-he is. He saved my life . . . but I put him in danger in so many different ways." Looking up, she asked, "Did you ever go into combat? Did you have to shoot an enemy?"

Nodding, Graham said quietly, "Yes, I did."

"You never told us," she said, gazing at him in wonder.

"Baby girl, it's not something a man ever wants to talk about to someone who doesn't know the territory."

"Right," Callie said, nodding between sniffles. "I-I had a nightmare earlier, and I woke myself up screaming."

"I heard you."

Callie's eyes widened. "Oh . . . God . . . I'm sorry, Grandpa . . ."

He lifted his hand. "No need, Callie. You went through a lot, from what I can tell."

"W-we both did," she said, her voice low with anguish. "I-I miss Beau so much, Grandpa. I wish with my heart, my soul, he could be here with me. He was there. He knows what happened . . ."

"What's stopping you from asking him to come for a visit?" Graham asked suddenly, surprising her.

"Uh, well, I don't think he'd come, Grandpa." She got up, beginning to pace, her hand against her mouth, more tears falling.

Graham sat watching Callie move back and forth, and his heart was raw with pain. He knew a lot more about what she was going through than he had let on, but he'd never tell her. More important, he recognized the signs of severe trauma, or what they now called PTSD. "Tell me why, Callie. Why wouldn't he come to see you? You said you had a good relationship with him before the ambush."

Over the last five days, Graham had begun piecing together things that Callie had let slip. She was like a huge jigsaw puzzle, and if he hadn't been a Marine Corps sniper, he wouldn't have put it together as he had.

Callie halted in front of Graham. "B-because . . . oh, Grandpa, don't tell anyone this, okay?"

"Promise, cross my heart and hope to die, baby girl," he said, making the symbolic sign with his hand over his Sherpa jacket.

"I-I placed Beau in danger. He got shot twice because of me." She sobbed and choked out, "I ran! I got scared and ran, Grandpa. He told me to crouch down behind a huge pine tree trunk and not to move. I was well hidden there. But when the Taliban on horseback got closer, I ran. I was so scared!" She began to sob earnest, humiliated by her actions.

Graham slowly unwound and walked over to her. She was a little thing compared with his six feet five inches. Without a word, he drew her gently into his arms, allowing her to press her face into his jacket and cry with wracking, body-shaking sobs. He took off his other glove, rubbing her back and patting her shaking shoulders. Now the rest of the pieces fell into place. This was what was really eating at Callie—that she'd run when Beau Gardner had hidden her so he could take care of the bad guys trailing them.

He pulled a white linen handkerchief out of his back pocket and pressed it into Callie's damp left hand. The pain in her cries ripped into an old wound he carried deep within himself. Never had he thought that one day, one of his beloved granddaughters would ever receive a wound similar to his. Rubbing her shoulder, he let her cry it out, because he knew from long ago that crying had gotten him through his own private hell as a Marine.

Finally, she stopped crying and blotted her eyes dry with his handkerchief.

"Sometimes, baby girl, we need a special person in our life who can help us through something like this," he told her gruffly. "And it sounds like this Gardner fella might be exactly what the doctor ordered for you, Callie."

She gave him a miserable look. "But I've disappointed him so badly, Grandpa. I'm sure he won't have anything to do with me. I got him shot because I ran and I didn't stay hidden."

Shrugging, Graham asked, "Did you tell him that?"

Sniffing, she mumbled, "No, but in so many words I did . . . I told him I knew I was a huge disappointment to him."

"What'd he say?"

"I-I don't know. I turned and walked away from him. I-I couldn't stand to hear what he might say to me. I know I'm a coward . . . I ran . . . I didn't trust what he told me, and I put his life in jeopardy because of it . . ."

Graham nodded, pursing his lips in thought. "First of all, you're a McKinley, and there aren't any cowards in our family that I know of, Callie." He touched her nose. "You were a civilian, completely untrained in military tactics, and you were scared for your life. Now, if you'd had training like Beau Gardner did and then you ran—yes, you would be disobeying a direct order." He placed his finger beneath her chin, looking deep into her suffering eyes. "But you weren't trained, Callie. You did the best you could at the time. You thought you were gonna die, didn't you?"

She gave a jerky nod. "I-I thought we were both going to die . . ."

"Can you tell me about the whole event, then? It might help me to help you."

Callie sank against him, closed her eyes, and finally let the story pour out of her. Her grandfather had never judged her, not ever. And she knew he was the only member of their family who had been in the military, so intuitively she knew he would understand.

When she was finished telling the story, she pulled out of his arms, blowing her nose. It hurt to look up to see the expression in his face, but when she did, Callie was amazed. His eyes were bright with unshed tears and there was such sympathy in his expression it nearly made her collapse with relief.

"Are you open to a suggestion, Callie?"

"Of course . . ."

"Why don't you email that young, heroic man of yours and plead with him to come here and spend Christmas with you? Tell him you need him. I'll bet he'll find some way to make it happen. He's on the sick list, and if he's got back leave coming, his CO should grant it to him, no problem." Looking deep into Callie's hopeful gaze, he added gruffly, "I believe that he will find a way to come home to you. Am I right?"

"B-because you know how the military works, Grandpa?"

He smiled a little and brushed her damp cheek. "No. Because I know how the human heart works. Go email him, baby girl. Something will break loose to get him here. Right now, you need him more than the military does, so go get him."

CHAPTER 17

CHRISTMAS MUSIC WAS playing throughout the Butte airport terminal as Beau made his way through security. He wore civilian clothes, not wanting to advertise he was military. His brown leather bomber jacket, jeans, black T-shirt, and motorcycle boots made him look like anyone else. After getting his CO to sign off at HQ giving him his thirty days' leave, he limped past the security guards and into the open terminal.

His heart was pounding with anxiety over Callie's email. She needed him. Could he come for a visit? Could he spend Christmas with her? Was there any way his CO could release him and allow him to come stateside? It was a cryptic email, but Beau took her plea seriously. Luckily, snow was falling heavily in the mountains and high valleys of Afghanistan, and the Taliban intrusion was coming to a halt. No one was going out on missions right now, so his captain was able to give him leave.

"Mr. Gardner?"

A man's gruff voice made him turn to the right. Although Beau was six feet tall, this man with silver and black hair was probably six feet five inches, with sparkling blue eyes and a thick handlebar mustache. He held his hand out and said, "I'm Graham McKinley, Callie's grandfather. I told her I'd pick you up. Thanks for coming, son."

Gripping the man's weathered hand, Beau said, "Good to meet you, sir. And please call me Beau."

The Montana rancher was wearing a gray Stetson, jeans, scuffed cowboy boots, and a championship bronc rider silver belt buckle. His cranberry long-sleeve shirt was hidden by the worn Sherpa jacket draped over it.

"I can do that, Beau. I'm the only one meeting you here. Callie's in too much emotional turmoil to come to a crowded, noisy place like this. I'm sure you understand." Graham gave Beau a sharp, measuring look.

"Yes, sir, I do understand."

"Good. You got luggage?"

"Just a duffel bag, sir."

Nodding, Graham said, "Let's mosey along this way, and we'll get it in baggage claim. After we stick it in the truck, we'll go find the best hamburger joint in the town, eat, and have a little chat."

Beau felt exhaustion tearing through him, and his need to see Callie overrode everything. But he appreciated that she had sent her grandfather, whom he knew she adored. Over at the baggage claim area, Beau stood near the carousel to wait for his luggage to be spit out by the machine. He noticed McKinley constantly looking around, keeping an eye on things. His bearing told Beau he'd been in the military at one time. "What branch were you in, sir?" he asked, curious.

McKinley's mouth turned up into a grin. "Marine Corps. Sniper." And then he looked at Beau, holding his gray gaze. "You and I share a common denominator. We're both black ops."

"Yes, sir, I was sure you were." Beau's regard for the rancher had already escalated. For being in his sixties, he was a large-boned man, leanly muscled and—regardless of his age—more able-bodied than most. Beau suspected it was from running a ranch. "How is Callie?"

"Needing you, son. But I don't think that's any surprise to you, is it?"

"No. And, sir, I believe you and I share common concerns about Callie," Beau said.

"That we do." Graham saw an olive bag drop onto the carousel. "Is that yours?"

Beau checked and said, "Yes, sir."

Graham nodded. "Good. Let's get it and get going, son. We have a lot to discuss."

On their way to the café outside of the city, Beau saw that Montana was covered in snow. McKinley didn't say much, but Beau could feel a lot going on inside the man. Most of all, he felt the love he had for Callie, and that made him relax. This man was a friend and a former black ops, to boot. Every operator shared a common base of understanding. There was respect, integrity, morals, and values unspoken between them. Beau was sure it was no accident that McKinley told him he'd been a Marine Corps sniper. They were almost always black ops. And he would bet his next paycheck that McKinley had seen his fair share of action.

At the truck stop, they found a booth in the back where it was quieter. Beau was starving and ordered two hamburgers and a double order of French fries. McKinley had a bowl of chili that looked like it could eat chrome off the bumper of his Ford pickup. He could tell that the rancher wanted to talk to him about Callie. After all, he was her grandfather, he loved her, and he wanted only the best for her.

Beau understood about family matters. In Seattle, he'd been able to call his parents, and they were happy and excited to hear from him at last. His other two brothers, Coy and Jackson, were home for the holiday, and Beau knew that their presence softened the blow that he wouldn't be coming home. His parents were great—they completely understood why he was in Montana instead of coming home to West Virginia for the holidays. He loved them for grasping the situation with Callie, and they fully supported his seeing her instead of them.

Wiping his mouth with a paper napkin, Graham McKinley eyed the young soldier opposite him. Now he could see why Callie was madly in love with the man. Beau Gardner, despite his West Virginia drawl, rugged good looks, and easy smile, was not a man to tinker with. Graham was very familiar with Delta Force operators and had worked with his fair share of them over the years he'd been a sniper. There was a confidence in Beau that Callie needed, he realized.

"Do you love my granddaughter?" he asked sharply, his eyes riveted on Beau's face.

Beau sat up, unable to keep the shock out of his expression over the unexpected, blunt question. Looking into McKinley's narrowed blue eyes, he said, "Yes, sir, I do love her. Very much."

"It's not a passing fancy on your part, son? I know black ops men draw women by the truckload."

Beau pushed the empty plate aside. "No, sir, Callie has never been a passing fancy to me."

"Tell me how you met," her grandfather said.

Beau realized McKinley was checking him out, testing him, seeing if he was really worthy of Callie. But Graham McKinley represented something even more daunting. As her grandfather, he could decide here and now whether or not he'd see Callie. He was going to protect his granddaughter at all costs, and Beau silently celebrated the man's attitude. Callie didn't need a man who only wanted sex from her. There had to be a lot more than that involved before Graham was going to allow him back into Callie's broken life. Unworried, he folded his hands.

Without preamble, Beau told him just about everything except their shared intimacy. The man sat there like a sphinx, eyes unblinking. He listened closely to everything Beau had to tell him. By the time he was finished, Beau could feel sweat trickling down his ribcage.

"Now, tell me what happened in Afghanistan to put her into this agitated state. She's told the family very little about that experience."

Beau hesitated. The whole fiasco was top secret, but looking into McKinley's flinty blue eyes, he decided, *The hell with confidentiality*. This man carried as many, or more, secrets as he did. Keeping his voice low, he told him.

Graham sat back when Beau had finished, waiting until the waitress poured them fresh coffee in their cups and left. He stared at Gardner, sizing him up, seeing an equal hardness in the younger man's narrowed gray eyes. "You left one thing out of your story, son."

Beau scowled. "I left nothing out." He saw the man's expression grow thoughtful, his mouth pursed. Beau wasn't about to divulge their loving one another. That was none of anyone's business.

"Yes, you did, and you know you did. I want to know why you didn't divulge that Callie had run from the position she was hiding in and threw your entire op into disarray. It left you with few choices except to deal with the consequences." He raised a gray brow. "It also got you shot twice."

Leaning back, Beau met the man's implacable stare. This was no ordinary Marine Corps sniper. No, his intuition told him that in his day, Graham McKinley had worked with all the black ops groups, not just the Marines. That put him in a highly specialized, top-tier position within the community. And damned if he didn't recall that someone named McKinley had been instrumental in an op during the Persian Gulf War in February of 1991.

A group of SEALs and Delta Force operators had been pinned down in a Kuwaiti oil refinery and were being picked off by several Iraqi Republican Guard snipers far above them. The Marine sniper, known only as the Ghost, had sneaked into the firefight like the shadow he was. He took the Iraqi snipers down one by one, thereby allowing the other black ops teams to operate within the refinery and complete their important mission—to eradicate the Iraqis trying to hold on to it. The Ghost had also held the highest position within the refinery and spotted thirty of Hussein's Republican Guard speeding toward them to take out the black ops teams.

When it was all over, the Ghost had killed many of the enemy troops. He'd singlehandedly saved a mission that could have gone bad. The black ops teams captured fifty other Iraqi soldiers, leaving the refinery intact, and the Ghost left with those teams and became a legend within the black ops community.

Beau knew snipers were called "force multipliers" for good reason, and now he was looking at the man who had saved so many American lives on that fateful night. This man was a bona fide hero in Beau's eyes. And if his memory served him correctly, the Ghost was later awarded the Navy Cross, the second-highest medal a military person could receive, next to the Medal of Honor itself, for his accomplishments.

Moving the cup around between his fingers, Beau returned the Ghost's steady gaze. Obviously, Callie had told him what happened, which didn't surprise Beau. There was a strong tie between her and her grandfather, and she had certainly told the right person, because if anyone would understand her actions, it would be Graham McKinley.

"You know, your granddaughter is carrying enough guilt around already, so I wouldn't, with all due respect, divulge the choice she made out there." His voice lowered. "I know you love her with your life. And if Callie hadn't already told you what she'd done at that ambush, you would not be hearing it from me. Ever."

Graham pulled in a deep breath and then took a sip of his coffee. He literally bristled with protectiveness toward Callie. Setting the mug down, he nodded thoughtfully. "That tells me everything I need to know about you, son."

Beau remained motionless, unsure of what McKinley meant by his statement. The rancher continued to assess him, like a surgeon contemplating a patient on the table, intent on learning all he could before operating. Beau suspected that McKinley lived very close to the surface of his skin, and he used his five senses to an extraordinary degree.

There was nothing else Beau could say to defend what he'd done to keep Callie's good name intact. Her family didn't need to know her decision. She was laboring under enough guilt as it was, because she'd urged Dara to go with her to that village.

"So," Beau said, challenging him, "where does this leave us, sir? Am I going to get to see Callie or not?"

Graham nodded. "Yes, you'll get to see her, son." He smiled a little, his eyes glinting. "Ordinarily, I don't put up with liars. But you lied for all the right reasons. You can see that my granddaughter is already on the edge of what I call the 'black hole.' I've been there too many times myself. I know what she's staring into, but then, so do you."

"Yes, sir, I do know."

"She trusts you."

"And I trust her."

"Even after you ordered her to remain hidden and not move, and she disobeyed?"

"She's a civilian, sir." Beau hesitated, his voice deepening as he held McKinley's implacable, unblinking gaze. "Answer me one thing. If I don't miss my guess, you were called 'the Ghost' back in the Persian Gulf War. So I don't think you miss a damn thing, sir. And you know civilians are not trained up to our military standards to defend the position they're given. The same standard that's applied to a military person is not applied to a civilian who might be caught in the same situation."

Graham refused to respond to Beau's revelation about the Ghost, and his respect for the young Delta Force operator rose another notch.

"She calls herself a coward," Graham tossed out. "What's your opinion?"

Beau snorted. "She's anything but that, sir. She was brave, never complained, never whined, and was a fighter in every sense of the word."

"Good. I like how you see her, because that's the way she is. Right now, I'm afraid, she's got a pretty severe case of PTSD." Graham grimaced. "Back in my day we knew about it, but everyone ignored it. We just continued to do our jobs, regardless."

"I agree with you."

"You love her."

Beau felt all the fire go out of him. "Without question, I do, sir. But I have no idea if Callie loves me. We've never broached the topic with one another. We didn't know one another that long before the ambush happened."

"She does love you," her grandfather said lazily, moving the cup between his large hands. "But she's got too much on her plate right now to realize it. Her focus is on her memories from that ambush. She can't seem to get past them."

"She's been through too much, sir, and she needs time to absorb the trauma. Then she can heal up from this experience. It's shattered her in a lot of ways," Beau said, relieved to be talking freely to someone who cared so deeply for Callie.

Graham nodded in agreement. "Tell you what I'm going to do. And I need you to go along with an idea I have. Just consider this a little black ops assignment, son."

CALLIE WAS SO nervous that her palms broke out in a damp sweat as she saw her grandpa pull into the main parking area near the homestead. Her heart was pounding with anxiety and excitement.

Beau was sitting in the passenger seat, and she felt shock ripple through her as she saw him climb out of the truck. Where was his beard? And his hair was military-short! He was actually handsome! Her heart blew open as she saw his casual, easy way of walking, a duffel over his left shoulder as he ambled toward the white picket fence. She clasped her hands, standing inside the main door, watching them approach. Her grandfather was smiling, and Beau was laughing at whatever he'd said. It was as if they were old friends reunited after a long separation.

She shifted from one foot to another, now eager to see Beau, to be near him again. And here he was, on a real visit, just for her! Callie was so grateful that her grandfather had urged her to send out that email to him—and he'd answered her almost immediately.

Thirty days! Beau would be with her for a whole month! She'd nearly fainted with joy and relief when she received another email from him a day later, telling her that his captain had authorized his leave. And he was here . . . now, with her.

Suddenly, fear rose up, followed by guilt and shame. And then, her love for Beau overrode everything else. The mix of emotions was almost too much for her to process. She took a deep breath and opened the door as they stomped their boots on the thick, bristly rug on the front porch. The bristles took off most of the snow.

Beau's head snapped up, and his gaze pinned hers as she opened the door and stepped out. Then all doubt dissolved, and she was overcome with joy, spreading like wings, lifting her out of her dark depression.

Beau grinned and moved forward as Callie threw open the screen door, calling his name. She still had her right arm in a sling and he halted, then opened his arms to her. The sheer delight in her eyes hammered at his pounding heart. She reached up and slid her left arm around his neck, bringing his mouth down upon hers.

Beau was as excited as she was—he loved that taste of apple pie and coffee, and a sweetness that was pure Callie. Her long hair was a loose, shining cape around her shoulders, and he inhaled her womanly scent as she eagerly kissed him in greeting.

Remembering that McKinley was standing nearby, Beau reluctantly eased from Callie's mouth. They were both breathing raggedly. "I told you I'd come," he said, grinning, holding her gently against him, his arm loose around her waist.

"Thank you," she whispered unsteadily. Callie pulled from his embrace and went over to her grandfather, kissing his cheek. "And thank you!"

"She's looking better already," Graham noted wryly, winking at her. "Come on, let's all go inside. It's cold out here."

It was three p.m., and the huge kitchen was bright and cheery as Beau followed them inside. He placed his bag at the corner of the room to keep it out of the walkway. There were frilly white curtains at the large glass windows that looked out at the ranch, and the snow-covered, rounded hills rose in the distance. The kitchen was painted a pale yellow, white tiles on the counter and backsplash.

Everything looked homey and antique. Beau especially appreciated the ancient iron wood-burning stove and the black iron skillets sitting nearby. The warmth in the kitchen gently mingled with the scent of freshly made apple pie and coffee.

Graham remained standing. "Baby girl, why don't you and your friend sit down over pie and coffee and chat? Grandma and I have some work to do outside. We'll see you two at dinner tonight."

Callie nodded, barely able to keep from bubbling over with happiness.

"Okay, Grandpa. Thank you so much for picking Beau up at the airport."

Graham smiled. "No problem, Callie. Just enjoy your time with this fine young man."

"That pie sure smells good," Beau murmured, eyeing it on the trivet sitting on the kitchen counter. He grinned and reached across the long trestle table, squeezing her hand. "When I kissed you I tasted it. Did you already have a piece?"

He saw her cheeks flush pink, her green eyes had been clouded blazing into life once more. Graham had warned him that Callie was nosediving into depression. He'd recognized the signs because he, too, had a tendency to sink into the same state.

Both Graham and Beau suspected she was stuck because she couldn't release the horrors of the ambush. Graham hoped that because Callie trusted Beau, he could get her to release whatever was troubling her.

"Busted," she laughed softly, shaking her head. "Yes, I stole a sliver of it earlier. Would you like a slice?"

"Yes," he said, "but let me help you. You're still one-armed at this point."

"I'm getting to hate this sling," she muttered. "The doctor said starting tomorrow I could go without it, and I can hardly wait." She pulled her arm out of the sling, showing him her new, removable cast. "The healing is going well. My doctor said this is waterproof so I can wash with it, which is wonderful."

Beau pushed the chair back and rose. "Well, it's a step in the right direction, gal. Why don't you show me where things are kept, and I'll cut us two slices of pie."

"Okay. I'm actually feeling hungry now," she said, getting up.

Callie had lost weight, and Graham had confided that she had no appetite, which bothered him, but Beau was buoyed to see her interest in joining him for apple pie—could it be a sign of progress already?

"This is a great place to live," he said, cutting the pie with a knife. "Everything's so big."

Callie brought down two plates. "Dara and I were so lucky to grow up here. Grandpa and Grandma have given us all a wonderful life."

He looked her way. "Are you feeling better now that you're home, Callie?"

She seemed to deflate with his question. Pulling two forks from the drawer, she said, "Yes and no. My parents are worried about me, and I-I can't tell them what happened . . . not yet." She bit down on her full lower lip. "I'm just not ready . . ."

Never, if Beau had anything to do with it, would her family know everything that had happened to Callie. It was her call, and he respected however she wanted to handle it. He remained silent, bringing the pie over to the table. After Callie sat down opposite him, the coffee and pie in front of them, he decided to remind her of something she'd said to him in Ops at Bagram.

"I need to understand something, Callie," he began, holding her gaze. "You said something to me in Ops, just before you left, about being a disappointment to me. I never had a chance to ask you what that meant." His voice faltered as he remembered. "And I could see it was something important, or you wouldn't have said it. Can we talk about that now?"

He saw her face become still, some of the darkness returning to her green eyes. She put her fork down. "How could you not be disappointed in me, Beau? I ran. I was a coward. I didn't listen to you when you hid me behind that huge tree on that mountain slope. I put you and me both in harm's way." She shook her head, giving him a wounded look. "I'm so sorry I did that. You'll never know how much."

He stretched his hand across the table, gripping hers. "Listen to me. First of all, I wasn't disappointed by anything you did out there, Callie. You must know that once and for all." He saw tears glimmer in her eyes, saw her fighting them back. "It would be one thing if you were in the military and I gave you the order to stay put, but you're a civilian, Callie. You were scared. And I'm sure that, as those riders came closer, adrenaline was pouring through your bloodstream. Fear makes us do things to survive, and that's why you ran. You were afraid they were going to find you and kill you."

He released her hand, seeing the devastation in her face. She had to hear the truth from him, or she'd go on telling herself she was a coward who ran away, a disappointment to the whole human race. None of that was true, but Beau had to get her to see it from his perspective as an operator.

Callie sat up, tucking her hands in her lap. Searching his open face, the look in his gray eyes, she whispered, "Really? You aren't mad at me? Or disappointed?" She saw his mouth tug upward.

"No, sweet woman', I'm none of those things where you're concerned. We have to get this talked out, Callie. Otherwise, it's going to be like an elephant in the room between us. I don't want that. I want to be here to help support you as much as I can. I know what you've gone through. I was there. I saw it all." Beau halted and shook his head. "If you never believe anything else I say, Callie, believe this: I care so damn deeply for you, my heart aches sometimes. I would do anything in the world for you. Let what happened out there on that ambush go. I'm telling no one about it—that's between you and me. It's not important to me to throw that information around. What is important is how you see yourself, and that you realize how I see you. Don't close the door on life, or me, or yourself, Callie. Let your life go on, and that includes your life and mine."

Sharp relief cut through Callie as she stared into Beau's narrowed gray eyes. His voice was low, fraught with emotion, and he wasn't trying to hide how he felt. She twisted her hands, palms damp. Seeing the sincerity, the raw feelings reflected in his eyes, his low, gruff words sank deep into her. She unknotted her hands, flattening them against the table. "You've never lied to me, Beau."

"No, and I never will, Callie." He reached out, his one large hand covering hers on the table. "Will you believe me? Will you let the past go on this? You're not a loser. You did nothing wrong. I've never blamed you or been upset or angry about what happened out there. I never will be." His fingers tightened marginally over her hands, holding her watery stare. "Let it go. It's the past, Callie. Only you and I know the truth of what happened out there. It will go to my grave with me. No one else needs to know."

Giving a bare nod, she stared down at their hands. She didn't care if she put her arm back in the sling right now. This was so much more important and she needed Beau's touch. Pressing her lips together, so many emotions clashing within her, she whispered, "Thank you, Beau . . . I was really lost for a while over this . . ."

He turned her hand over, gathering it gently between his own, holding her confused stare. "Yeah, I know. And it's to be expected, Callie. You're not trained to be an operator out there. You did the best you could, and it was more than enough. In my eyes, you're so damned brave. You were a fighter when we had to run. You never gave up or gave in. You were there with me every step of the way. Look at all the things you did right with me to get us out of that hot mess. Okay?" He added a small, hopeful smile to go along with his low, thick words.

To his surprise, he saw Callie take his passionately spoken reasons to heart. There was a lightening in her eyes and he could see the tension draining from her pale face, as if a priest had given her absolution for her sins. Never had he wanted her to believe him more than right now. They had to jump this hurdle together and then put it behind them forever. If he could convince her she'd done nothing wrong, that she was simply reacting out of survival instinct, then Beau knew this wouldn't continue to haunt her for the rest of her life. And he loved her too much to see that happen. He would fight with his heart, his soul, to put this idea she held to rest and bury it forever between them. Otherwise, there was no hope for their being together in the future and he knew it.

"Callie, I have dreams of us being together," he began. "And I hope you have dreams for us, too." His hands tightened a little around hers, because Beau wanted a life with this woman. The surprise in her eyes told him that she'd given up on having any relationship with him until just right now.

"That's a dream I thought," she said, choked up, "had died out there . . ."

"Dreams are about hope, Callie." He held her wounded gaze. "I dream for both of us, but now I think you realize you can dream right alongside me, too.

That there's a lot of hope of a future if we want it."

AT DINNER THAT night, the family gathered as usual, and Callie watched her parents react to meeting Beau for the first time. She saw hope in her mom and dad's eyes now that he'd come for a visit to see her. They knew in general how important Beau had been to her life being saved in Afghanistan. It was clear from their reactions toward him that they were completely grateful to him and glad that he would stay with them throughout the holidays.

It was her grandparents, who sat at either end of the table, who made Callie feel even happier. Beau gravitated to Grandmother Maisy, who was warm and outgoing. It made her heart swell, because everyone at the dinner table had fallen in love with quiet, humble Beau Gardner, just as she had. His manners, his boyish smile, and his easygoing nature captured everyone in the best of ways. More relief tunneled through her when she realized her family fully accepted Beau into their lives. They saw him as the true hero he was. Pride filtered into her chest, and her heart was filled with love for him.

Callie got the shock of her life when her grandfather announced at the dinner table that night that he thought she and Beau might think about taking the small cabin near the main ranch house. But no one at the table seemed particularly stunned by his suggestion. The cabin had two bedrooms and had always been a cozy house for relatives who came to visit in the summer.

Her mother, Stacy, and father, Connor, nodded and acted like it was fine idea. She looked at Beau, who also seemed surprised with the arrangement. Maisy said, "I think that's a good idea, Graham. Callie and Beau need some alone time to sort things out. Things are so go-go-go in the main ranch house here, it doesn't make for quality communication time between two people."

Beau sat with Callie on one side of the table, facing her parents. He could feel Callie's reaction and hear it in her voice—was she embarrassed by the idea? Scared to be alone with him? Secretly pleased? He saw Callie's cheeks grow a deep pink, her glance in his direction shy but hopeful-looking. He gave her a nod, hoping to ease her discomfort.

"Sure, that sounds okay," he told the family, "but it's really Callie's decision."

Clearing her throat, Callie managed to say, "I think it's a great idea, Grandpa."

Graham nodded. "Thought you kids might see it as an opportunity that presented itself. Your family came together earlier and we talked about it. We think if you two young people have some time alone, it might be helpful to both of you. You're always welcome over here, of course."

Callie felt her skin prickle as she blushed. The doors to her heart swung wide open as she met her grandfather's twinkling blue gaze. She cast a glance over at Beau, who kept his face carefully arranged as well. She knew the decision was hers to make. Her family had never pushed her into anything before and she realized they saw a need for Beau and her to have some privacy with one another. She wanted to cry in that moment, because they all realized her need for Beau to walk back into her life, which she hadn't admitted to until just recently, had always been there. That was how messed up her mind and emotions were, and she wished she could strain them out properly and not be like she was presently. If not for her grandpa's urging her to contact Beau and ask him to join them for the holidays, Callie knew she wouldn't have asked Beau to visit. She was in too deep and dark a place to be thinking straight. Thank goodness her family was. Giving them all a grateful look, she whispered, "Yes, I would love to do that. It's a great idea." She turned, looking up at Beau. "Are you okay with it?"

"More than okay, Callie." His face lost that unreadable look, his gray eyes growing tender as he held her gaze. "I want whatever you want. It's more important how you feel about this. Us."

"I'm more than okay with it," she admitted to him, seeing his eyes turn soft with love for her. And it was love. She knew it whether they'd ever broached the topic or not.

Graham cleared his throat. "Dara and Callie," he told Beau, "used that cabin as their castle, their playroom, while growing up. When we had our relatives drop by, they would use it. The rest of the time the girls painted, drew, and read out there. It was like their fairy-tale castle, where they could go to get away from us older people." He gave Callie a warm look. "Am I right, baby girl?"

Callie smiled a little. "You're right, Grandpa."

"Well, it's all set up for you. Your grandmother and I have put clean sheets on the beds, we've stocked the fridge, and the heat is on. All you have to do is take some of your clothes and toiletries out there after dinner, and you'll be all set."

"Can we come and eat here with all of you?" Callie asked, feeling a bit awkward. Her grandfather had never banished her to the cabin before.

"I would expect you two young ones to show up for dinner whenever you want. And if you don't want to? That's fine, too." Graham gave her a kindly look. "It's entirely your call, Callie. Beau is here to support you. And it's not like we won't be around, and it's not like you can't come over and see us. We love you. It's just that we all think that, under the circumstances, this might be a nice retreat for you."

Maisy said, "Callie? If you decide you would rather stay here, you can come right back into the house and claim your bedroom, all right? We're not kicking you out of the house here," and she smiled warmly.

That made Callie feel better. "For a moment I felt like you were trying to get rid of me," she admitted quietly, nervously moving her fingers in her lap. She knew her screams at night would wake the household.

"Nothing could be farther from the truth," Connor said, opposite Callie at the table. "The four of us were looking at things that might help you through your period of struggles, Callie, that's all."

Beau turned, placing his hand over hers briefly. "You won't be alone over there, Callie. I'll be there, too."

And that made all the difference in the world to her, but she didn't want to divulge the depth of her love for Beau to anyone else . . . not yet. She and Beau had so much to talk out between themselves.

"And that's good," she offered, her voice wobbly with emotion, giving him a grateful look. Just the calm in his steady gaze settled Callie's anxiety. She wanted Beau to keep holding her hand, but he reluctantly released it.

"Nothing changes around here, Callie," Graham informed her. "There are still stalls to clean, there are cattle to check on, and there are bales of hay to haul out to them by tractor. All the normal things that go on around here will be there if you want to partake in them. Same goes for Beau. But you don't have to."

She nodded, feeling better about being sent to the cabin. In truth, she looked forward to the privacy with Beau. Callie wasn't sure what would happen, which put her on edge in a new way. The low, emotional words he'd spoken to her this afternoon had sent a healing balm throughout her. He wasn't disappointed in her! He didn't blame her for running. That lifted the biggest load off her shoulders that she was carrying.

She would never feel good about what she'd done, but at least Beau had forgiven her. More than anything, he cared deeply about her. She felt his passionately spoken words flow through her heart so powerfully she couldn't speak, and his raw need for her beneath those words had made her whole body come alive.

"Besides," Maisy said, "we're decorating our Christmas tree tomorrow night, and we fully expect the two of you to be there to help us do it."

"Yes," Graham said, grinning. "And you get to make the popcorn chains for the trees like you always do when you're home, Callie."

She loved that memory and said with a smile, "I'd love to do that, Grandpa. It brings back a lot of good times." It was always the happiest time of the year for Callie, and this time, Beau was here. Her heart felt such euphoria that all her anxiety, dread, and depression were gone for a moment, and looking into Beau's eyes, she suspected that the darkness in her soul might soon begin to lift. Her heart sensed he was an integral key to her healing process.

CHAPTER 18

"NICE CABIN," BEAU told Callie as they entered it after dinner. The lights were on, and he liked the coziness of the place. It was open concept, with a kitchen near the front door and huge windows a person could look out while doing dishes at the sink. He did note that there was a dishwasher, which was always appreciated.

"I love this place. I always have," Callie said, closing the front door.

He nodded, dropping his duffel near the door. "My brothers and I liked to climb trees. In fact, our pa helped us build a tree house that we couldn't wait to climb into . . . so I kind of understand how you feel about this place." He smiled, then noticed she had gone silent. "How are you doing right now?" he asked, moving over to her and sliding his hands across her slumped shoulders.

"Am I that easy to read?" She frowned.

He leaned over and hugged her lightly. "Only to me, Callie," he reassured her. "I sense you. We seem to have this invisible connection. I don't know the words exactly, but I pick up on what you're feeling."

"Is that black ops training?" she asked curiously.

He gave her a wry smile. "Hardly. It's more like connecting to the woman who makes the sun rise and set for me.'"

She went still, six inches separating them because of her sling. "That's so beautiful," she whispered, searching his eyes. "Is that how you see me?"

Threading his fingers through her loose, silky hair, he groaned, "From the night I first saw you, Callie, you've meant the world to me." Beau was desperate to share, in the strongest way possible, how much he loved her without using the actual words.

Her eyes shone, and he saw happiness begin to reemerge. Damn it, he knew she loved him, and so did she. There were just too many signs. Callie wasn't in touch with them right now, but he was. "In fact, for the next thirty days I'm going to show you in every possible way how much you mean to me, Callie."

She reached up and trailed her fingertips across his jaw, feeling the growth of shadow beneath them. It made Beau look dangerous—far more so than when he'd worn that beard of his. His face was angular, hard, and rugged. With his gray eyes, he did indeed remind her of an eagle who missed nothing. "That sounds too good to be true," she whispered.

He gave her a slight smile. "Hey, I'm here just for you, Callie. If you tell me what you want, I'll try to make it happen, okay?"

Nodding, she whispered, "I know I've said this before, but sometimes I think you're a figment of my overactive imagination."

"I'm real," he assured her. If she looked down, she'd see his very real erection pressing against the zipper of his jeans beneath his jacket. "There are two bedrooms. Which one do you want?"

Beau wanted desperately to take her to his bed, but it had to be Callie's idea, not his. He watched her hesitate, torn. He could feel her wanting to be with him, not be alone. Whatever Callie decided was all right because Beau did not want to push or force her into being with him. He could see her struggling to separate her feelings from her mind. Right now, they ruled her, and logic and clarity were secondary. He'd seen his own teammates in this condition in years past when they were shot or were too close to an explosion going off. At those times, Beau knew the only thing he could do was ride it out with his injured teammate, give him a lot of room and compassion. That helped the healing process more than anything, and he knew it would help Callie. He ached for the anguish he saw come to her eyes, because he could feel her wanting to be with him.

Lifting her hand, she pressed it against his chest. "I feel so broken in some ways, Beau. I know what we shared at Bagram was beautiful. Wonderful. I dream about it."

"Look," he rasped, settling his hands on her shoulders, "you're in shock. It takes time to dissolve, Callie. There's no right or wrong here. I'll take the room to the left."

Feeling uneasy, she gave a jerky nod. "I never knew what shock was or what it could do, Beau."

"I've seen it up close for myself and some of my teammates, Callie. You'll have to trust me on this one."

She allowed her hand to slip off his chest. "Okay, I guess I'll take the one on the right."

"Sounds good." Beau picked up his duffel. "What do you feel like doing now? Are you tired?" He'd seen her begin to tire while Maisy was serving dessert to the family.

"It's eight p.m.," she said, more to herself than to him. "I go to bed early, Beau. I still don't have my usual energy back. I get tired so easily now, it drives me crazy."

He hefted the duffel over his shoulder. "Shock does that, too. Then let's hit the sack. I'll take a shower first, okay?"

"Good, because there's a bathtub in there and I want to soak in it for a while before I try to sleep."

Beau heard the emphasis on "try" but said nothing. Graham had given him a lot of valuable information on Callie, and he was going to put it all to use. And if he'd had any doubt that McKinley was the Ghost, that had been put to rest. Toward the end of their conversation, Beau had bluntly asked him if he was or not, and he'd received a slight nod of Graham's head, nothing more. Beau knew the look in his eyes: it came from killing people. And he knew from talking with the Delta Force snipers that it was the same for all of them. They never forgot one of their victims' faces. They killed in the most intimate of ways: seeing the target's face through the sniper scope before the trigger was pulled. Beau was sure McKinley had his own fair share of ghosts from the past that haunted him to this day.

As he dropped the duffel onto the queen-size bed with a white, downy comforter across it, Beau knew he had his work cut out for him with Callie. Fortunately, Graham was there in the background like the angel he was for his granddaughter, watching and assessing her struggles and behavior. As a sniper, no one was better at correlating details, and even just being around Callie this long, Beau agreed with Graham's assessment: Callie was not only fragile but brittle. He could feel the sharp edges around her, as if one small event would crack her wide open and she'd shatter into a million pieces.

He'd seen others reach that same point of no return. And some he'd seen actually deconstruct. Graham wasn't sure Beau could give her what she needed—maybe no one could—and Beau himself wasn't sure. He did keep thinking about something Matt Culver had told him: "Let your heart lead you." So for now, that was going to be his inner voice, leading them both, hopefully, to a better place.

BEAU WAS UP cooking breakfast when Callie came out of her bedroom. She had on a pair of sheepskin slippers and wore a long, pink flannel granny gown that fell to her slender ankles. On top of that, she wore a cream-colored chenille robe. He smiled over his shoulder as he saw her emerge from the room. Her hair was mussed, making her look beautiful and wanton to him.

This morning, he was pleased to see no shadows beneath her green eyes. That was a step in the right direction; she had slept long and hard.

"Hey, sleepyhead," he called as she shuffled across the rug in the living room, heading for the kitchen. "Welcome back to the world of the living." He turned the bacon in the skillet and then poured her a cup of coffee.

"I'm not awake yet, Beau . . . but thank you . . . ," she murmured, accepting the cup.

"I see you're not wearing the sling on your arm. How's it feel?" he asked, returning to the bacon frying in the skillet. She stood there, hip against the counter, both hands around the mug of coffee, sipping it with relish.

"It feels so freeing," she murmured, turning and looking out the window. Frost was forming on the edges in almost crochetlike patterns. "Looks like the weather has finally passed."

"Mmm," he said, draining the grease from the bacon and placing the strips into a nearby bowl. "Are you up for a little adventure this morning?" He wiggled his brows and grinned.

"What kind of adventure?" she asked, hesitant but intrigued.

He saw her wariness. "A fun one," he assured her. He hooked a thumb over his shoulder toward the living room and the large picture window. "I was thinking we might find a Christmas tree today. I'll cut it down, make a stand for it, and we can have one here in the cabin, too. What do you think?"

Graham had made a point of saying that he should get Callie outdoors and encourage her to do the daily ranch work. Since she'd come home, she'd pretty much stayed in her room, and he didn't feel that was good for her. Beau agreed.

"Well?" he prodded.

She smiled. "Yes, I'd love to do that."

"Now," he murmured, taking the skillet off the burner and shutting it off, "we're going to trim your family's tree tonight over at their homestead."

"Good. And if we find one today, we could trim our own tree tomorrow evening. Just you and me?"

Nodding, Beau retrieved four fresh eggs and broke them into another bowl. "That sounds good."

"Just having you here," she added softly, "gives me hope . . ."

He held on to his emotions. Giving her a glance, he said, "What do you mean by that, Callie?"

Graham had told him that unless someone asked Callie a lot of questions, she would never explain herself. It wasn't that she didn't want to—that was normal for her.

"I didn't want to leave you at Bagram," she admitted quietly, stealing a glance at him to see his reaction. "I just wanted to leave Afghanistan and that horrible ambush behind. But I didn't want to leave you, Beau."

He added some milk, salt, and pepper to the eggs, stirring them briskly with a whisk. "That makes two of us. I wanted so damned badly to escort you home, Callie. I knew how raw you were feeling. I knew the crowds, the jostling, and the noise were going to hammer you."

"They did," she sighed. "Dara was in much better shape than I was. And I'm glad. I'm guilt-ridden enough about dragging her through that experience."

Beau poured the egg mixture into the skillet. He then crumbled up the bacon into it. "You have to let that go, Callie. Dara survived. She's not angry at you, and she doesn't blame you for what happened."

Looking up at him, Callie asked, "How do you know this?"

"Because I talked to Matt by phone when I reached Seattle. I had four hours before my flight and made calls to my family and then to him. I found out Dara is doing very well. And I asked him point-blank if Dara held you responsible for what happened to her." He held her wavering gaze. "He said no, she didn't blame you, Callie." He gave her a swift kiss on the cheek. "So it's time to stop riding that horse, pardner. Okay?" he said firmly, giving her a look that pleaded with her to think about it.

"I asked her about it before we left Afghanistan," Callie admitted. "But I didn't believe her. That's on me."

"You tend to stew on things," Beau said gently, watching the omelet cook. "And I'm here to short-circuit that for you, Callie. You can't keep carrying loads that aren't yours to carry."

"You're right," she admitted, frowning. "I don't know why I do it."

"Doesn't matter," Beau said, holding her gaze. "What matters is that you recognize what's happening and then dump it. And if you don't realize it, I'm here to help you see what you're doing to yourself. It was hard enough for you to survive that ambush, Callie. That's enough to carry around in you without adding other people's lives into the equation, don't you agree?"

"As you can tell, I'm pretty much an emotional person, and thinking isn't something I do first. It's actually the last thing I do."

"But I like you that way," he reassured her. Beau knew he couldn't just tear her down without building her up. He wanted today to be a new day for Callie, and he'd said enough. "Hungry?"

"Everything smells good," she admitted tentatively.

"Your grandfather says you've had the appetite of a sparrow. And I can see you've lost more weight, so my first priority is to get you to eat."

"Yes, and drink. Remember, I don't hydrate often enough?"

"How true. I don't think you'll ever forget that charley horse you got when we were on the run, will you?"

A slight smile tugged at her lips. "No, I won't. And you'd be proud of me, Beau. Since coming home, I drink a lot more water than I ever did before."

It felt good to know he had a positive influence on her. He scooped up the omelet and said, "Come on, let's eat. It's our first breakfast together here . . ."

★

CALLIE FELT AS if a final, huge load had lifted from her shoulders as she and Beau scouted a small hill with plenty of pine trees to choose from. The sky was a deep winter blue, holding a slight breeze, the sun shining brightly above them. They'd left shortly after lunch, and Callie had never felt happier. Beau had grabbed her gloved left hand, helping her slog up the hill toward their future Christmas tree in nearly knee-deep snow. She was careful with her right arm, still very protective of it. And she noticed how Beau's arm went around her waist as they made it to the top, breathing hard. She longed for physical closeness to him.

"How about that one?" Callie asked, pointing to a blue spruce that was about five feet tall.

Beau held a hand saw and squinted, his dark glasses protecting his eyes from the glare across the snow. "Looks good to me. Want it?" He turned, meeting her smile. Callie looked winsome, as if she were as whole and happy as he'd known her to be before the ambush. Today, her cheeks were flushed pink, light was dancing in her green eyes, and there was a smile on those soft lips he wanted so desperately to kiss. Her hair was free and loose, glinting red, gold, and burgundy in the overhead sunlight, a red knit cap on her head.

"Yes, that's the one," she said, moving awkwardly through the snow.

Beau had longer legs and made it over to the tree first. He placed his arm beneath her left elbow, helping her move closer to inspect it.

"It's really perfect," she murmured. Beau had worn a dark green baseball cap and a green knit muffler she'd given him to keep his ears and neck warm. He looked strong, confident, and masculine in his leather jacket and jeans. She could not get over how different he looked without his beard and long hair. The change was amazing. Wonderful. Enticing.

Every time he held her gaze, she drowned in his dove-gray eyes, which were clearly filled with yearning—for her. She'd been afraid she would never feel any strong emotion again since returning home, but now Callie felt the coals of hunger burn brightly in her belly. Last night, her last thought before falling into a deep, healing sleep was that she wished Beau were tucking her up against his tall, strong body, holding her in sleep. Holding her safe.

"Okay, this is the one," he drawled, and got down on his hands and knees, pulling the snow away from the trunk.

Callie watched him quickly saw the tree trunk. It fell into the snow, glittering, tiny flakes flying into the air, dancing like diamonds in the sunlight. The day felt magical, filled with hope. She couldn't keep her eyes off Beau. He seemed lighter, happier. Why wouldn't he be—no one was shooting at him, and they weren't being hunted, either. Still, it was a delightful discovery to see him suddenly turn boyish, smiling and laughing easily with her. No one would ever have guessed he was a deadly Delta Force operator.

He pulled the tree down the hill and Callie followed. Never had she felt so light since the ambush. Her heart turned in gratitude to Beau for telling her that she wasn't a disappointment to him. She still felt bad, however, because even now, he limped because of the bullet wound he'd sustained in his calf. That was a direct result of her decision to run and not remain hidden.

Callie didn't know how Beau could still like her despite the life-and-death choices she'd made for both of them out on the slope of that mountain. Just one look into his eyes, however, told her he loved her. And yet, he'd not touched her. He didn't need to in order to lift her out of the darkness that had ruled over her since the ambush—all it took was a look, a word.

After he put their chosen spruce tree in the back of the Ford truck and closed the tailgate on it, she came over to him. He turned toward her, breathing hard, his cheeks slightly ruddy from the work it took to haul that tree to the truck. Callie was scared, but she followed her heart and slowly lifted both her arms, settling them around his broad set of shoulders. They were alone, out in a series of hills, the pastures to the south.

"Beau?" she whispered, holding his suddenly intense gaze as she moved against him, her breasts against his chest, her hips against his, "I want to kiss you . . . ," and she leaned up on her tiptoes, closing her eyes, feeling his mouth claim hers. The world anchored to a halt for Callie as Beau swept his arms around her slender body, holding her tightly to him. She could sense his awareness of her broken right arm, and he was careful not to reinjure her. Still, his mouth took hers with a hunger that robbed her of her breath for a moment. The blinding emotion behind his lips claiming hers made her moan with pleasure as she pressed her breasts wantonly against his jacket. Heat flamed to life between her legs, and she felt a deep ache below as his mouth opened hers even more. He was like a hunter who had found his quarry, his mouth seeking, finding, taking, and giving to hers. Their breaths were sporadic, moist, and warm against one another's faces as she tightened her grip around his neck, never wanting that searching kiss of his to end.

Beau lifted his hand, threading his fingers through her hair, angling her just enough to allow his tongue to touch hers, to get her reaction, feel her tense and then hear her response deep in her throat. The moment her tongue tangled with his, he nearly lost it. He was starved for the taste and the feel of this woman! She was warm, willing, and just as hungry as him. And if he didn't stop right, now Beau was going to take her right here, in the snow.

But that wasn't what he wanted for their first time since that ambush. He wanted her in a place that was warm, intimate, and private—a place where he could slowly introduce her to his deepest self in every possible way. He wanted to love this woman until she swooned from pleasure only he could give her.

Reluctantly, Beau eased his mouth from hers, staring into her barely open eyes, seeing the green fire and gold flecks in them. He felt her loosen her hands around his neck, felt her gloved fingers trail down his arms. Releasing her, Beau captured her shoulders, staring down at her. "I've been wanting to kiss you like that for a long, long time, Callie'." His voice rumbled with arousal, thick with hunger.

She sighed, closing her eyes, whispering, "Don't ever stop kissing me like that, Beau. My knees . . ." She opened her eyes and laughed a little, embarrassed. "My knees feel weak!"

Pride moved through him. Beau desperately wanted to love her so thoroughly she would never want to consider another man in her life. "Well," he growled, sliding his arm around her waist, guiding her toward the passenger side of the truck, "I can't have you falling down, can I?"

"No," she said, smiling warmly up at him. "You can't. Tonight we trim the family Christmas tree. I'm so happy you're here, Beau," she added, her voice bubbling with joy.

He opened the door for her, helping her climb in. Callie still cradled that right arm and continued to be protective of it. "I'm looking forward to it, too," he told her.

On the way back, Beau drove slowly because the gravel road was heavy with ice and snow. "Tell me about your family Christmas tree trimming party."

She smiled, taking off her gloves. "I always volunteered to make the long strings of popcorn to hang around the tree. When Dara was here, she got the job of putting bulbs on the tree along with Mom and Grandma."

"And your granddad? What does he do?"

"Oh, he's so tall he can easily string the lights around the top of the tree," she said.

"Sounds a lot like what our family does," he confided, smiling over at her. She had taken off her red knit cap, her hair loose, giving her a wild, natural look. There was no more tension in her face, and Beau was grateful. He'd had just one kiss. One. And he wanted so many more with her.

"You said your brothers, Coy and Jackson, were home now on Christmas leave?"

"Yeah. My pa will go out with them and they'll find the right tree. Ma makes peanut brittle while we're gone. It's a nice dessert to come home to."

"Sounds really yummy," Callie agreed. "What then?"

"Well, we trim the tree. Ma kept all our little-kid efforts from grade school. You know how you always had classes around Christmas where you made things to hang or wrap around the tree?"

"Yep," she laughed, "I do. My mother has all our attempts in special boxes. She doesn't hang them, but she said they're there for each of us. We'll get our box when we get married. She told us when we have children, we can then show them how to make their own ornaments for the trees we'll be trimming as a family." She sighed. "Dara and I always dreamed of getting married and having families."

"You sound sad."

"Dara's twenty-nine and I'm twenty-seven. We're getting up there as far as getting pregnant. I sure wouldn't want to be pregnant at forty."

His mouth twitched. "I think Matt is going to ask Dara to marry him on Christmas Day."

"No!" Callie gasped, turning toward him, her eyes huge. "Seriously, Beau? Is that what he told you?"

"Yep." Beau's smile grew. "He knows it's too soon, but he's going to give Dara a set of rings that belonged to his Turkish grandmother. He was a favorite of hers, and she asked that the rings be given to Matt after she passed."

"That's so wonderful," Callie whispered. "Dara deserves that kind of happiness."

Beau held her teary gaze. "So do you, gal." And if he had anything to say or do about it, he was going to get this stubborn redheaded wench of his to marry him.

Callie sat back, frowning. "I thought I knew what I wanted out of life, Beau. I was very happy being a volunteer for the Hope Charity."

"But you're changing your mind?" Beau was beginning to see the array of changes that the ambush had made in Callie.

He drove the pickup into the main parking area of the ranch and then around the homestead. The cabin sat about five hundred feet away from it.

"I'm changing," she admitted, her brows moving down as she studied her hands, which were clasped in her lap. "I'm not sure about much of anything right now, to be honest. I feel like I'm making a major transition, and I'm in it and can't see where I'm going."

"It's too soon to sort this all out, gal," he reassured her as he parked the truck and turned off the engine. He opened his seat belt and placed his arm behind her slumped shoulders. Callie was cycling down again. He was damned glad he could pick up those subtle changes in her. "You had a life-changing experience, Callie. And it takes time to figure out how it's going to affect how you see yourself and your world." He moved his hands lightly down her unruly red hair, its silken strands always drawing him close so he could touch it.

"And you know this how?"

He drew in a deep breath and said, "The first time I got shot, it shattered me in ways I couldn't possibly imagine, Callie. I almost bled to death out in the field because it hit a pretty major artery even though it was classified as a flesh wound. Some major arteries are real close to the skin. Luckily, we had a great medic and he saved my life. I thought"—he looked down at her—"I was invincible. I never really thought about dying, even though I was in one of the most dangerous fields in the military. It just hadn't crossed my mind."

He saw her eyes lighten a little. Beau was beginning to understand that he needed to share from his own experience in order for Callie to open up to him. "I lay in a hospital bed recovering and having a lot of time on my hands to think about the what-ifs. Suddenly, life became a lot more precious to me. I began appreciating little things, things we take for granted every day. I became closer to my parents and my two younger brothers. Everything I loved in my life became more dear to me."

"That's what is happening to me, Beau. Exactly."

He gave her a sad smile. "Yes, the symptoms of healing are the same. You nearly die or think you're going to die, and your world order gets shaken up. You begin to question the career that got you into this fix in the first place. I'd only been in Delta Force for a year when I got wounded. I talked to Matt about it. He's very wise, and he told me to take it slow and not make any sudden, knee-jerk decisions. He even suggested I make a couple of lists. One list was what was important to me. And the other was things I used to think were important to me but weren't anymore. He said to throw out the last list and only keep what was important to me from now on."

"And now that you've been wounded a second time?"

"It's making me review everything again, gal." He grazed her cheek with his fingertips. "And you're going through the same lists I am. We need to compare our lists when we feel it's right."

CHAPTER 19

C HRISTMAS MUSIC PLAYED in the background as the McKinley family went about trimming their ten-foot-tall Colorado blue spruce in one corner of the ranch living room. With the high ceilings, Beau thought the Christmas tree went well with the floor-to-ceiling fieldstone fireplace now roaring with flames, warming the entire first floor of the huge cedar-log home.

Stacy and Connor McKinley were bringing out boxes of ornaments from the attic. Beau, because he was tall like Graham McKinley, had been assigned the job of placing the lights on the tree. He kept an eye on Callie, who was sitting at the granite island stringing long lines of popcorn for a final touch. Everyone was feeling warm and happy, just as a family should.

Maisy was in charge of the mulled red wine simmering with cinnamon, nutmeg, and cloves along with thick, fresh slices of oranges floating on top. There was also dark, rich hot chocolate for those who didn't want to imbibe alcohol. Maisy had also made Christmas cookies earlier, hand-decorated each one, and put them on a huge green platter on the granite island next to the drinks.

Beau was impressed with how strong the spirit of Christmas ran in this family. But he couldn't deny that all this activity made him homesick. He knew his family would be trimming their tree any day now, and let's face it—he hadn't been home for the holidays in three years.

Well, maybe he'd make it next year. Still, being able to share this season with Callie made up for everything. Since their kiss on his arrival, she had become less anxious and nervous, and Beau wished he could find out what was going on inside that gorgeous head of hers. Slowly, she was allowing him entrance into her deeper thoughts, and that was good for both of them.

As he and Graham slowly worked the lights around the tree, Beau decided to talk quietly with Callie' grandfather. "Sir? Has Callie always kept her feelings inside her?"

Graham, who wore jeans and a dark green, long-sleeved shirt with a black leather vest, nodded. "Yes, she's pretty much an 'inny.'" When he saw Beau's confused expression, he said, "Callie's an extrovert, for sure, but when it comes to her emotions, she hides them from everyone. She's always been that way, from the day she was born."

Grimacing, Beau made sure their voices couldn't be heard by anyone else as they slowly walked a string of lights around the middle of the tree branches. "How do I get them out of her?"

Chuckling, Graham said, "That's the big question, son. The only thing her parents found worked was to keep asking her a lot of questions."

"Why does she hide herself like that?"

"I don't know. Dara isn't like that at all." Graham looked across the massive room. "I think Callie takes after her father, Connor. He's pretty introverted by nature and stopped up emotionally, too."

Grunting, Beau nodded. "In some ways, she reminds me of an operator."

"Yes, hide everything and keep on moving," Graham agreed. He leaned down and brought up the next string, plugging it into the last one. "You making any headway with her since going over to the cabin?"

"Some," Beau said. "But it's a slow process."

"Callie's stubborn on all fronts. Not that she can help it. It's just the way she is. Being like that can give you a lot of enduring strength, but when you hit a brick wall like she has, it confuses her, and she doesn't know what to do with all those emotions charging up through her. So she sits on 'em."

Beau couldn't disagree. "I see a difference if I get her outdoors and doing something."

"Yes, as a little girl growing up here, she was an outdoors type. Dara, less so. But Callie had so much energy to burn off, she was always helping me or the wranglers with our normal daily duties." Graham and he had moved behind the tree and the large window, out of view of the rest of the family. He halted and turned to Beau. "Keep getting her outside and working. Clean stalls. Go for horseback rides. I can take both of you with me when we load the hay on the tractor-trailer to go feed the cattle. She'll do better when she's got a physical outlet. And it looks like her arm is doing better."

"It's still tender and she can't use it for much, but yes, it's better," Beau told him.

"We're going to have good weather for the next five days, so be thinking of ways to get Callie out of that cabin and into the fresh air."

Nodding, Beau said, "I will, sir. Thank you."

CALLIE SMILED AS Beau wandered over and stood at her left shoulder, watching her stringing the popcorn. "Got the lights strung on the tree?"

"Yep. Your granddad is an ace at it. He made it easy."

"He's only got fifty years of doing it," she said, smiling.

"Want some mulled wine? Smells good," Beau said, lifting his nose. Callie had chosen a gold sweater that had glittering silver threads gleaming through it, which brought out the beauty of her face and her sea-green eyes. She'd worn jeans and calf-high black leather boots. Beau had a tough time keeping his hands off her.

"That sounds good," Callie murmured. She watched Beau move with that casual grace of his. The fit of his blue chambray shirt and jeans made her yearn for him, and she remembered how he looked without clothing—even better than with them, and that was saying a lot!

There was a quiet confidence and ease to Beau that she appreciated so much. Every time she looked at his hands, she wanted him to touch her, explore her, and she found herself thinking almost constantly about how it had felt making love to him. After their kiss at the door, she knew that she wanted to feel him close again, as close as possible. She just didn't know when.

Meanwhile, being around him all the time was giving her the stability and calm she needed right now. He was like an unobtrusive shadow moving in between her family members, never disturbing the energy or what was going on. She supposed it was his black ops background. Beau was just like her grandpa, or vice versa. Callie swore they came from the same mold and began to wonder more about her grandfather's military experience. He never talked about it.

"Here you go," Beau said, sliding over a white mug steaming with the mulled wine in it. He took a stool next to her, his cup in his hand.

"Thanks." She took a tentative sip. "Mmm, my mother makes the best mulled wine, doesn't she?"

"I've never tasted it before," Beau admitted, "but it's good. I like the orange flavor in it." He eyed the strings of popcorn. "Looks like you're making good headway with that."

She smiled and looked at the strings she'd laid out, ready to be put on the tree. "I'm an old hand at this. When Dara was here, she and I would do this together."

"Do you miss her right now?"

Shrugging, Callie picked up the mug, absorbing Beau's nearness. "I know she's happy having Matt with her. Plus his family is flying in for the holidays." She gave him a tender look. "I feel like I've already been given the best Christmas present ever: you." She saw Beau's cheeks go ruddy and he became almost bashful for a moment as she felt him take her sincere compliment into his heart. In that moment, Callie realized just how sensitive he could be and that as a Delta operator, he had never shown this side to her. Reaching over, she grazed his shaven jaw. "Really, you are a gift to me, Beau."

He caught her hand, placing a kiss on her opened palm, looking into her glistening green eyes, which held love in them for him. Beau could feel it radiating off Callie and heard it in her wispy, emotional voice. He almost let fly with the fact that he loved her but at the last second swallowed it. When he told Callie those words, he wanted to be alone with her. "You've been a Christmas gift since I saw you dance at Bagram, gal. Nothing's changed. Did you know that?" Beau saw her eyes go soft, her lips parting. If he'd been anywhere but here, he'd have kissed her until she melted into him.

"I like the idea of being someone's gift. That's nice . . . thank you."

Beau had to get off this line of conversation or he was going to blurt out how he really felt about Callie. "Have you talked to Dara lately?" Beau saw that Callie's green eyes were clear. He liked the warmth simmering between them. Had one kiss shared between them done all of this? He wrestled with ways to find out what Callie was thinking and feeling. He reluctantly released her hand so she could reclaim it.

"We talk every day."

"Good, because right now you need that kind of support."

Her mouth quirked. "Yes, I do." She reached out, touching his jaw. "But you have helped me so much by just being here, Beau."

"Well, you've got me for a whole month, so I hope I don't wear out my welcome," he teased. He saw Callie's eyes grow shadowed, then clear. Was it fear? He decided to press it. "What was that look about?"

"Oh," she muttered, shrugging. "In my idealistic dream world you wouldn't go back to the Army. You'd always be here with me."

Inwardly, Beau anchored over that unexpected admission from her. His heart blew open. Did Callie mean it? The sincere look in her eyes said yes. Throttling his emotions, keeping them under control, he tried to sound unaffected by her words. This had to be the shock talking through Callie. Beau didn't think she honestly realized what she'd just said to him. He would ask her later, when they were alone. He knew from his own wrestling with shock that he'd sometimes say things without realizing the depth or importance of what he'd shared with one of his teammates. It didn't mean Callie was lying, however-er. Shock made a person say things they truly felt or believed. Under normal circumstances, those things would never come out of their mouth. But shock did funny things to a person's brain and emotions. If only Callie really meant what she'd said. "Nothing wrong with dreams and idealism, gal," Beau said gently. "What other dreams do you have?"

Callie looked around the large living room, her eyes softening even more. "I didn't realize just how much I missed my ranching life. At age eighteen I left, because I wanted adventure. I thought life on our ranch was really dull and boring."

"I see. So you went to work for the Hope Charity?"

Nodding, Callie sipped the warm wine, the taste of the spices on her tongue. "I did. My parents wanted me to go to college, but honestly, I hated school. I'm a hands-on kind of woman. I learn by doing. I didn't learn from books. Dara did, but I didn't."

"Your grandpa was saying you were a lot like your father. Do you think you are?"

She gave her father, Connor, who was sitting on a living room couch with her mother sorting through decorations, a loving look. "Me and my dad are definitely a lot alike. Dara is a carbon copy of Mom."

"Your dad's a surgeon. That's hands-on, don't you think?"

She laughed quietly and nodded. "Yes, but I don't have his smarts."

"You have lots of intelligence, Callie. I saw it in Afghanistan. I see it here. You have your dad's desire to learn by doing. I'm sure that with every surgery he performs on a patient, he learns something new."

She tilted her head, drowning in his shadowy gray eyes. "Yes, you're right, I do. I've always been this way."

"Your grandpa was saying it's going to be pretty nice weather for the next five days. I was wondering if you might teach me how to ride. You have that great indoor arena next to the horse barn. Think you could teach me how to stay in a saddle?"

"I'd love to!" she said, perking up. "I know you said you and your brothers rode the neighbor's mule."

"Yeah," he said, grinning, "but that doesn't mean I know how to ride a decent-size horse." He lost his smile and held her green gaze. "Callie, I'd really like to go horseback riding with you. You could show me your ranch, the trails you use. I know the snow is deep in some places, but in other areas, it isn't. What do you think?"

She clearly loved the idea. Her eyes bright, she said, "I can't wait!" Now the life had returned to her face, and Beau was determined to keep it there. His ass might get saddle sores, but he didn't care. And Graham was right: getting Callie outdoors, or doing something she was good at, would draw her out. Then he could honestly begin to see where she was at.

CALLIE WOKE UP screaming. It was dark and she gasped for air, finding her legs trapped beneath the tangle of covers. Kicking them off, she whimpered, pulling her legs out from beneath the blanket. Oh God, she hated these nightmares! It had been such a wonderful evening with her family trimming the tree. There had been so much laughter and singing of Christmas carols, and so many warm memories from the past.

A soft knock came at the bedroom door. Callie groaned, pushing off the bed, and wiped her damp hair away from her face. She turned on the light with a trembling hand and opened it. Beau stood in the hall, dressed in a T-shirt and boxer shorts, his eyes filled with concern.

"Sorry," she mumbled. "It was a nightmare, Beau. I didn't mean to wake you. Oh, I knew this would happen. I'm so sorry . . ."

"It's all right," he said soothingly.

"W-what time is it?" she asked, feeling like a storm-tossed ship at sea.

He glanced down at the watch on his wrist. "Oh three hundred. I mean, three a.m."

Hearing the thickness of sleep in his voice, she felt awful for waking him. "Was your door closed?"

His mouth crooked. "Yeah, but I have wolf hearing, Callie. Is there anything I can I do to help you?"

Her heart opened to him as he stood there, ready to help and support her, whatever the hour. "I-I don't know," she whispered. "When I get these nightmares, I have to get up or it'll come back if I try to go back to sleep." She rubbed her face, ashamed to admit it to him. "When I five, I got scared by a grizzly along a stream. My father was with me, but I felt such terror. The grizzly was at least eight hundred pounds and so close to us. I just froze."

"Yes?"

"I had horrible nightmares for nearly a year after that, Beau. Dara and I shared a room at that time. I kept waking her up. She'd get angry and stomp off to Mom and Dad's bedroom, wake them up, asking them to take me out of the room so she could sleep. I felt so humiliated . . . so ashamed . . ."

He reached out, caressing her slumped shoulder, seeing the shame and understanding now how far back it really went. "How often did you get them after that?"

"Three or four times a week for about a year. It was an awful time for me, Beau. I'm sure Dara and my family were stressed by my doing it, too."

"I believe your parents and grandparents would understand, Callie. They love you. I'm sure they worried for you and wished they could do more to help you."

She smiled faintly. "Grandpa would always take me out of the bedroom, carry me down the hall, and make me hot chocolate. And then he'd go and get Dara. The three of us would sit at the table drinking it. He'd take us back to our room, tuck us in, kiss our cheek, and we'd dropped off to sleep."

"That's because Graham understood better than anyone, Callie, what trauma and shock do to a person. He knew and he was a great support for you."

"I love him so much." She lifted her chin, looking into his shadowed eyes. "And you're so much like him, Beau."

He smiled a little and continued to caress her shoulder, seeing her respond positively. "This nightmare you just had? Was it because of that time as a five-year-old or the ambush?" he asked quietly, reaching out, smoothing strands of hair away from her pale face.

"The ambush . . . damn it, I just hate when this happens! I'm so tired, and I need to sleep, Beau. And I'm not taking sleeping pills, because I hate them even more," she said with distaste.

"Tell you what, gal," he said. "How about this? Climb back into your bed, and I promise, no funny stuff." He held up his hands. "I'll just tuck you next to me and hold you so that you go back to sleep. Maybe the nightmare won't come back that way."

She licked her lower lip, thinking a moment. Then she said, "Yes . . . I'd like that."

"Okay," he murmured, "I'll hold you, Callie. Nothing more." He looked deep into her distraught eyes. "Okay?"

"Y-yes, that's good. Thank you . . ."

Beau wasn't sure whether Callie would go along with his suggestion or not. But she'd surprised him with her answer. More than anything, Beau had to be as good as his word. He knew his body would react to her closeness even though she wore a frumpy pink flannel nightgown that fell to her ankles. "Okay, let's go," he urged her.

Callie felt a lot of her terror reduce as she slid into her bed beside Beau, who covered them both up. He'd promised not to do anything but hold her. A good part of her didn't want that at all. But another part of her did. It was a step that Callie was willing to take with Beau. She wasn't emotionally ready to take that last step. At least not tonight, although her lower body was already reacting to his closeness, his scent, and the feel of him sliding behind her, fitting her gently against his body.

As he slid his arm beneath her neck and brought her back against his front, she sighed and closed her eyes. Already, she could feel his erection against her, but the way he tucked her down the length of his strong body suggested he wasn't trying to take advantage of her or the situation.

"Now," Beau said gruffly, her head beneath his jaw, her hair silky against his cheek, "you can go back to sleep, Callie. Close your eyes. I'll hold you, and no more nightmares will bother you."

She was utterly emotionally exhausted and closing her eyes. Beau felt warm, hard, and wrapped a strong sense of protection around her. "I will," she whispered. "Thank you, Beau . . ." And it was the last thing she remembered.

It wasn't so easy for Beau to go sleep. He held Callie, absorbing her warmth, her curves beneath that fuzzy nightgown of hers. She dropped off into a deep sleep almost immediately, and he found himself wanting to always protect her. She never complained. Rarely said anything about the terror that still inhabited her. Callie had never reached out for help like most people would. She behaved more like a military operator than a civilian woman, Beau thought. How much crap did he hold within himself? Did he ever air it? No. And neither did Callie.

He nuzzled his cheek into her hair, inhaling her sweet, womanly scent. His arm was around her waist and he could feel the slow, shallow rise and fall of her chest. His fingers itched to slide the nightgown upward and feel her slender legs beneath, to kiss her, feel her wanton response once more.

He loved Callie, and that feeling was growing stronger by the day. Last night, Beau had seen her relaxed as never before. Her family connection was strong, and everyone had showered her with hugs, kisses, and love. They'd all made her a part of the tree trimming.

Beau liked that her family supported her, although from time to time, he saw worry in Stacy's eyes for her wounded daughter. And Maisy had the same look of concern. More than anything, Beau saw the strong connection between Callie and Graham McKinley. They were more alike than either had realized. Beau smiled to himself. There was definitely an operator personality to the two men and Callie. Maisy and Stacy, on the other hand, were extroverts, open, warm, and reminded him of his own maternal and nurturing mother, Amber.

Eventually, Beau fell asleep. The scent of Callie in his nostrils, his hand against her belly, splayed out across it, the two of them fitting together beneath the warmth of the covers, was a dream come true.

BRIGHT SUNLIGHT SPILLED into Callie's bedroom, awakening her. She made a muffled sound, feeling warm and happy. Turning over, her mind groggy, she remembered Beau holding her last night. Slowly sitting up, she saw he was gone, her bedroom door closed. Squinting, she looked at the clock on the dresser opposite the bed. It was ten a.m.!

Gasping, she threw off the covers, her bare feet meeting the cold cedar floor. She had never slept so late! Pushing off the bed, she quickly gathered her clothes, opening the door. Down the hall she could hear Christmas music coming from a radio in the living room. Where was Beau? She didn't see him as she crossed the hall to the bathroom. She needed to get awake first. Take a hot shower, wash her hair, and get dressed, in that order.

By the time she emerged nearly an hour later, she met Beau coming in the front door. He was carrying a huge load of cut pine in his arms for their fireplace. He stomped off the snow from his boots, looking handsome in his leather jacket and the green muffler around his neck, his baseball cap in place.

"Hey, sleepyhead," he teased, shutting the door, grinning at her. "Finally woke up, huh?" He took the wood to the fireplace, opened up the screen, and tossed a few logs into it.

"Hi, Beau. I think I need coffee," she mumbled, giving him an apologetic look in return.

"I just made a pot," he said, straightening. "You were in the shower when I came in last time."

"Bless you," she whispered, moving to the kitchen.

Chuckling, Beau took off his cold-weather gear, hanging it on hooks next to the door. Callie's shining hair fell around her shoulders, and she wore a dark blue sweatshirt with Christmas decorations on the front, making her look more like a child than a woman. It was obvious that she loved Christmas.

His body ached as he watched her move in those jeans that made her hips and long legs so damn tempting. She never wore tight clothes, preferring clothes that fit her comfortably. They couldn't hide her charms from him, though.

She had poured him a cup of coffee when he sauntered into the kitchen. "Hungry?" he asked.

"I am," she admitted. "What about you? Have you eaten?"

"A long time ago. Go sit down at the table," he coaxed. "I made scrambled eggs and diced ham with sliced red and green peppers earlier. I put it in the fridge. I can warm it up for you if it sounds tempting."

Giving him a grateful look, she moved to the table and sat down. "Sounds wonderful, thank you."

He nodded and opened the fridge, taking out the bowl. "That's pretty much the intention, gal."

"You're spoiling me, Beau. You know that?"

He arched a brow as he put some olive oil in a black iron skillet. "Every once in a while, I find we all need a little spoiling. It's good for our soul. Why do you say that?"

Heat nettled her cheeks. "Well . . . I just thought that because you're so caring . . ."

He took a fork, pulling the egg concoction out of the bowl and into the warming skillet. "I care about only you, Callie. Okay?" He gave her a sharp look to reinforce his statement. He saw her green eyes flare with hope, and much more.

He decided to take the light approach. "You seemed to sleep real well after

I climbed into bed with you. Did you?"

She rolled her eyes. "I felt as if I'd died." Then she muttered, "Delete that. I did sleep. I slept a full seven hours after you held me last night, Beau. And no more nightmares. Usually, if I try to go back to bed, it picks up where it left off and I get a repeat."

"Hmm," he teased, giving her a wicked look. "Maybe I should hold you more often in bed . . ." He saw her lips pull into a slight smile, her eyes telling him that she was considering exactly that.

"I'm giving it serious thought, Beau."

He said nothing but grinned as he warmed up the eggs in the skillet. Callie was careful with her heart and Beau understood that. He felt good that he'd been a man of his word and had not tried to seduce her last night. God knew, he'd wanted to. What kept him from doing it? He wanted Callie's trust, the way she'd given it to him before at Bagram. Last night, he'd taken a huge risk by making the suggestion to hold her in bed. He hadn't expected her to agree, but she had. If only he could get inside this woman's head and heart. Patience was the key. Could that one time with her outweigh her trauma and shock? Or not? He was going to find out.

"I was out in the indoor riding arena with Graham this morning," he told her, putting the warmed eggs on a plate. "I asked him which horse would be a good one for me to learn to ride on."

"Oh, that's great. What did Grandpa say?"

He brought the plate and flatware over to Callie. "He said there's a twenty-five-year-old quarter horse named Dude who would be good for me."

"Dude is quiet and smart," Callie agreed.

"Want some toast?"

"That would be great, Beau. Thank you." She was still drowsy. Getting a good night's sleep though, a full seven hours, uninterrupted, made her feel so much better—it was amazing. After he brought over a plate of toast and strawberry jam, Beau joined her. He sat at her right elbow, watching her eat with her right hand.

"How's the arm doing this morning?"

"Better. I can feel it's still weak, but it's so nice to be able to eat with my right hand again."

"Do you think you can still teach me to ride?" he teased.

"I think so. After you learn the basics, shall we go for a short trail ride this afternoon? It looks sunny out."

He turned to look out the window. "Yes, that would be great. Right now, it's about thirty degrees outside."

"We'll dress warmly," she promised. Looking over at their tree, she said, "Tonight, let's trim it. Sound good?"

"Sure. It looks like there are plenty of leftover decorations from the family tree."

"There are," she agreed, enjoying her food. "We'll go over and get some boxes of stuff later."

Beau nodded. He watched Callie eat with real enjoyment for the first time since he'd arrived. She seemed happy. And relaxed. And she was going to be his.

BY TWO P.M., Beau was on Dude, in a comfortable western saddle riding next to Callie, who was on Ghost, the gray cutting horse. He wondered if Graham McKinley had given him that name and smiled secretly. Beau would have put money on it and planned to ask the Marine just that later when he saw him.

Beau's butt was sore, but at least he'd learned how to steer Dude and not make a complete fool of himself. Riding a horse was a helluva lot of different than throwing a leg over a mule's broad back. The afternoon was perfect, with no wind, a warm sun, and a deep blue winter sky vault above them. Callie was leading him from the indoor arena toward a flat trail that skirted the massive pastures where the cattle remained. It was a wide trail, and two horses could easily walk together. Beau liked that their legs occasionally touched one another. The change in Callie was remarkable and filled him with hope. Graham had been right about getting her outdoors.

"I noticed in the main house that there was a room with a long metal barre at the wall with mirrors behind it," he said, holding her gaze. "Is that where you work out and belly dance?"

"Oh, yes," she said, smiling. "I go over there every other day and work out. I know you operators are always working out on heavy gym equipment there at Bagram, but I would go over to the women's gym and do the same thing. Only"—she held up her gloved hand—"I didn't do weight lifting. I did a lot of warm-up and stretching exercises before putting on some Turkish belly-dancing music, plugging in my iPod earbuds, and then dancing."

"Wish I could see you do that."

She smiled. "Tomorrow? I work out about three p.m. every other day. You can come over and watch how athletic belly dancing really is."

"I'd like that. You were incredibly graceful and hot when you danced at Bagram." He saw her cheeks grow pink beneath his gruffly spoken compliment.

"Thanks. I think you're getting a heck of a workout around here, Beau. Every time I see you, you're helping Grandpa. There's a lot of work that goes on in the winter, and he's shorthanded during the holiday season. A lot of his wranglers go home at that time."

"I like helping out. You're feeding me and keeping a roof over my head, so why shouldn't I pay you back in some way?" His pulse bounded as she gave him a blinding smile and he saw the gold dancing in the depths of her eyes. More hope filled Beau, because more than anything, he wanted to help Callie get through this trauma period.

Never mind, he was falling even more helplessly in love with her every hour they were together. The ache to love her grew every day within him. They were slowly moving toward one another, and he could feel her wanting him. Beau was sure Callie knew he wanted her. It wasn't like he could hide his physical reaction to her. And he was positive that last night she'd been well aware of his hard erection against her backside.

Every day, they moved closer to one another. And every day, Beau was grateful to be here with her. When would she give the signal to him? He knew he was physically attracted to her, but his heart and his soul were equally invested in her as well. Beau had never felt what he felt for Callie before. He couldn't see his life without her being a permanent part of it.

CHAPTER 20

B EAU HAD NEVER seen a belly dancer work out, so he was more than a little curious as Callie led him into her dance room at the main house the next afternoon. They had already spent the morning cleaning out box stalls, with Beau doing most of the heavy work because Callie's broken arm could not handle the weight of a pitchfork full of straw and horse poop. But she did help by currycombing each horse as he cleaned out six stalls. They worked well together, and both of them felt a new connection beginning to form between them.

The sunlight poured into two large windows opposite the barre where Callie was beginning her stretching exercises. Beau sat down on the shining cedar floor, its red and gold colors showing its age and beauty. The door to the exercise room was open, and Maisy popped in.

"Oh, good," she called to Callie. "It's great to see you back at work," and she grinned, waved to them, and continued down the hall.

Beau observed Callie, now wearing gray sweatpants and a loose red T-shirt that hung to her slender waist. Her molten hair was up in a ponytail. Her bare feet gave her an especially vulnerable look this morning.

The room was cool but not cold, and Callie's iPod sat nearby on the floor. She had looked up from her stretching as her grandmother had greeted her.

"Have you not been doing your usual exercises?" Beau asked.

"No," Callie admitted. "When I got home, I felt paralyzed. Like a wounded rabbit, all I wanted to do for the first five days was hide in my bedroom. I slept a lot, but it was all broken sleep peppered with nightmares."

Nodding, Beau said nothing. Callie looked delicious as she held her hand on the barre and then did what she called a "fencing position stretch," getting her thighs warmed up for the demands that would be put on them later. The windows behind him showed off the bright azure sky, and the western sunshine poured into the area, warming it naturally. In two more days, it would be Christmas.

They had decorated their tree last night and it turned out to be a lot of fun, giving their cabin a festive look.

Now Graham came to a halt in the doorway, his hands on his hips.

"About time," he called out to Callie.

She grinned. "Hi, Grandpa. Yeah, if I don't get back to doing this, I'll lose all that muscle I need for dancing," she said, and smiled over at him.

"That's true. Well, it's good to see you working out again, Callie." Graham buttonholed Beau. "I'm going into Butte—got to make a run for more sweet feed. Want to go along?"

Beau stood. "Yes, sir." He gave Callie an apologetic look. "Maybe I can stay next time for your workout, gal."

She wiped the dampness off her brow. "Sure, no worries. You guys go have fun! And hey, stay out of trouble." Laughter bubbled out of her.

Graham winked at her. "Nah, our type attracts it. But we'll be on our best behavior, baby girl. See you later." He lifted his hand, disappearing down the hall.

Beau smiled and caught up with Graham. He'd been trying to get into town the last few days because he wanted to buy Callie's family Christmas gifts. Graham knew about his plan and had promised to take him to town. Just his luck that it would happen now! Beau had been looking forward to seeing Callie belly dance once more.

ON THE WAY into town, Graham said, "Callie's coming out of her shell."

"Yes, sir, she seems to be." Beau enjoyed the drive into the city. The freeway was now clear of snow and ice and the landscape around them was blinding, with white snowbanks dotted with evergreens in thick groves.

"The fact that she's back doing her belly-dancing exercises tells me a lot." Graham slowed down as he hit the outer limits of the town. "What about her nightmares? She was getting them just about every night when she first came home."

Beau wasn't going to tell him about the one night he'd slept with Callie. "They seem to be getting less frequent. The last two nights, she's slept through the night and hasn't woken up screaming."

Graham grunted and then said, "Is that hard on you?"

"Yes, sir. But we know the drill. There isn't a black ops man who doesn't have some trauma every now and then. It actually helps me to help Callie."

"True," Graham said. He turned down a street. "There's a shopping mall up ahead. You said you wanted to get Callie a gift for Christmas. I'll drop you here and then drive over to the feed store. It will take me about an hour. I'll meet you out at the front door then, all right?"

Beau nodded, seeing the shopping mall coming up on their right. "Yes, sir, that would be fine. Thanks."

BY THE TIME Beau returned to the ranch, it was five p.m., and he thanked Graham for the ride and trotted around the parking area and off to the cabin. Smoke was rising from the chimney in the pink dusk light. Just above the western horizon, he could see a thin slice of a recent new moon. It was quiet and beautiful as he stomped his boots free of snow and entered the cabin.

"Good timing!" Callie called from the kitchen.

Beau met her smile and closed the door. "Smells good. What's for dinner tonight?" He shucked out of his winter coat and hung everything on the pegs on the wall. He had a sack in his hand and he took it down to his bedroom, returning afterward.

Sauntering into the kitchen, he inhaled the tangy scent. "What are you making? It really smells great." he said, leaning over her shoulder at the stove. Callie was wearing a frilly pink apron, which Maisy, the seamstress in the house, had made for her.

"I made us meatloaf with real mashed potatoes, and I'm making the gravy right now."

"Never bother a woman makin' gravy," he said, leaning down, pressing a kiss to her temple. He wanted to do more, but he wasn't going to destroy a good meal by turning her around and kissing her senseless. Which is exactly what Beau wanted to do. "How about I set the table for us?"

"Go ahead," Callie said, giving him a warm look. She stirred the gravy in the pot with a whisk. "What did you get in town?"

"Oh, a few things I needed," Beau said, purposely vague. He pulled down the plates from the cabinet. "How did your workout go?"

"Good, but after not doing it for two weeks, I can feel the difference."

"You'll get back into working out every other day, and your body will snap right back into it. Muscle memory."

"Says the Delta Force operator," she said with a chuckle.

Beau felt the warmth in the cabin, but really it was Callie's presence. She looked fetching in her jeans and bright green sweater, her hair still in a ponytail. The pink apron made her look very domestic, and he could definitely get used to this.

"Graham and I unloaded about a thousand pounds of sweet feed into the main horse barn when we got back," he told her, laying out the flatware on the table.

"We were running low," Callie explained. "There's another front coming in two days from now. He likes to be stocked up in case we have a blizzard."

"There's always work on a ranch," he agreed.

They fell into a companionable routine. Beau set the table, made them a salad, and got their drinks. Callie brought the large meatloaf on a platter, pulled the mashed potatoes out of the warmer, and put fresh, hot rolls on the table. Beau pulled out a chair for Callie to sit in, then sat at her elbow, serving her first.

"This reminds me so much of my own family," he confided. "Ma has an old iron Ruby wood-burning stove like we have in the cabin, as well as at the main house. Brings back lots of good memories."

"Dara and I learned to cook on the wood stove," Callie told him, enthusiastically digging into her dinner. "We didn't have electric or gas until we left home. And believe me, there's an art to cooking and baking on a wood stove."

"Oh," he murmured, "I know. Ma made us three boys learn to cook on it, too."

"I would love to meet your family someday, Beau."

His heart pulsed. "I think we can make that happen," he said. In his head, he had a vision of bringing Callie home to his family, introducing his wife-to-be. Every day, Callie was responding positively to his being in her life, along with Graham's strong suggestion to get her outdoors and working.

Everyone healed differently, Beau realized. For athletic, type A people like Callie, movement was the key. For someone like Dara, sitting around and reading a good book, being alone and quiet, helped her heal. Beau was glad Callie was so athletic and loved being outdoors, because he did, too.

"Our families seem to be so similar," she said, cutting into her meatloaf.

"They're both country folks, and both have a wood cooking and baking stove, animals, and a garden." He met and held her gaze, seeing yearning in her eyes for him. "You're in the mountains of Montana and we're in the hills of West Virginia. You have cattle and horses and we don't."

"But your pa tans hides. That's working with animals in a different way."

"True enough."

Their dinner was a special gift to Beau. He loved their time talking and sharing. Afterward, he cleared the dishes and put them in the dishwasher. He'd bought some chocolate chip cookies at a bakery at the shopping mall, and produced them along with coffee.

Then, their intimacy was gone. Callie tired easily and she apologetically excused herself, going to the small office down the hall from the two bedrooms. Beau knew she called Dara every night and sometimes, they would talk for nearly an hour. He smiled a little as he cleaned up the kitchen and prepared it for breakfast the next morning. He ached to be in bed with her tonight but made no move, gave no verbal cues.

To push Callie would be crazy and he knew it. Yet, there were only three weeks left, and already he was grieving that he'd have to leave her behind. At least when he did, he knew she would be safe. He'd be going back to Afghanistan, but she would be home, surrounded by loving family, no bullets being fired at her. That gave him a sense of peace he wouldn't have had if Callie had decided to go back to Kabul and work at the orphanage.

He watched television out in the living room for about an hour, his gaze straying toward the popping, crackling fireplace. Having shut off the kitchen light, Beau enjoyed the flames leaping and jumping, creating different shadows around the room. There was peace in this cabin. And happiness. Even though Callie was in the office and probably catching up on Facebook with her Hope Charity friends, this cozy place felt like home. Their home.

Beau didn't want to go there, but his heart did. This cabin would be perfect for them. It was small, nurturing, and intimate. For the first time since he'd entered the Army, he allowed himself to dream of a future—with Callie. He was nearly dozing when he awakened, hearing Callie's slippered feet coming down the cedar hall toward the living room.

He saw she was in her favorite old flannel granny gown and her chenille bathrobe. He must have dozed for a while, because she smelled of just having come from a bath, her cheeks a flushed pink.

"Sorry," she said. "I didn't mean to wake you, but it's nearly eleven p.m. I'm hitting the sack." She leaned over where he sat, kissing his cheek. "Good night, Beau . . . Thank you for being here for me . . ."

That feminine scent of hers drove him crazy with need of her. Beau wanted to reach up, slide his hand behind her nape, and draw her down and really kiss her. Her hair tickled his face as she pulled away from him. "I'll get a shower and hit the sack, too," he mumbled, hearing the drowsiness in his voice.

"Okay," she said, straightening. "See you in the morning. Good night . . ."

Beau sat there, seeing the yearning in her eyes for him. But she said nothing. Disappointed, he slowly sat up, rubbing his face as the door to her bedroom quietly shut.

CALLIE'S SCREAM HAD Beau snapping upright in bed. He moved, throwing the covers off, her cry scaring the hell out of him. Having no idea of time, he had left his door ajar as always, wanting to keep tabs on Callie in case she got up or needed something. He went to her door, knocking softly.

It opened. Callie's hair was mussed, her face drawn, tears in her eyes.

"Nightmare?" he asked thickly, reaching out, opening his arms to her. She was in her nightgown, looking so damned vulnerable. Every particle in his body surged forward, wanting to protect her.

Callie nodded, her lower lip trembling as she came into his arms. Groaning, he took her full weight, her arms going around his waist as she buried her head against his chest beneath his chin. Sweet. So sweet. And rounded, curved, and so damned feminine. He felt his erection growing quickly, and there was no way to hide it from Callie, whose round belly lay against it. He leaned down, kissing her temple, inhaling her subtle wildflower scent deeply into his lungs.

Her fingers dug into his back as if she were still fighting the nightmare, and he felt her quiver almost imperceptibly.

"I-I need you, Beau," she sobbed against him. "I need you . . ."

"Shhh, you have me, sweet woman'. I'm here," he whispered, stroking her back, feeling the flannel beneath his fingertips, feeling the luscious curve of her spine. Beau stopped himself from allowing his hand to stray below her waist. How badly he wanted to cup those beautiful, well-rounded cheeks of hers. And then his world tilted.

Callie pulled back, sliding her hands in a frame around his face, pushing up on her toes, her lips finding his mouth, and Beau's whole world exploded into heat, light, and bolts of electricity. He was taken aback at first by her assertiveness, pressing against his lips, demanding entrance, the hunger urgent within her, infecting him, sending his heart racing with anticipation.

Her kiss was totally unexpected; his body howled with keening fire that raced up through him, knocking out his mind and throwing him into the primal male hunter zone. Her lips were setting explosions off in his lower body, tightening him, thickening him, until he took her, now—at last—in command.

She arched into him. Beau understood what she wanted and he was more than willing to surrender to her needs. Her lips were full, sliding against his, her tongue boldly tangling with his. In moments, Beau eased from her. Only their heavy, ragged breathing and the pounding of their hearts could be heard as he stared down at her.

"Callie," he groaned, "is this what you really want? Are you telling me you're ready?"

She gave a slight nod of her head. "Love me, Beau. I need you . . . please?"

Her barely whispered words, heavy with ache, damn near totaled him.

"Okay," he growled, and in one smooth motion, he picked her up in his arms. He was taking her to her bed, and nothing would stop him now. His whole world was made of fire, boiling heat combined with a deep hunger begging to be satiated.

Beau sat Callie on the edge of the mattress and in moments, his T-shirt and boxer shorts were gone. Callie quickly removed her gown, allowing it to slide to the floor.

Beau couldn't breathe for a moment as he stared down at Callie. She sat like the curvaceous goddess she was, her hair a crimson waterfall around her shoulders, halfway down to her beautifully formed breasts. His gaze took in those perfect berry-colored nipples, standing so tight and ready to be touched and tasted. Just as he remembered. And then everything stopped.

As Beau laid her down on the bed, coming alongside of her, he stilled the movement of her hips, which urged him to take her. "Are you still protected, Callie?" he demanded, trying to keep a shred of common sense before their raging need consumed all thought.

"Yes."

He swallowed hard, watching the play of shadows across her body, watching her dark, lust-filled eyes. "I don't have a condom on me."

He saw amusement in her eyes for a split second. She reached up, trailing her fingers down across his chest.

"That's okay," she said, breathless.

Beau felt her urgency, understood that a nightmare had fueled this reaction in her. His mind was dissolving beneath her hands, her hips against his, making him groan. Graham's words, "She'll come to you when she's ready," pounded through his head. What he didn't want was for her to run to him, to hide in sex from whatever was chasing her. He discounted that almost immediately as her mouth closed seductively over his, brushing against his lips, a hum of pleasure caught in her throat as he returned that kiss.

There had been many times when she'd sought his protection, a sense of safety he knew he could give her. Beau was positive that was part of her need for him. But there was something so much more, and he felt it in each turn and twist of her body against his own.

As he laid her gently on her back, her red hair spilling like a fiery cascade around her face and shoulders, he saw love glistening in her eyes. For whatever reason Callie was ready to take this final step with him. It was a precious moment filled with wonder, followed immediately by a ravenous need for her in every possible way. He wanted to plunge into her, take her and make her his, but his heart cautioned him to go slowly, to allow her to set the pace, let her tell him what she wanted and how she wanted it.

Her fingers trailed down his side, caressing his hip, wrapping softly around his erection. A deep growl emanated from his chest as he tore his mouth from hers, staring down into her languorous eyes, which were shining with her love for him. Even if Callie never whispered those words to him, Beau knew without a doubt in that molten moment that she loved him.

She smiled as he leaned down, kissing her exquisite collarbones, feeling her respond, hearing those little sounds of pleasure that spurred him on. As he drew closer to her breast, he cupped it with one hand, feeling the soft weight of it in his palm, how well it fit there, that taut peak begging for attention. Capturing it with his lips, he suckled her, feeling her tense, a small cry tearing out of her, hips thrusting against his.

Yes, she was ready for this, and he could feel the quiver moving through her. He lifted his head, finding the other nipple, giving it equal attention, and she started to come apart in his arms, her fingers slipping from around his erection. A powerful surge of desire tunneled through Beau, along with an overwhelming need to love Callie. She had been through so much and had toughed it out within herself for so long. He could feel her reaching out, encompassing him, drawing him to her on every level.

Her breathing was ragged, her leg pulling against his, guiding him over her. He lifted his mouth from that nipple and eased between her opening thighs, kissing the center of her firm, well-muscled torso. Her fingers dug into his shoulders, pushing him downward, and he liked her assertiveness.

Nestling his mouth against her curls, the scent of her sex a perfume to his nostrils, kissing her, teasing her, he slid his fingers down her left thigh, easing her open even more. Now she was utterly vulnerable to him. Callie was panting, calling his name, moaning, pushing her hips up toward his mouth as he moved his tongue through those saturated curls.

There were so many ways to love a woman, and Beau knew them all. As he slid his fingers through her wet folds, she cried out. So slippery, her body was more than ready to receive him. Easing forward, his body covering her, she locked her legs around his, pulling his erection toward her entrance, and he allowed her to guide him.

He settled across her damp body, felt her pounding heart against his chest, the sweet tightness of her nipples dragging through the sprinkle of dark hair across his chest. Sliding his hands around her face, his fingers tangling in her silken hair at her temples, he stared down into her half-opened eyes, which burned with starvation for him. He felt it. He saw it. Everything was perfect. Right.

He nudged his hips forward, his erection moving into the slickness of her waiting entrance. Callie's eyes shuttered closed, a low moan tearing from between her kiss-swollen lips, hips arching to meet him.

He held her prisoner beneath him, feeling her wantonness, her wetness spilling over him as he slowly moved into her, grimacing as her tightness gripped him. Over and over, he told himself to go slow and to introduce himself to her body.

Callie had chosen to trust him with her deepest feelings, her strongest needs, even after nearly being raped by the Taliban. As the heat of that realization soared through his soul, wrapping around his heart, he slid deeper into her, hearing that sigh of profound pleasure.

Gritting his teeth, Beau felt her body shift, tighten, and then accept him as her juices spilled around him. The slow, rhythmic movement of her hips against his, the way she gripped his upper arms, her back arching upward, wanting all of him in her, exploded through his wariness of possibly hurting her by accident. Beau could never live with that. Callie had been hurt enough. He didn't need to be a raging bull out of control right now. And it was a special hell he resided in because he was allowing her to reacquaint herself with him on every level. There was such sweetness in it that he felt his pounding heart weld the love he had for her even more deeply into himself as she wrapped her strong legs around his hips.

Callie had always been brave, even under fire, and she was brazen as a woman, confident with her femininity. There was no holding back on her part, just utter enjoyment, the bliss now shining in her soft expression, her eyes closed, the corners of her mouth lifting upward with satisfaction as he rocked deeply into her, taking her, sweeping her along as he felt her shift. And then she surrendered to him in every way, blasting whatever reserve existed between them both. And all the love he felt for her rushed through him, breathless and filled with the knowing that he could complete himself only with her.

His brow was damp, face tight with fighting for control, fighting not to come until he'd fulfilled Callie. He could feel her body starting to spasm, felt her juices surround him, her channel gripping him so tightly he groaned. With each thrust, he pushed more deeply into her. He silently thanked all those years of belly dancing for Callie's ability to milk his body, move so sensuously with his that it felt they'd fused utterly with one another. His fingers tightened against her scalp and he heard her breath hitching, felt powerful contractions surround him.

Beau knew she was going to come. Pumping powerfully into her, reaching that spot deep within her, he heard her cry out, her fingers gripping his biceps, her body spasming against his.

Beau wasn't prepared for the twist and feminine power of her hips slamming into his as Callie reached an orgasm. He used his strength to continue to plunge into her, teasing her sweet body, giving her those delirious cries of release, feeling her hands knead deep into his shoulders. And just as she started to wane, started to relax just a little afterward, he allowed himself to spill hotly into her small, tight confines.

He gripped her hair, his brow against her own, breathing harshly, teeth clenched the heat spiraled up his spine and then slammed down through it. The release made him grunt, and he sucked air in between his teeth as she responded, her hips drawing him deep into her, holding him, draining him of everything he had stored up for so long.

Callie swam in a cauldron of heat, lights flashing behind her closed eyelids as she continued to feel tidal waves throughout her lower body. They were fused to one another, Beau a heavy, warm blanket against her, making her smile with gratification. She slid her fingers up and over his taut shoulders, his breath warm against her breasts, his fingers tangled within the strands of her hair as he lay frozen in pleasure above her.

All this time, she had waited for him and wanted him. Her head had told her it was too soon—she needed to heal—but her heart told her it was past due. Maybe it was a sign of her continuing to heal from the trauma? It felt like it to Callie. She gloried in Beau's damp male body against her own, felt comforted by his arms around her shoulders, drawing her against him, kissing her hair, her temple, her cheek, and finally, his mouth caressing her lips.

Their breaths mingled and their chests rose and fell with exquisite synchronicity. Everything about Beau, from his hard, lean body capturing hers to his tenderness as he continued to kiss each eyelid, her nose, her brow, made her slide into a wordless oblivion where only their hearts ruled and embraced one another. And finally, she was truly home.

CHAPTER 21

C ALLIE SLEPT AFTERWARD in Beau's arms. It was a dreamless sleep, and when she awoke, she felt Beau stir, sensing she was awake. Outside, dawn was sluggishly breaking the hold of the dark winter sky. Her body hummed with satisfaction. It felt so wonderful to have him holding her, the hard warmth of his body against her own. She lay with her head on his shoulder and made a soft sound of contentment.

Beau moved, propping himself up on one elbow. He kept the blankets around her because the room was chilly.

She met his sleepy eyes, seeing the renewed hunger in them, knowing he wanted to make love to her again. That was obvious with his erection thickening once more against her hip. "It's Christmas Eve," she said, her voice thick and drowsy.

"And you're the greatest gift I've ever received, sweet woman'." Beau leaned over, pressing a kiss to her lips.

Languishing in the tender strength of his mouth sliding against her own, Callie closed her eyes, curving her arm across his torso, holding him close to her. He smelled so wonderful to her, that special scent that was only him. Beau's fingers moved slowly through the strands of her mussed hair. Her heart burst open with such fierce love for this man, for his patience with her, his understanding that she was still working through the most major trauma in her life. And he was here, just when she needed him most. He was loving her, caring for her, giving her a safe harbor when she so desperately needed one. As he eased from her lips, she saw fulfillment in his shadowy gray gaze as he studied her in the silence.

"This is a Christmas I'll never forget," he told her, and she saw a sheen of moisture in his eyes.

She smiled and slid her fingers across his cheek, feeling the stubble of beard beneath them. "Me either." Slowly, Callie sat up and tucked the blankets around her waist, holding Beau's gaze. He was all male, an animal lurking just beneath his skin, a consummate hunter, and the perfect lover for her.

"I talked to my grandpa yesterday morning while you were busy," she confided.

"Oh? About what?" Beau was finding that her grandfather, more than her surgeon father, was her go-to confidant.

"About my life. What I'm going to do with it. I know my grandpa was in the Marine Corps overseas, but that's all I know. I can talk to him about my feelings—I guess the PTSD, as he referred to it, that I got because of the ambush. He was asking me a lot of questions."

Beau suppressed a smile. Good for Graham! "Like what?" he asked, moving his hand across her warm lower belly.

"He asked what makes me happy and what I see myself doing for the next year of my life. That made me think about where my passion lies."

"He's a heavy hitter with questions," Beau said, seeing the serious light in Callie's eyes. "And he goes for the jugular." In more ways than one, but Beau would keep the man's past a secret even from her. If Graham ever wanted to divulge his life as a sniper to Callie, it would have to come directly from him.

"He's always been that way," Callie said. "I love him so much. He always tells me he has my back, and I know he does." She slanted Beau a glance. "I swear, you two were twins separated at birth and sent to different families, you're so much alike."

Chuckling a little, Beau said, "I like him a lot. He's reliable, honest, and operates from common sense. He reminds me a lot of my pa, as a matter of fact. Those two would get along like a couple of horse thieves."

Laughing, Callie said, "I love all your country sayings."

"I grew up with 'em," he said with a shrug. "So tell me, how did you answer his questions?" He watched as her expression changed and she grew serious.

"My family has always wanted to serve those who have less than we do," she began quietly. "When I was eighteen, I signed up with the Hope Charity because they were in a lot of third-world countries. I wanted to make a difference. I got sent to Afghanistan for five years straight and loved what I did for the orphanage over there. I loved every one of those children."

Beau saw her eyes grow sad and he reached out, lacing his fingers through hers. "And then real life intruded," he said softly.

"Did it ever," Callie said, her throat constricting, shaking her head. Her fingers curved around his. "I asked Grandpa if he'd ever had a trauma like this hit him when he was in the Marine Corps. He said yes, it had. I asked him if he quit the Marine Corps because of it." She chewed on her lower lip, looking away from Beau for a moment, battling her emotions. Finally, she met his gaze. "He said he wouldn't tell me what happened to him over there, but that it wasn't something he ever wanted to do again. He decided at that point not to make the Marine Corps his career. He got out at and came home to run the ranch. He's at peace, he told me. And he's happy here doing ranching and doesn't regret his decision."

Beau knew about that particular black ops mission at the refinery in Kuwait, and he understood Graham's decision. Snipers lived a very different life compared to the normal grunt in the trenches. And there wasn't a month that went by that he didn't see every man he'd killed in combat. "Well," he said gruffly, "everyone has that line in the sand, Callie. If it gets crossed, then I think everyone stops and takes stock of where they're at. That's when you decide what you want to do with your life, and you hit one of those lines."

"I sure did. I asked Grandpa when he knew, and he said, 'Right after the mission was completed.'"

"And how about you?" Beau coaxed gently, watching the play of emotions across her face.

"Right away." And she gave him a wry look. "After the mission was completed, in our case."

"So are you in a settling-in period? Are you rearranging your life to pursue something that's calling strongly to you instead?"

Callie stared over at him, feeling Beau's warmth and support wrap around her, holding her safe and secure. "I'm still sorting it out a new plan for my life." She hesitated, holding his gaze. "I told Grandpa something I haven't told you yet, Beau. And I've been afraid to say it. Grandpa asked me why." She shrugged helplessly. "I told him I was afraid you'd reject me."

Beau frowned. "What?" There was disbelief in his voice.

"I know it sounds stupid. Grandpa told me I owed you what was in my heart and head, and that I shouldn't keep withholding it from you." She placed her other hand over his so it was sandwiched between hers. "Beau, I love you. I don't know when it happened, or why, but it did. At first, I didn't want anything to do with you because I knew you were chasing me. You saw me dance at Bagram and you wanted me in your bed. I knew that."

Shock tunneled through him, and he kept his face carefully arranged, but his heart was doing somersaults of joy. "What changed your mind about me, Callie?"

"Watching you with the babies at the orphanage. Doing the diapering, cleaning out the diaper pails. I've never seen a man do any of those things. Ever. And sometimes, I'd be walking by the room where you were changing a baby, and I could see the love in your face for that tiny child. It was real. You were real."

She lifted her hand and pressed it against her heart, her voice wobbling. "You are the kindest, most sincere, and caring man I've ever met, Beau. I told

Grandpa about what you did there at the orphanage, and he said that I ought to lasso you, hog-tie you, and never let you go."

Beau grinned, holding her glistening green gaze. "Callie, I love you too. I've been holding on to that admittance for a long time, gal. I knew you weren't ready to hear it yet from me. And then we had that ambush to contend with. So much has happened to you . . . to us . . . in such a short time I just didn't feel right in letting you know how I felt. I was afraid I'd scare you off."

She wiped her eyes. "I knew you loved me, Beau. Grandpa said you do, too. I guess I cried a lot on his shoulder then, because when he asked me how I saw my life going forward, I felt afraid."

"Afraid of what?"

"Afraid that you didn't love me, that it wasn't that level of seriousness between us. Grandpa reassured me that it was, and he told me to get up my Montana gumption and go lay it at your feet." She leaned over, kissing his brow. "I knew then I had to stop this waffling nonsense and tell you how I really felt about you, Beau. I got out of bed and was going to go to your room, wake you up, and tell you everything."

He smiled a little. "But then I showed up at your door, didn't I?"

She felt the warmth of his smile flowing through her, making her feel calm and happy. "Yes, and when I opened the door and you were standing there, something happened inside me, Beau. My heart literally burst with so much need for you that I leaned up and kissed you."

"Which was one hell of a surprise to me," he admitted, drinking in her openly loving gaze.

"I know I can be awfully forward at times," she admitted. "I was going to tell you I loved you, why I had waited, and share my conversation with Grandpa. You were standing there, and I needed you so badly that all I could feel was wanting to love you, to have you love me back."

He caressed her cheek. "And that was fine, Callie. In my line of work surprises are just part of my everyday life. And you kissing me out of the blue wasn't exactly tough to take, gal." He leaned over, kissing her smiling lips, feeling her heat, her eagerness to love him once more.

Beau was going to shake Graham's hand later. "Your grandpa was right, Callie. I do love you. It's been a special hell for me because just being in this cabin with you, I honestly see us living here, having dinner every night with one another, talking about the day's events, me helping you in the kitchen. Small things, but they're important." Because Beau had realized a long time ago, it was the small, everyday things that counted the most.

Nodding, Callie said, "You have three weeks left here. I really, really want to make the most of them with you, Beau. I want to sleep with you every night. I'm tired of being scared. I'm tired of running. Grandpa told me I had to stop and make a stand. Make decisions, because I was capable of making them."

"I like his suggestions to you, Callie."

"Do you?" She searched his eyes, sniffing.

Beau released her hand, retrieved a box of tissues sitting on the nightstand, and handed one to Callie. "I do," he told her, remaining serious, because he could still see remnants of the fear that he'd somehow reject her.

Callie was so unsure of herself, her confidence having taken a major hit due to that ambush, but her heart was running strong and true. And Graham McKinley, bless him, had seen the overview, just like a sniper saw not only every detail but the major pattern they added up to. He was helping Callie thread her way through the trauma, helping her discover what was still whole and healthy within her.

Callie blotted her eyes, giving him a look of apology. "God, I'm such a weepy sop, Beau."

"I love you just as you are," he said, shushing her and touching her cheek. "Tears are always good. Better out than in."

"Are you okay with us sleeping together?"

His mouth hitched. "Gal, that's a dream come true for me."

"The other night when you slept with me, I wanted so badly to turn around, kiss you, love you."

"I felt it," he said, then added wryly, "And I'm sure it was no secret that I wanted you."

She managed a choked laugh, nodding and wiping her eyes. "I thought it was too soon, Beau."

"Yeah, I did, too." He gave her a tender look, moving his thumb across her damp cheek. "You've been under tremendous strain. Your whole life got uprooted, Callie, and then we fell in love. Not exactly a great formula for success. And I didn't want to add to your stress. You were carrying enough. I thought I'd wait it out. I could be here for you, let you know daily in small ways that I did love you. I didn't know if you were even open to me on that level, to tell you the truth."

"I love you so much," she snuffled against his shoulder, squeezing her eyes shut, holding him as tightly as she could.

Beau smiled against her hair, running his hand across her shoulders. "Let the past go, gal. It doesn't have any impact on me, my heart, or how much I love you . . . how much I want a life with you."

His words were exactly what Callie needed to hear. He was so strong, hard-muscled, tender with her right now because Beau had that incredible ability to sense where she was really at. The last of her guilt dissolved in that moment as he held her and slightly rocked her.

Time stopped and Callie languished within his embrace. More than anything, Callie wanted Beau in her life right now because in three weeks he would be going back into harm's way. She couldn't even think about that now . . . the prospect tore her apart inside.

CHRISTMAS EVE DINNER at the main house was like a dream come true for Callie. Beau sat at her side at the long trestle table in the dining room after helping her mother and grandmother bring over the sumptuous feast. There were turkey and ham, mashed potatoes, gravy, chestnut stuffing, sweet potatoes slathered in marshmallow sauce and pecans, cranberry relish, yeast-risen rolls, carrot and raisin salad, and so much more. The talk was lively, spiced with laughter, and Callie hungrily absorbed every moment.

How could she have left the ranch she grew up on, and how could she leave her family again?

Maisy tapped Beau on the shoulder from where she sat. "You don't know our family protocol around here for Christmas," she said, smiling warmly at him. "On Christmas Eve, we give each other one gift. On Christmas morning, we all gather after a breakfast that Stacy, Callie, and I will make for everyone, and then the rest of the gifts are opened. Are you okay with that, Beau?"

"I sure am."

"What's it like with your family at Christmas?" Stacy asked him. She sat opposite Beau at the long table.

"My ma and pa are pretty set about opening all gifts on Christmas morning after we have breakfast," he told everyone.

"Were you able to send everyone in your family a gift?" Graham asked from the other end of the table.

"Yes, sir, I did. They'll be delivered a day after Christmas, but I think my family will be glad to get the gifts."

"We should have gotten you into town sooner," Graham said.

"It's okay," Beau said, giving Callie a warm look. "I called them yesterday and let them know what was happening, and they understood."

"We're glad to have you here with us," Maisy told him. "Callie's blooming under your care." Her eyes brimmed with happiness.

Callie felt heat rush into her cheeks. She and Beau had said nothing about their intimacy or their declaration of love for one another. She wanted to break the good news to all of them on Christmas morning. She glanced over to see her grandfather's blue eyes sparkle with secret knowledge. Did he already know? That wouldn't surprise Callie at all. She swore her grandfather was psychic and could read her mind.

"Sometimes," Graham said to no one in particular as he cut the turkey slice on his plate, "certain people are just meant for one another, Maisy." And then he grinned a little. "For instance, like you and me. We met and fell head over heels with one another before we knew what hit us. Right?"

It was Maisy's turn to blush. Her lips twitched as she ladled more gravy onto her mashed potatoes. "Yes, dear, that did happen. You were a brazen, overconfident Marine, walking into the store where I worked in Butte. You were so full of yourself."

Graham chuckled indulgently. "Well, I knew I was going to have you in my life even if you didn't know it yet."

Bemused, Maisy laughed. "What was it you called me? A spitfire?"

"You still are," Graham said, his eyes alight with tenderness. "Your hair might have gone from red to silver, but you're a redhead in spirit."

Callie grinned. "I love hearing how people met and fell in love."

"Well, Maisy wasn't exactly turned on by me. My enlistment was up, and I left the Marine Corps and had come home to help out at the ranch. I met her in the hardware store. Now, Maisy and I went to the same schools growing up, but she worked out on her parents' ranch."

"Yes, and you were always the mean little boy pulling on my braids, Graham. I really, really disliked you growing up."

"Yeah," he mumbled, hiding his smile. "But I grew on you over time, didn't I?"

Beau laughed with Callie. He liked the wicked, loving look Graham gave his fiery wife down at the other end of the table. There was love in this family, even though all the people involved were different. They all held this ranch sacred, and that gave him a good feeling. Because his family, though they didn't own a huge cattle ranch, was the same way with their homestead in the hills of West Virginia. And both families had more than one generation in the same home, which was important to Beau.

After dinner, the men cleared the table. The women had cooked, so it was their turn for some time off. Beau helped Graham and Connor clean up, clearing the table and putting items into the dishwasher. The women sat in the living room, chatting and laughing. Beau might have felt homesick, but it was lessened considerably by Callie's family, who easily absorbed him into their midst.

Beau sat with Callie on a leather couch in the living room that faced the roaring fireplace. He was interested in how the McKinley family celebrated their Christmas. With soft holiday music in the background, Graham and Maisy met at the huge Christmas tree and faced the group.

"Now, we choose a gift for everyone," Graham told Beau. "As you can see, there are lots of gifts under this tree, but each person is allowed to open one from each person."

"Sounds good to me," Beau said. He saw a *lot* of gifts beneath that tree. He leaned back on the couch, Callie near him, their hips touching. He smiled over at her as he eased her left hand into his. There were two gifts from him to Callie. Earlier, he'd asked Graham to choose the larger of the two tonight. The small one would be opened on Christmas morning.

For the next ten minutes, the grandparents chose a gift for everyone. Pretty soon, Beau, to his surprise, had one from each member of the McKinley family. They sat on the coffee table in front of him, and he was glad he had gone to the shopping mall to buy each of them something. He'd have felt terrible if they'd given him gifts without his having some for them.

Callie had equally as many gifts sitting in her stack. Among them was his red-wrapped gift with a gold bow on it. Would Callie like his gift? He hoped so.

Callie tried to contain her excitement. She loved opening gifts! There was an air of anticipation as everyone in the living room sat with his or her presents. Graham ambled back to the other couch with Maisy and they sat down.

"Okay, everyone, let's do it," he said.

Callie made a happy sound and the first gift she took was the one from Beau. His heart beat a little harder. He'd chosen her gift to open but left it lying in his lap as he watched her enthusiastically tear open the red wrapping. She was like a child, and a grin edged his lips. The tearing of wrapping paper was going on everywhere in the room. Beau looked around and saw that everyone else was as intent as Callie on opening their gifts! It had to be a family trait, he decided.

His ma was one of those people who very carefully unwrapped a gift, making sure she didn't tear the paper because she'd save the wrappings and use them again. Not the McKinley family. He suppressed an affectionate laugh as he watched them.

Callie gasped as she opened the white tissue paper, and her eyes grew wide as she stared down at Beau's gift.

"Oh!" she cried, lifting out a long purple chiffon scarf with small, shining silver coins along one edge of it.

"Do you like it?" Beau asked, holding his breath. Her eyes were bright with joy as she held it up.

"I love it! This is from Turkey! How did you get this, Beau?" She stood up and then wrapped the chiffon scarf around her shoulders, showing everyone in the room the belly-dancing gift he'd given her.

"Through Matt Culver," he said, sitting back, watching her lovingly stroke the material with her fingers. "I won't ever forget you wearing that purple belly dancing outfit," he admitted, meeting her smile.

"But," she said, "this is from Turkey. When did you get it through Matt?"

"Oh," he drawled, "quite a while ago. Matt knew one of the famous seamstresses in Kuşadasi, Turkey, who makes belly-dancing outfits for the professionals in the country."

Tilting her head, she whispered, "You knew long ago that you . . . you . . . ," and she swallowed, not wanting to tell anyone yet about their secret.

Beau nodded. "I knew instantly, Callie. And what happened was that I asked Matt for his contact. She has a website, so I spent some time on the HQ computer and picked this scarf out for you. It's one of a kind. Everything she does is by hand."

Callie was so impressed, so charmed by his thoughtful gift, that she couldn't stop sliding her fingers across the expensive material. And knowing the prices of belly-dancing outfits, she realized this one did not come cheap. The silver coins had been drilled individually and carefully placed in the material. It had taken hours and hours of handwork to place the coins that gleamed along one edge of the scarf. "It's so well made!" She sighed. "Well, I'm going to have to find a new dance where I can wear this scarf."

"I'm hoping so, and I want to see you wear it," he told her, giving her a wolfish look. Clearly, Callie loved his gift, and inwardly Beau drew a sigh of relief.

"I will," she promised, sitting down next to him, carefully folding it up and setting it on the coffee table. "Thank you, Beau. You have no idea how much it means to me!" She wanted to lean over and kiss him, but until they told the family tomorrow morning, Callie could only reach over and squeeze his large hand.

"Open my gift to you, please?" she asked breathlessly.

"You're such a little girl over presents," he chuckled, taking hers into his hands. It was a fairly big, bulky gift, and Beau carefully opened it. Callie was sitting there with an anxious look on her face.

"I wanted you to have something I knitted for you," she said. The expression on Beau's face was one of deep gratitude as he lifted the black knitted scarf that she had made for him.

"I'll wear this a lot," he told her, holding it up and then wrapping it around his neck and shoulders. "And it feels soft and warm."

"Black is a good color on you," she said, thrilled that he liked her gift.

"Goes with an operator's territory," he teased. The joy in Callie's eyes lifted him as nothing else ever would. Lowering his voice, he said, "Tonight, I'm gonna thank you for this gift." He saw her lips turn up into a wide grin.

"Oh, and I'm going to gift you for that beautiful scarf, believe me."

"Well," he drawled, sliding her a wicked look, "I guess we'll make tonight a special present to one another." And he felt his lower body respond hotly to that promise. Beau figured they weren't going to get much sleep tonight. But who cared? It was Christmas, after all.

CHAPTER 22

T HE NEXT MORNING, there was such an air of festivity, Beau had to smile. Christmas music played on the radio, and Maisy hummed along as she and Graham distributed all the gifts to the entire family. This time, the group sat on the two large leather couches, the gifts piled around their feet or on the glass and cedar coffee table. It was nearly ten a.m.; the day was cloudy and it was going to start snowing soon, Beau thought.

He was bone-tired, but he didn't care. Callie and he had made love two times the night before, and they'd finally fallen exhausted into one another's arms near 0400. If not for the clock on the dresser beeping at 0700, they'd have missed Christmas breakfast with the McKinley family at 0830.

Callie had loved her purple scarf with the silver coins so much, she'd chosen a bright red, long-sleeved silk scoop-necked tee and a long black wool skirt to wear with it. Not only that, she'd allowed her hair down, a crimson cape of its own around her shoulders, put on makeup that made those glorious green eyes look even more like emeralds, and worn her dark brown leather boots. She looked sexy as hell in that long scarf, the tiny silver coins flashing and tinkling against one another as she moved. She'd even worn her only pair of silver Turkish earrings, the same ones she'd worn the night she danced at Bagram. Beau almost didn't let her out of the cabin, fantasizing about slowly undressing her in their bedroom. Callie had seen that look in his eyes and, laughing, waved her finger at him. There was no way they were missing the family gathering on Christmas morning!

Beau found himself with another five gifts from the McKinley family. He had gotten each of them one gift. Callie had two, but the second one was special, and he tucked it on the other side of his body where she couldn't see it. More than once, Callie looked through all the gifts, trying to find one from him. Beau suppressed a smile. Damn, but his woman was a fox on the hunt! Madly in love, he'd never felt happier. Her long red hair was mussed, long tendrils on each side of her face giving her the look of a wild, uninhibited woman. He ached to take her in his arms and kiss her into oblivion.

Amid the ripping, tearing sounds of wrapping and ribbon flying all over the place, Beau watched and grinned. There was a surprised yelp from Callie, and she jumped up to hug her parents and grandparents for their gift, a new red Ford pickup. When Callie had left at eighteen, she'd sold her truck. Beau hid his smile, observing how much her family loved her. Callie was effusive, open, all heart and love. Beau had seen the same open quality at the orphanage in the way she'd loved all those little tykes just starving for a bit of attention. Callie might not have been their mother, but she'd mothered each and every one of them. Beau knew she missed them and he could, at times, feel her aching for them, worrying about them. She was a natural mother. As he sat there, he imagined Callie pregnant with his child. The thought was like an earthquake through him, tearing down what he thought he wanted out of his life. Since meeting her, everything in his life was changing, different, better.

When everyone had opened their gifts, the wrapping, ribbons, and boxes lying scattered around the living room, Beau stood up. All eyes moved to him. Graham was in his large leather rocking chair and he lifted his chin, his blue eyes glinting. Beau held out his hand toward Callie.

She looked up at him, at his hand, and then took it, confusion in her expression. The only thing Beau could hear right now was the snapping and crackling of the fire in the huge fireplace across the room. He gave Callie a tender look, pulling her to her feet.

"I have one last Christmas gift for you," he said, leading her out to the center of the room. His throat tightened as he looked at the McKinleys, his heart beating harder for a moment. He continued to hold Callie's left hand.

"Callie and I have gone through an awful lot in a very short amount of time. Sometimes, experiences either draw you together faster, or they tear you apart at the same speed." He swallowed and glanced down at her upturned face. She stood close to him. Beau could feel her heat, feel her concern, because she didn't know what he had planned for her. Or them.

He turned, his gaze sweeping her family, his gaze on the parents. "I love your daughter and you need to know that. I suspect some of you already know it." His mouth pulled upward a little. His gaze moved to Graham, who remained still in his rocker, his gaze soft now, resting on Callie.

"What Callie and I experienced, and by the skin of our teeth survived, changed both of us. I'm sure she can tell you how it affected her. It changed me, too. It also made me know without any doubt that Callie is the woman I want forever. I want to wake up with her every morning, in our bed, at my side. I want to share her laughter, how she sees her world, and share her incredibly generous heart." His voice grew strained and he faced Callie, touching her cheek. "I know this is too soon, gal, but I wanted to give you a gift from my heart to yours. And you just let me know when you're ready, okay?"

Beau slipped the purple-foil-wrapped gift into her hand and took a step back, watching her expression. Tears glimmered in Callie's eyes and she sniffed, giving her family a look of apology. Her fingers trembled as she untied the pretty silver bow. Holding on to it, she opened the paper. Inside was a purple velvet box. Beau took the paper and bow from her hands so she could open it.

Callie gasped as she stared down at the opened box. Inside was a platinum wedding ring, and with it a solitaire engagement ring of purple tanzanite from Africa, the same deep purple color that she loved so much.

Her hand flew to her throat and she gulped. "Oh . . . Beau . . . ," she whispered brokenly.

He smiled nervously. "Do you like them, Callie?" Because as God was his witness, he'd never wanted her to like anything more than those rings. His hands grew damp as she swallowed, tears running down her flushed cheeks, grasping the box between her breasts, over her heart.

"Like them?" she managed in a choked whisper. "I've never seen anything so beautiful."

"Will you marry me, gal? When the time's right?" he rasped, leaning down, claiming her lips, tasting the salt of her tears on them.

Callie sobbed as she drew away and threw her arms around his neck. Beau smiled, burying his face into her hair, holding her tightly against him. He heard movement around him but was focused only on Callie and how she felt against him, the joy he'd seen leap to her green eyes, that expression of pure love on her face for him. Just for him.

He released her just enough to stare down into her eyes. "Tell me."

"Yes, yes, I love you. And I do want to marry you, Beau Gardner. More than anything in the world."

For a moment, Beau was so lightheaded with the joy shearing through him, he thought he might pass out. Then he felt the same joy stabilizing him. He had no more reason to doubt or fear her feelings. Just looking at Callie and the deeply loving gaze she shone on him, he knew she was all his.

"Congratulations, son," Graham said, walking over to them, clapping Beau on the back. "Welcome into our family. We couldn't want a better grandson-in-law." He held out his hand to him.

Beau released Callie but kept her at his side. He shook Graham's roughened hand. "Thank you, sir. My only aim in my life is to make Callie happy. She deserves only good things to happen to her from now on."

Maisy came up next, hugging Callie. She was crying, too. Then she turned and hugged Beau. "You're going to make Callie a fine husband, Beau. You're the best of friends, and that's such a great foundation to start from."

Stacy and Connor came up next. Stacy gave her daughter a happy look, hugging her, kissing her hair and cheek. She was crying, too. Connor shook Beau's hand, his voice wobbling with emotion, welcoming him into their family. And then Connor held his daughter gently, for a long time, kissing her cheek. When he released her, he said, "You've got impeccable taste, Callie. Beau already fits in here with all of us."

"Yes," Stacy sighed, sliding her arm around Connor's waist. "You make such a beautiful couple. From the very first moment you arrived, Beau, we saw such a positive difference in Callie. Before, she was depressed and lost. But as soon as you showed up, she started rallying. She made the decision to fight the shock and get better." She reached out, touching Beau's arm. "You're her sunlight."

Beau nodded, deeply touched by everyone's emotional welcome and congratulations. "Well, if I'm Callie's sunlight, she's my heart's compass."

Callie looked up at him, dazed by his eloquence, and kissed his cheek. "You always say the most beautiful things, Beau," she whispered, giving him a tender look.

"Come on," Graham coaxed the couple. "Sit down on the couch here. Callie, wouldn't you like to look at that pretty engagement ring of yours a little more closely?"

Callie stared down at the box she had clutched in her hand. "Very much so, Grandpa."

Beau led her to the couch. This time, Beau sat down in the corner of the couch, his arm going around Callie. From now on, they could show their affection for one another with the rest of her family. "Going to try it on, gal?" he teased her.

Callie nodded, overwhelmed by so many emotions. She carefully pulled the engagement ring from the plush box. "Tell me more about it, Beau. What gemstone is it? It's truly beautiful."

"Well," he drawled, "that gemstone comes from Africa. It's called tanzanite, and it's a very rare stone. In fact, the deposit of this mineral in the magnesium mines where a seam of this gemstone was found has run out, so whoever has the gem now has something no one else will ever have again." He picked the ring from her fingers and then eased his arm from around her waist. Gently lifting Callie's left hand, he said, "Want to try it on for size?"

"Y-yes," she said eagerly, "of course I do!"

The ring slid on, a perfect fit. The gemstone was a square cut. As Beau saw the beauty of the purple flashing through it from the light in the living room, he said, "This reminds me of the night you danced at Bagram, all light, shimmering beauty. I don't think I took one breath while you danced," and he smiled down at her, unable to fully believe that she was going to be his wife.

Her fingers wrapped around his. "This is such an incredible gift, Beau. I love it, and I love you, so very much."

BEAU LAY IN bed with Callie after they had loved one another. It was Christmas night, and they'd had a final dinner with the family midafternoon and then come home to their cabin. She lay naked in his arms, their hearts still beating hard as he nuzzled his face into that cloud of her silky red strands. He breathed in her womanly scent and growled, holding her tightly against him.

"I'm so weak," Callie laughed softly, smiling and closing her eyes, her head on his damp shoulder.

"Makes two of us," Beau agreed, never happier.

The bedroom was warm because the door was open and the fire was roaring in the living room. Beau had opened the curtains, and from where he lay on the bed, he could see the snowflakes twirling outside the partly frosted window.

A new blizzard was blowing in tonight and that meant that everyone would get up early to feed the livestock and horses. But it was going to be a quiet day of rest for the most part.

"I love my rings," Callie whispered against his neck.

"I'm glad you do," he said, easing back and placing a pillow by his shoulder so she could lie on it. "That ring has purple fire in its depths. Reminds me of the fire in you, Callie."

"Tell me how you got the rings, Beau."

"Oh," he sighed, "it's quite the story. I told Matt that I wanted to get a purple engagement ring for you. Of course, we were stuck at Bagram, out in the middle of nowhere. He knew a Turkish jeweler that his family uses in Kuşadasi, Turkey. We sat down at the computer and he Skyped with him. The jeweler is a very old gentleman, silver haired and very kind. I explained that I wanted a purple gemstone for you. He asked me about you." Beau leaned down, kissing her nose. "I thought it was very nice of him to ask. So I told him all about you, about that wild purple and silver belly-dancing outfit you danced in. I could see his eyes light up, and he said he had just the stone for you. He came back with it and showed it to us. Matt suggested I go with a platinum ring. I agreed. So the jeweler made the set for you. Matt has his resources and the rings were sent to me by courier to Bagram."

"When was this?"

"Right before we got ambushed," Beau admitted unhappily. "I had plans that when we got back from that village that evening, I was going to take you to that special restaurant you liked so much. I was going to propose to you after dinner, but it didn't happen."

Callie slowly sat up, pushing some of her hair off her shoulder. The glow from the fireplace danced shadows and light up and down the hall, some of it reflecting into their bedroom. Looking deeply into Beau's amused, shadowed eyes, she said, "You were probably wondering if you'd ever give them to me, weren't you?"

Beau reached out, moving his hand down her arm, feeling the velvet strength of it. "I wasn't even sure we'd survive the attack, gal. The rings were the last thing on my mind. When we finally got out of that hot mess, I brought the rings with me when I came to see you. I wasn't sure I'd even show them to you. I wasn't sure where we were at with one another." He searched her face, now quietly reflective. Her lips were slightly swollen from the kisses he'd given her, lower lip almost pouty, making her look even more fetching to him.

"What a story," Callie said, shaking her head, amazed. "Well, you sure surprised me this morning. I never expected you to ask me to marry you, or to have that gorgeous set of rings. I'm just stunned by the beauty of the tanzanite." She held the ring up, watching the firelight catch shards of the fire within the purple gemstone. "I want to share with you about my plans, Beau."

He became serious. Callie had spent her young life in the service of the Hope Charity. Beau knew she had quit, but he wasn't sure which direction she wanted to go.

"Tell me," he coaxed, holding her gaze.

"You already know I quit Hope Charity. My mother and grandma sat down with me a few days ago, to discuss my life plans. Mom said that I'd served the world since I was eighteen. She asked me if now that I'd met you, maybe it was time to start looking differently at my dreams and goals."

"You're lucky to have such a tight-knit family, Callie, that can help you with big life changes that come everyone's way."

Somber, she nodded, seeing the concern in Beau's gaze. "I am and I know it. I told them that I was in the midst of a huge change within myself because of the ambush. But right now, I wanted to stay at the ranch and work. I need this kind of work because it's helping me to heal, Beau."

"I know it is. I see it daily in you, Callie."

"There's a small charity in town. I'd like to devote some time locally because I love to help others who have so much less than I do." She caressed his jaw. "But my life is changing before my very eyes. I'm marrying you. I want children. A family. And I know what it takes to be a full-time parent." She chewed on her lower lip for a moment, in deep thought. Finally, she whispered, "You and I come first. Our dreams we dream together come first. I've always had a good head for numbers. Grandma Maisy said she'd teach me how to do the accounting for the ranch. I could have a job, be a help to the ranch in general, and still be home to raise our children, Beau. What do you think?" She searched his eyes.

"I think it's a great plan, Callie." He picked up her fingers, tangling his between hers. "You'll probably always do some kind of service work, and that's fine with me. I like that you're making us and our family-to-be as first. And learning accounting would be helpful. I'm not that great at that kind of thing." He gave her a grin. "I'd much rather work with Graham and learn the ins and outs of becoming foreman of this ranch someday down the road apiece."

"I like how everything is falling into place," Callie agreed quietly, holding his warm gaze. "We'll both work at our new jobs, learn them, and someday, maybe a decade from now, be good enough to take over the reins of running this ranch. Then Grandma and Grandpa can retire and live with us."

"Sounds like a workable plan," Beau agreed. He took a deep breath and released it. "I've only got a few more weeks with you, Callie," he offered quietly, looking at her stricken expression. His fingers moved gently down her arm and he slipped her hand into his, holding it. "I've got five months to go on my enlistment. Our team is leaving Bagram in March of next year. There will be very few missions between now and then because of the snow in the passes. Everything will be very quiet at Bagram. I'll probably go out of my skull with boredom." He grinned boyishly.

"What happens after March, Beau?"

"My team returns stateside. We always have a lot of training to do, but first I'll get a week to come home to you here, at the ranch."

"A week," she sighed. "I'll miss you so much until then . . . "

Beau could already feel her moving into worry over his being overseas. "Look, Matt will be with me through March. That's when his enlistment is up and he leaves the Army and goes home to work for his parents' charity, Delos. I'll have three months here stateside, and then the Army will cut me loose."

"That would be June?"

"June 1, to be exact."

"That would be a wonderful time to get married, wouldn't it?" she suggested coyly.

"Yes, I'd like that. And that's far enough away that it would give my folks time to drive up here to be part of our wedding. They wouldn't miss that for the world." His grin widened.

She absorbed his joy as he spoke about his family. "I was thinking that after we get married, we might spend part of our honeymoon with your folks so I can spend some quality time with them and see where you grew up. I'd love to meet all your family. They had you, so I know they're special people." She laid her hand on his chest, her palm over his heart. "Anyone as special as you has to have a very, very wonderful set of parents, Beau."

He placed his hand over hers. "They're great people, Callie. Salt of the earth. Kind. Hardworking. I know they'd cherish a visit from us. As a matter of fact, my pa and a number of men on Black Mountain built a second cabin on my parents' property years ago. They built it hoping at least one of the three boys might come home with his bride and they could stay in it."

"Oh, that sounds wonderful. Could we do that? Stay there?"

He shrugged. "I don't see why not."

"And maybe," Callie said, thinking out loud, "next Christmas, we could travel down there and spend the holiday with your folks. I know they miss you, too."

"Sure, we could trade off years having Christmas up here and then down there. I know my folks would appreciate that."

"When you come home, Beau, you'll start to work as wrangler with Grandpa guiding you."

"Well"—he gave her a wicked look—"I need to learn to ride a horse first, and then be a wrangler and learn the ways of cattle ranching. I told him I might fall off a time or two before I got the hang of riding, but I'll do it."

"That sounds absolutely perfect," Callie sighed. "Grandpa wants to retire someday, and my dad has no interest in running the ranch."

"Yeah, I kinda figured that."

"But you have the earth in your soul, Beau. You're so much like Grandpa."

"We get along right well with one another," he agreed quietly. "He's a real hero and a mentor to me. I enjoy being around him."

"I think that Grandpa always wished Mom had had a son instead of two girls." She smiled a little. "And I see the warm relationship you two have with one another. You're kind of like the son he never had, Beau. You two get along so well, it's amazing. He's not like that with most people."

"Well, we're cut from the same military cloth, gal. That breeds a bond right there. I might be Army and he's a Marine, but we have that unspoken brother-hood between us."

She sighed and lay down at his side, nuzzling him and kissing his neck. "When I talked to Dara earlier . . ."

"Yes?"

"She told me she got engaged to Matt. I think that's so wild that we both got engaged on the same day!"

"'Kismet' is what my ma would call it," he laughed, seeking her lips, which parted to accept his, filled with promise. Filled with love. As he eased away, he said, "Your sister has a fine man who will make her a wonderful husband, so don't worry about her, Callie."

"Oh, I always liked Matt." She laughed a little. "I mean, it was pretty obvi-ous he'd fallen for Dara. The way he looked at her when he met us in back of the chow hall after we'd finished our dance told me everything."

"They'll be a beautiful couple together, but so will we. Dara will be happy working down there at her hospital in Alexandria, and Matt's happy working with his parents for their charity nearby. It will work out."

"Yes, and you'll be up here riding the fence line, herding cattle and getting a sore butt," she laughed.

Beau eased her onto her back, watching the shadows and light caress the valleys, hills, and curves of her luscious, warm, and loving body. "I'll gladly suffer a sore butt to live my life with you, Ms. Callie McKinley."

She sighed and framed his face with her hands, looking deep in his eyes. "Beau, how do you feel about getting me pregnant right after we marry? I don't want to wait to have children. I want at least three. Maybe four."

"Heck," he teased her, "we can have our own family of new ranch hands over time."

Callie laughed and hugged him to her, feeling the warm weight of his body moving over hers. She was aware that he wanted her again and she could feel herself wanting him just as much. "Four little buckaroos. Think you can handle them?"

His smile deepened. "I've got your grandpa and grandma, who I'm sure will be tickled pink, and so will your parents. But Graham and Maisy will spoil them all rotten."

"They sure will," she whispered, searching his gleaming eyes. "And you're so good at diapering."

He chuckled indulgently, kissing her brow, nose, and cheek. "I'm fine with the idea, Callie. I've always dreamed of having a big family. I come from one myself."

"This is like a dream coming true," Callie said, suddenly serious, "after almost dying."

"Well, Christmas is a special time, gal. Always has been. Always will be."

She felt his lips begin to worship her once more. "You are the ultimate gift, Beau. Without you, I wouldn't be here. And for what you are, and what you have given me," she whispered fervently, "I will love you forever."

THE BEGINNING...

Don't miss Lindsay McKenna's next DELOS series novella,

Hold Me

Available from Lindsay McKenna and Blue Turtle Publishing and wherever you buy eBooks!

Turn the page for a sneak peek of *Hold Me!*

Excerpt from

Hold Me

C ALLIE TRIED TO stuff her fears deep down inside herself. She stood with her fiancé, Beau Gardner, an Army sergeant in Delta Force, at the Butte, Montana airport. He was leaving on this cold January, the skies clear, typical of a Montana winter morning. His arm was curved around her shoulders. It felt comforting to her, but the terror that he was going back to complete his fifth tour over to Afghanistan, raged through her. He could be killed. Callie felt his fingers move soothingly up and down her upper arm as she leaned against his tall, hard body. Was he reading her mind? She tried to appear relaxed and calm, but there was a hellacious storm of anxiety inside her.

People were making their way home from the Christmas and New Year holidays. Beau was dressed in civilian clothes and Callie didn't think anyone in the bustling airport would know he was a deadly operator. He had saved her life when her civilian charity van was attacked by Taliban on the way to a 'safe' Afghan village to render medical aid to its people. She had worked for Hope Charity, spent six months out of every year in Kabul, the capitol, where she worked with fifty orphaned Afghan children. She loved her work with them, even knowing that Kabul wasn't truly safe, either.

She sighed, resting her brow against his Levi jacket, closing her eyes and squeezing him around his narrow waist. Instantly, Beau responded, dropping a light kiss on her hair and holding her a bit more tightly for a moment, as if to reassure her. He knew she was worried about him going back over there. His enlistment wasn't up until June of this year and it was only January. Six months. Callie knew that in the winter, the Taliban attacks slowed down or stopped because of the heavy snowfall didn't allow the enemy to travel around the country very easily. They all trooped back to Pakistan to wait until the spring thaw in April, to return and begin systematic attacks against anyone, Afghan, American or otherwise, who did not believe as they did.

"You doing okay?" Beau asked as he leaned down, his lips brush the curve of her ear.

"I'm doing okay," she lied. The last thing Callie wanted was to have Beau's attention and focus on her and not his job in black ops missions. She heard a rumble in his broad chest.

"You're such a beautiful liar, Ms. McKinley, but I love you anyway."

She absorbed his West Virginia drawl, loving the low, husky sound, feeling how much he loved her. Callie thought she knew what love was through a series of mistakes with other men. At twenty-seven years old, Beau had more or less crashed into her life when she was working at Hope Charity in Kabul. Rousing herself, she lifted her head, angling it so she could meet his amused looking gray eyes focused solely on her. Lips twisting, she whispered, "I'm not lying, Beau."

"You're a first class worry wart, sweetheart. I'll be fine," he promised, dropping another kiss on her wrinkled brow. "I'll be home before you know it. I'll be meeting you right here in this regional airport." He lifted his head, angling his chin. "And Grandpa Graham will be here with you."

Callie rallied a small smile. Her Grandpa Graham, once in the U.S. Marine Corps sniper and black ops when younger, was standing near the swinging doors, looking around like he always did. She supposed it was his top secret security background that made him more alert to the situations around him. "Yes, Grandpa will be here with me, for sure. But the whole McKinley family will probably be here to meet you, too. Everyone loves you. You know that." And her Montana ranch family truly did love Beau. He fit in well to the ranching way of life. His own folks, Cletus and Amber Gardner, lived on Black Mountain in West Virginia. They were from a long line of Hill people who had lived over a hundred years on that mountain. Beau might not have come from a ranch life, but he was used to living close to nature, was rural in his soul, a hunter and fisherman, and helping his father who was a furniture maker.

"Yes, I love your family," he agreed, rocking her in his arms, squeezing her once more to comfort her. "I can hardly wait for you to meet MY family. They're dying to meet you."

"Ugh, don't use that word 'dying,' Beau," and she wrinkled her nose.

"Oh . . . sorry . . . well, yes, they want to meet the woman I'm gonna marry after I get home in June. The good news is that they're driving up here to be with us when we get married at the Eagle Feather Ranch. It's going to be a great big shindig, for sure," and he smiled down into her eyes.

Beau's love drenched Callie and she saw it in his gaze, in the way he was holding her against him, rocking her just a little, as if he were rocking a scared child in order to calm it. And right now? Callie felt exactly like that scared child. No matter how much she tried to mentally tell herself Beau was going to be all right once he returned to Bagram and conducting winter missions, her heart screamed the opposite. Her emotions were on tap, anyway, because she'd gotten a good dose of PTSD from that ambush late last year, running and hiding and trying to get back to Bagram with Beau's help and protection. "I can hardly wait," she whispered, her voice off key.

The Books of Delos

Title: ***Last Chance*** (Prologue)

Publish Date: July 15, 2015

Learn more at: delos.lindsaymckenna.com/last-chance

Title: ***Nowhere to Hide***

Publish Date: October 13, 2015

Learn more at: delos.lindsaymckenna.com/nowhere-to-hide

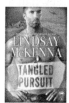

Title: ***Tangled Pursuit***

Publish Date: November 11, 2015

Learn more at: delos.lindsaymckenna.com/tangled-pursuit

Title: ***Forged in Fire***

Publish Date: December 3, 2015

Learn more at: delos.lindsaymckenna.com/forged-in-fire

Title: ***Broken Dreams***

Publish Date: January 2, 2016

Learn more at: delos.lindsaymckenna.com/broken-dreams

Title: ***Blind Sided***

Publish Date: June 5, 2016

Learn more at: delos.lindsaymckenna.com/blind-sided

Title: ***Secret Dream***

Publish Date: July 25, 2016

Learn more at: delos.lindsaymckenna.com/secret-dream

Title: ***Unbound Pursuit***

Publish Date: July 25, 2016

Learn more at: delos.lindsaymckenna.com/unbound-pursuit

Everything Delos!

Newsletter

Please sign up for my free quarterly newsletter on the front page of my official Lindsay McKenna website at lindsaymckenna.com. The newsletter will have exclusive information about my books, publishing schedule, giveaways, exclusive cover peeks, and more.

Delos Series Website

Be sure to drop by the website dedicated to the Delos series at delos.lindsaymckenna.com. There will be new articles on characters, publishing schedule and information about each book written by Lindsay.

Quote Books

I love how the Internet has evolved. I had great fun create "quote books with text" which reminded me of an old fashioned comic book . . . lots of great color photos and a little text, which forms a "book" that tells you, the reader, a story. Let me know if you like these quote books because I think it's a great way to add extra enjoyment with this series! Just go to my Delos Series website delos.lindsaymckenna.com, which features the books in the series.

The individual downloadable quote books are located on the corresponding book pages. Please share with your reader friends!

Made in the USA
Columbia, SC
21 September 2018